A CARTOON NETWORK ORIGINAL

PRINCESS AND PRINCESS

ROSS RICHIE CEO & Founder
MATT GAGNON Editor-in-Chief
FILIP SABLIK President of Publishing & Marketing
STEPHEN CHRISTY President of Development
LANCE KREITER VP of Licensing & Merchandising
PHIL BARBARO VP of Finance
ARUNE SINGH VP of Marketing
BRYCE CARLSON Managing Editor
MEL CAYLO Marketing Manager
SCOTT NEWMAN Production Design Manager
KATE HENNING Operations Manager
SIERRA HAHN Senior Editor
DAFNA PLEBAN Editor, Talent Development
SHANNON WATTERS Editor
ERIC HARBURN Editor
WHITNEY LEOPARD Editor
CHRIS ROSA Associate Editor
CAMERON CHITTOCK Associate Editor
MATTHEW LEVINE Assistant Editor

SOPHIE PHILIPS-ROBERTS Assistant Editor
AMANDA LaFRANCO Executive Assistant
KATALINA HOLLAND Editorial Administrative Assistant
JILLIAN CRAB Production Designer
MICHELLE ANKLEY Production Designer
KARA LEOPARD Production Designer
MARIE KRUPINA Production Designer
GRACE PARK Production Design Assistant
CHELSEA ROBERTS Production Design Assistant
ELIZABETH LOUGHRIDGE Accounting Coordinator
STEPHANIE HOCUTT Social Media Coordinator
JOSÉ MEZA Event Coordinator
HOLLY AITCHISON Operations Coordinator
MEGAN CHRISTOPHER Operations Assistant
MORGAN PERRY Direct Market Representative
CAT O'GRADY Marketing Assistant
LIZ ALMENDAREZ Accounting Administrative Assistant
CORNELIA TZANA Administrative Assistant

ADVENTURE TIME: Princess and Princess, January 2018. Published by KaBOOM!, a division of Boom Entertainment, Inc. ADVENTURE TIME, CARTOON NETWORK, the logos, and all related characters and elements are trademarks of and © Cartoon Network. (S18) All rights reserved. KaBOOM!™ and the KaBOOM! logo are trademarks of Boom Entertainment, Inc., registered in various countries and categories. All characters, events, and institutions depicted herein are fictional. Any similarity between any of the namesw, characters, persons, events, and/or institutions in this publication to actual names, characters, and persons, whether living or dead, events, and/or institutions is unintended and purely coincidental. KaBOOM! does not read or accept unsolicited submissions of ideas, stories, or artwork.

BOOM! Studios, 5670 Wilshire Boulevard, Suite 450, Los Angeles, CA 90036-5679. Printed in China. First Printing.

ISBN: 978-1-68415-025-0, eISBN: 978-1-61398-702-5

Created by Pendleton Ward

Written by **Jeremy Sorese**
Illustrated by **Zachary Sterling**
Colors by **Laura Langston**
Letters by **Warren Montgomery**

Cover by **Britt Wilson**

Designer **Chelsea Roberts**
Assistant Editor **Matthew Levine**
Associate Editor **Chris Rosa**
Editor **Whitney Leopard**

With Special Thanks to Marisa Marionakis, Janet No, Curtis Lelash, Conrad Montgomery, Kelly Crews, Scott Malchus, Adam Muto and the wonderful folks at Cartoon Network.

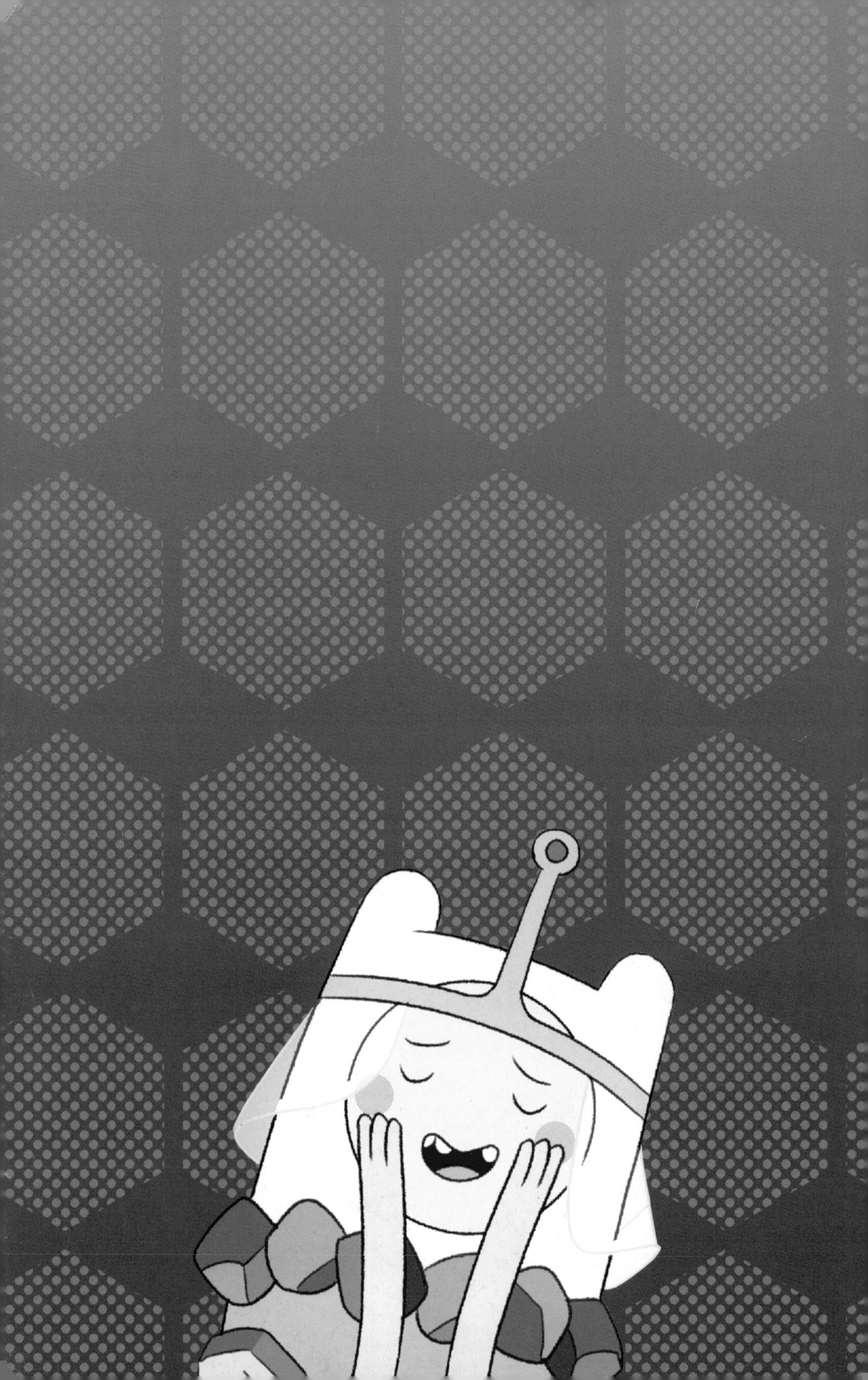

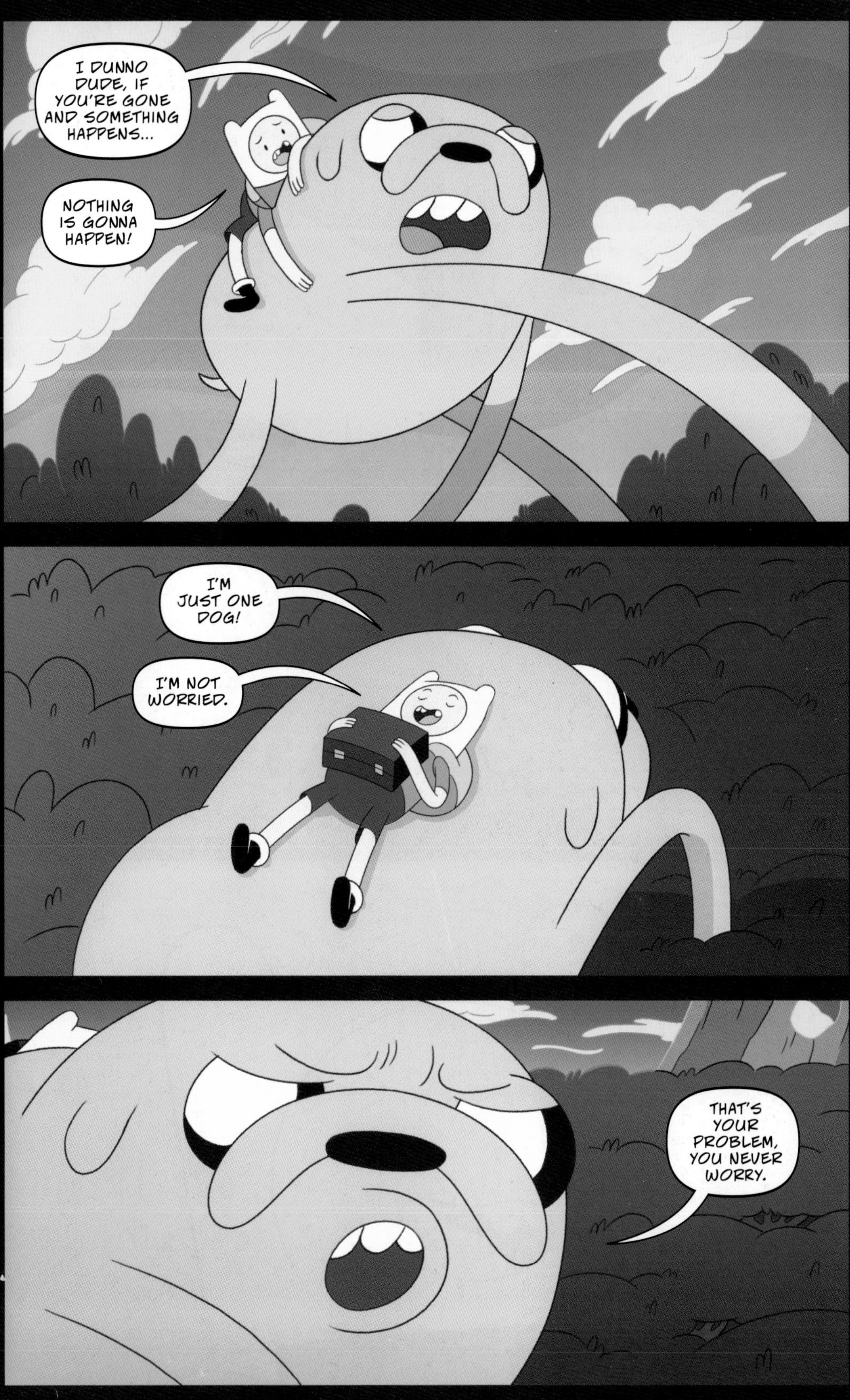
I DUNNO DUDE, IF YOU'RE GONE AND SOMETHING HAPPENS...
NOTHING IS GONNA HAPPEN!
I'M JUST ONE DOG!
I'M NOT WORRIED.
THAT'S YOUR PROBLEM, YOU NEVER WORRY.

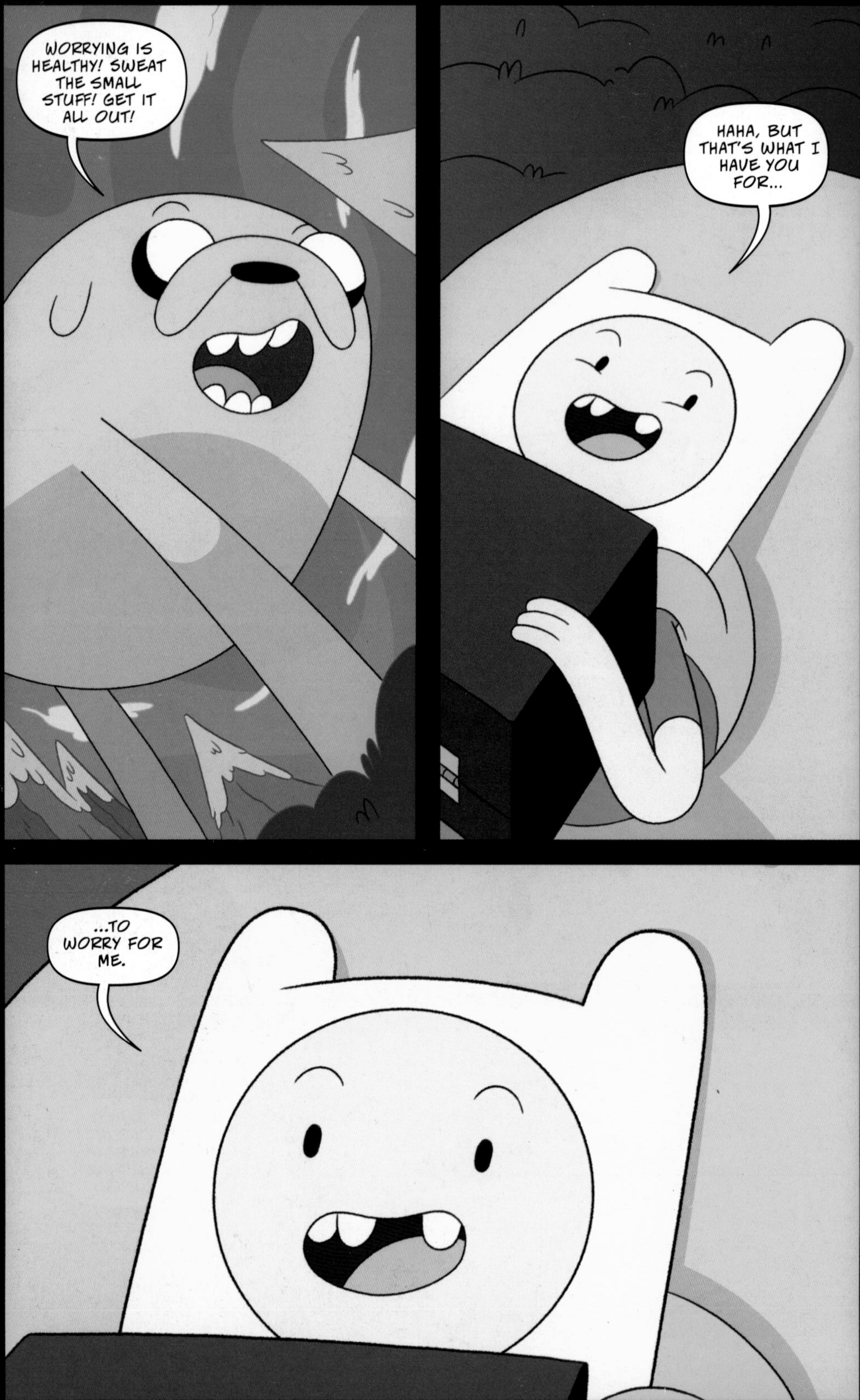
WORRYING IS HEALTHY! SWEAT THE SMALL STUFF! GET IT ALL OUT!
HAHA, BUT THAT'S WHAT I HAVE YOU FOR...
...TO WORRY FOR ME.

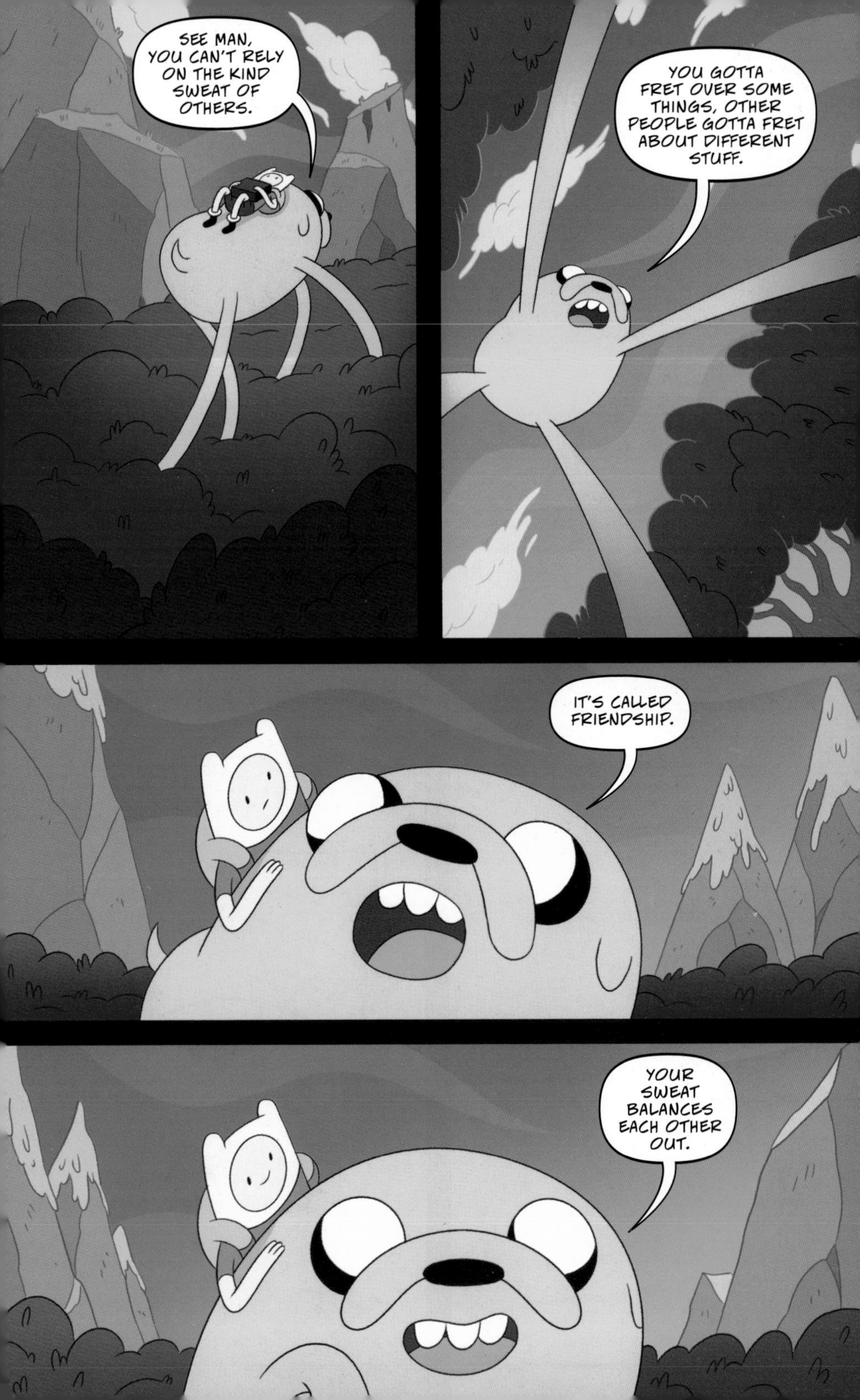
SEE MAN, YOU CAN'T RELY ON THE KIND SWEAT OF OTHERS.
YOU GOTTA FRET OVER SOME THINGS, OTHER PEOPLE GOTTA FRET ABOUT DIFFERENT STUFF.
IT'S CALLED FRIENDSHIP.
YOUR SWEAT BALANCES EACH OTHER OUT.

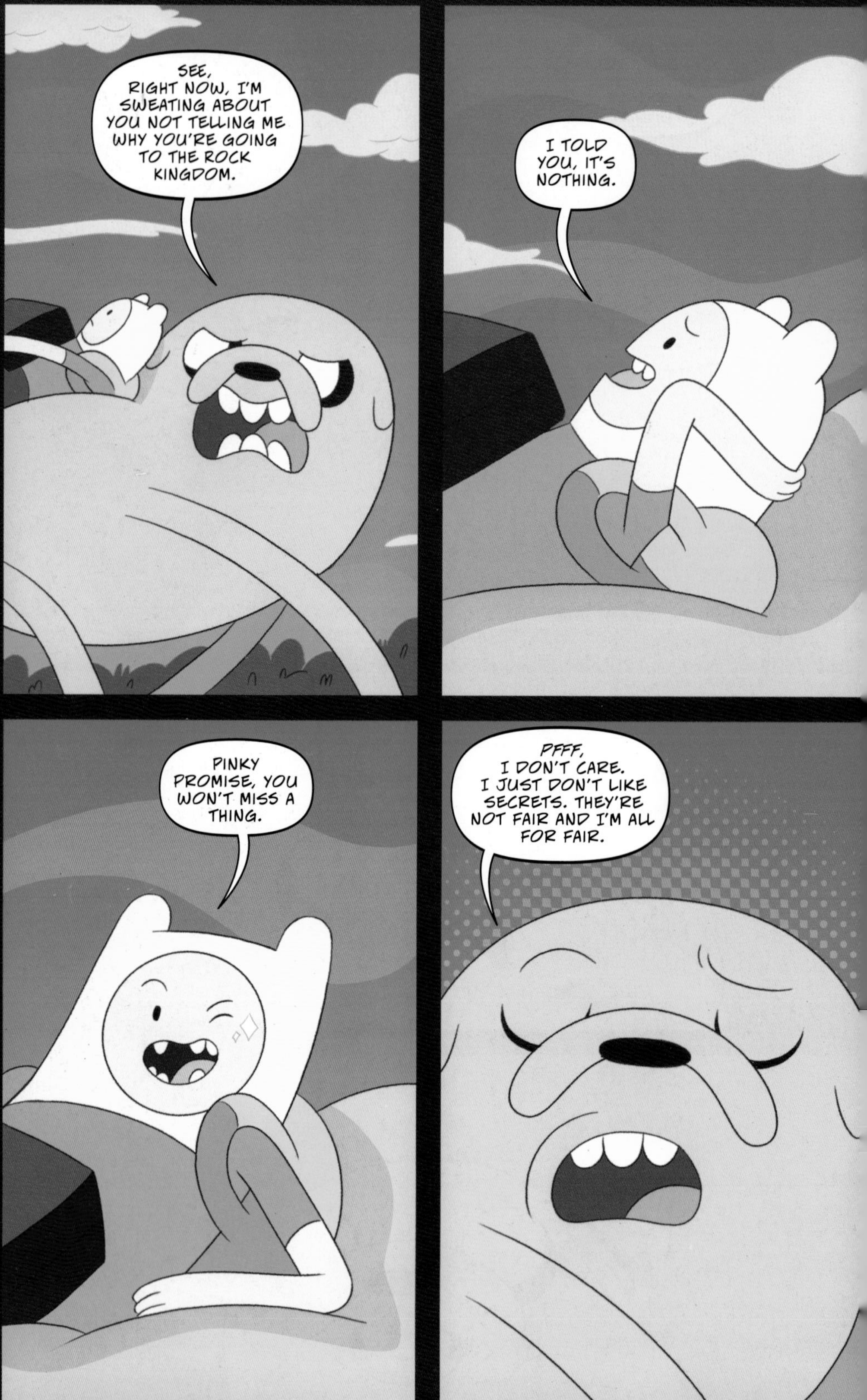
SEE, RIGHT NOW, I'M SWEATING ABOUT YOU NOT TELLING ME WHY YOU'RE GOING TO THE ROCK KINGDOM.
I TOLD YOU, IT'S NOTHING.
PINKY PROMISE, YOU WON'T MISS A THING.
PFFF, I DON'T CARE. I JUST DON'T LIKE SECRETS. THEY'RE NOT FAIR AND I'M ALL FOR FAIR.

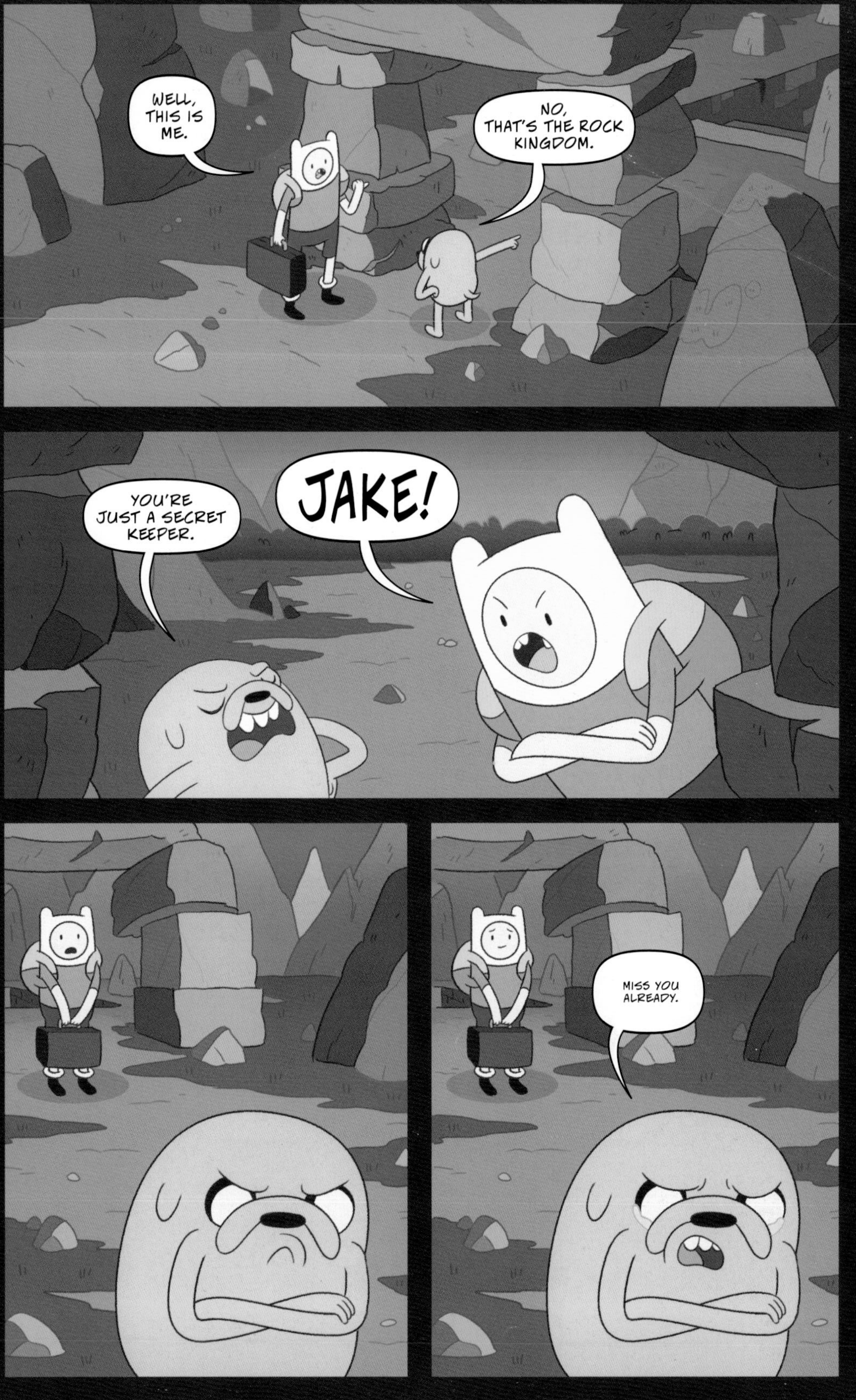
WELL, THIS IS ME.
NO, THAT'S THE ROCK KINGDOM.
YOU'RE JUST A SECRET KEEPER.
JAKE!
MISS YOU ALREADY.

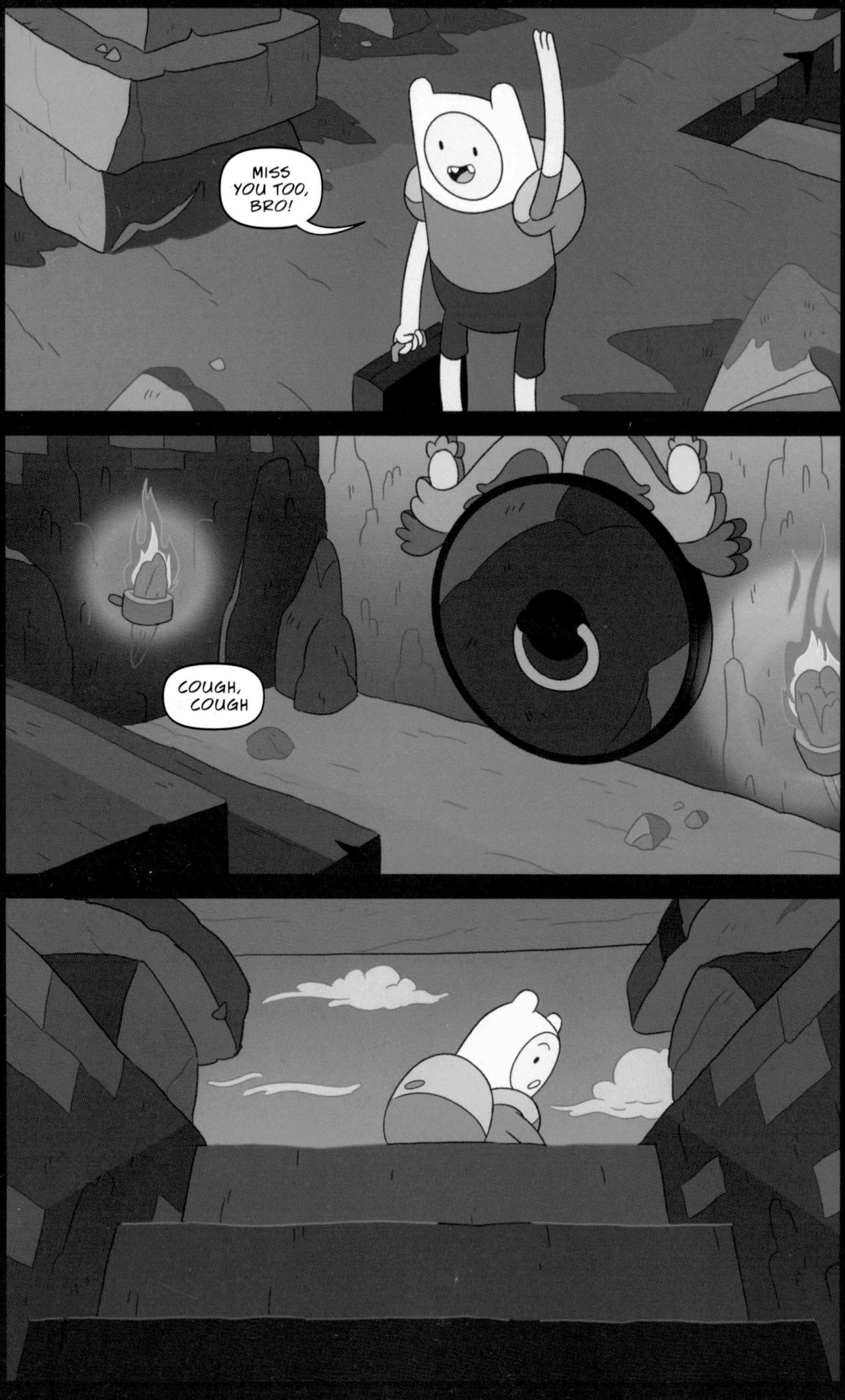
MISS YOU TOO, BRO!
COUGH, COUGH

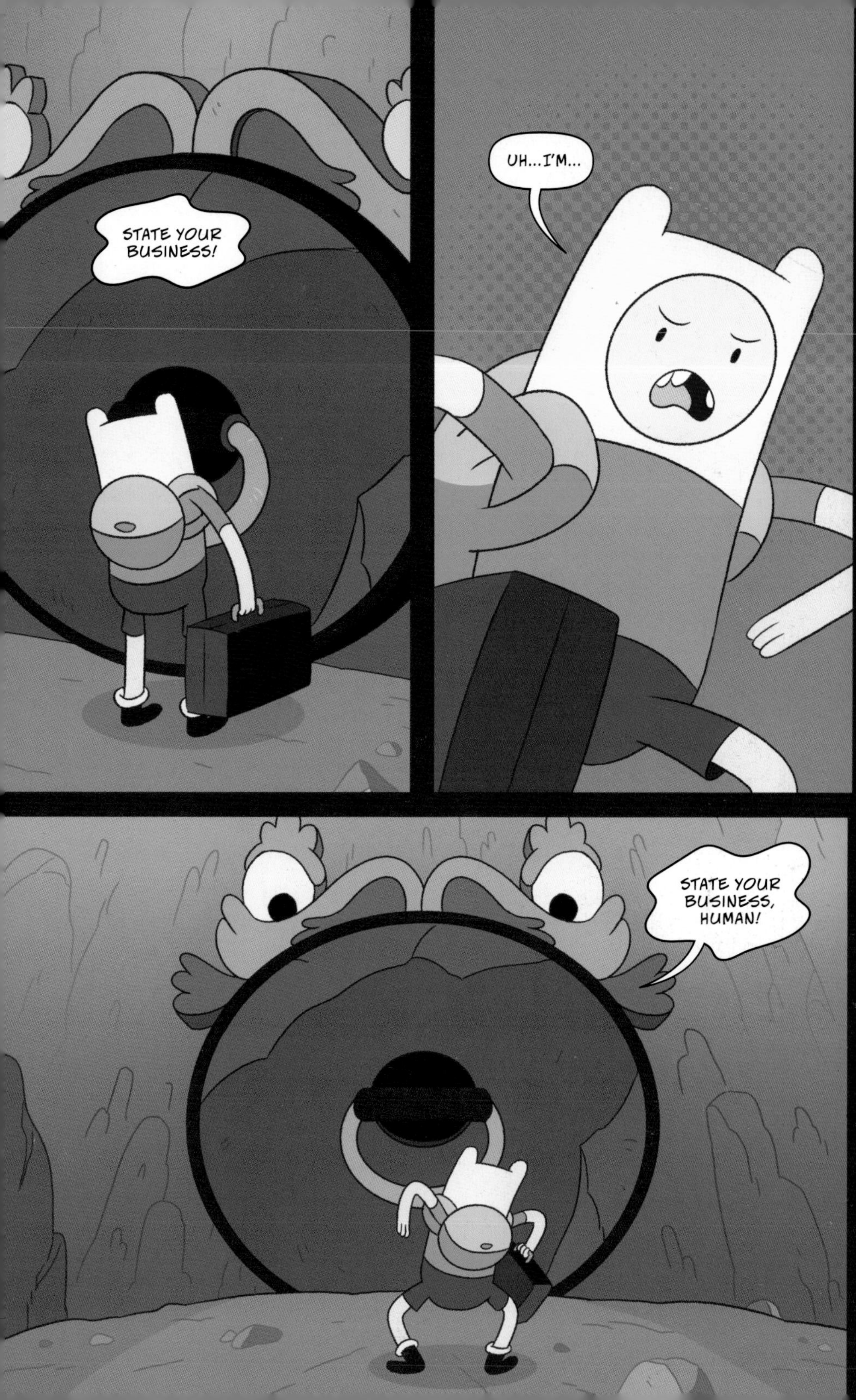
STATE YOUR BUSINESS!
UH...I'M...
STATE YOUR BUSINESS, HUMAN!

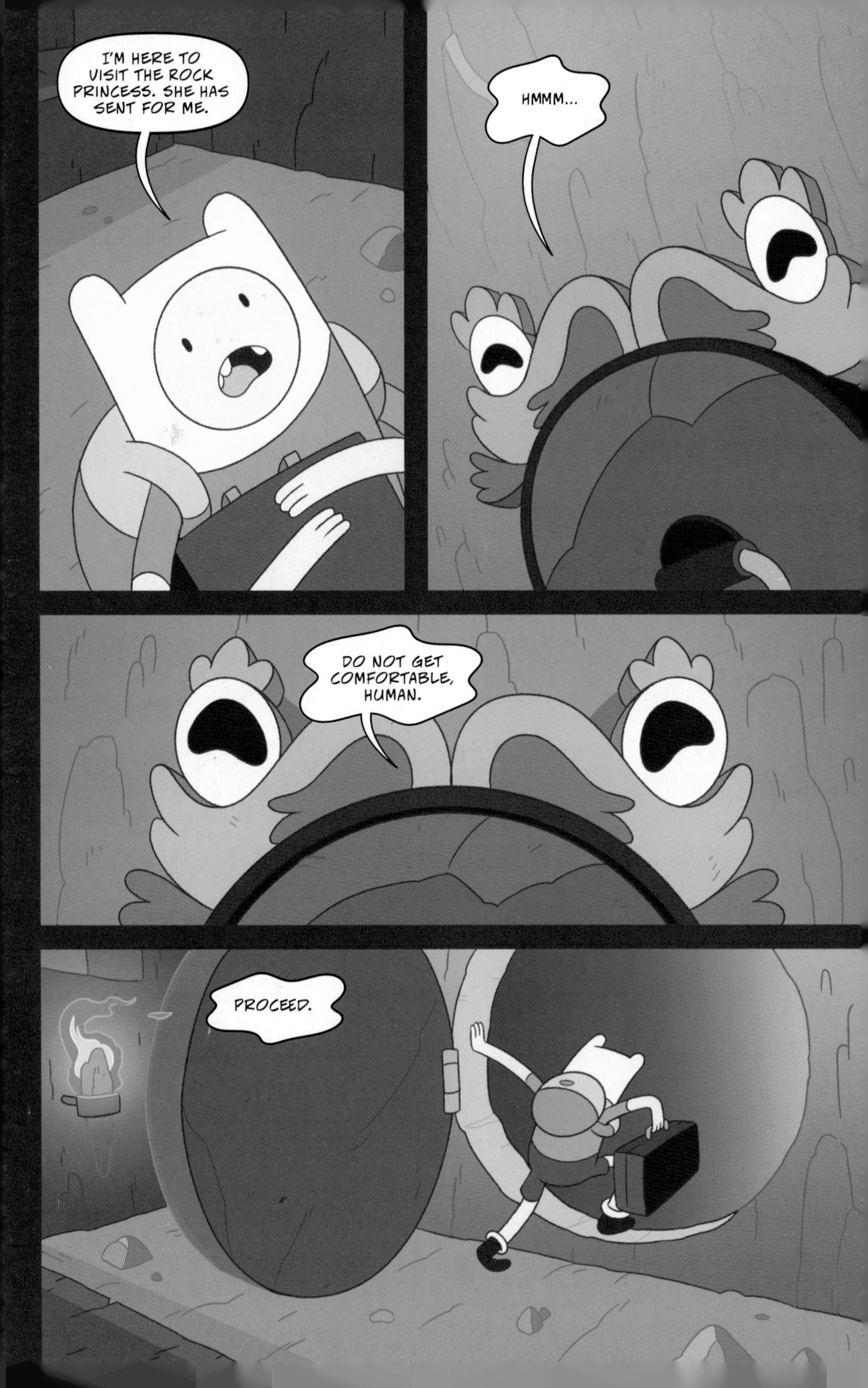
I'M HERE TO VISIT THE ROCK PRINCESS. SHE HAS SENT FOR ME.
HMMM...
DO NOT GET COMFORTABLE, HUMAN.
PROCEED.

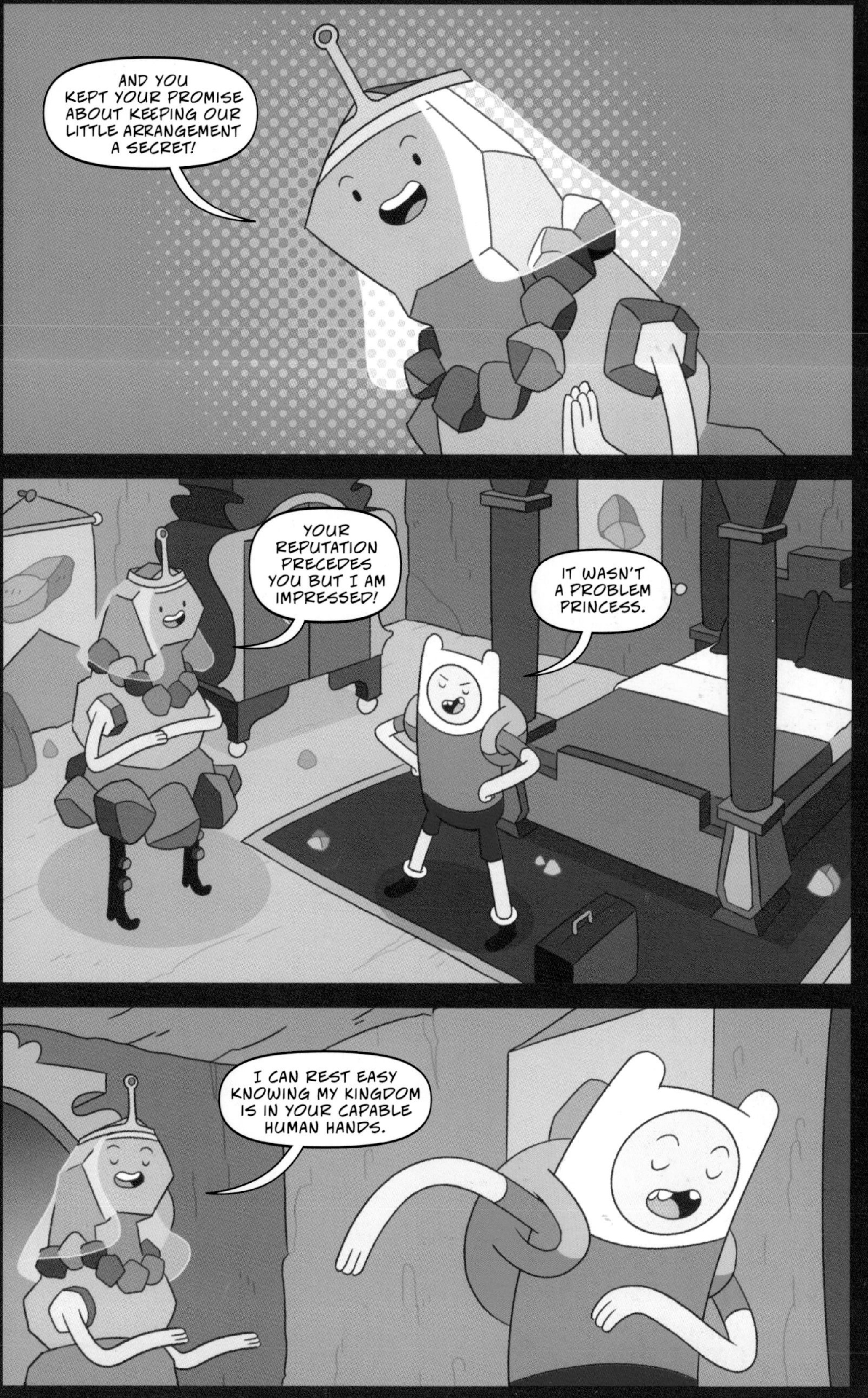
AND YOU KEPT YOUR PROMISE ABOUT KEEPING OUR LITTLE ARRANGEMENT A SECRET!
YOUR REPUTATION PRECEDES YOU BUT I AM IMPRESSED!
IT WASN'T A PROBLEM PRINCESS.
I CAN REST EASY KNOWING MY KINGDOM IS IN YOUR CAPABLE HUMAN HANDS.

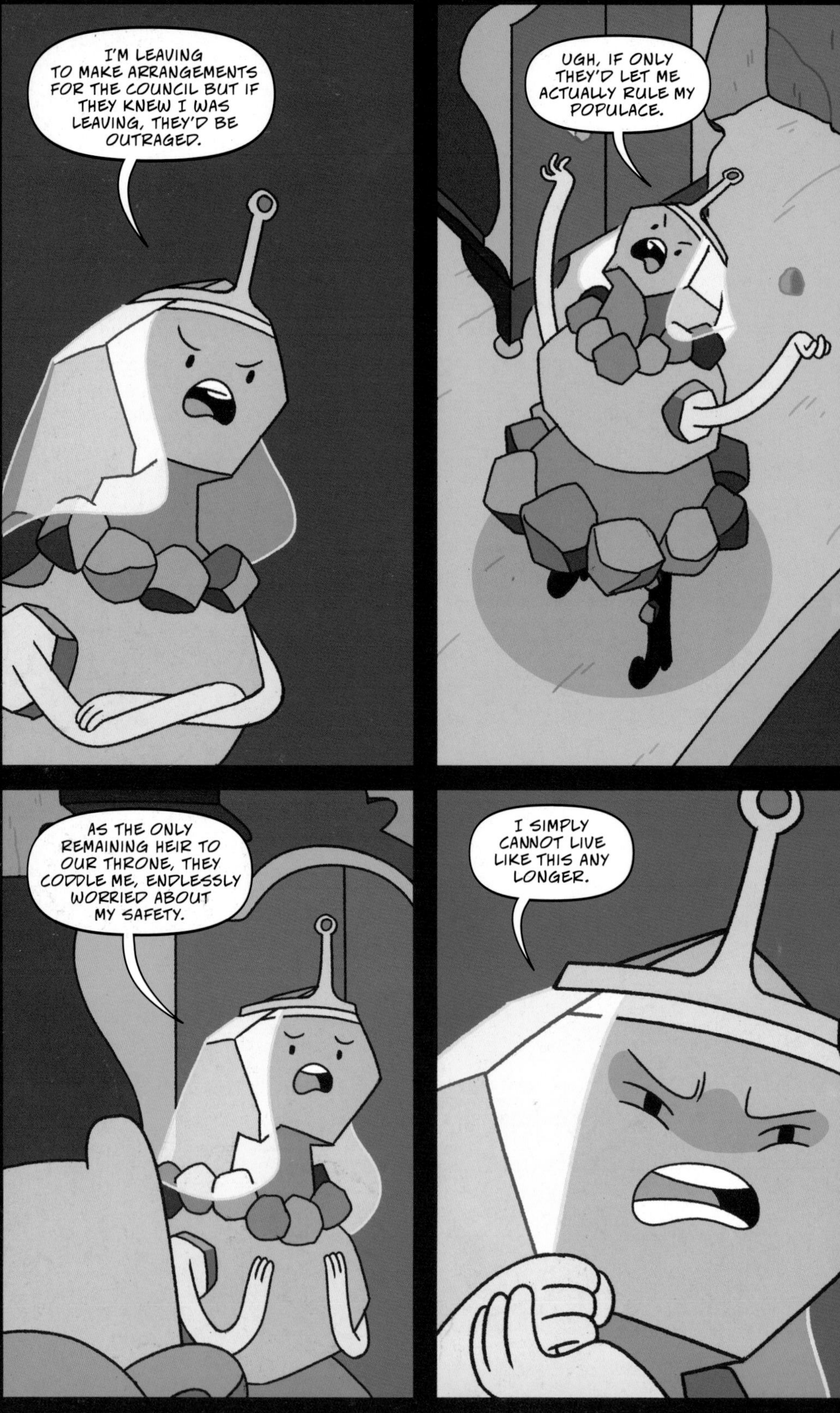
I'M LEAVING TO MAKE ARRANGEMENTS FOR THE COUNCIL BUT IF THEY KNEW I WAS LEAVING, THEY'D BE OUTRAGED.
UGH, IF ONLY THEY'D LET ME ACTUALLY RULE MY POPULACE.
AS THE ONLY REMAINING HEIR TO OUR THRONE, THEY CODDLE ME, ENDLESSLY WORRIED ABOUT MY SAFETY.
I SIMPLY CANNOT LIVE LIKE THIS ANY LONGER.

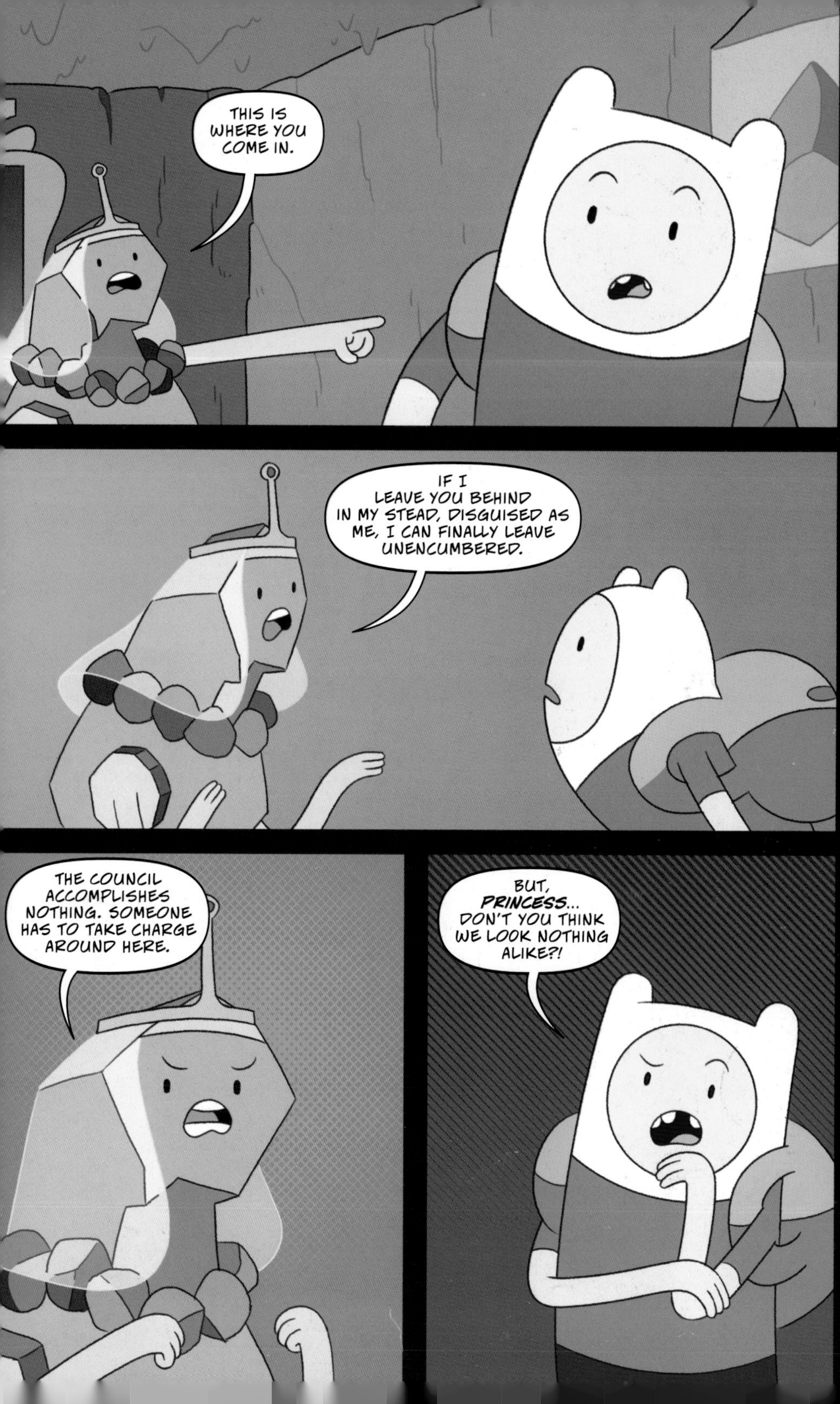
THIS IS WHERE YOU COME IN.
IF I LEAVE YOU BEHIND IN MY STEAD, DISGUISED AS ME, I CAN FINALLY LEAVE UNENCUMBERED.
THE COUNCIL ACCOMPLISHES NOTHING. SOMEONE HAS TO TAKE CHARGE AROUND HERE.
BUT, PRINCESS... DON'T YOU THINK WE LOOK NOTHING ALIKE?!

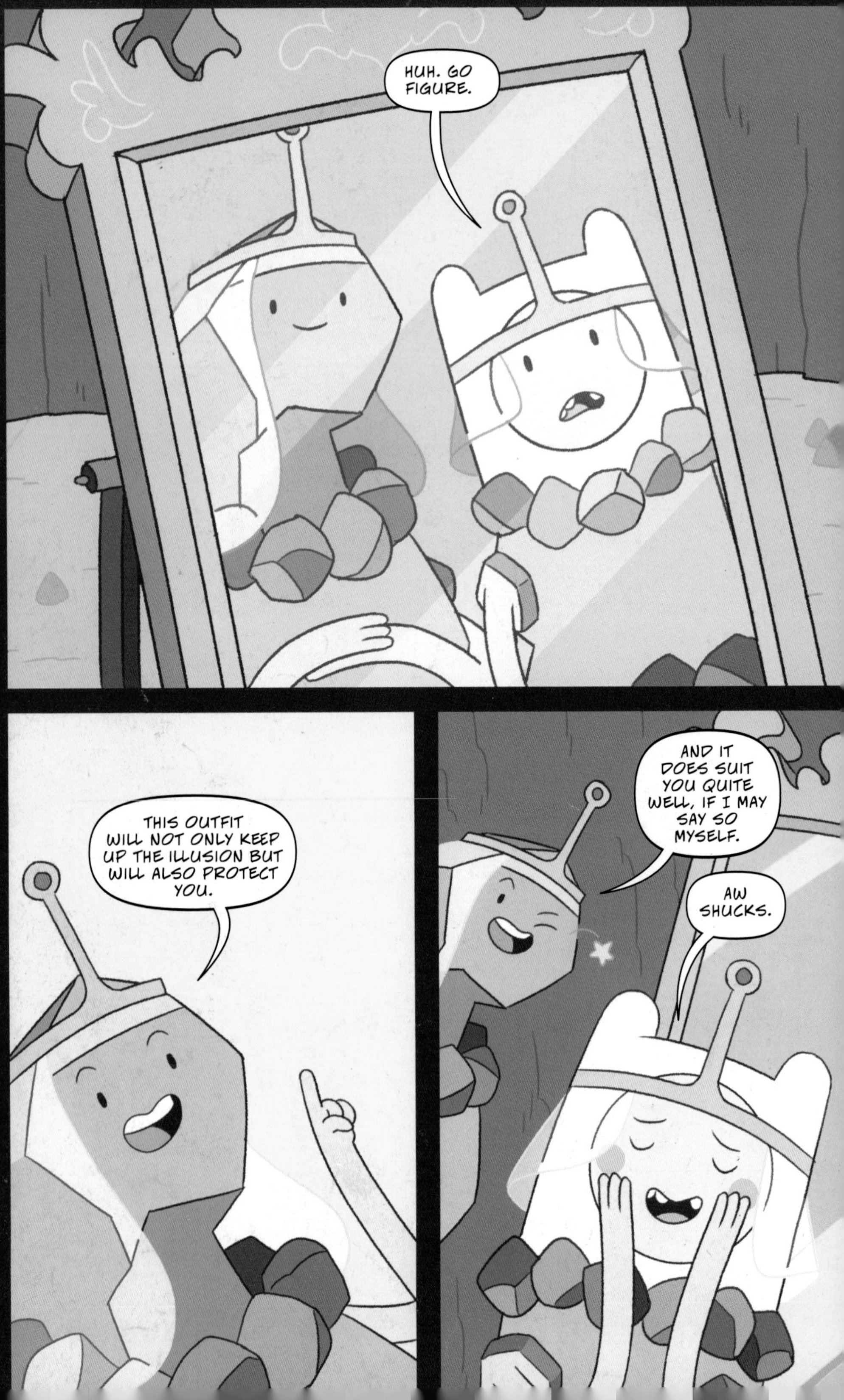
HUH. GO FIGURE.
THIS OUTFIT WILL NOT ONLY KEEP UP THE ILLUSION BUT WILL ALSO PROTECT YOU.
AND IT DOES SUIT YOU QUITE WELL, IF I MAY SAY SO MYSELF.
AW SHUCKS.

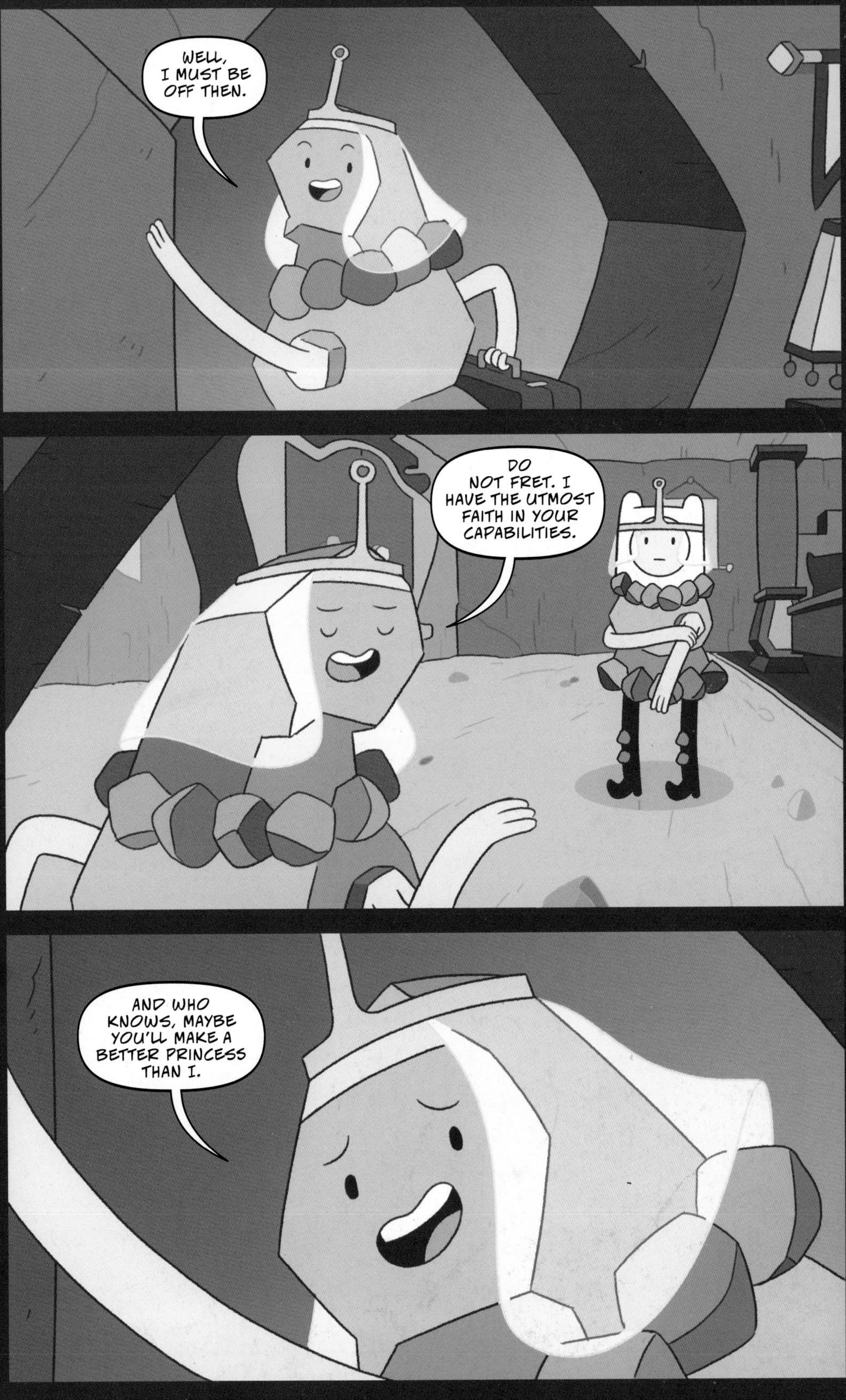
WELL, I MUST BE OFF THEN.
DO NOT FRET. I HAVE THE UTMOST FAITH IN YOUR CAPABILITIES.
AND WHO KNOWS, MAYBE YOU'LL MAKE A BETTER PRINCESS THAN I.

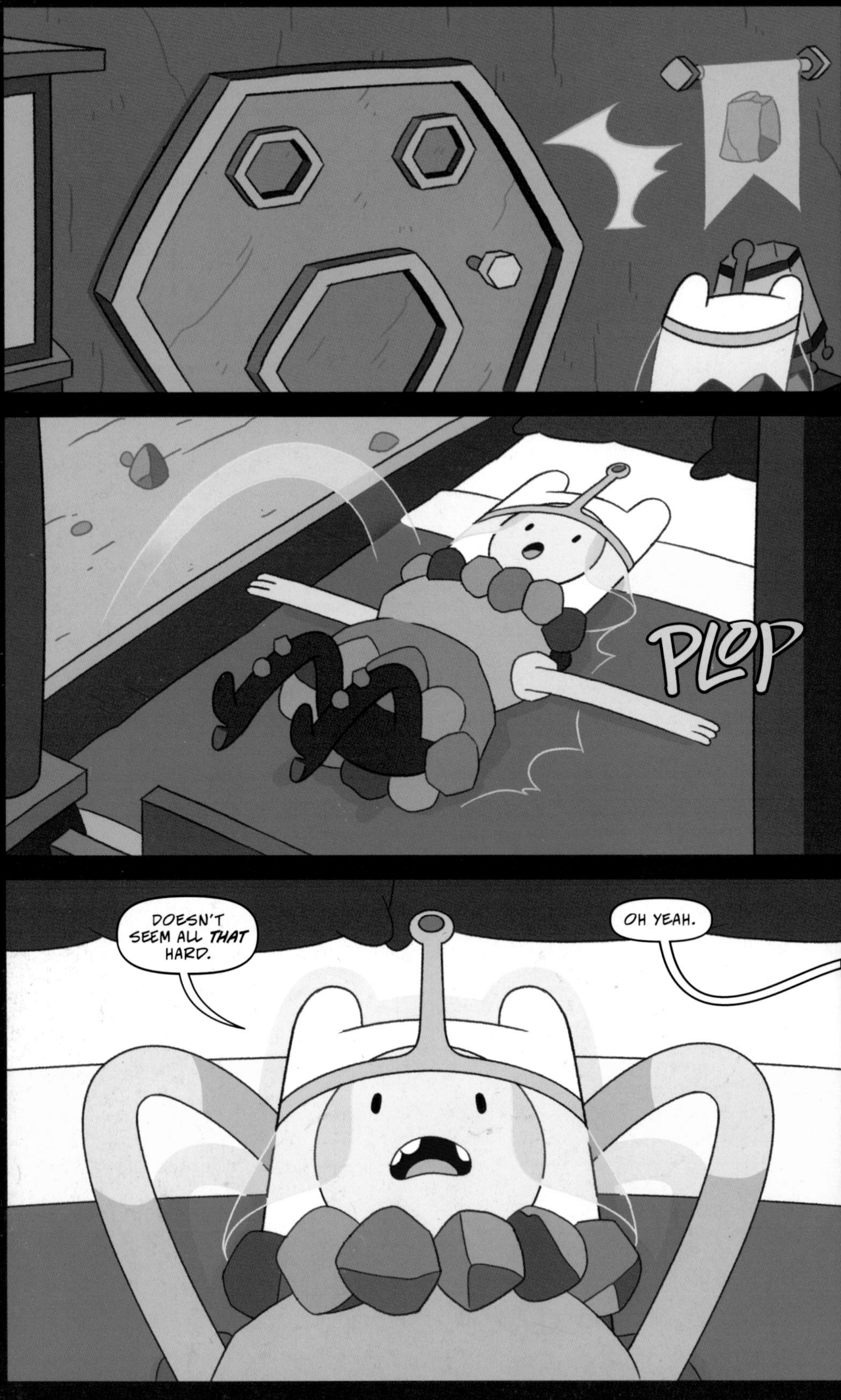
PLOP
DOESN'T SEEM ALL ***THAT*** HARD.
OH YEAH.

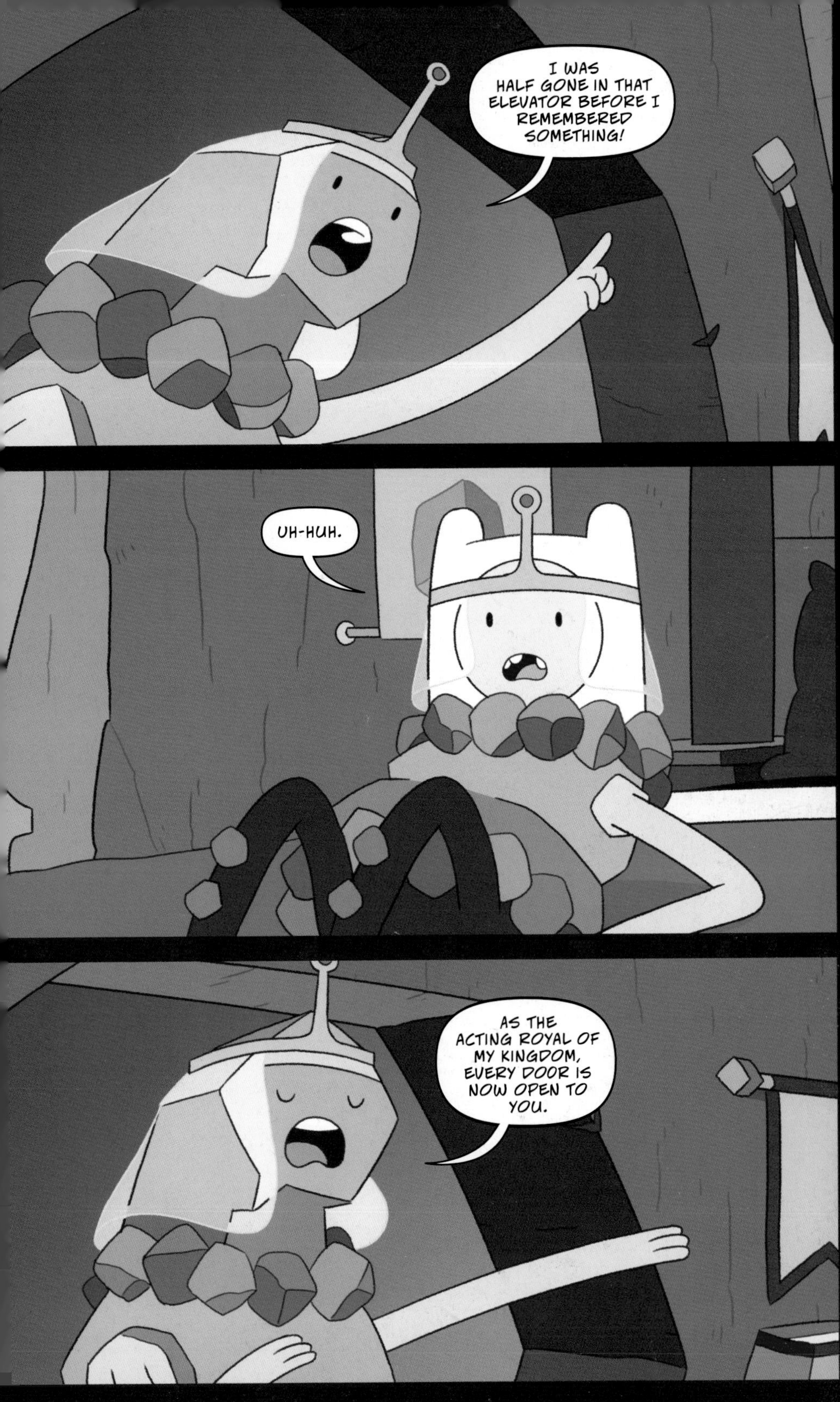
I WAS HALF GONE IN THAT ELEVATOR BEFORE I REMEMBERED SOMETHING!
UH-HUH.
AS THE ACTING ROYAL OF MY KINGDOM, EVERY DOOR IS NOW OPEN TO YOU.

YOU'VE ALREADY MET THE KEEPER, THE GUARDIAN OF THE WHOLE KINGDOM...

FIG.1 KEEPER

...BUT THERE'S ALSO MY INNER SANCTUM. THESE DOORS ARE MY CLOSEST ADVISORS AND KNOW OF OUR 'ARRANGEMENT' IF YOU EVER NEED HELP.

FIG.2 INNER SANCTUM

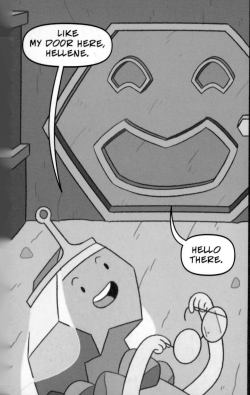

LIKE MY DOOR HERE, HELLENE.

HELLO THERE.

OH! UM...NICE TO MEET YOU HELLENE.

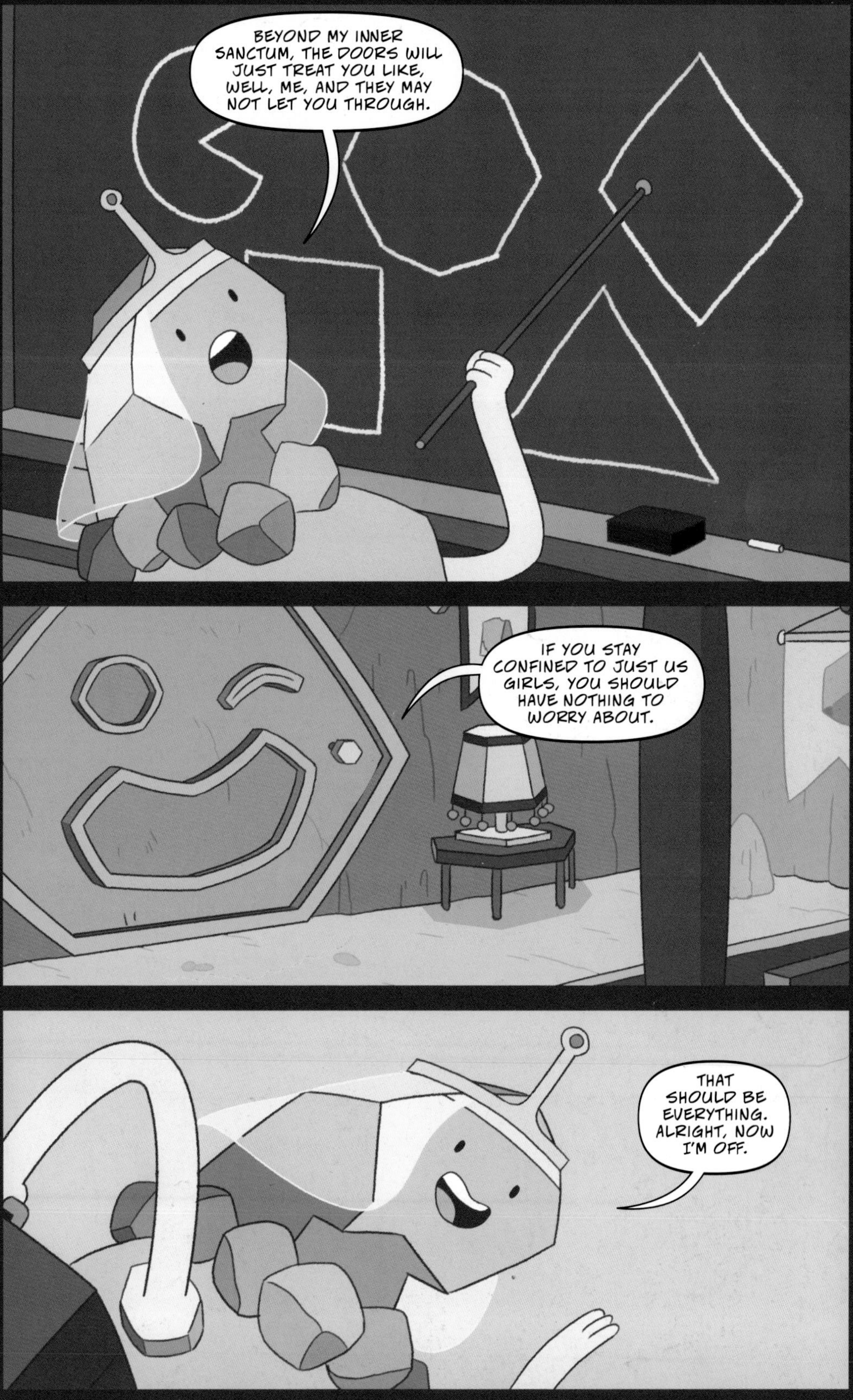
BEYOND MY INNER SANCTUM, THE DOORS WILL JUST TREAT YOU LIKE, WELL, ME, AND THEY MAY NOT LET YOU THROUGH.
IF YOU STAY CONFINED TO JUST US GIRLS, YOU SHOULD HAVE NOTHING TO WORRY ABOUT.
THAT SHOULD BE EVERYTHING. ALRIGHT, NOW I'M OFF.

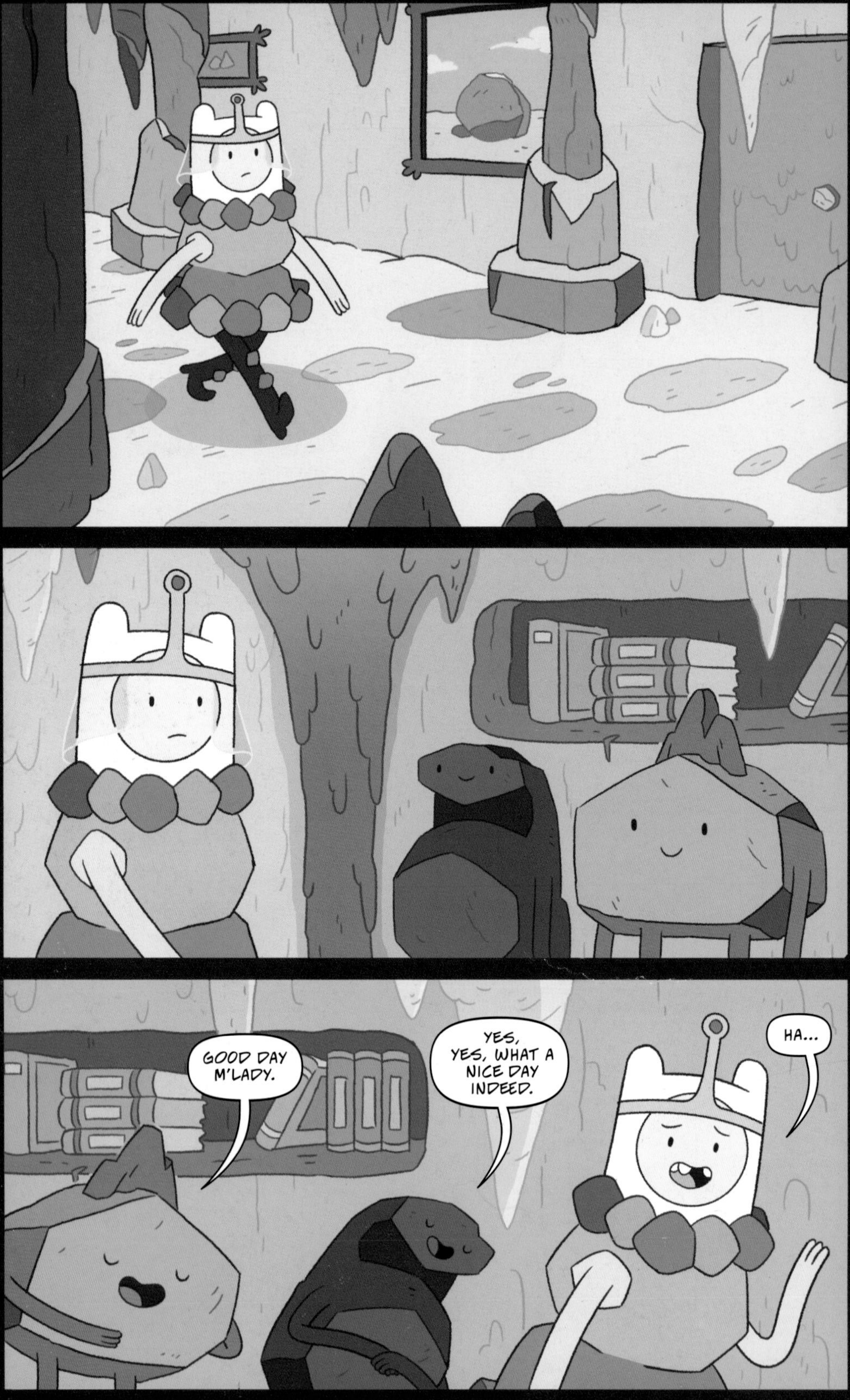
GOOD DAY M'LADY.
YES, YES, WHAT A NICE DAY INDEED.
HA...

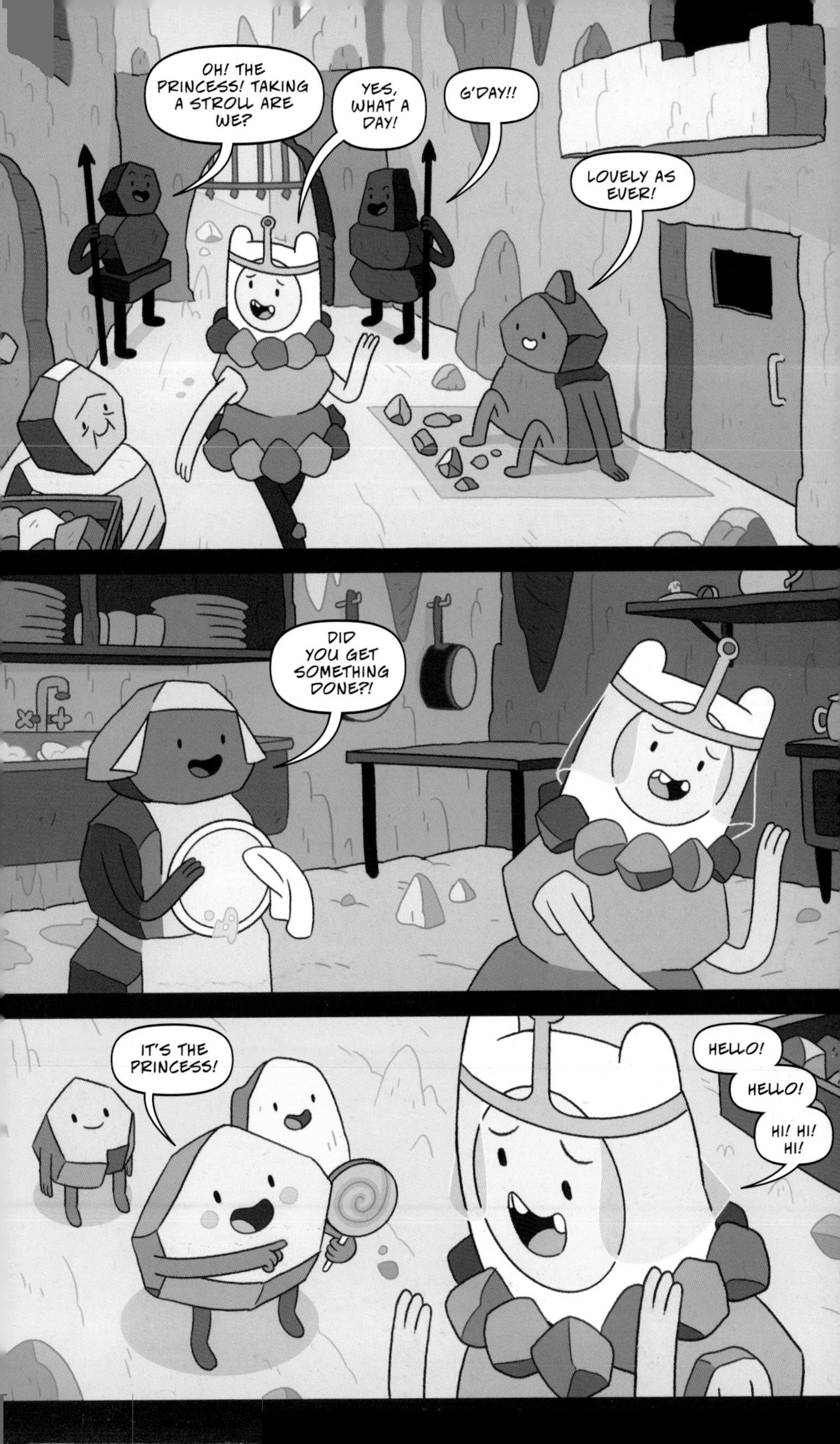
OH! THE PRINCESS! TAKING A STROLL ARE WE?
YES, WHAT A DAY!
G'DAY!!
LOVELY AS EVER!
DID YOU GET SOMETHING DONE?!
IT'S THE PRINCESS!
HELLO!
HELLO!
HI! HI! HI!

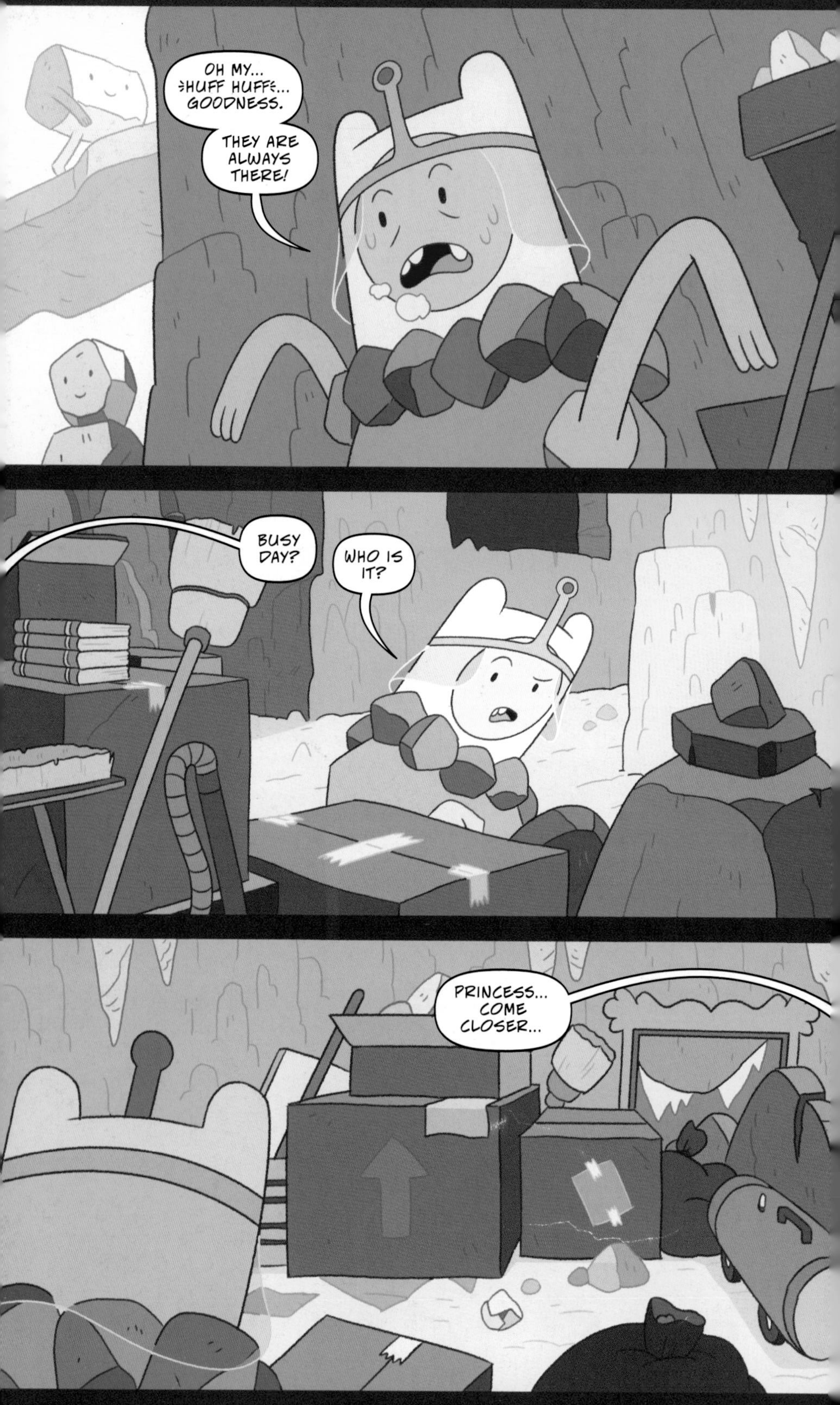
OH MY... HUFF HUFF... GOODNESS.
THEY ARE ALWAYS THERE!
BUSY DAY?
WHO IS IT?
PRINCESS... COME CLOSER...

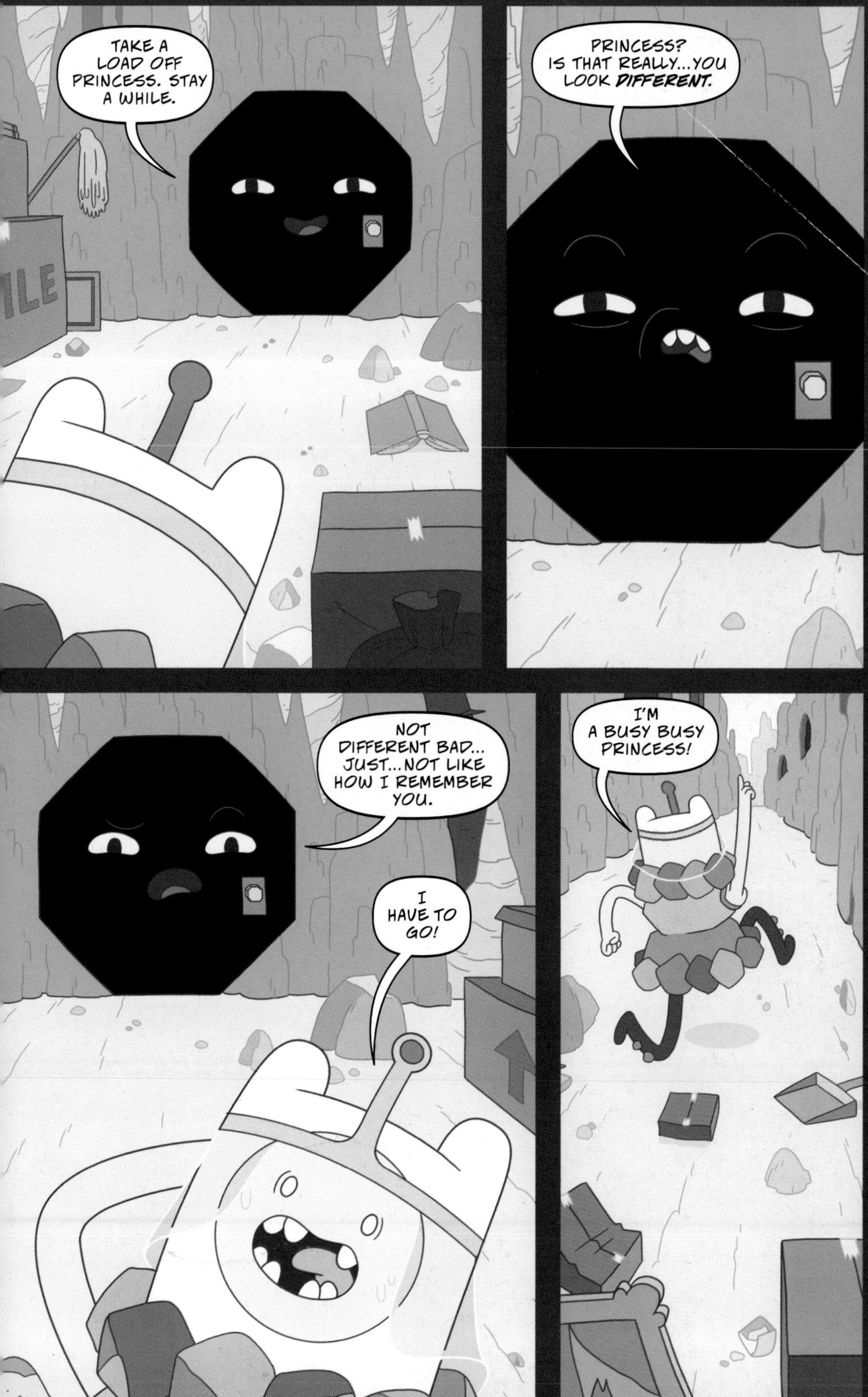
TAKE A LOAD OFF PRINCESS. STAY A WHILE.
PRINCESS? IS THAT REALLY...YOU LOOK *DIFFERENT.*
NOT DIFFERENT BAD... JUST...NOT LIKE HOW I REMEMBER YOU.
I HAVE TO GO!
I'M A BUSY BUSY PRINCESS!

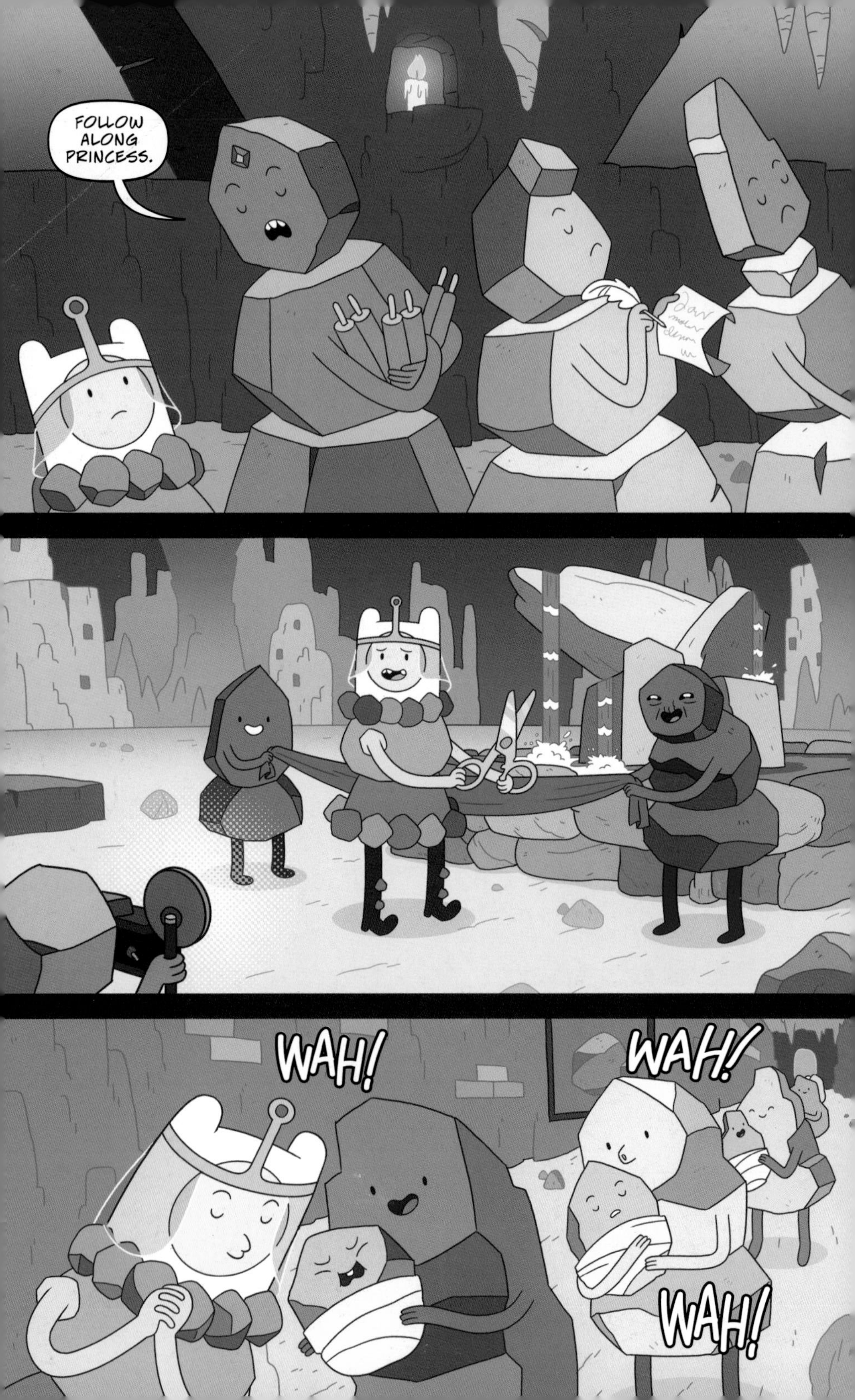
FOLLOW ALONG PRINCESS.
WAH!
WAH!
WAH!

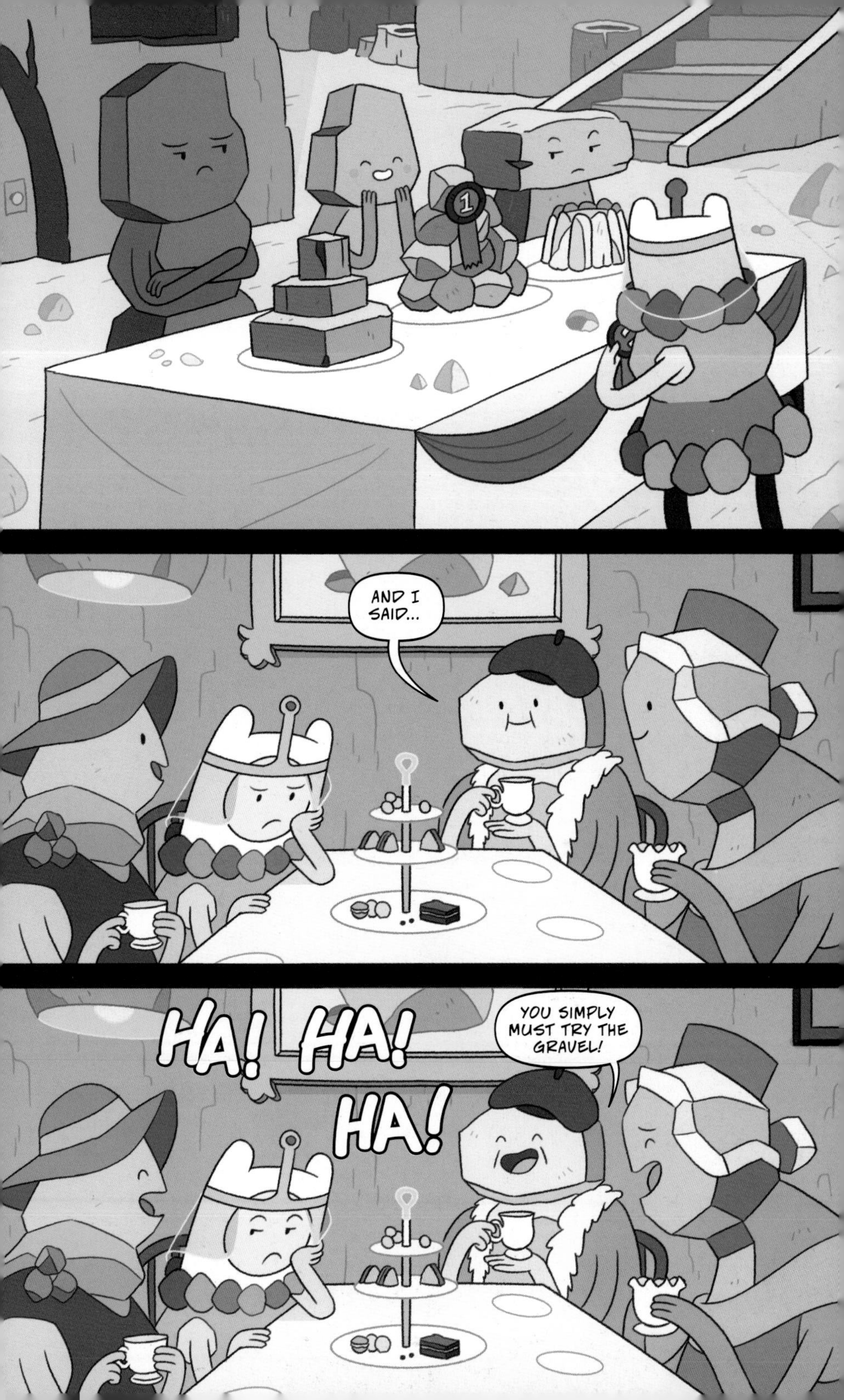
AND I SAID...
HA! HA! HA!
YOU SIMPLY MUST TRY THE GRAVEL!

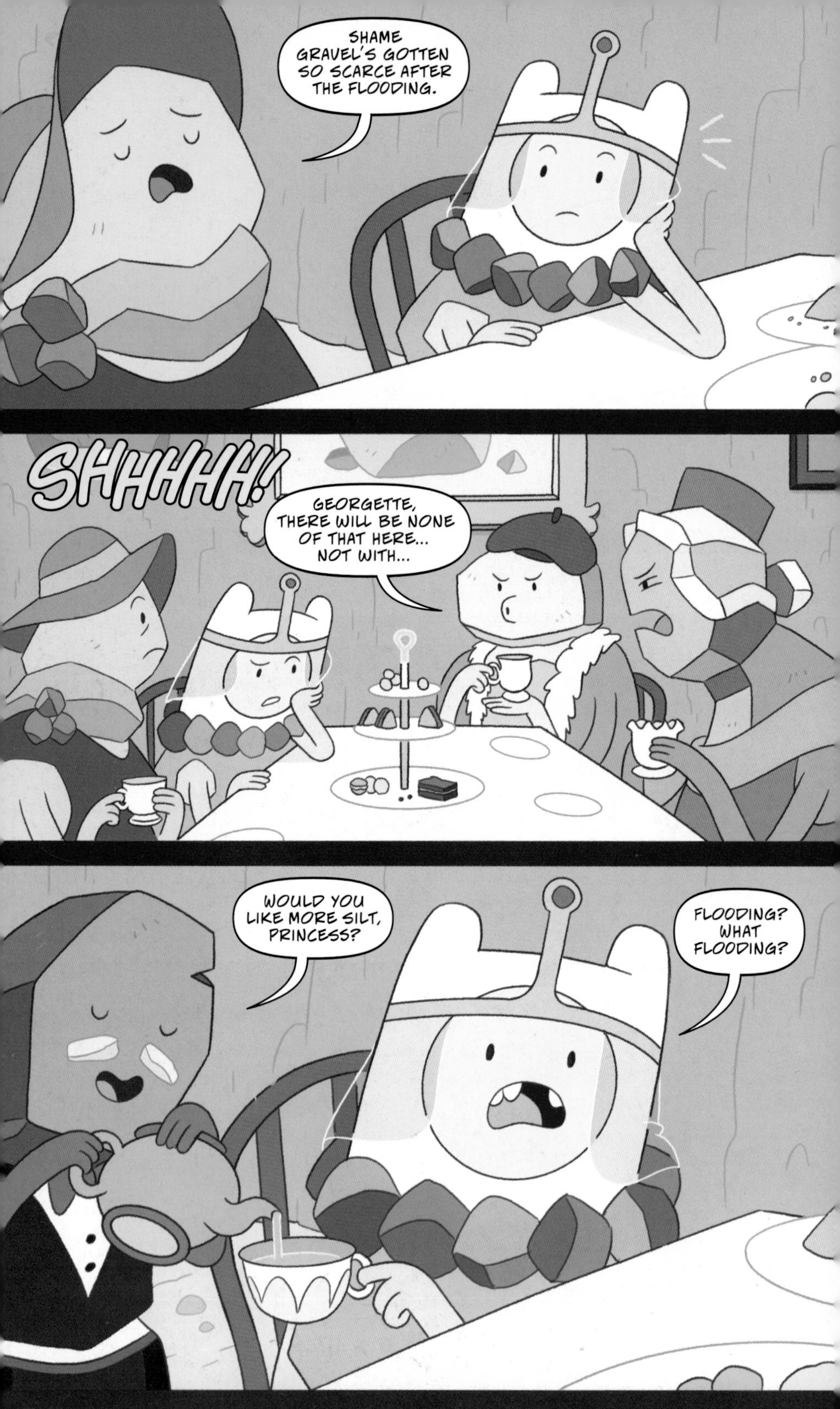
SHAME GRAVEL'S GOTTEN SO SCARCE AFTER THE FLOODING.
SHHHHH!
GEORGETTE, THERE WILL BE NONE OF THAT HERE... NOT WITH...
WOULD YOU LIKE MORE SILT, PRINCESS?
FLOODING? WHAT FLOODING?

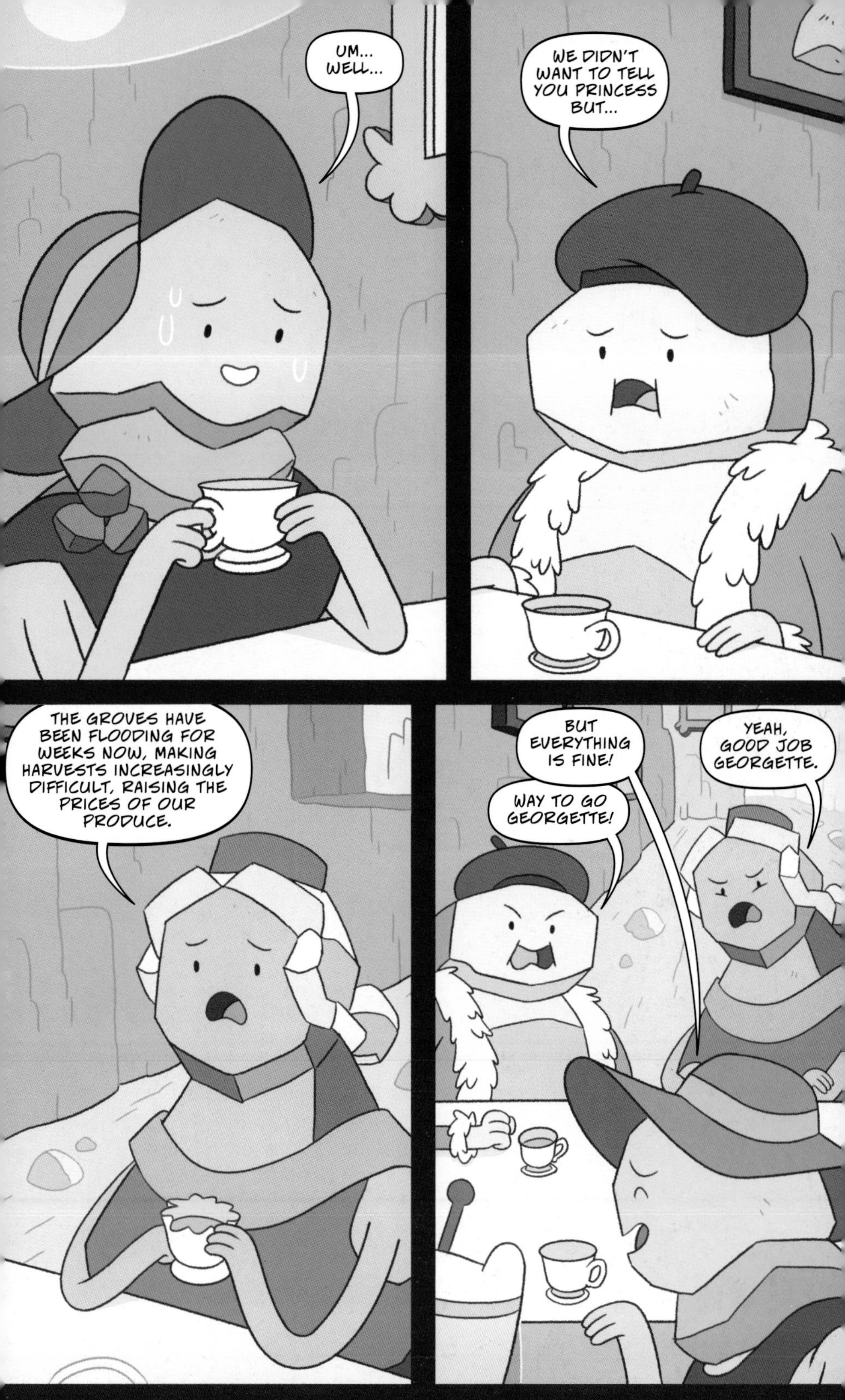
UM... WELL...
WE DIDN'T WANT TO TELL YOU PRINCESS BUT...
THE GROVES HAVE BEEN FLOODING FOR WEEKS NOW, MAKING HARVESTS INCREASINGLY DIFFICULT, RAISING THE PRICES OF OUR PRODUCE.
BUT EVERYTHING IS FINE!
WAY TO GO GEORGETTE!
YEAH, GOOD JOB GEORGETTE.

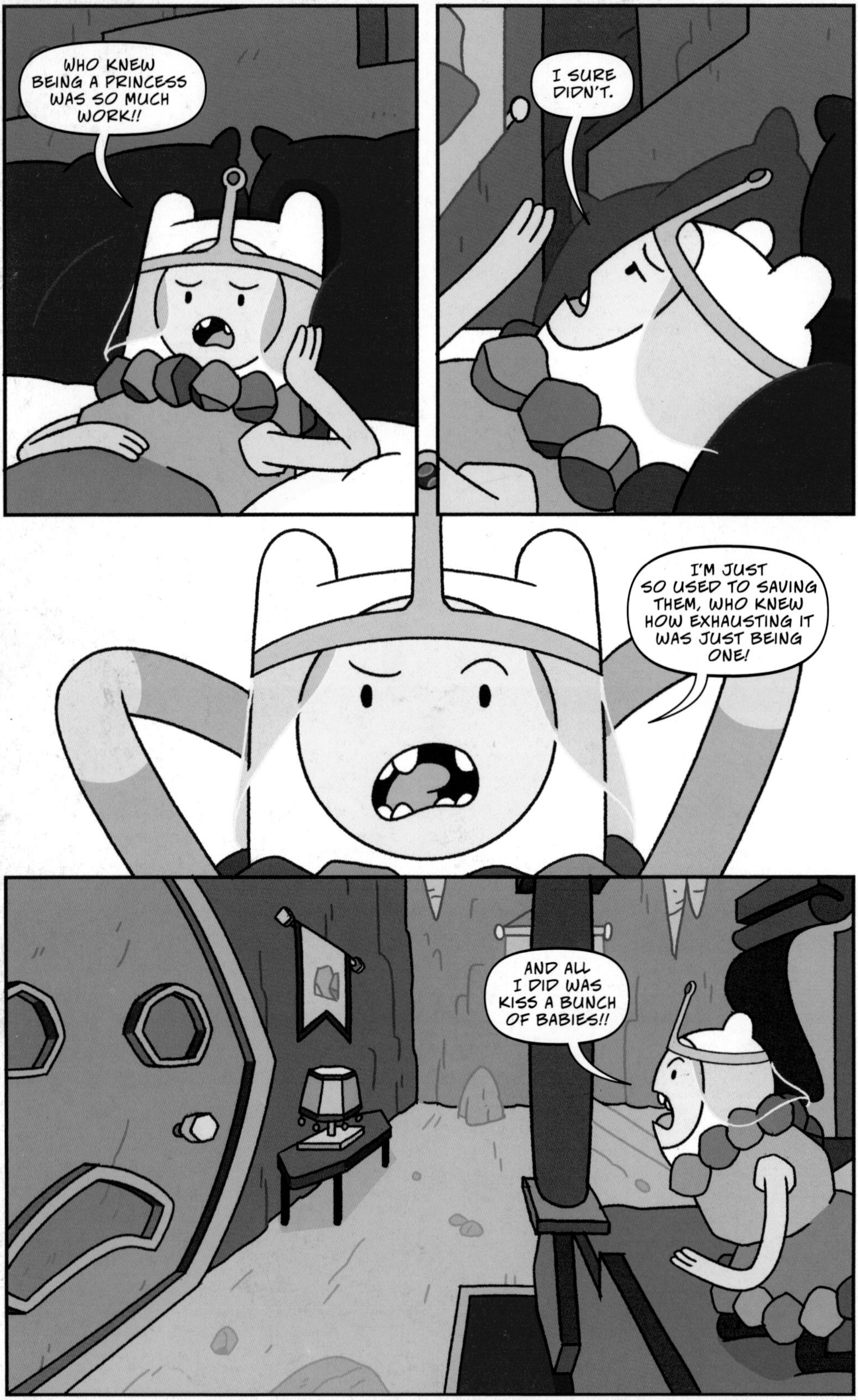
WHO KNEW BEING A PRINCESS WAS SO MUCH WORK!!
I SURE DIDN'T.
I'M JUST SO USED TO SAVING THEM, WHO KNEW HOW EXHAUSTING IT WAS JUST BEING ONE!
AND ALL I DID WAS KISS A BUNCH OF BABIES!!

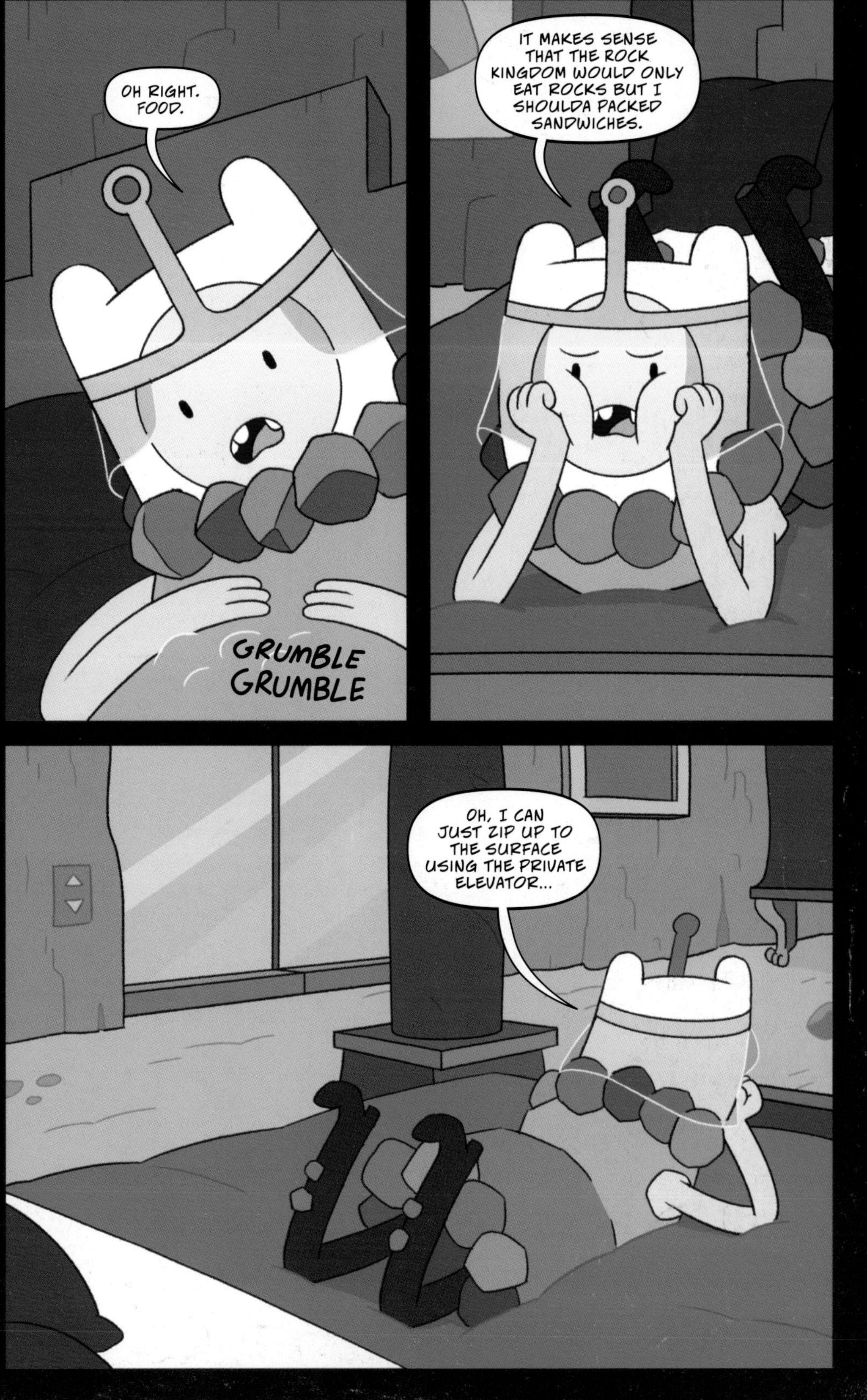
OH RIGHT. FOOD.
GRUMBLE GRUMBLE
IT MAKES SENSE THAT THE ROCK KINGDOM WOULD ONLY EAT ROCKS BUT I SHOULDA PACKED SANDWICHES.
OH, I CAN JUST ZIP UP TO THE SURFACE USING THE PRIVATE ELEVATOR...

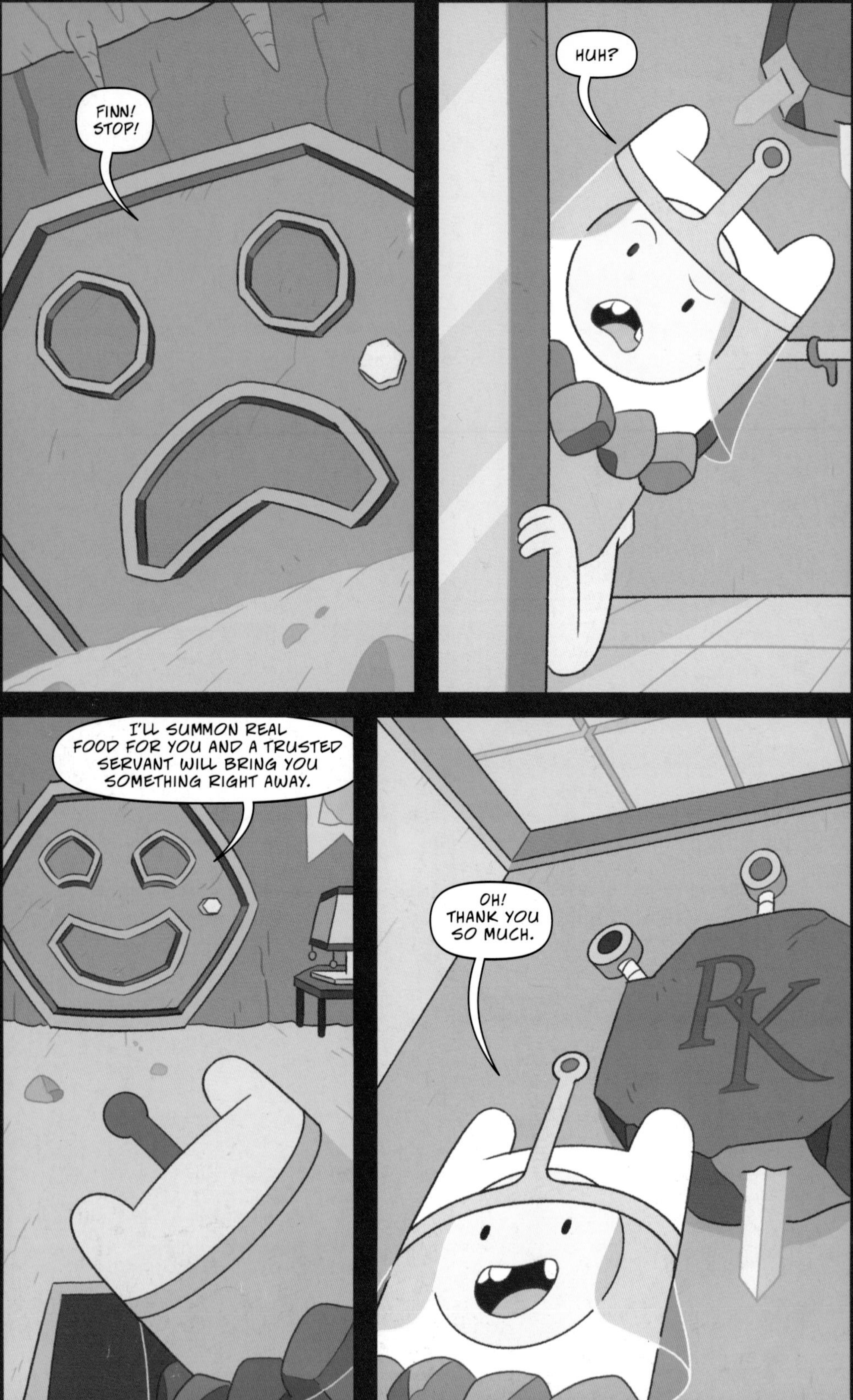
FINN! STOP!
HUH?
I'LL SUMMON REAL FOOD FOR YOU AND A TRUSTED SERVANT WILL BRING YOU SOMETHING RIGHT AWAY.
OH! THANK YOU SO MUCH.
RK

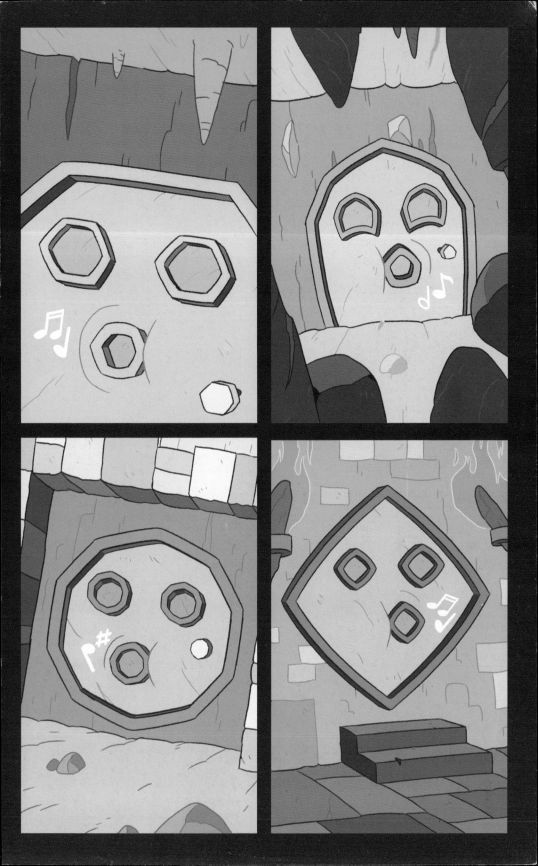

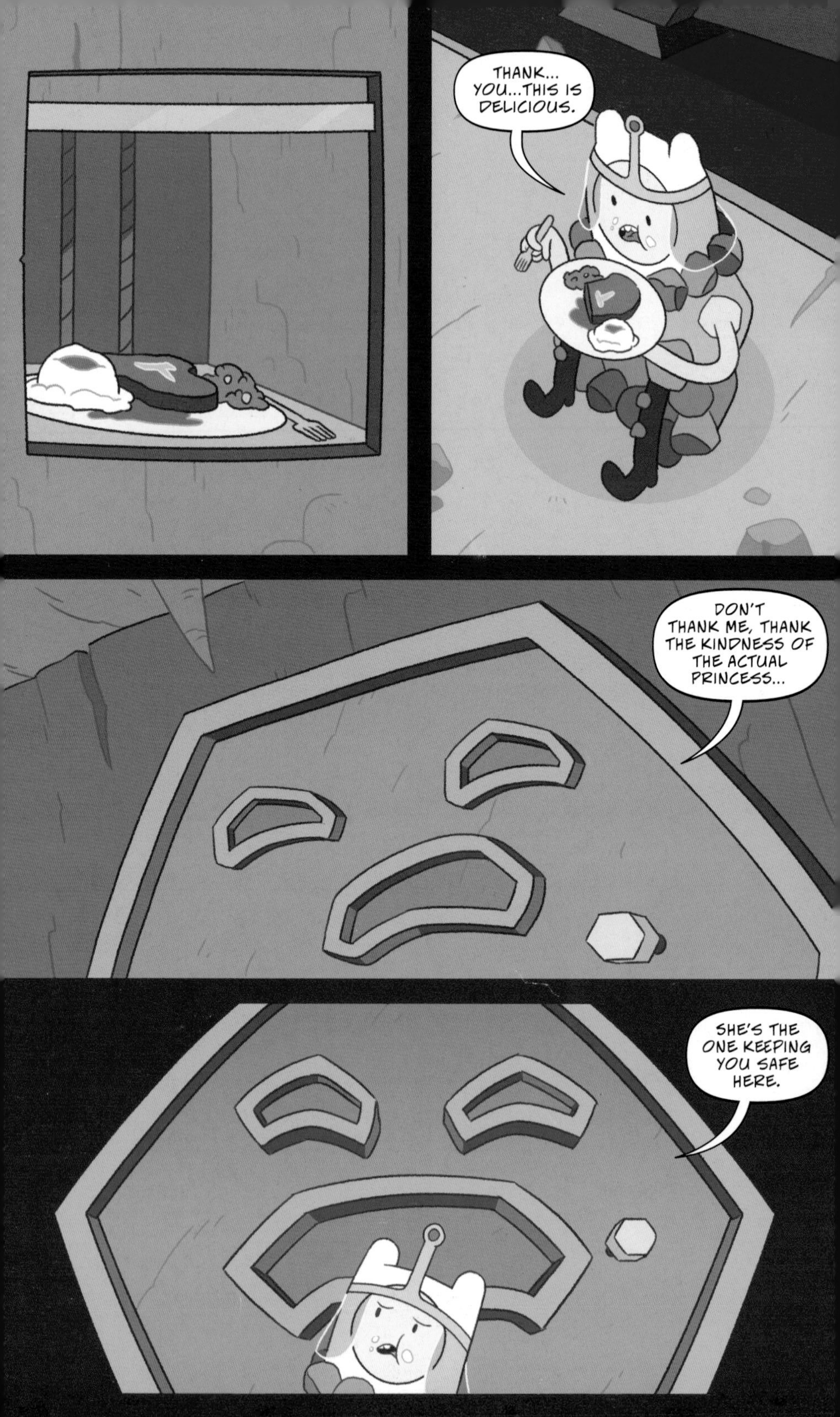
THANK... YOU...THIS IS DELICIOUS.
DON'T THANK ME, THANK THE KINDNESS OF THE ACTUAL PRINCESS...
SHE'S THE ONE KEEPING YOU SAFE HERE.

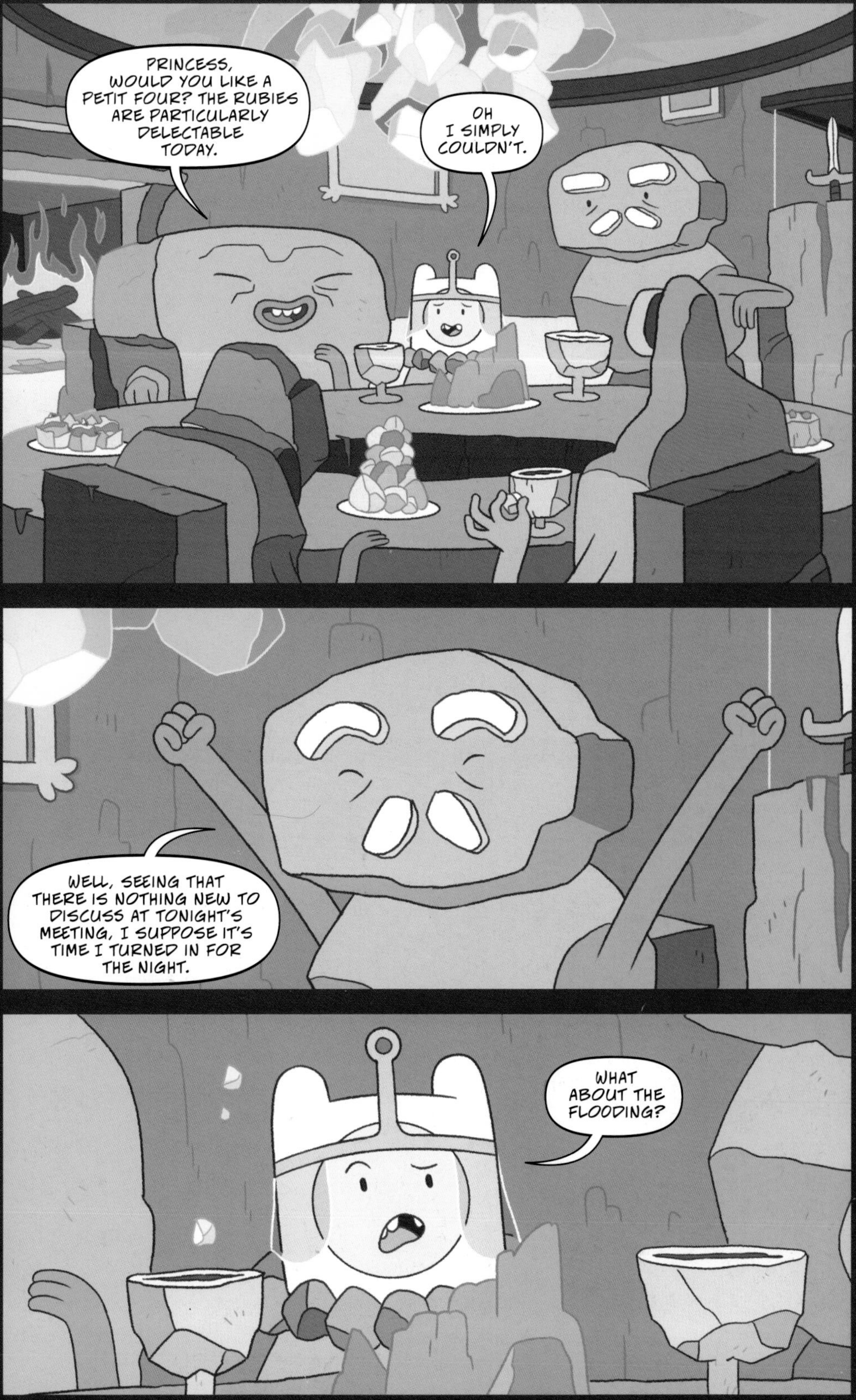
PRINCESS, WOULD YOU LIKE A PETIT FOUR? THE RUBIES ARE PARTICULARLY DELECTABLE TODAY.
OH I SIMPLY COULDN'T.
WELL, SEEING THAT THERE IS NOTHING NEW TO DISCUSS AT TONIGHT'S MEETING, I SUPPOSE IT'S TIME I TURNED IN FOR THE NIGHT.
WHAT ABOUT THE FLOODING?

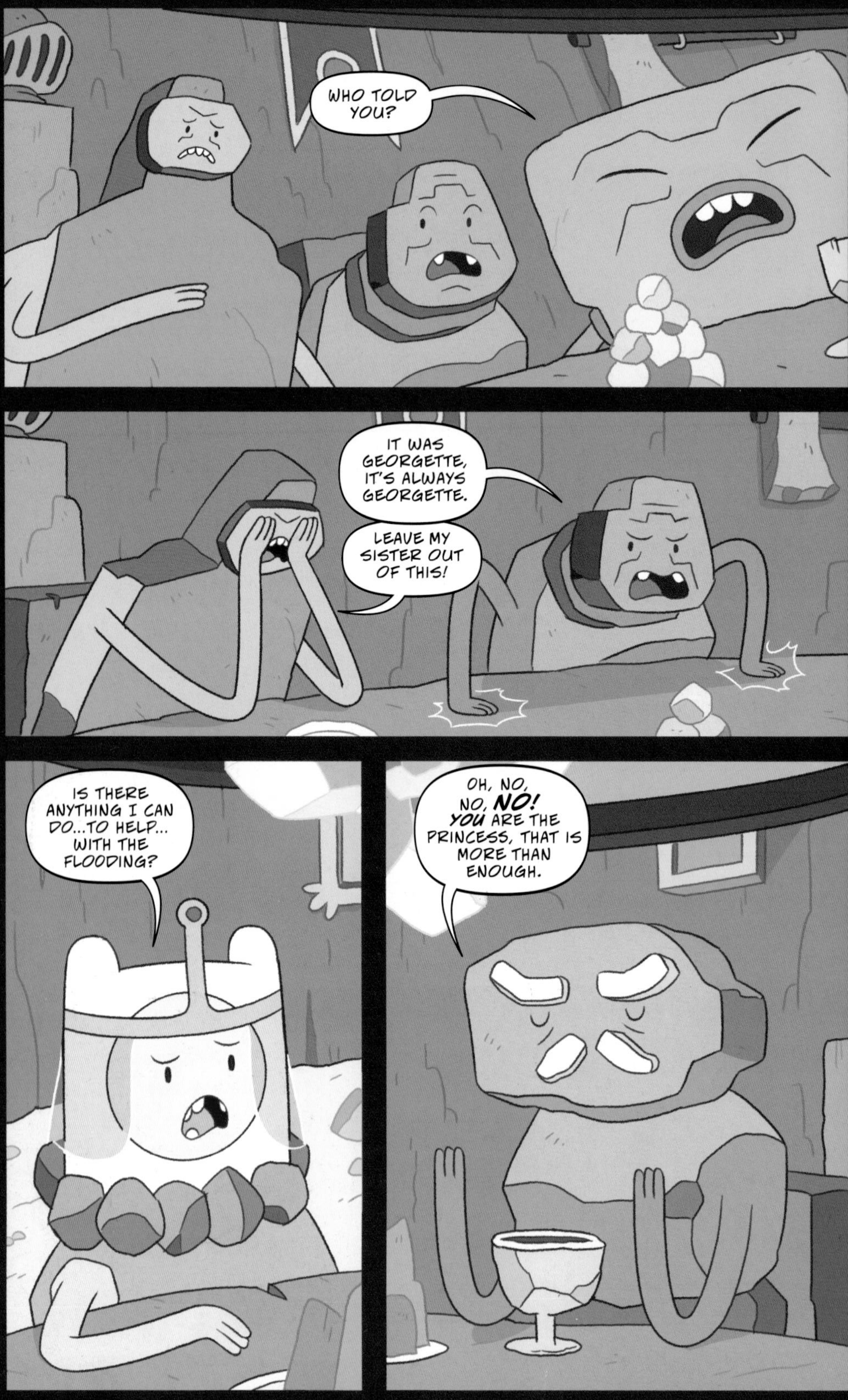
WHO TOLD YOU?
IT WAS GEORGETTE, IT'S ALWAYS GEORGETTE.
LEAVE MY SISTER OUT OF THIS!
IS THERE ANYTHING I CAN DO...TO HELP... WITH THE FLOODING?
OH, NO, NO, **NO!** ***YOU*** ARE THE PRINCESS, THAT IS MORE THAN ENOUGH.

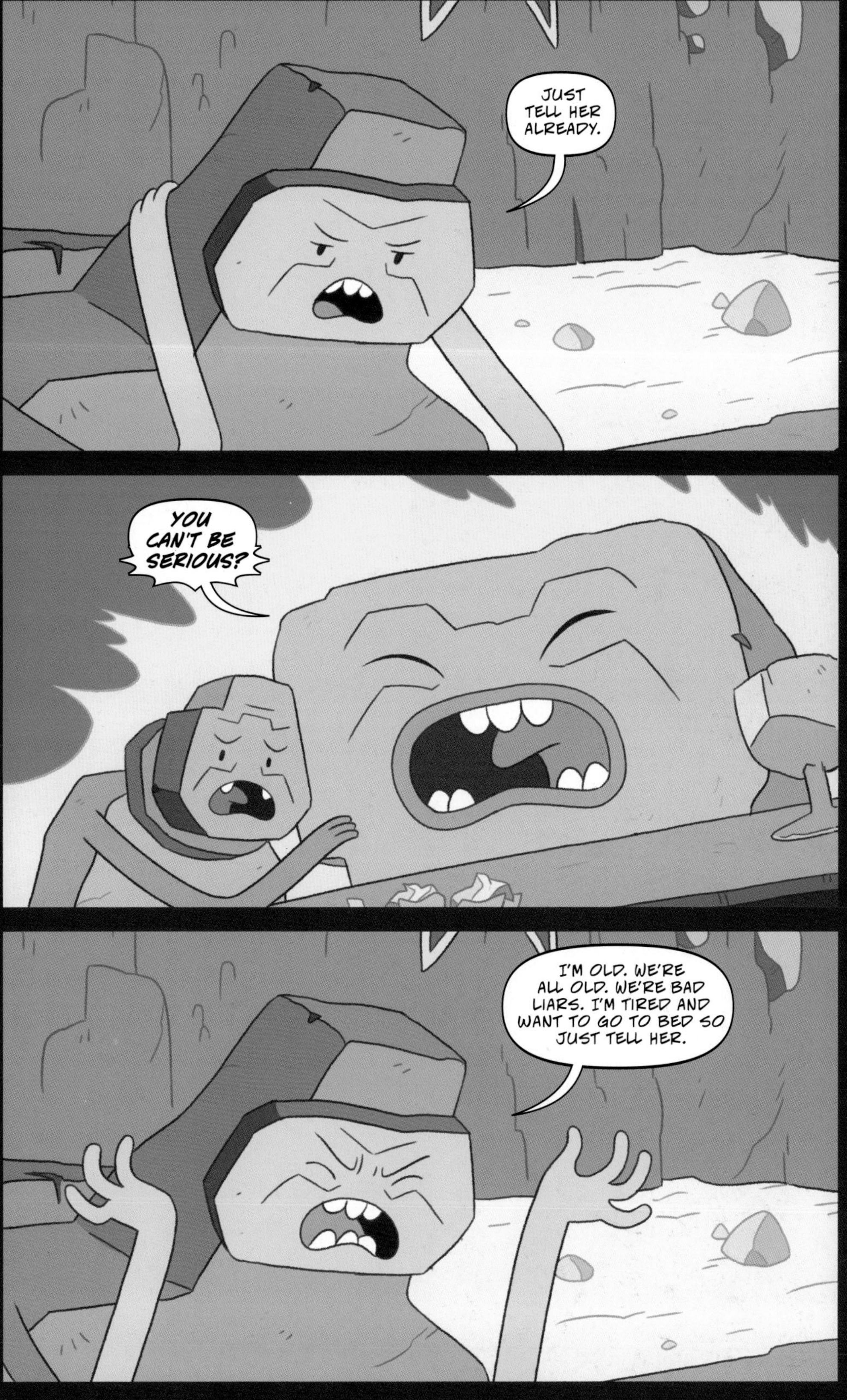
JUST TELL HER ALREADY.
YOU CAN'T BE SERIOUS?
I'M OLD. WE'RE ALL OLD. WE'RE BAD LIARS. I'M TIRED AND WANT TO GO TO BED SO JUST TELL HER.

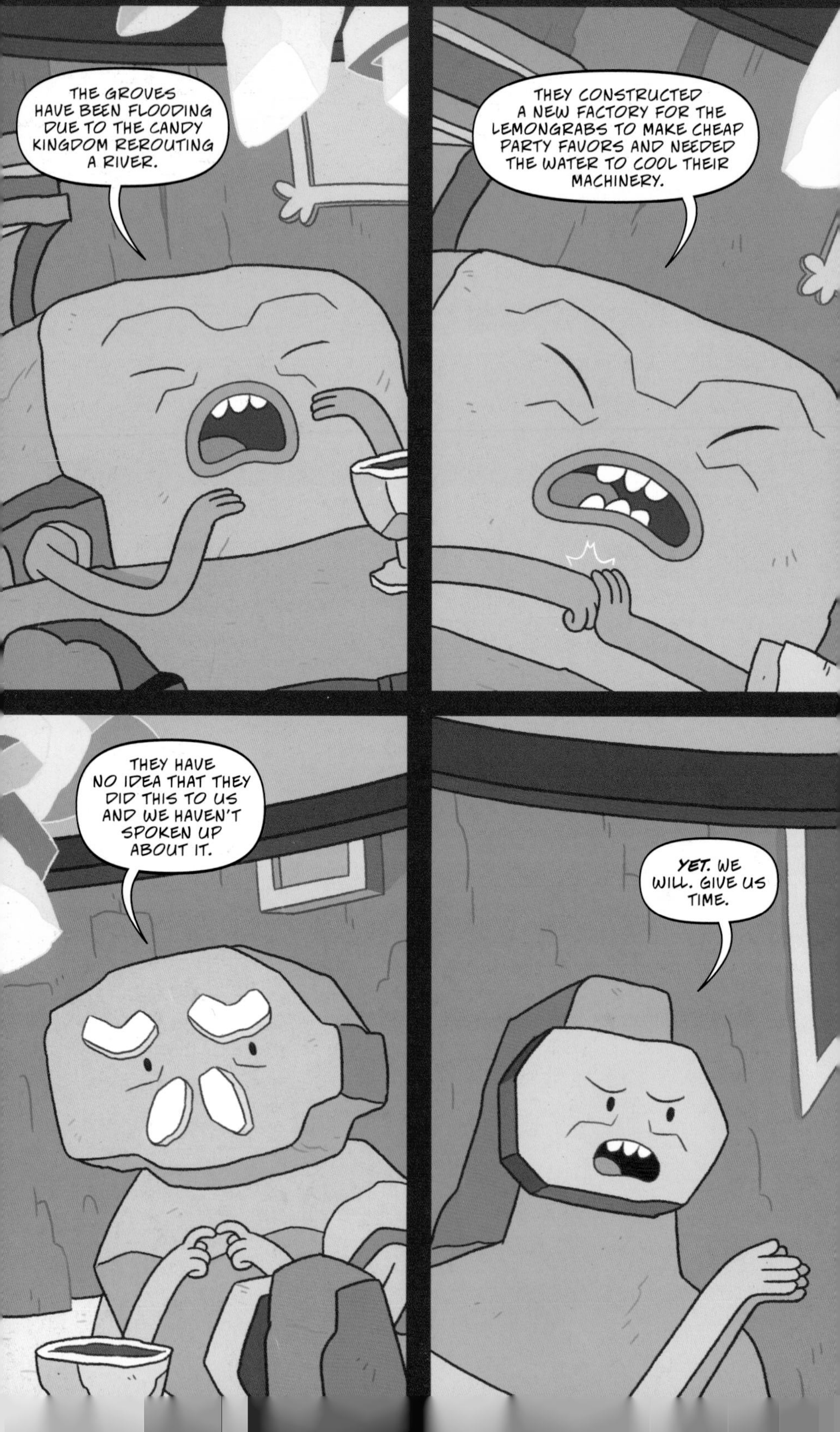
THE GROVES HAVE BEEN FLOODING DUE TO THE CANDY KINGDOM REROUTING A RIVER.
THEY CONSTRUCTED A NEW FACTORY FOR THE LEMONGRABS TO MAKE CHEAP PARTY FAVORS AND NEEDED THE WATER TO COOL THEIR MACHINERY.
THEY HAVE NO IDEA THAT THEY DID THIS TO US AND WE HAVEN'T SPOKEN UP ABOUT IT.
YET. WE WILL. GIVE US TIME.

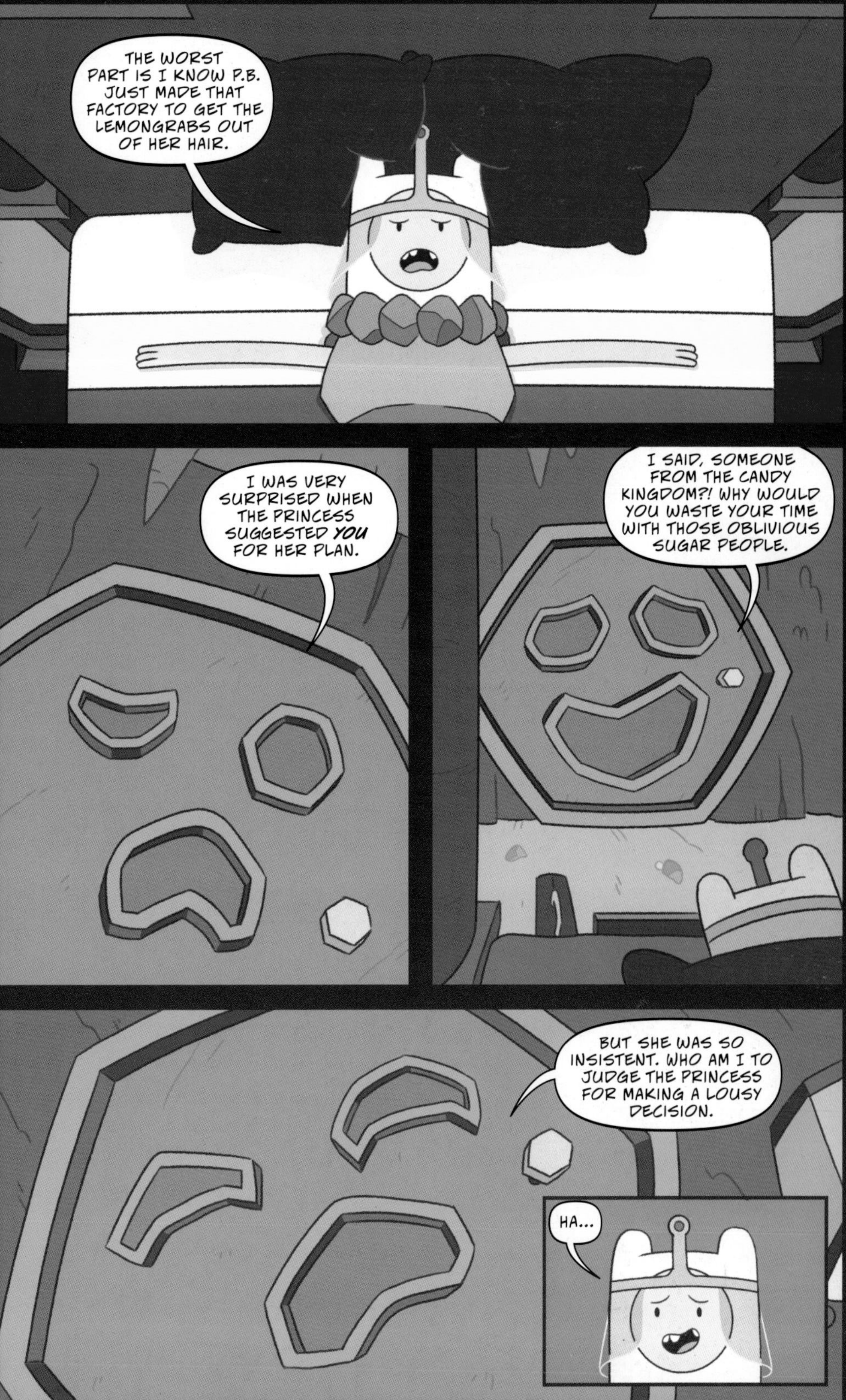
THE WORST PART IS I KNOW P.B. JUST MADE THAT FACTORY TO GET THE LEMONGRABS OUT OF HER HAIR.
I WAS VERY SURPRISED WHEN THE PRINCESS SUGGESTED *YOU* FOR HER PLAN.
I SAID, SOMEONE FROM THE CANDY KINGDOM?! WHY WOULD YOU WASTE YOUR TIME WITH THOSE OBLIVIOUS SUGAR PEOPLE.
BUT SHE WAS SO INSISTENT. WHO AM I TO JUDGE THE PRINCESS FOR MAKING A LOUSY DECISION.
HA...

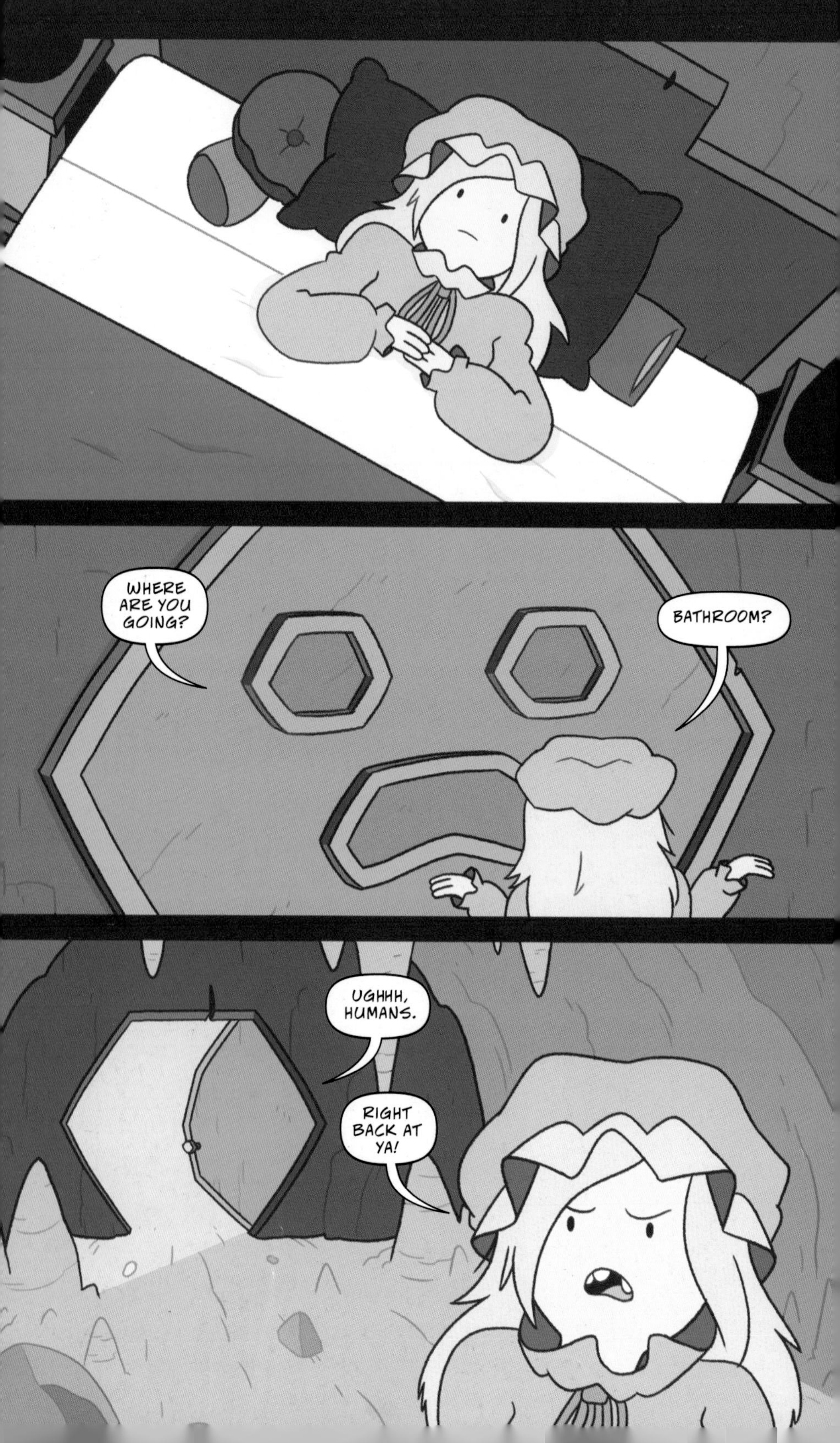
WHERE ARE YOU GOING?
BATHROOM?
UGHHH, HUMANS.
RIGHT BACK AT YA!

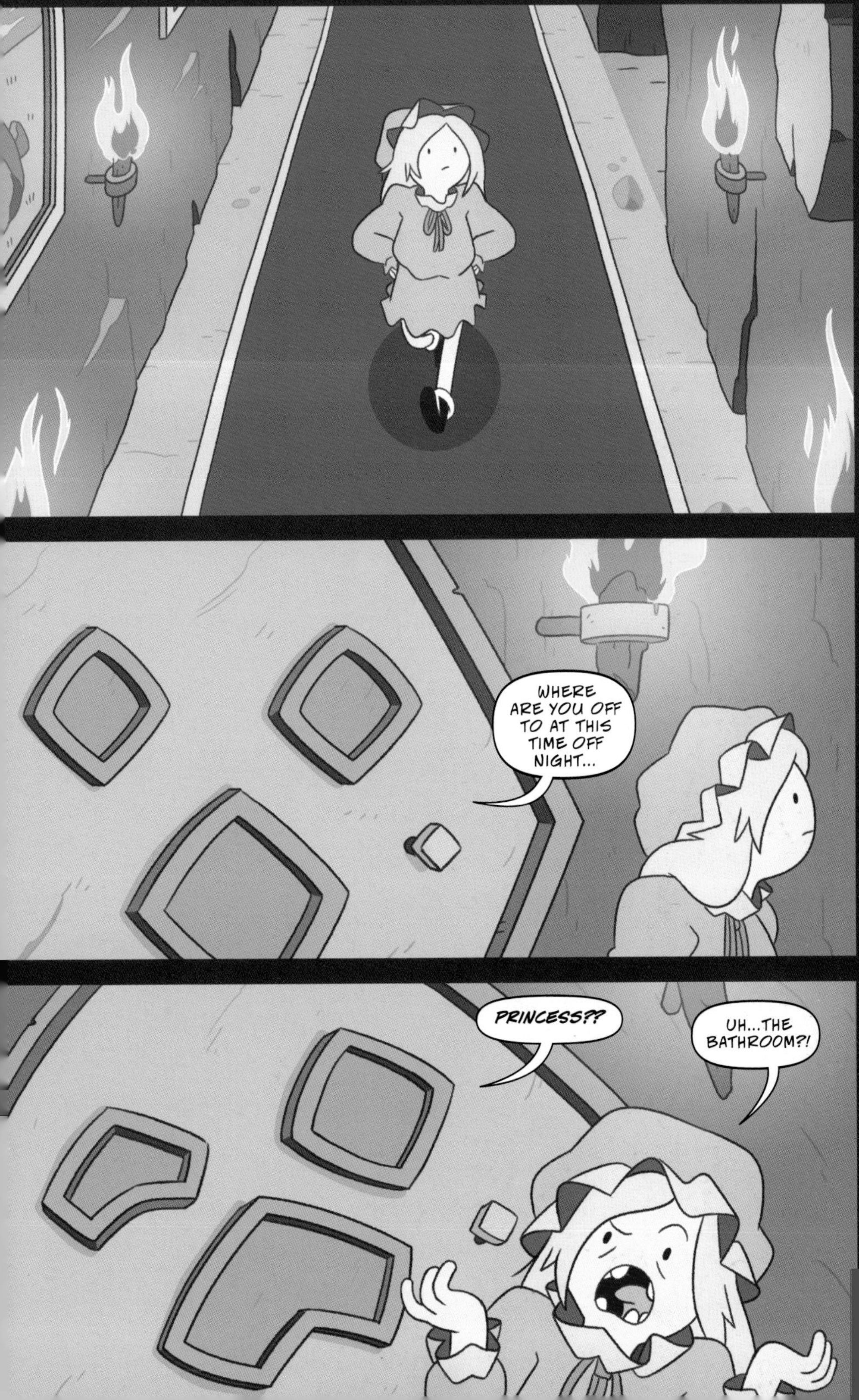
WHERE ARE YOU OFF TO AT THIS TIME OFF NIGHT...
PRINCESS??
UH...THE BATHROOM?!

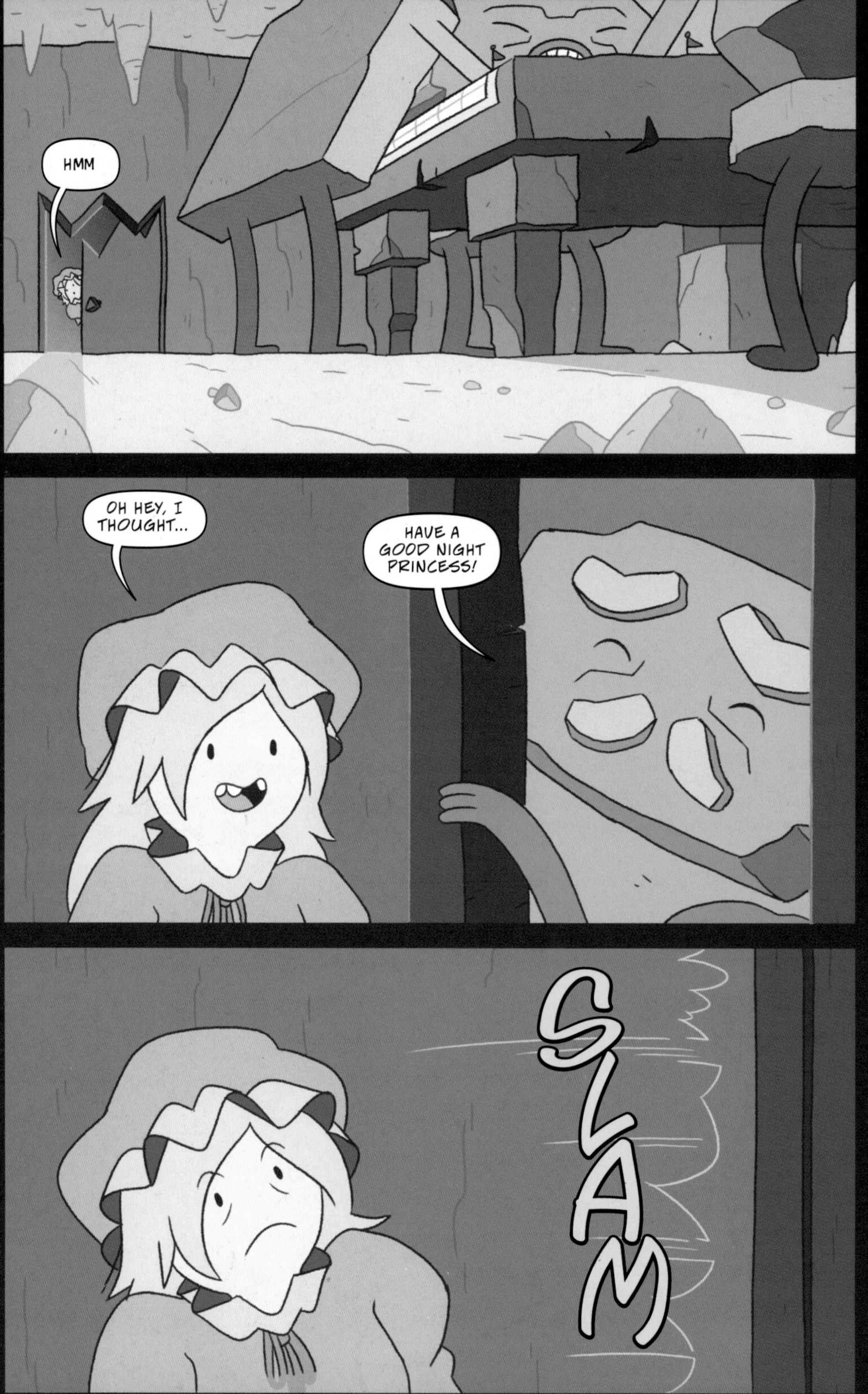
HMM
OH HEY, I THOUGHT...
HAVE A GOOD NIGHT PRINCESS!
SLAM

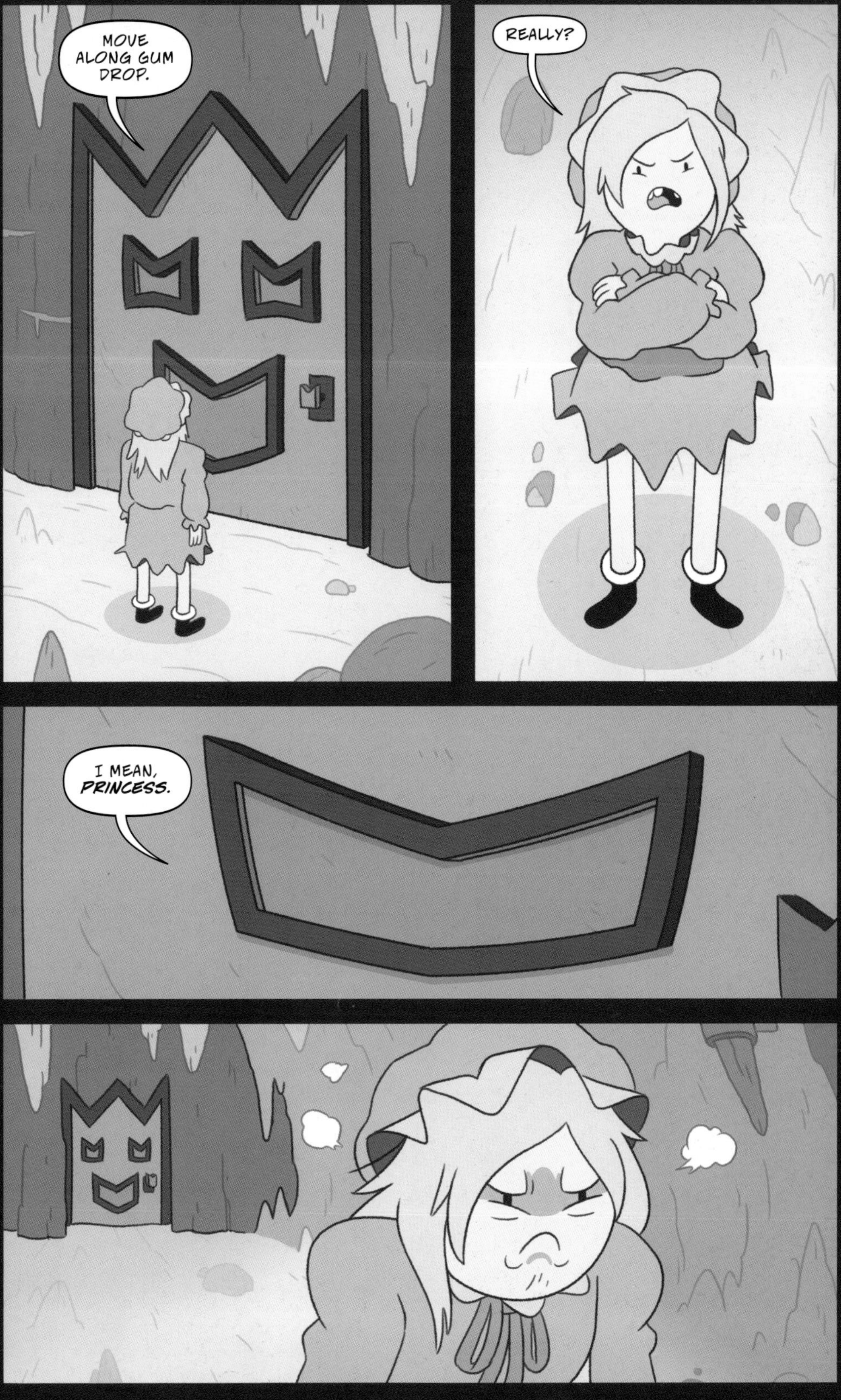
MOVE ALONG GUM DROP.
REALLY?
I MEAN, *PRINCESS.*

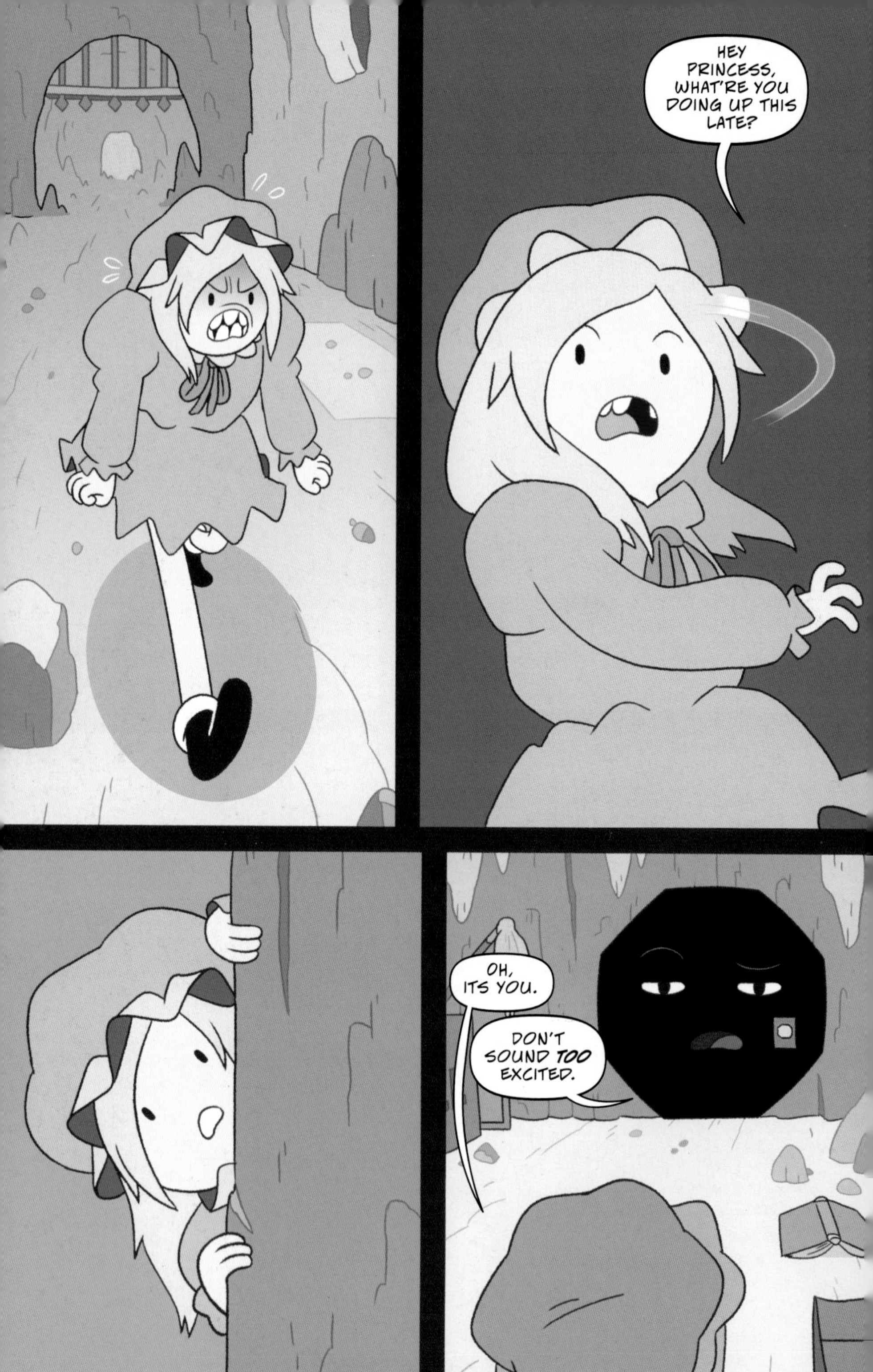
HEY PRINCESS, WHAT'RE YOU DOING UP THIS LATE?
OH, ITS YOU.
DON'T SOUND **TOO** EXCITED.

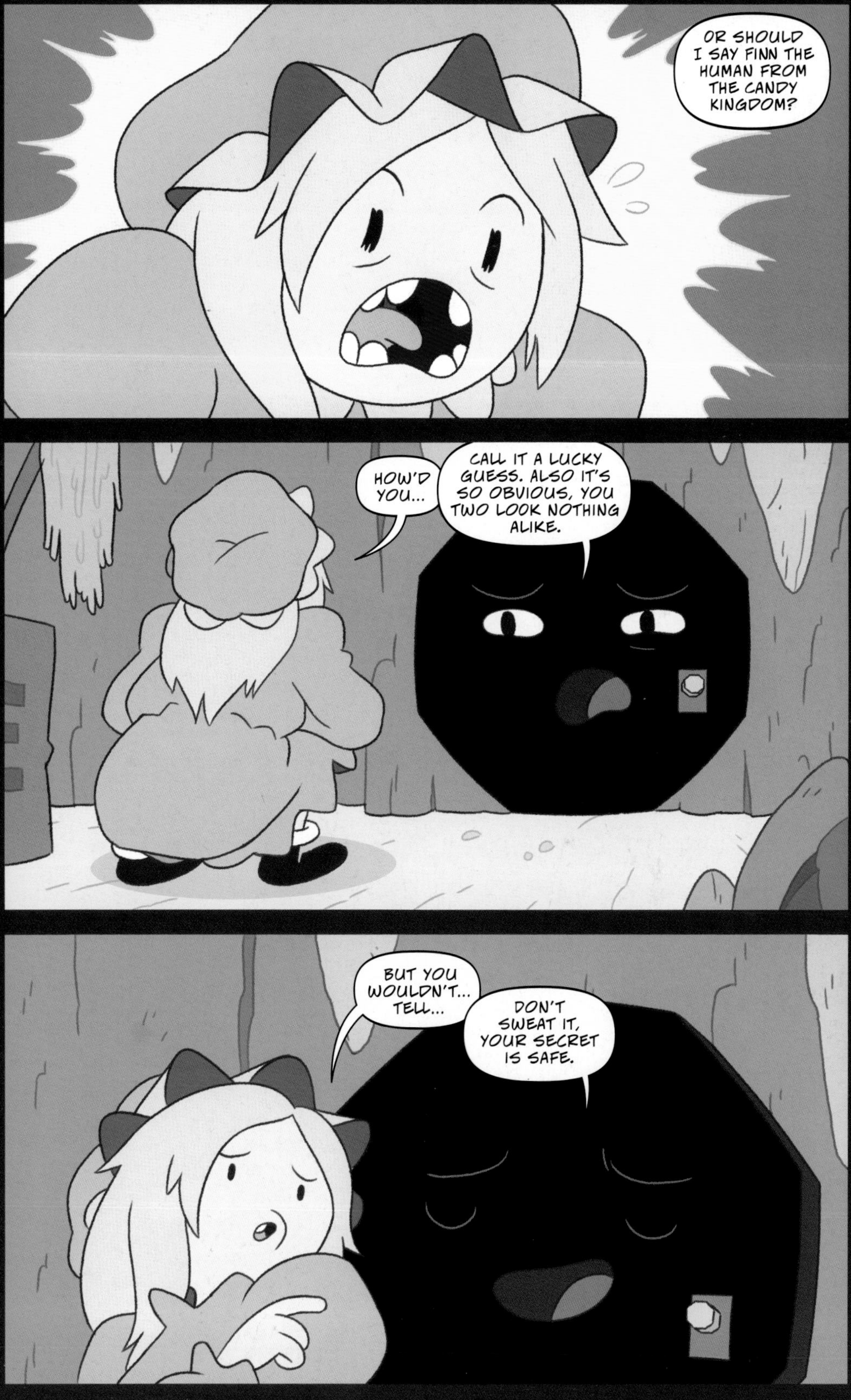
OR SHOULD I SAY FINN THE HUMAN FROM THE CANDY KINGDOM?
HOW'D YOU...
CALL IT A LUCKY GUESS. ALSO IT'S SO OBVIOUS, YOU TWO LOOK NOTHING ALIKE.
BUT YOU WOULDN'T... TELL...
DON'T SWEAT IT, YOUR SECRET IS SAFE.

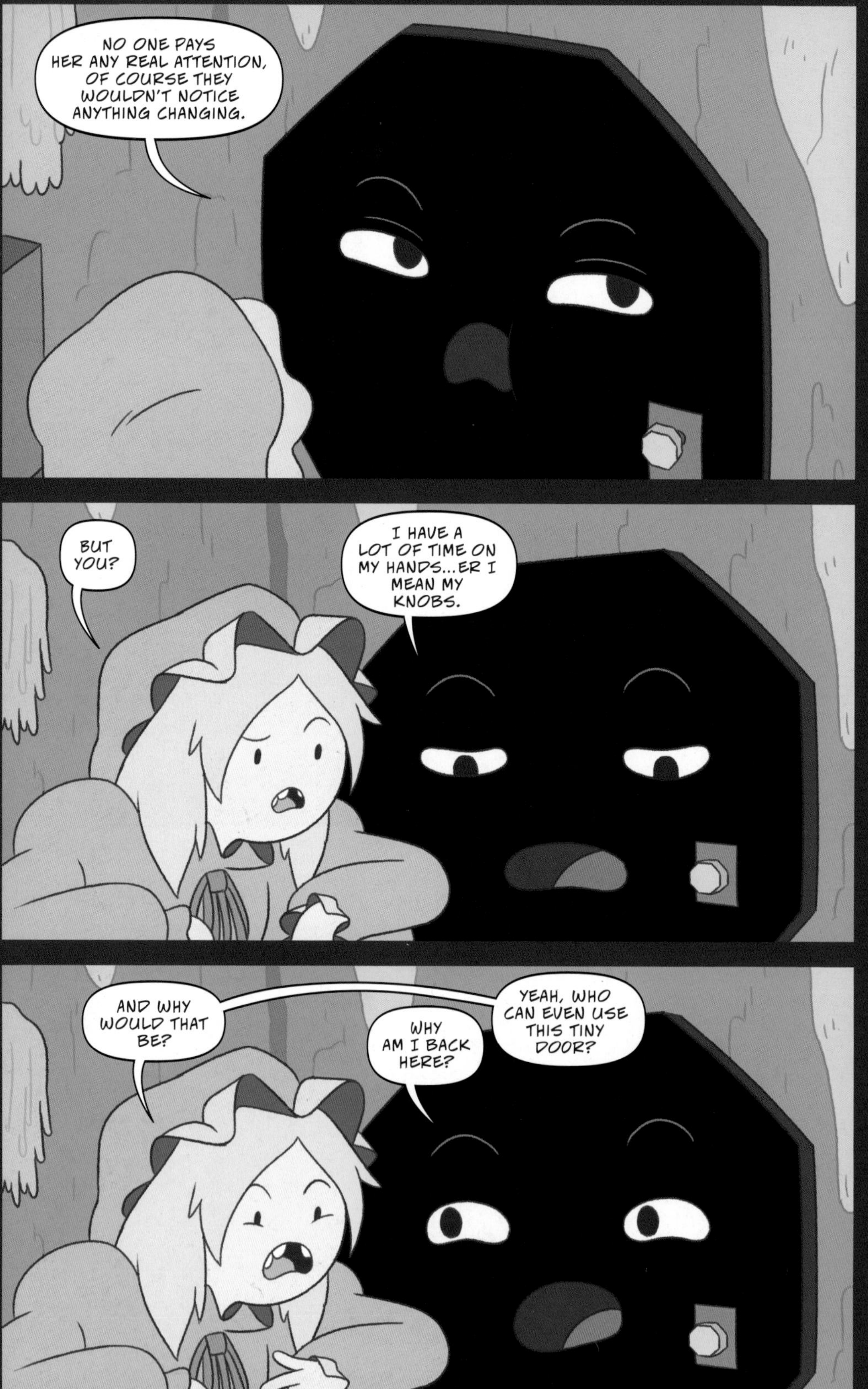
NO ONE PAYS HER ANY REAL ATTENTION, OF COURSE THEY WOULDN'T NOTICE ANYTHING CHANGING.
BUT YOU?
I HAVE A LOT OF TIME ON MY HANDS...ER I MEAN MY KNOBS.
AND WHY WOULD THAT BE?
YEAH, WHO CAN EVEN USE THIS TINY DOOR?
WHY AM I BACK HERE?

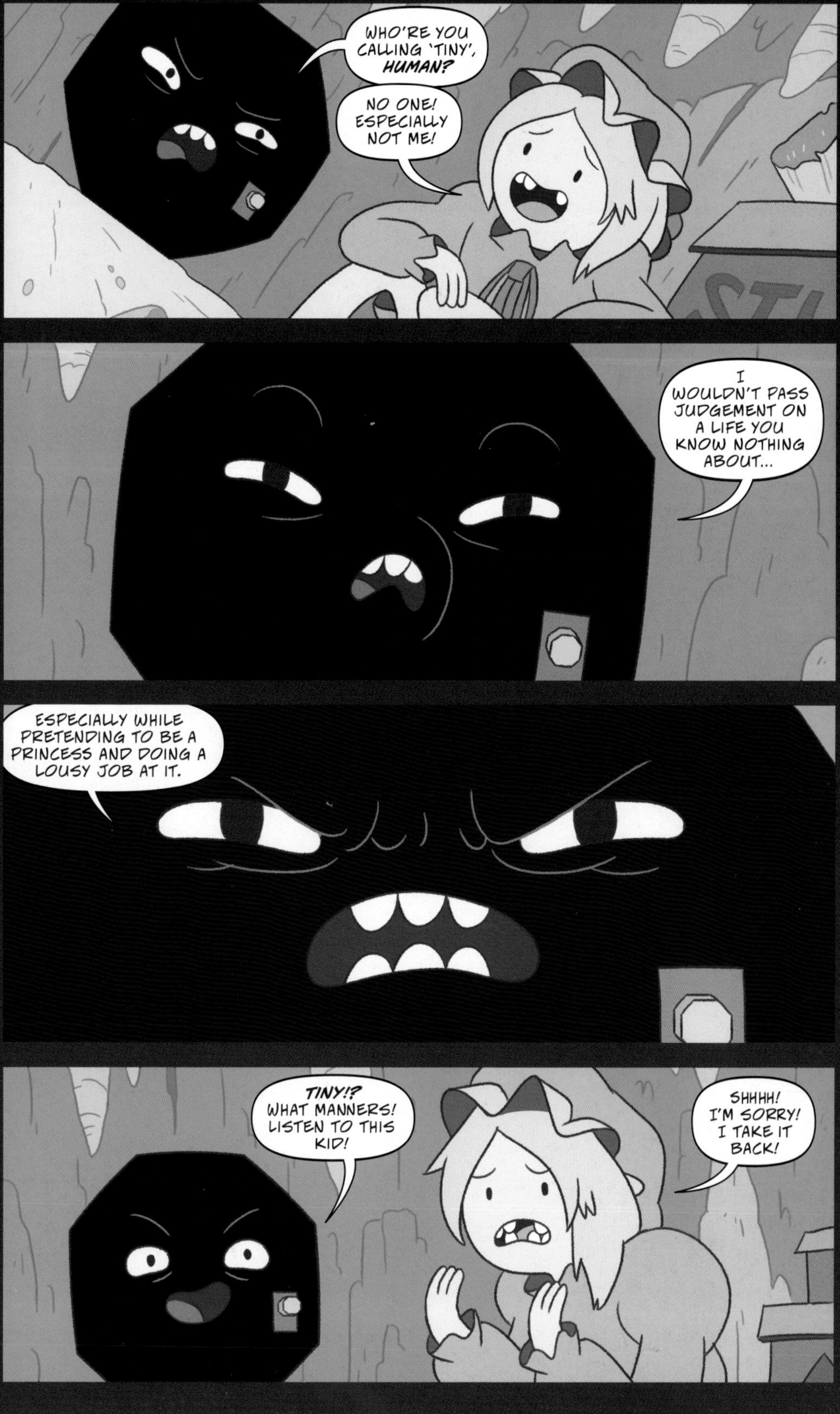
WHO'RE YOU CALLING 'TINY', **HUMAN?**
NO ONE! ESPECIALLY NOT ME!
I WOULDN'T PASS JUDGEMENT ON A LIFE YOU KNOW NOTHING ABOUT...
ESPECIALLY WHILE PRETENDING TO BE A PRINCESS AND DOING A LOUSY JOB AT IT.
TINY!? WHAT MANNERS! LISTEN TO THIS KID!
SHHHH! I'M SORRY! I TAKE IT BACK!

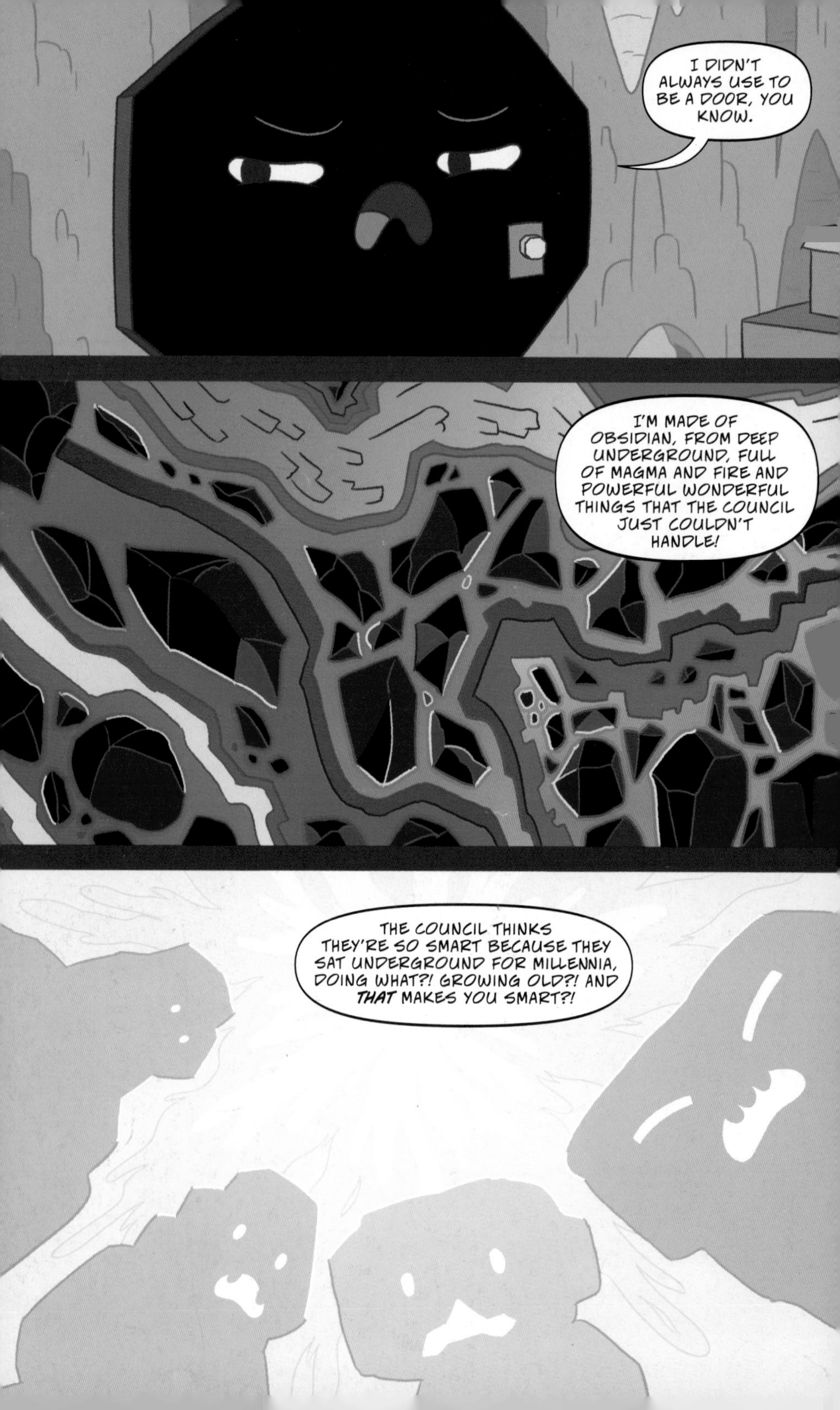
I DIDN'T ALWAYS USE TO BE A DOOR, YOU KNOW.
I'M MADE OF OBSIDIAN, FROM DEEP UNDERGROUND, FULL OF MAGMA AND FIRE AND POWERFUL WONDERFUL THINGS THAT THE COUNCIL JUST COULDN'T HANDLE!
THE COUNCIL THINKS THEY'RE SO SMART BECAUSE THEY SAT UNDERGROUND FOR MILLENNIA, DOING WHAT?! GROWING OLD?! AND *THAT* MAKES YOU SMART?!

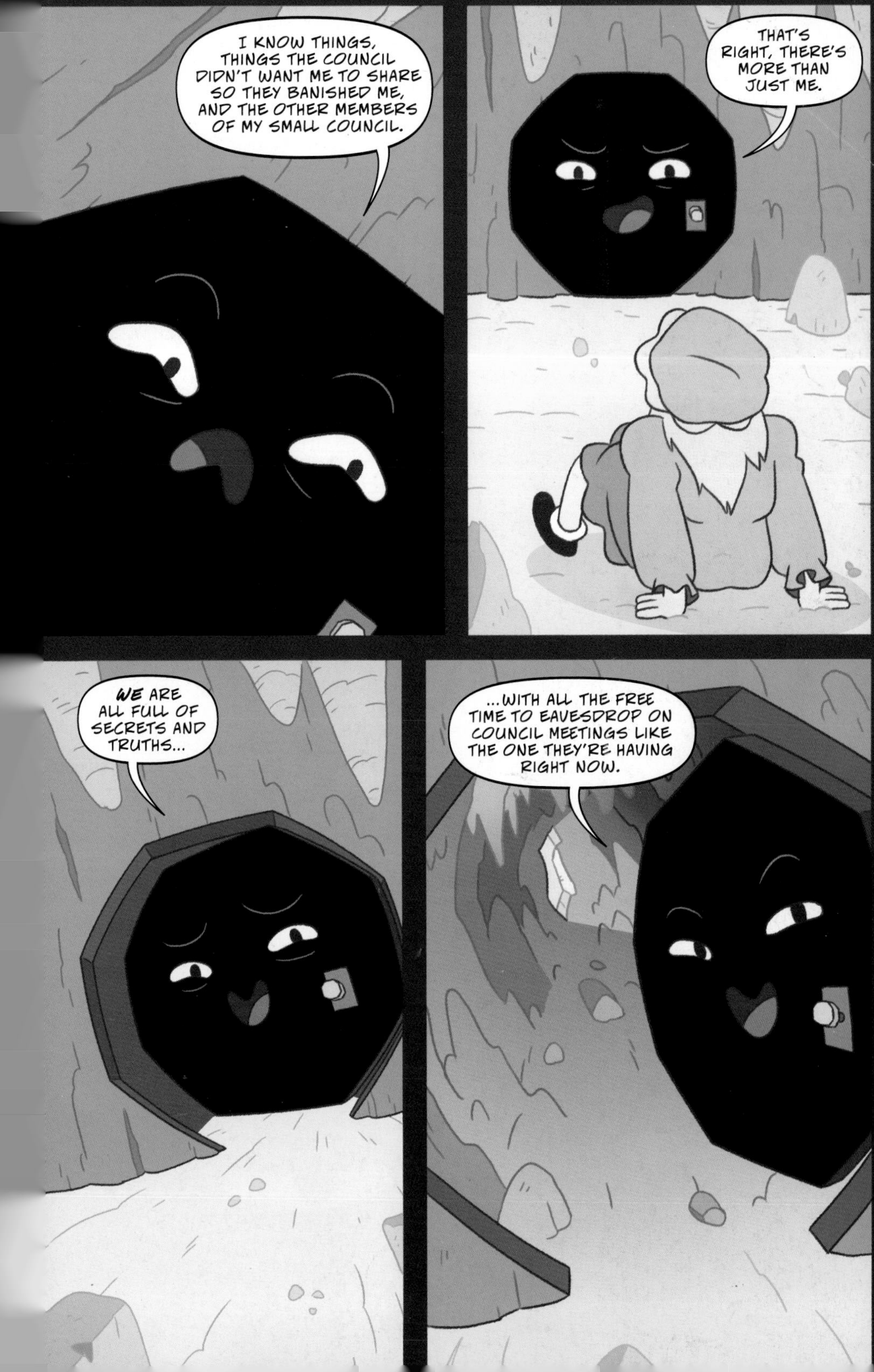
I KNOW THINGS, THINGS THE COUNCIL DIDN'T WANT ME TO SHARE SO THEY BANISHED ME, AND THE OTHER MEMBERS OF MY SMALL COUNCIL.
THAT'S RIGHT, THERE'S MORE THAN JUST ME.
WE ARE ALL FULL OF SECRETS AND TRUTHS...
...WITH ALL THE FREE TIME TO EAVESDROP ON COUNCIL MEETINGS LIKE THE ONE THEY'RE HAVING RIGHT NOW.

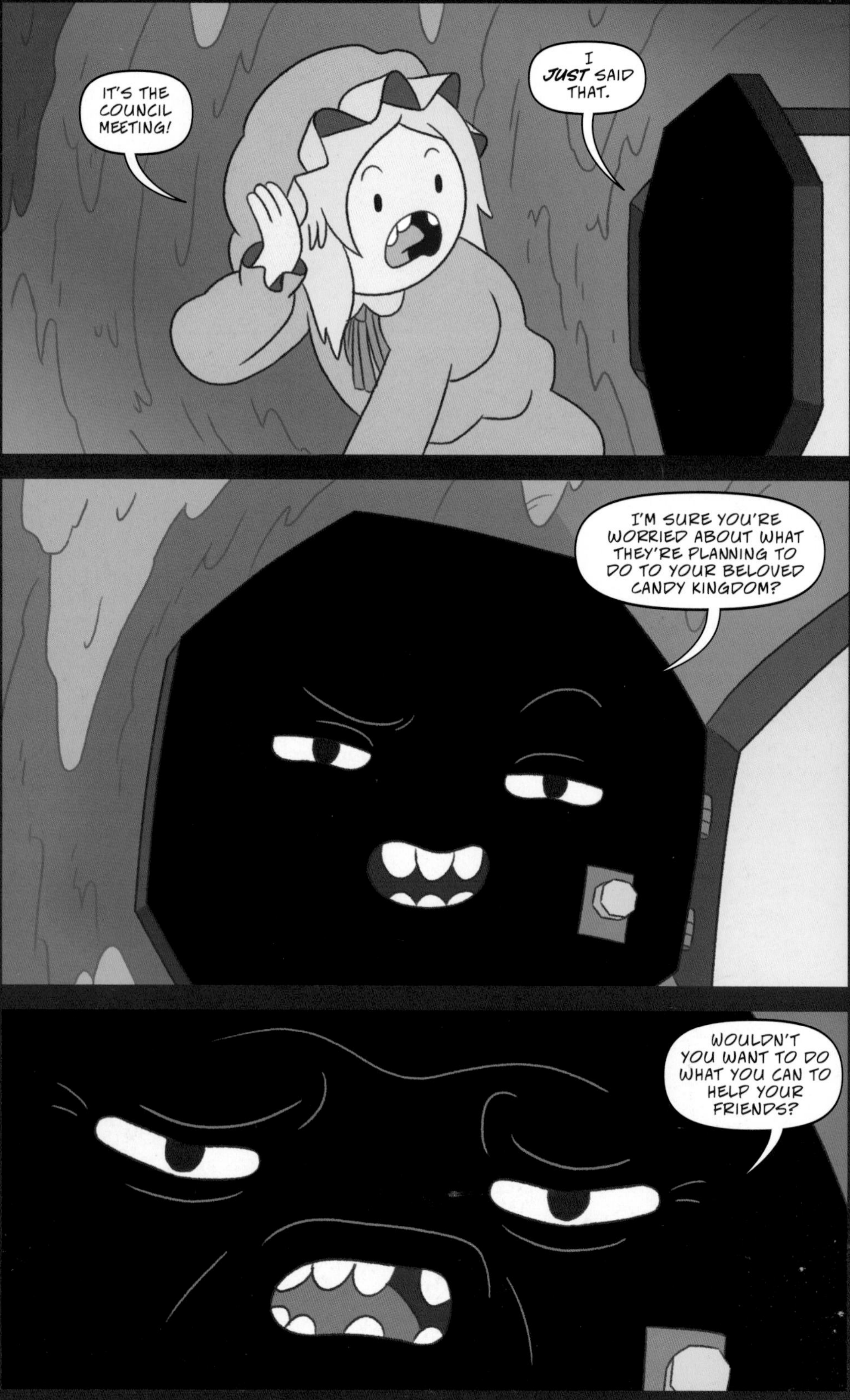
IT'S THE COUNCIL MEETING!
I JUST SAID THAT.
I'M SURE YOU'RE WORRIED ABOUT WHAT THEY'RE PLANNING TO DO TO YOUR BELOVED CANDY KINGDOM?
WOULDN'T YOU WANT TO DO WHAT YOU CAN TO HELP YOUR FRIENDS?

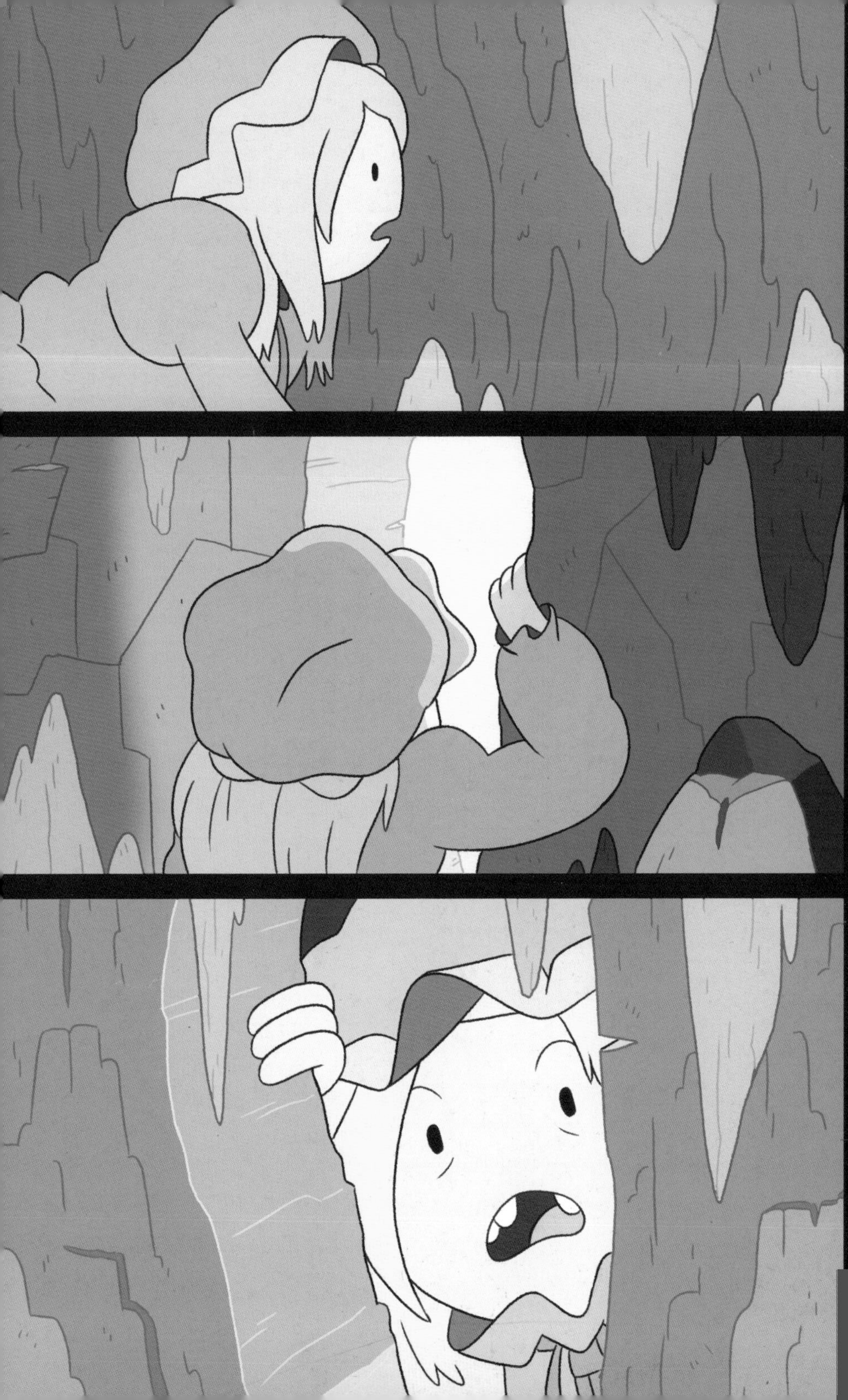

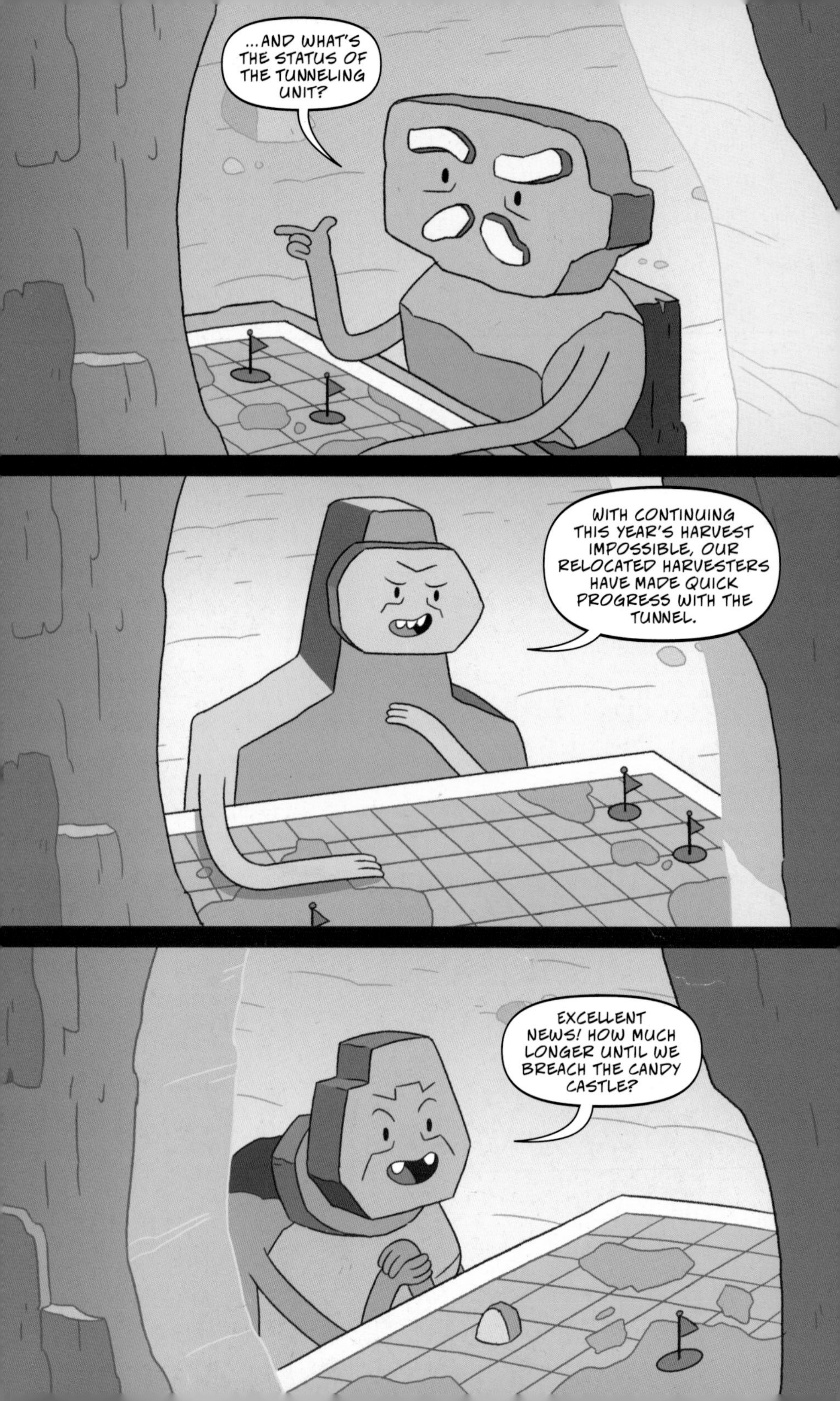
...AND WHAT'S THE STATUS OF THE TUNNELING UNIT?
WITH CONTINUING THIS YEAR'S HARVEST IMPOSSIBLE, OUR RELOCATED HARVESTERS HAVE MADE QUICK PROGRESS WITH THE TUNNEL.
EXCELLENT NEWS! HOW MUCH LONGER UNTIL WE BREACH THE CANDY CASTLE?

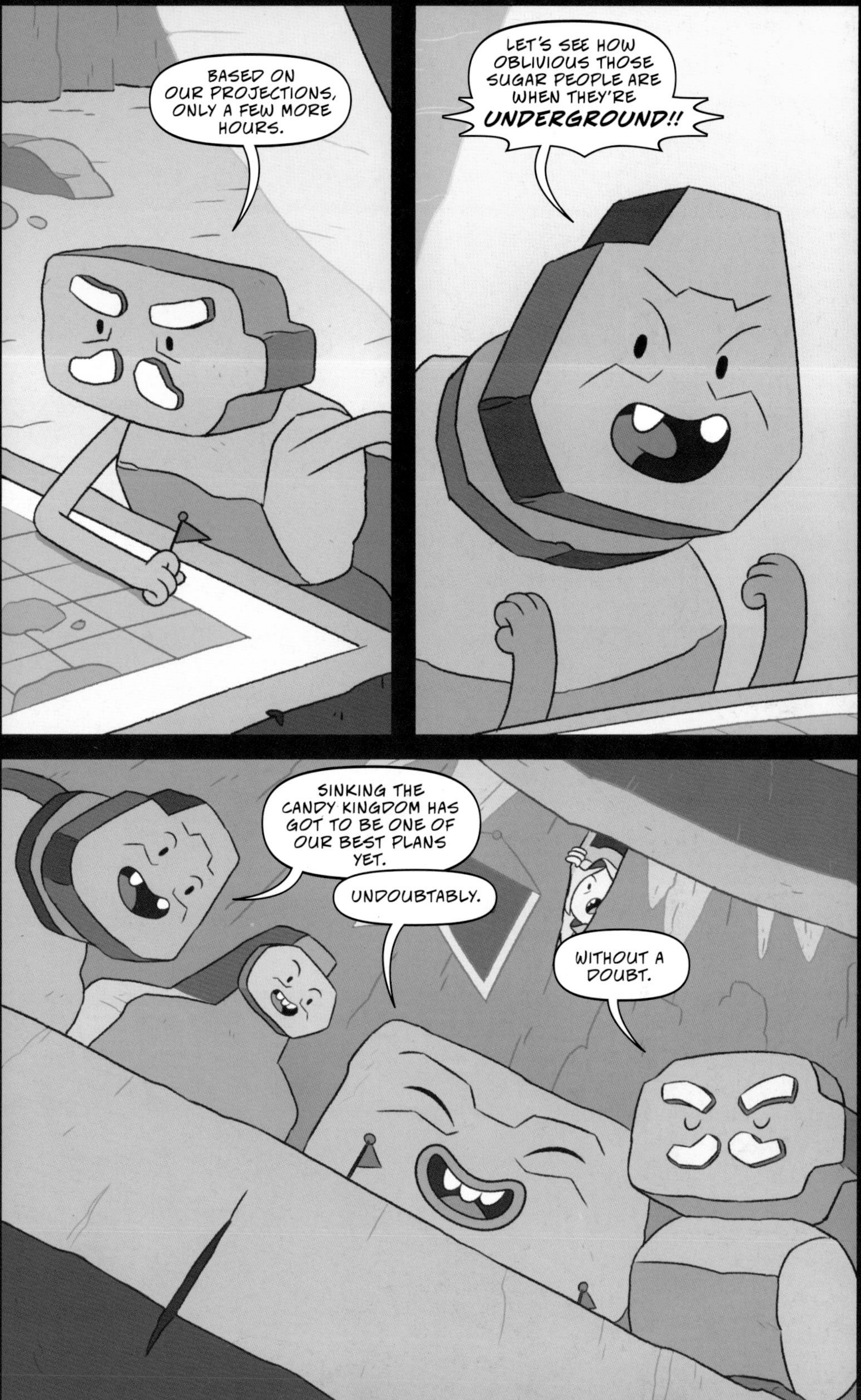
BASED ON OUR PROJECTIONS, ONLY A FEW MORE HOURS.
LET'S SEE HOW OBLIVIOUS THOSE SUGAR PEOPLE ARE WHEN THEY'RE UNDERGROUND!!
SINKING THE CANDY KINGDOM HAS GOT TO BE ONE OF OUR BEST PLANS YET.
UNDOUBTABLY.
WITHOUT A DOUBT.

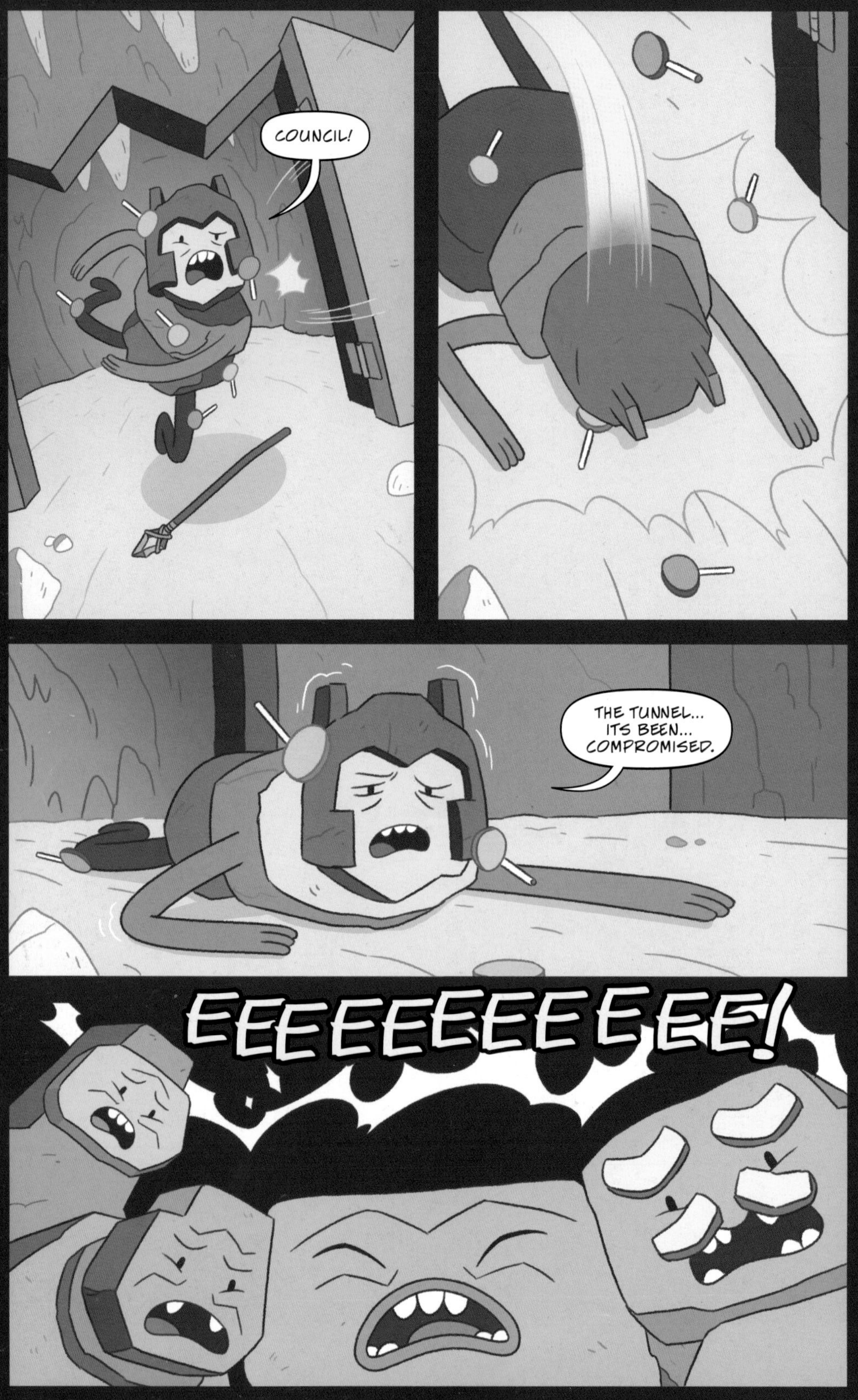
COUNCIL!
THE TUNNEL... ITS BEEN... COMPROMISED.
EEEEEEEEEEEEE!

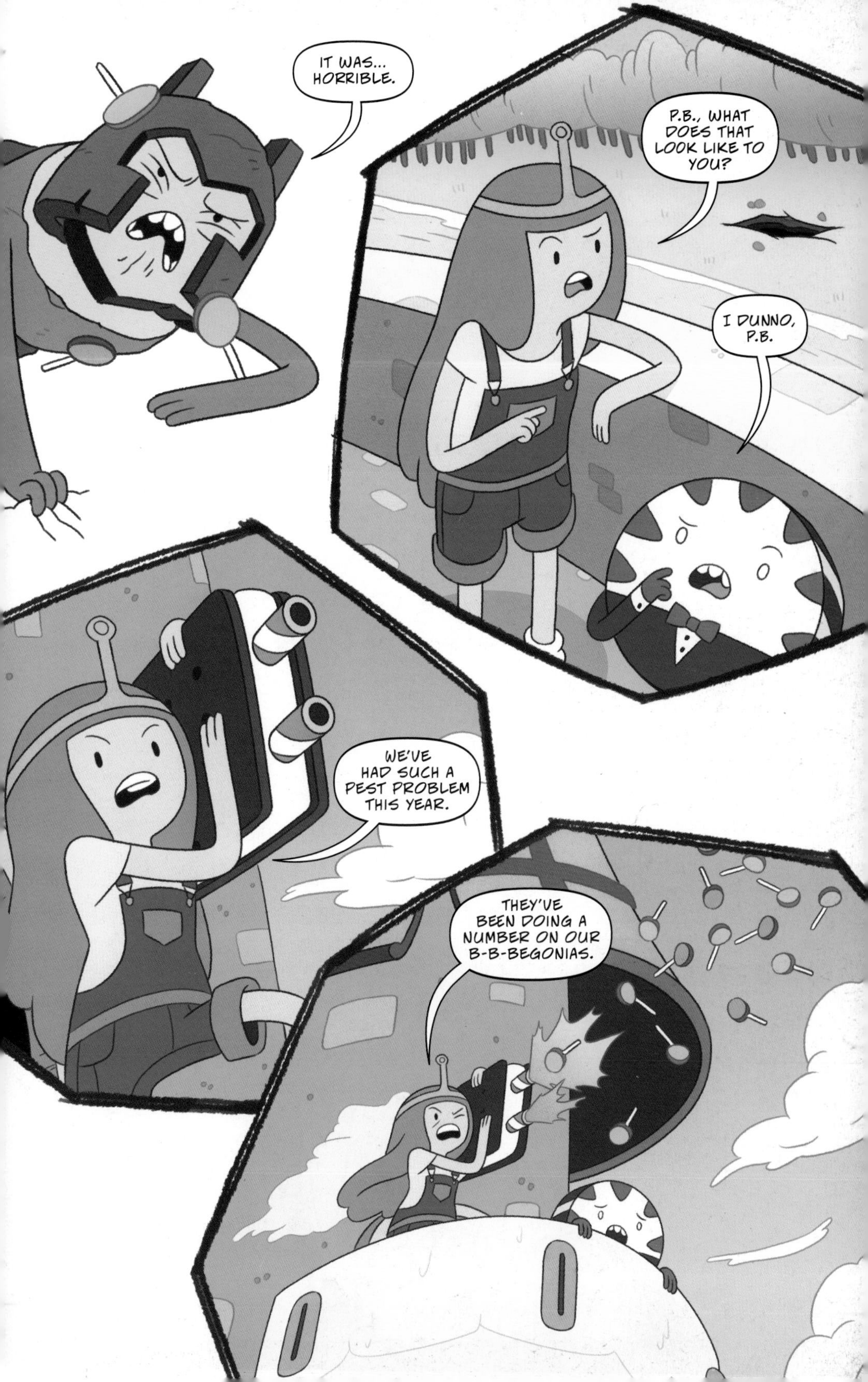
IT WAS... HORRIBLE.
P.B., WHAT DOES THAT LOOK LIKE TO YOU?
I DUNNO, P.B.
WE'VE HAD SUCH A PEST PROBLEM THIS YEAR.
THEY'VE BEEN DOING A NUMBER ON OUR B-B-BEGONIAS.

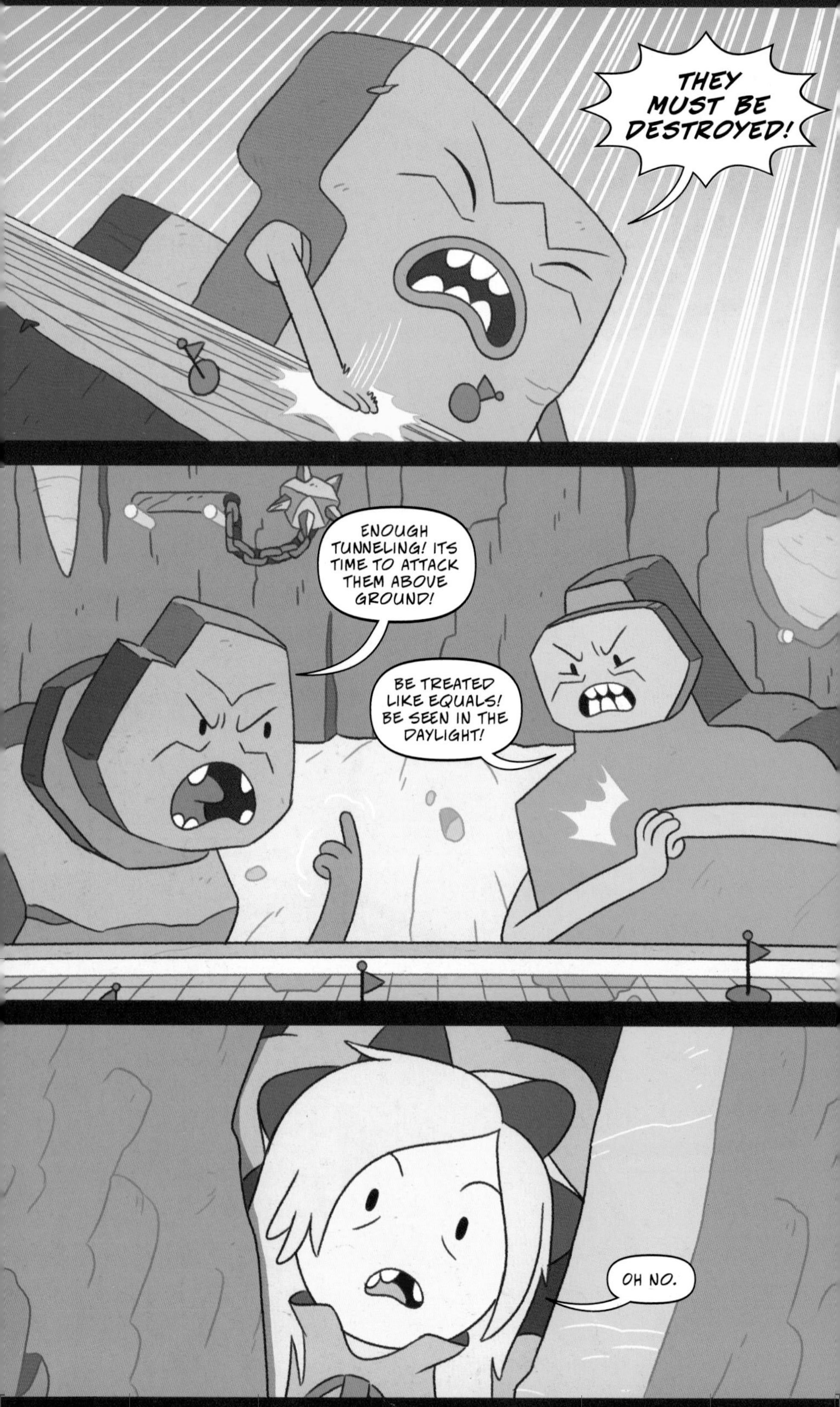
THEY MUST BE DESTROYED!
ENOUGH TUNNELING! ITS TIME TO ATTACK THEM ABOVE GROUND!
BE TREATED LIKE EQUALS! BE SEEN IN THE DAYLIGHT!
OH NO.

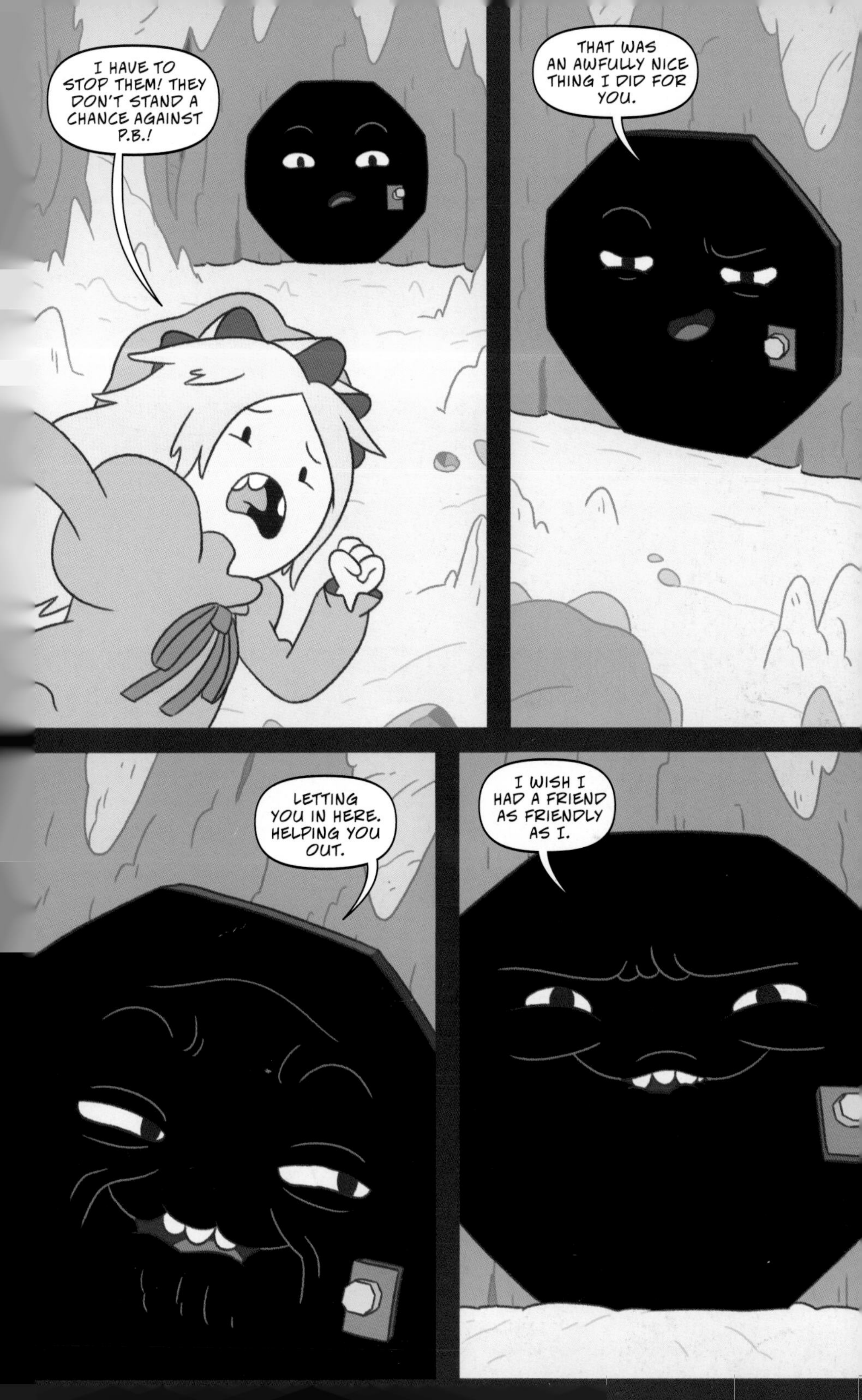
I HAVE TO STOP THEM! THEY DON'T STAND A CHANCE AGAINST P.B.!
THAT WAS AN AWFULLY NICE THING I DID FOR YOU.
LETTING YOU IN HERE. HELPING YOU OUT.
I WISH I HAD A FRIEND AS FRIENDLY AS I.

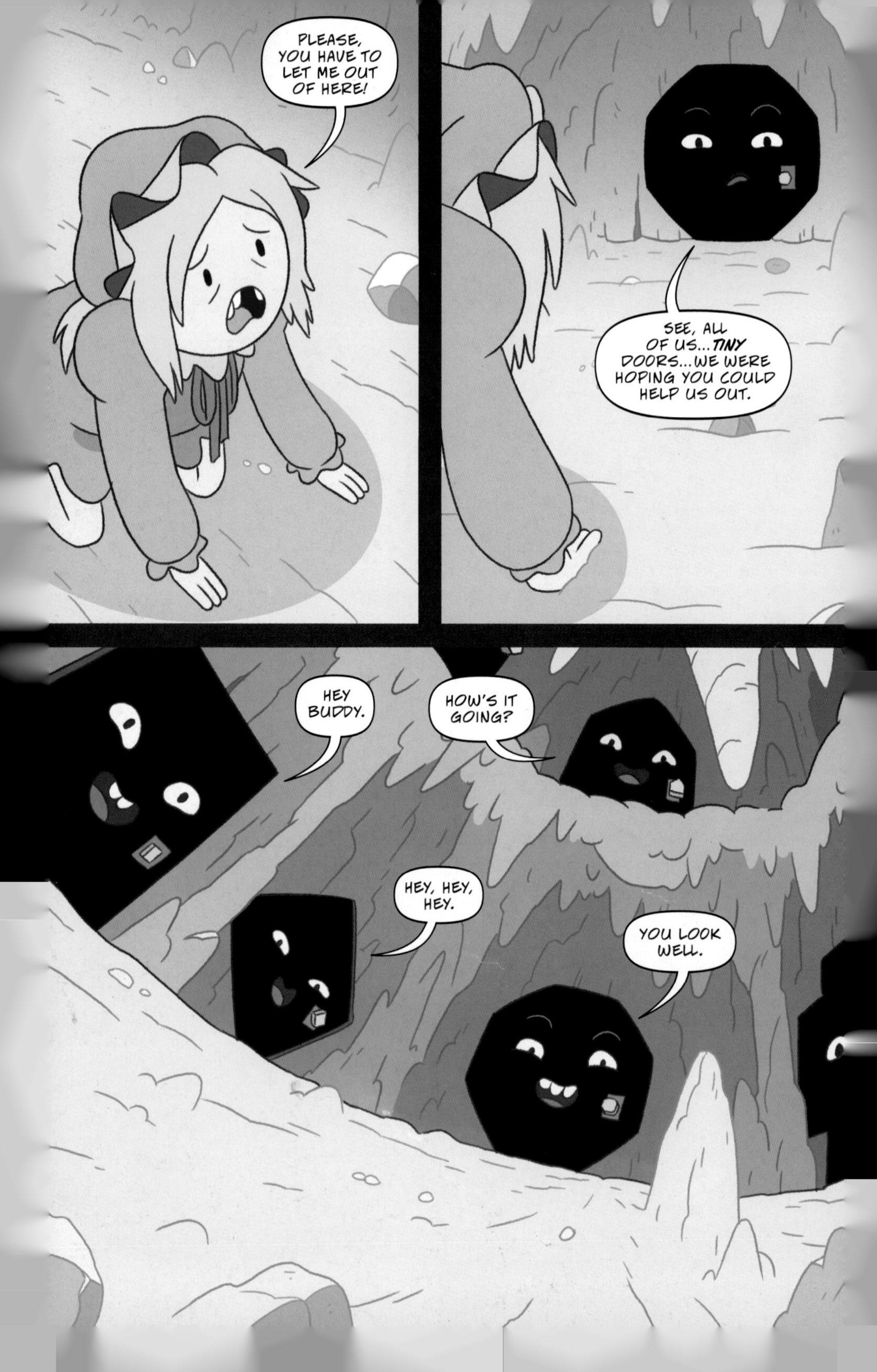
PLEASE, YOU HAVE TO LET ME OUT OF HERE!
SEE, ALL OF US...TINY DOORS...WE WERE HOPING YOU COULD HELP US OUT.
HEY BUDDY.
HOW'S IT GOING?
HEY, HEY, HEY.
YOU LOOK WELL.

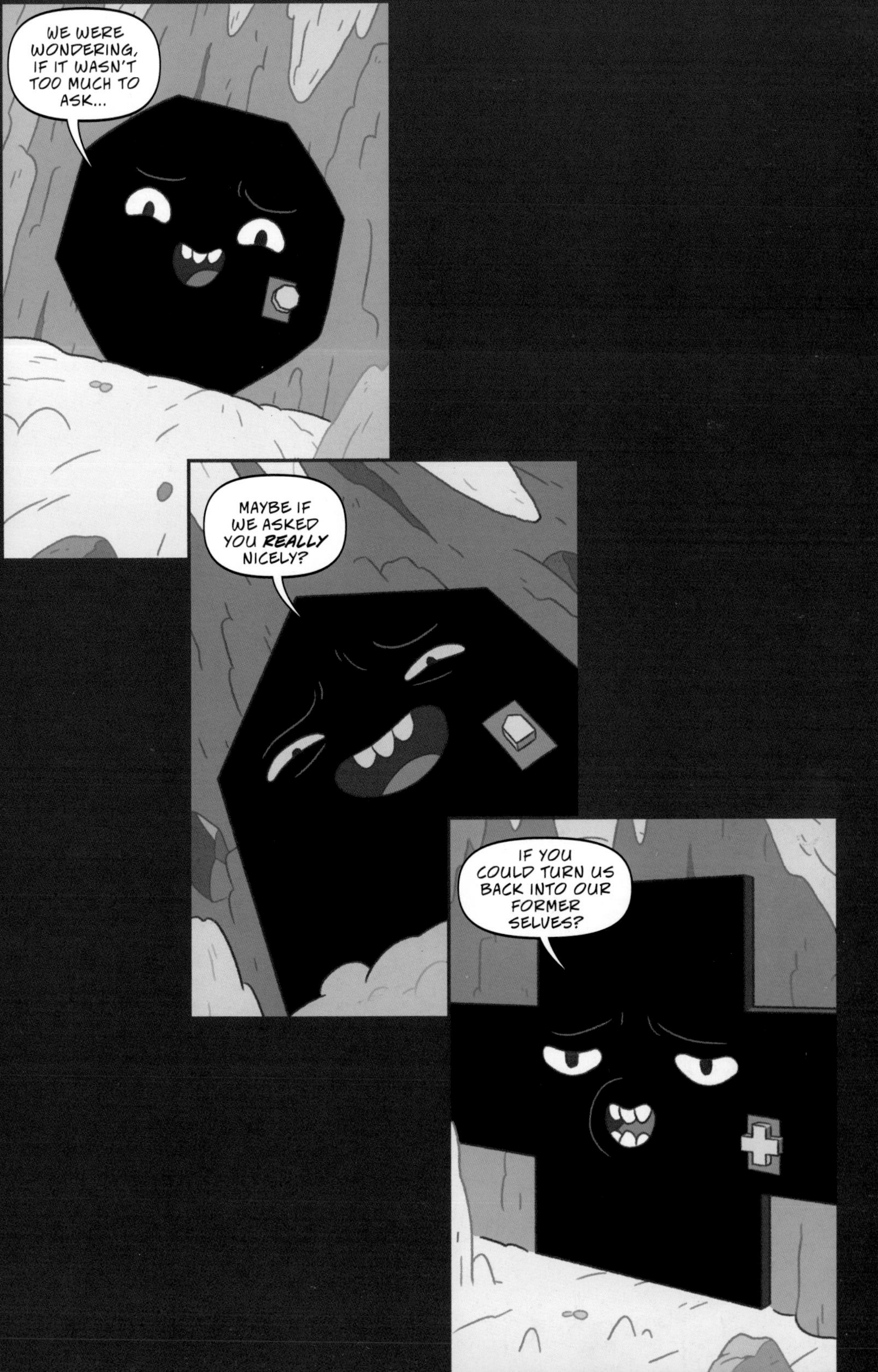
WE WERE WONDERING, IF IT WASN'T TOO MUCH TO ASK...
MAYBE IF WE ASKED YOU REALLY NICELY?
IF YOU COULD TURN US BACK INTO OUR FORMER SELVES?

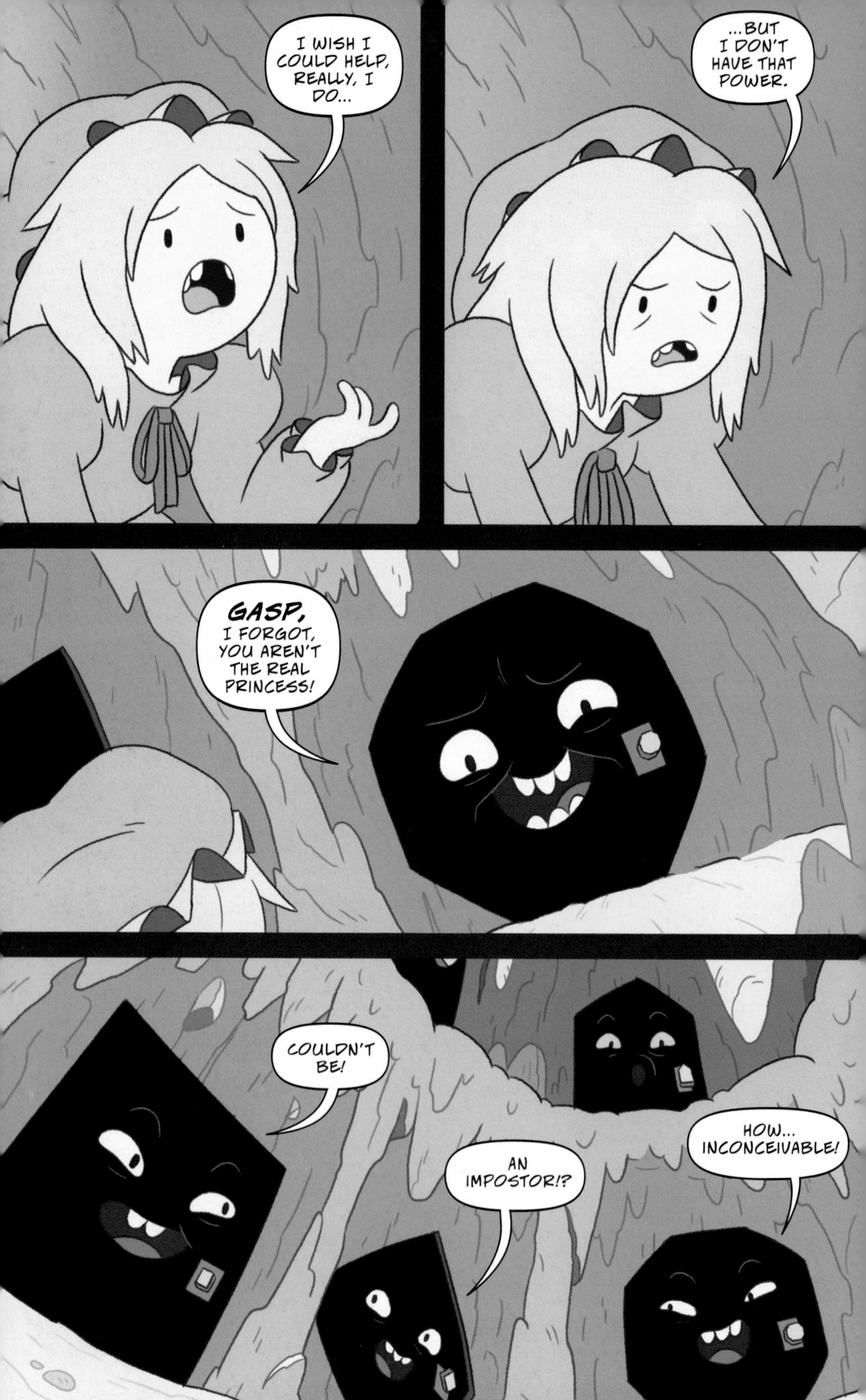
I WISH I COULD HELP, REALLY, I DO...
...BUT I DON'T HAVE THAT POWER.
GASP, I FORGOT, YOU AREN'T THE REAL PRINCESS!
COULDN'T BE!
AN IMPOSTOR!?
HOW... INCONCEIVABLE!

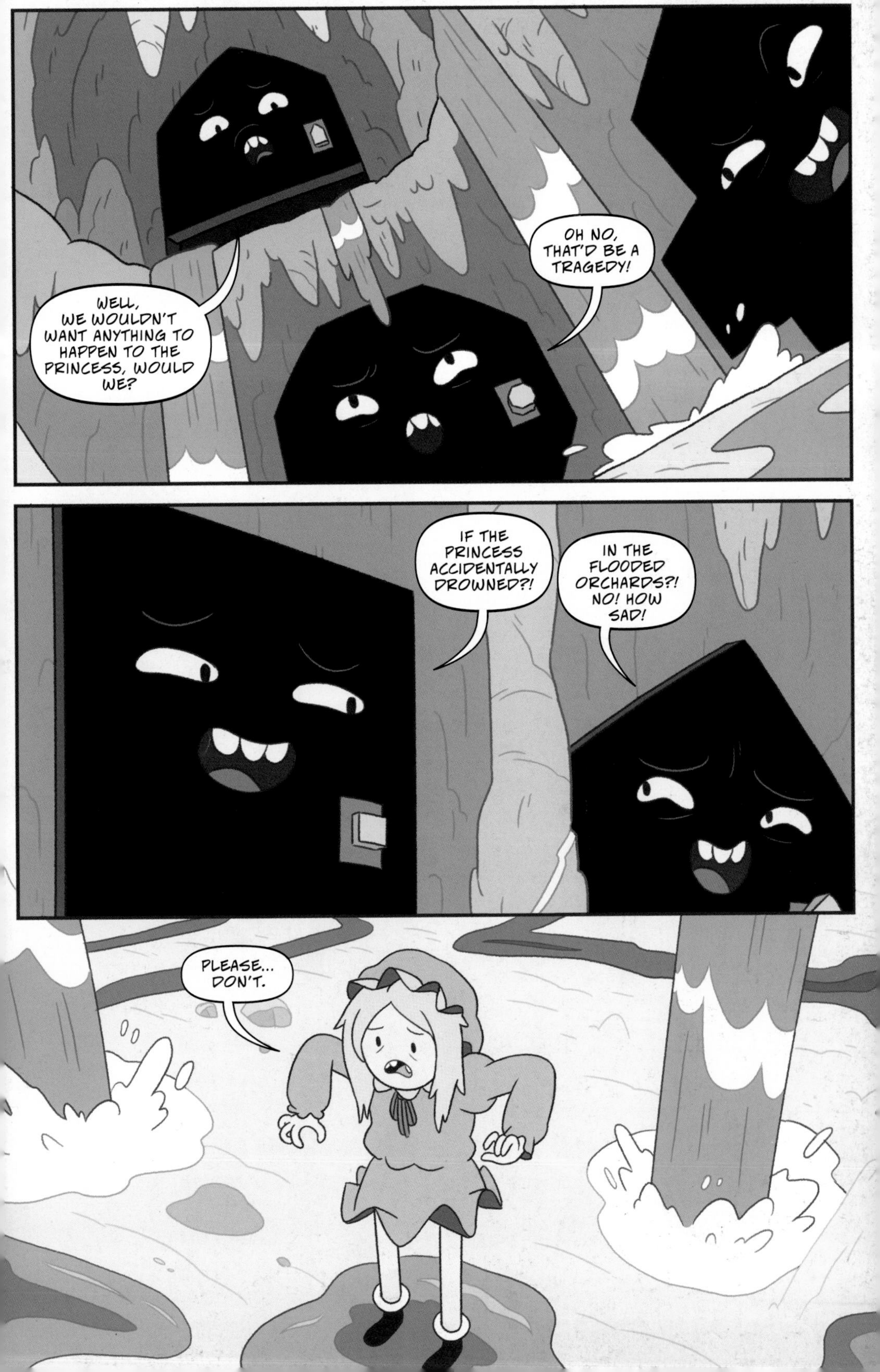
WELL, WE WOULDN'T WANT ANYTHING TO HAPPEN TO THE PRINCESS, WOULD WE?
OH NO, THAT'D BE A TRAGEDY!
IF THE PRINCESS ACCIDENTALLY DROWNED?!
IN THE FLOODED ORCHARDS?! NO! HOW SAD!
PLEASE... DON'T.

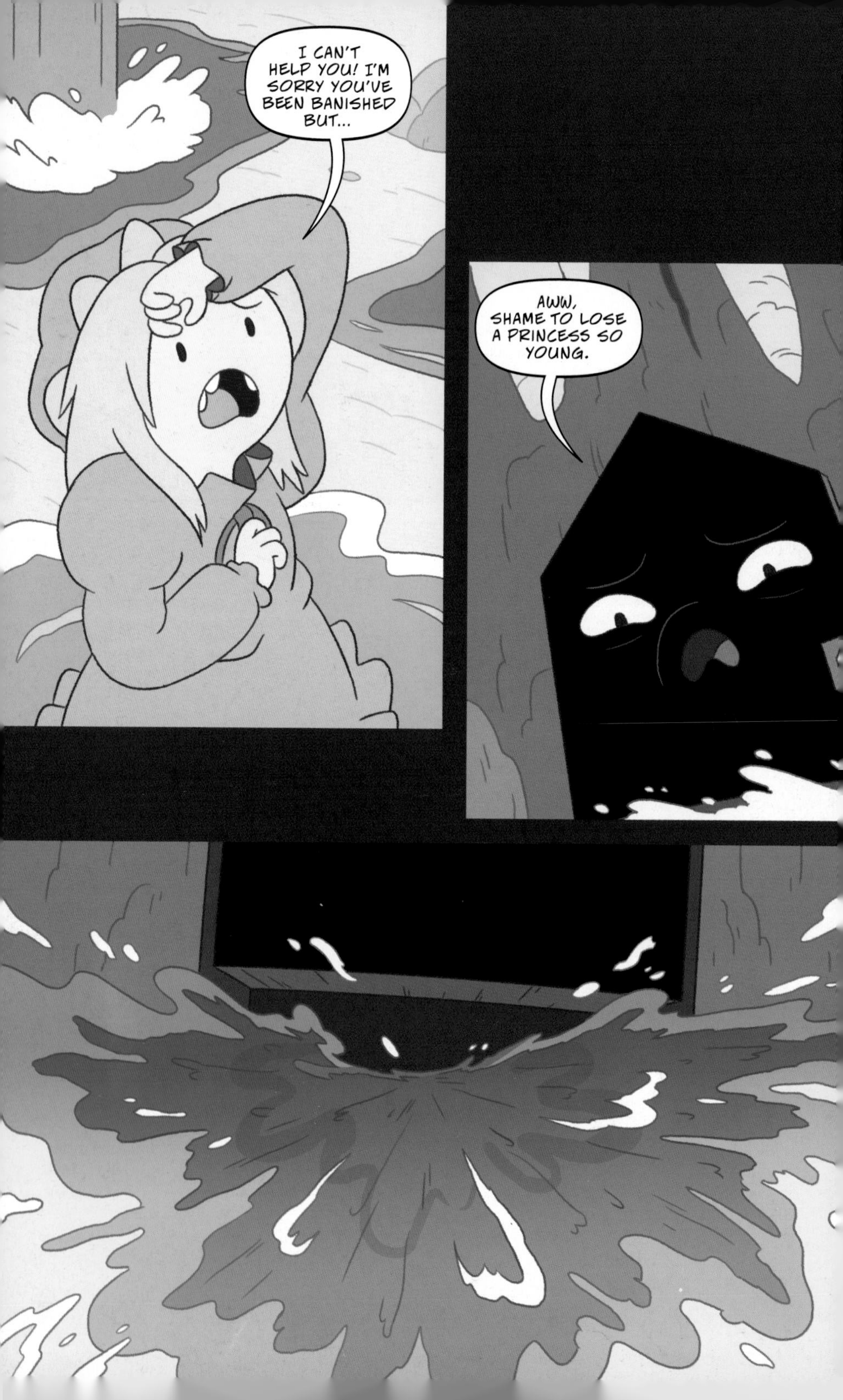
I CAN'T HELP YOU! I'M SORRY YOU'VE BEEN BANISHED BUT...
AWW, SHAME TO LOSE A PRINCESS SO YOUNG.

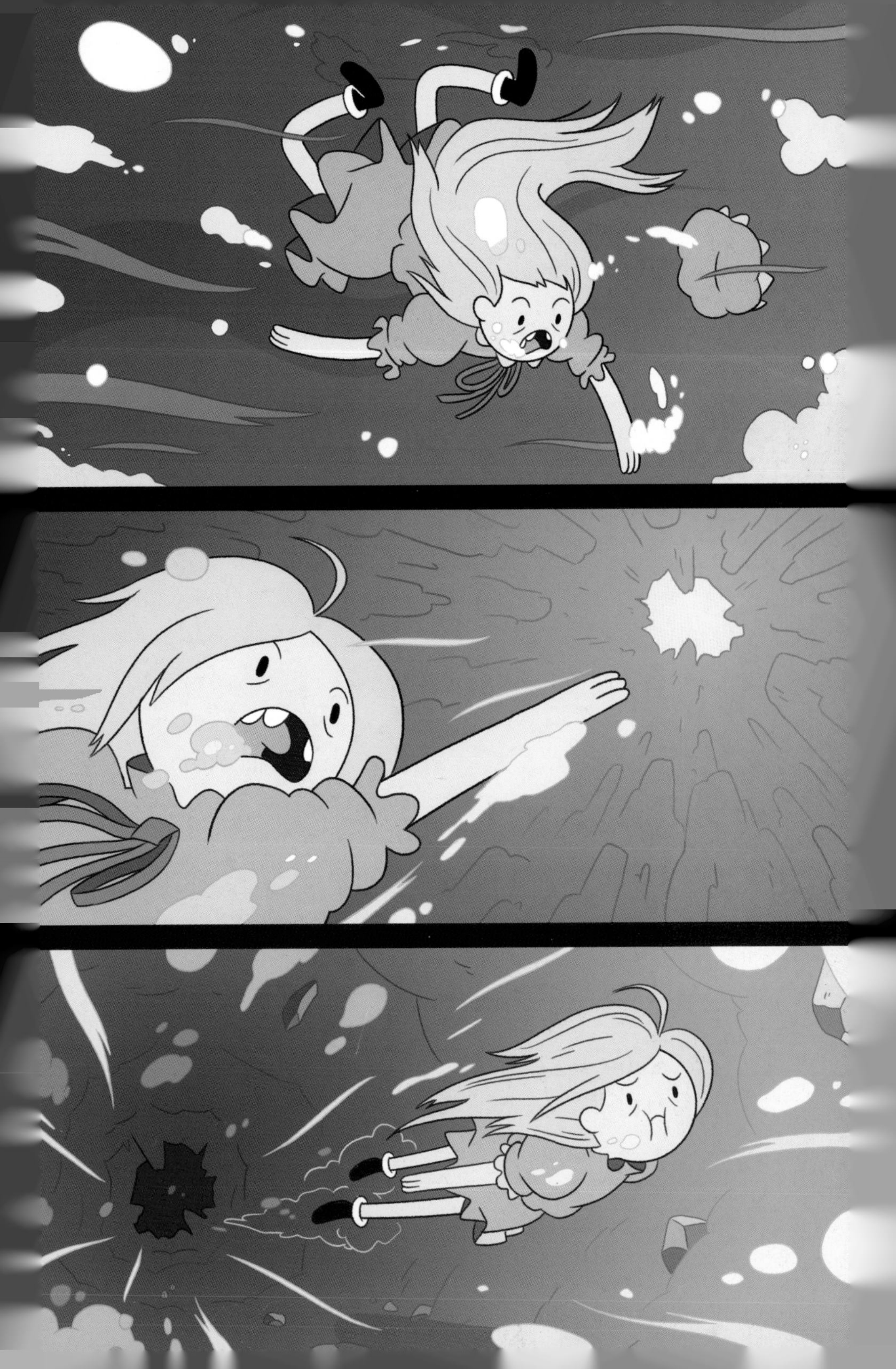

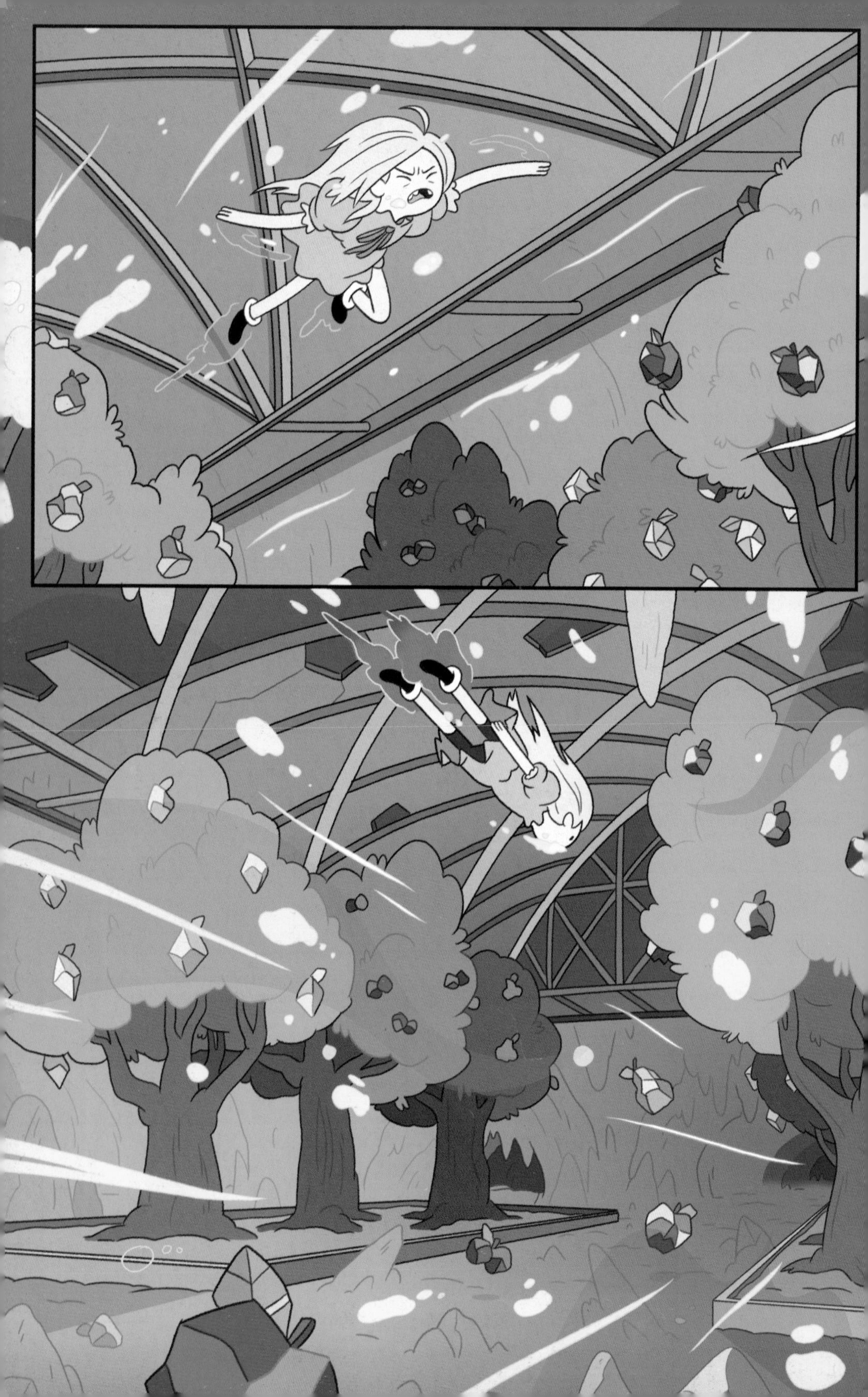

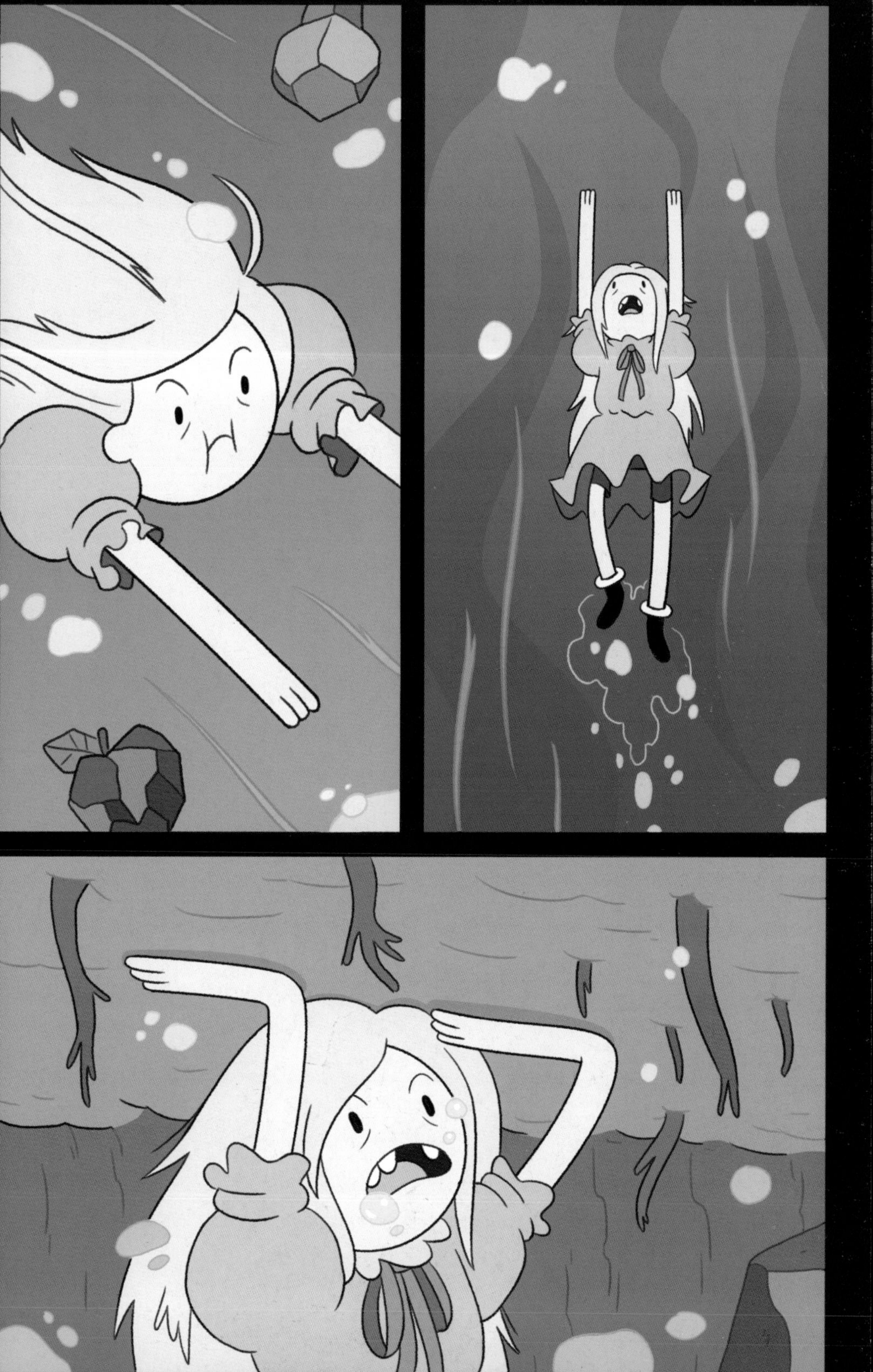

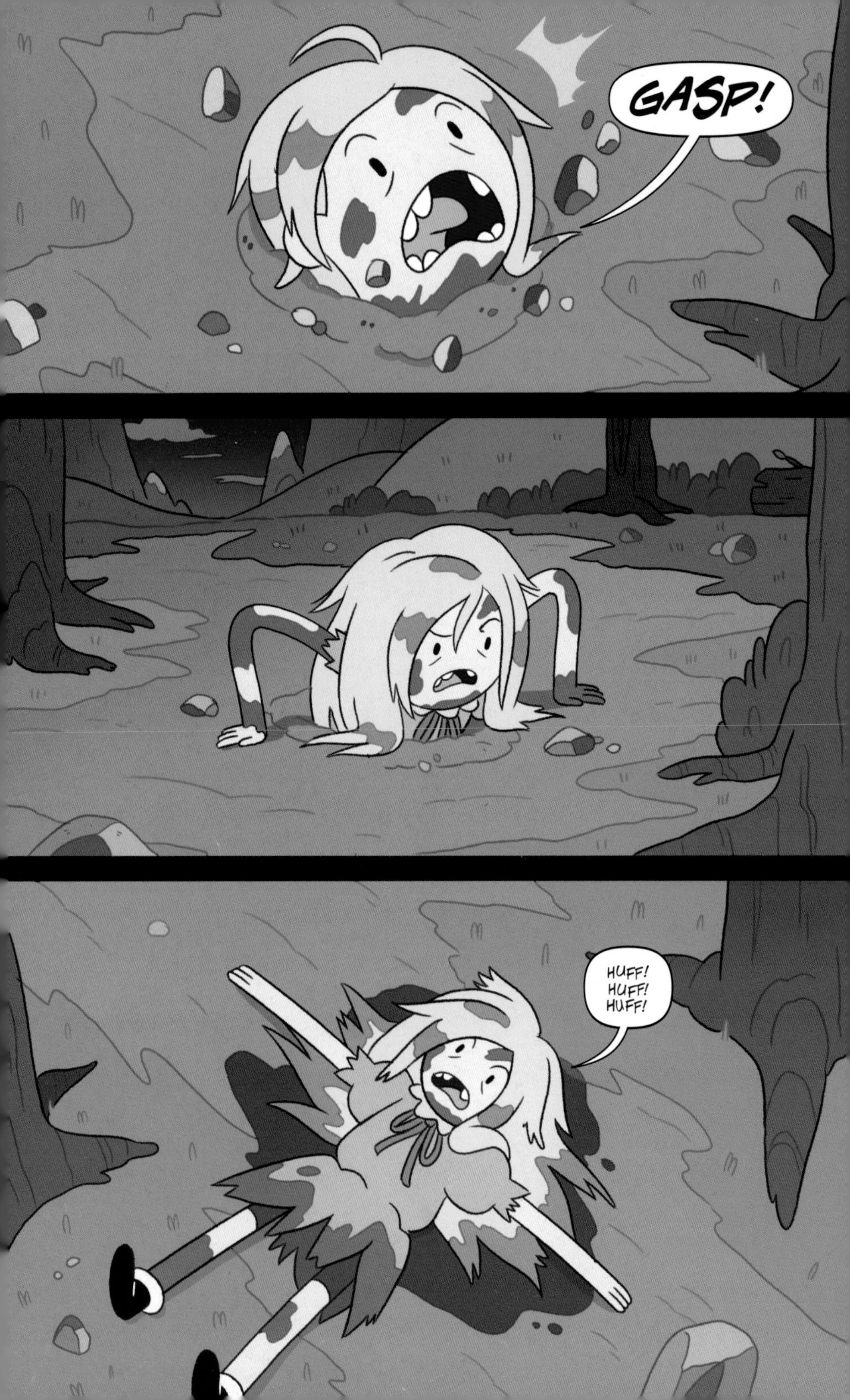
GASP!
HUFF! HUFF! HUFF!

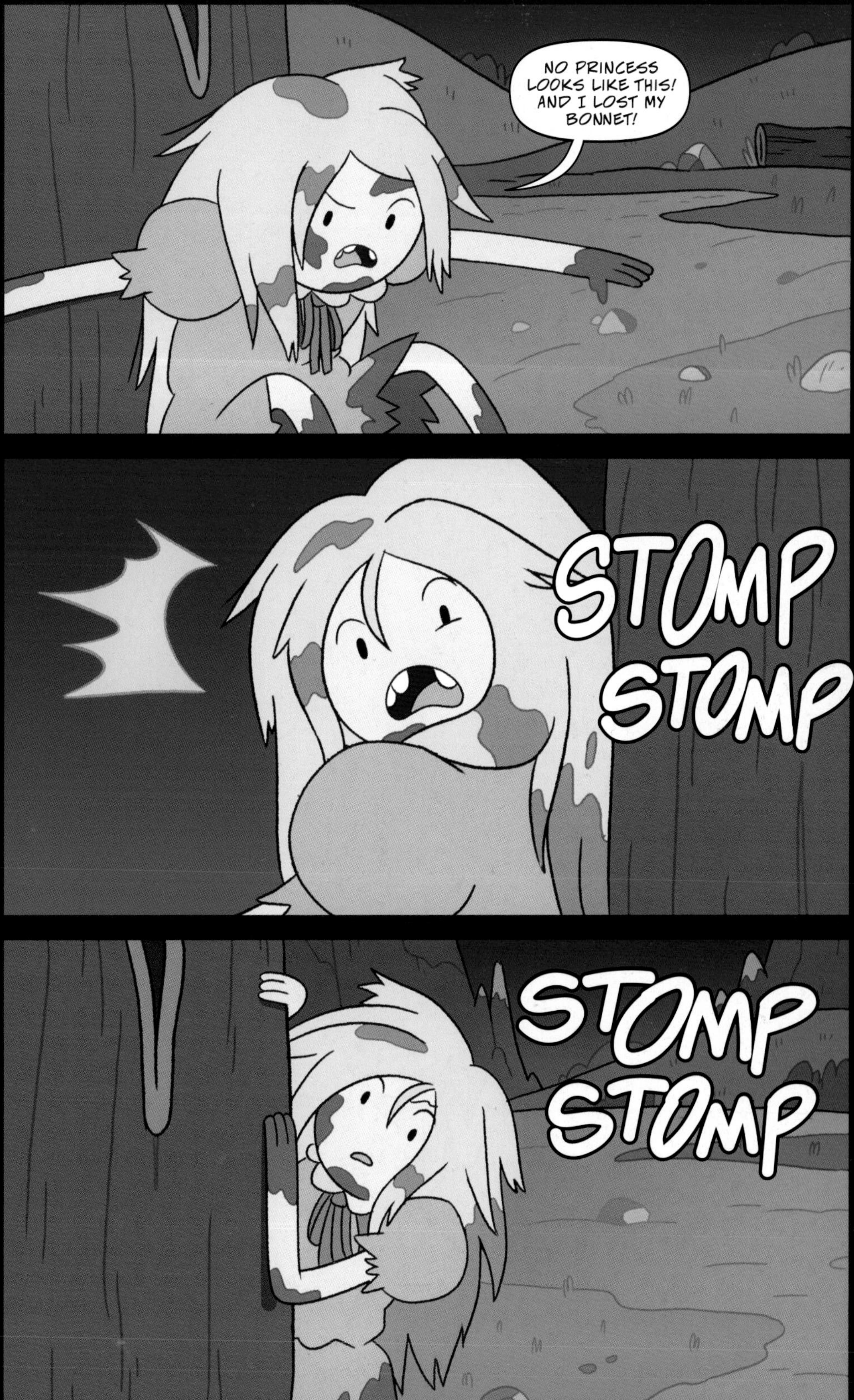
NO PRINCESS LOOKS LIKE THIS! AND I LOST MY BONNET!
STOMP STOMP
STOMP STOMP

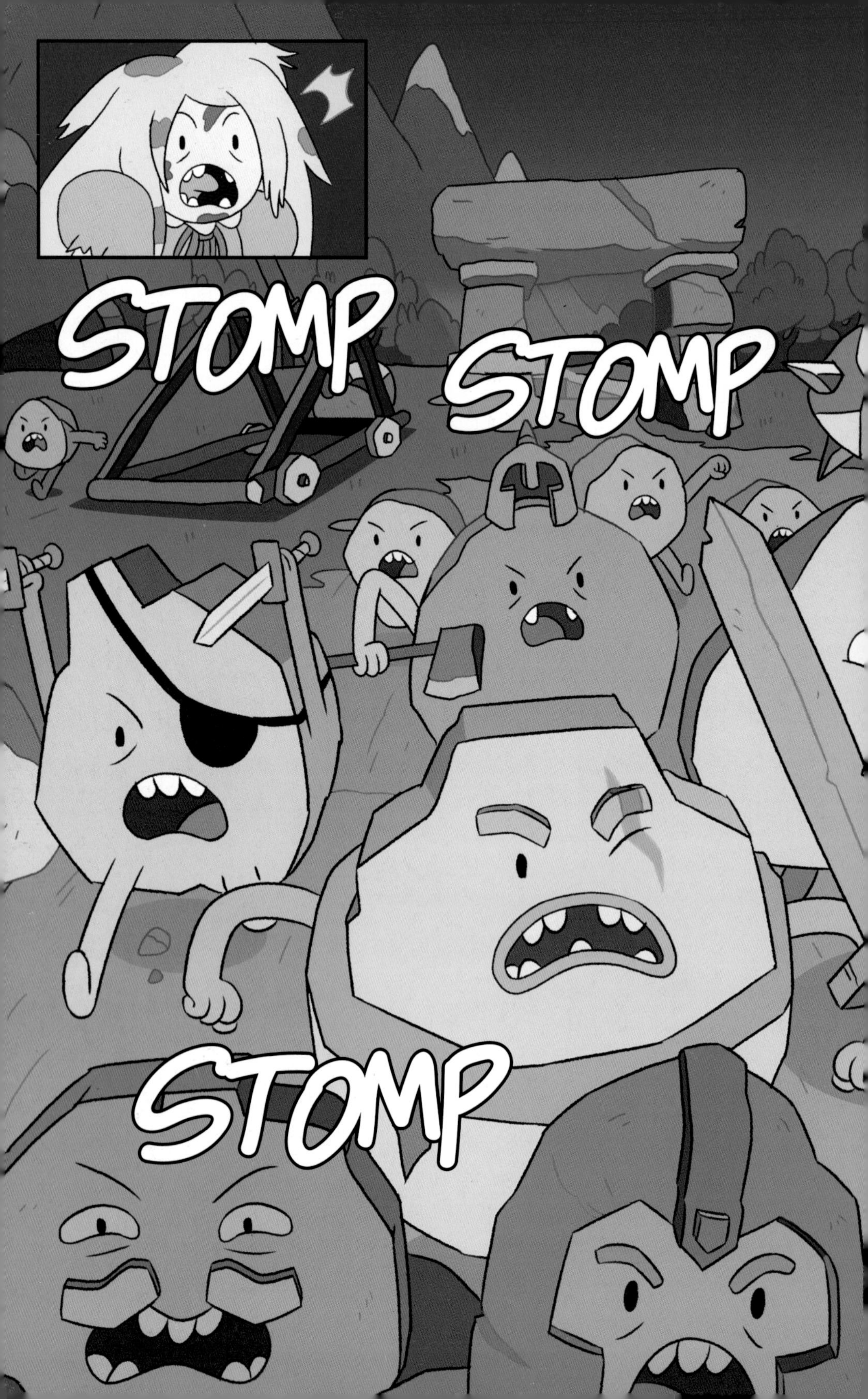
STOMP
STOMP
STOMP

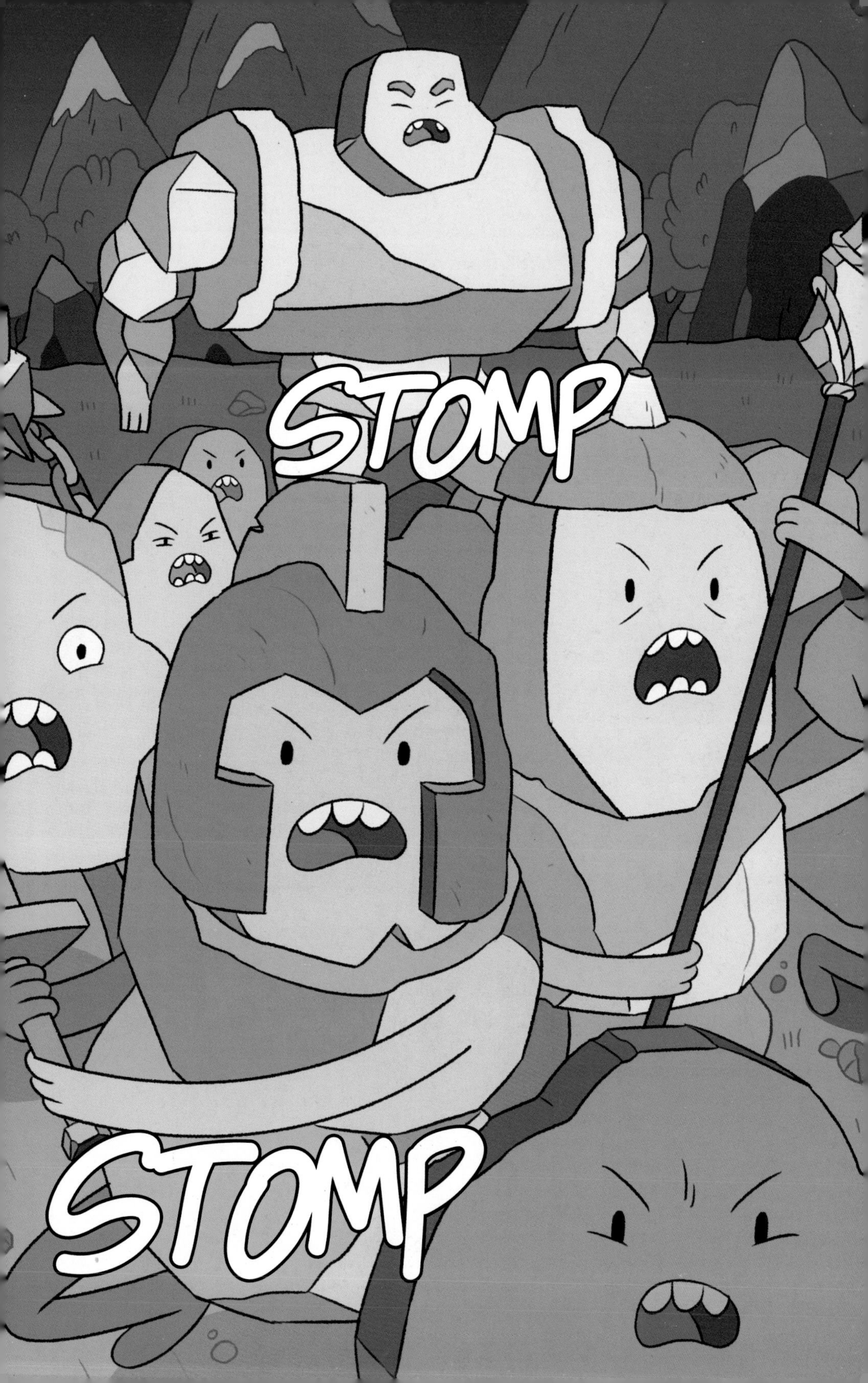
STOMP
STOMP

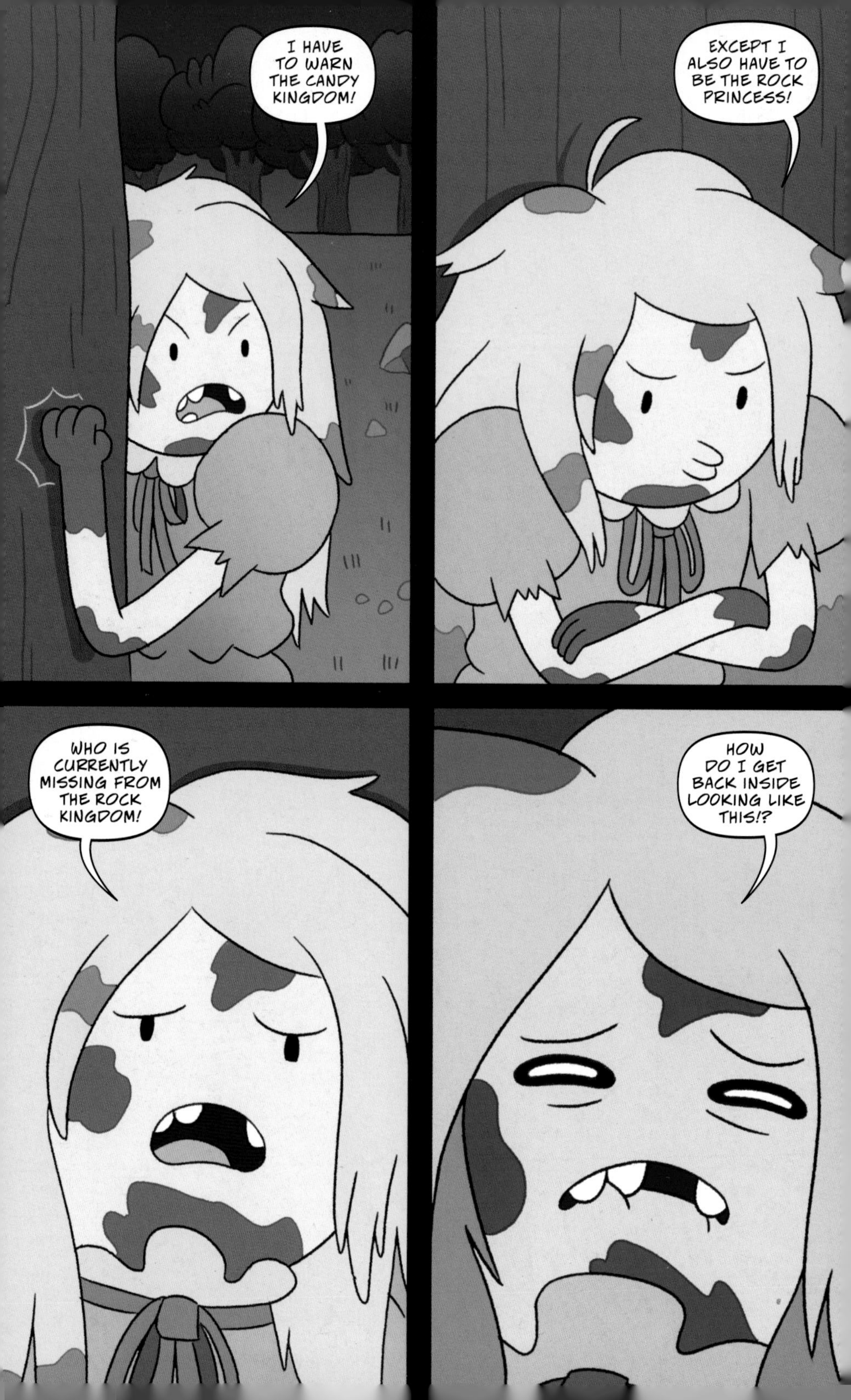
I HAVE TO WARN THE CANDY KINGDOM!
EXCEPT I ALSO HAVE TO BE THE ROCK PRINCESS!
WHO IS CURRENTLY MISSING FROM THE ROCK KINGDOM!
HOW DO I GET BACK INSIDE LOOKING LIKE THIS!?

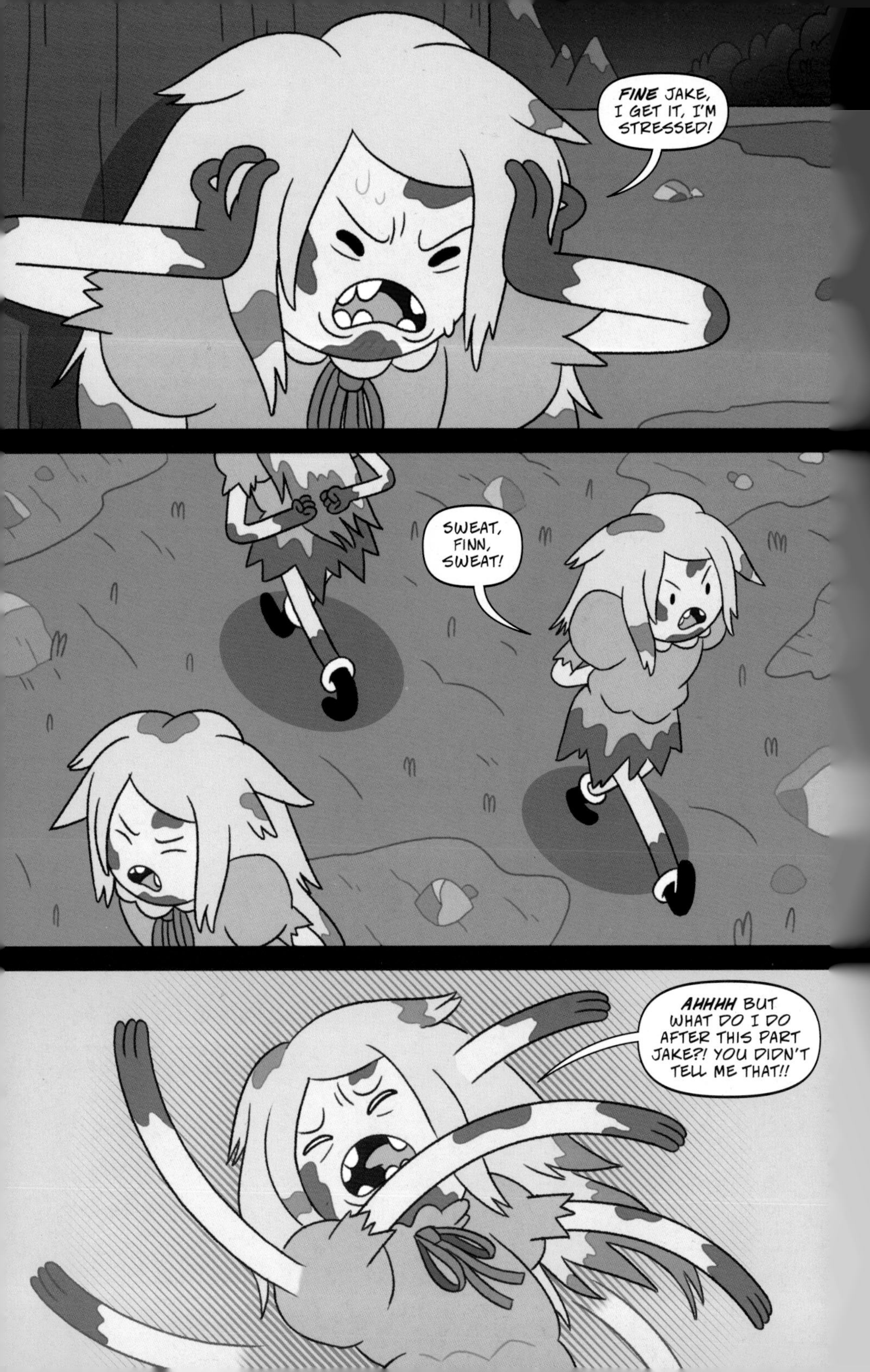
FINE JAKE, I GET IT, I'M STRESSED!
SWEAT, FINN, SWEAT!
AHHHH BUT WHAT DO I DO AFTER THIS PART JAKE?! YOU DIDN'T TELL ME THAT!!

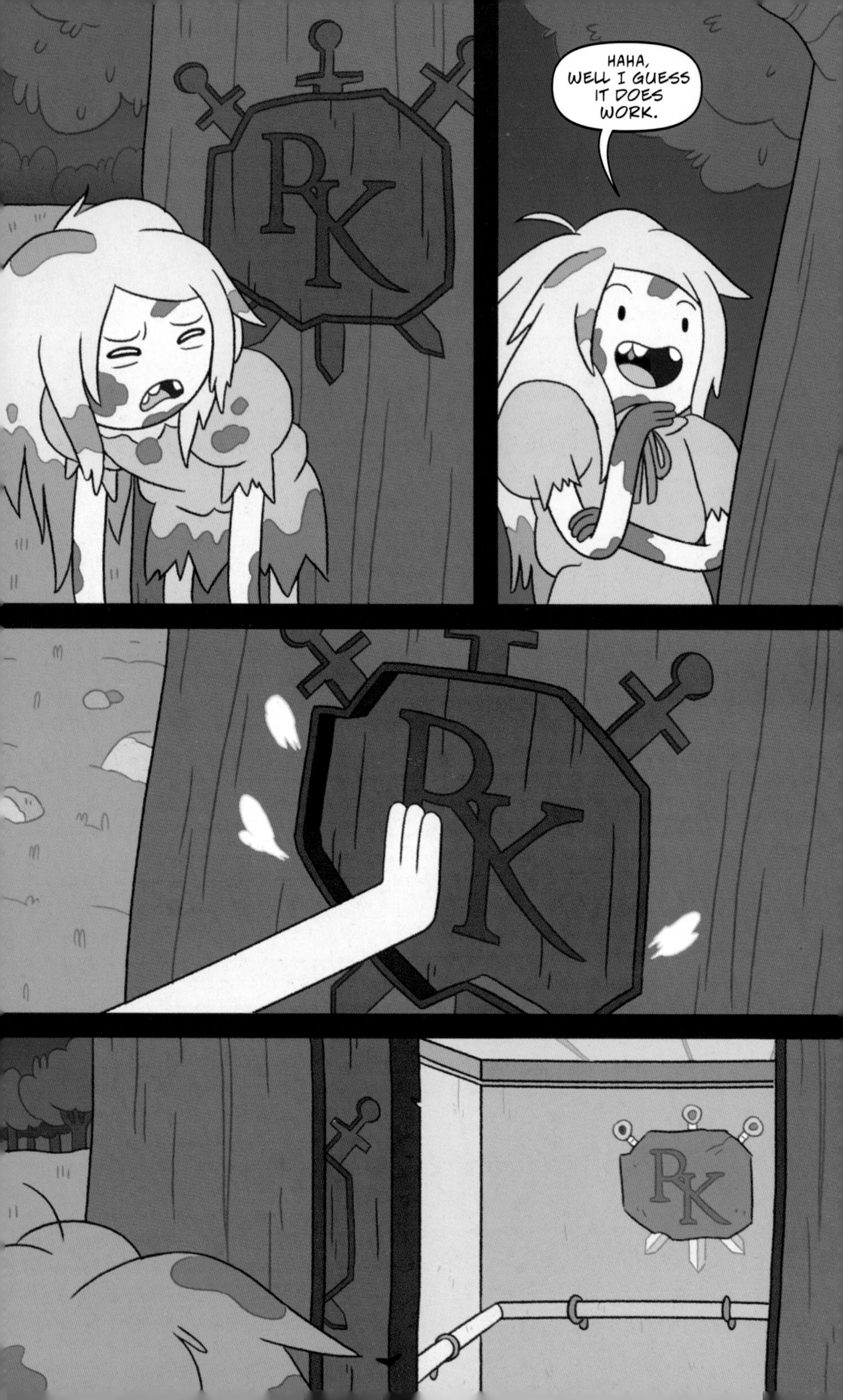

HAHA, WELL I GUESS IT DOES WORK.
RK
RK
RK

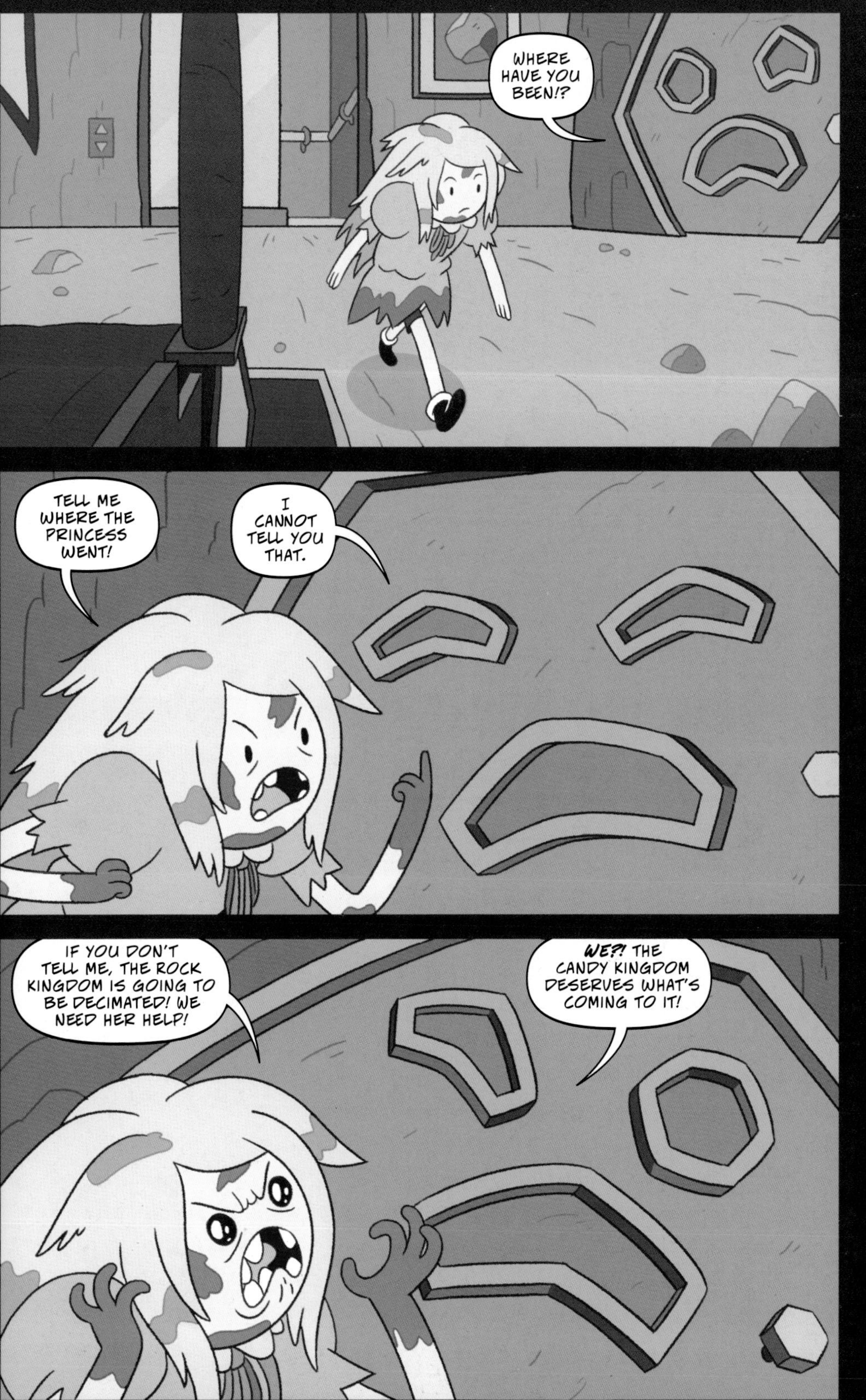
WHERE HAVE YOU BEEN!?
TELL ME WHERE THE PRINCESS WENT!
I CANNOT TELL YOU THAT.
IF YOU DON'T TELL ME, THE ROCK KINGDOM IS GOING TO BE DECIMATED! WE NEED HER HELP!
WE?! THE CANDY KINGDOM DESERVES WHAT'S COMING TO IT!

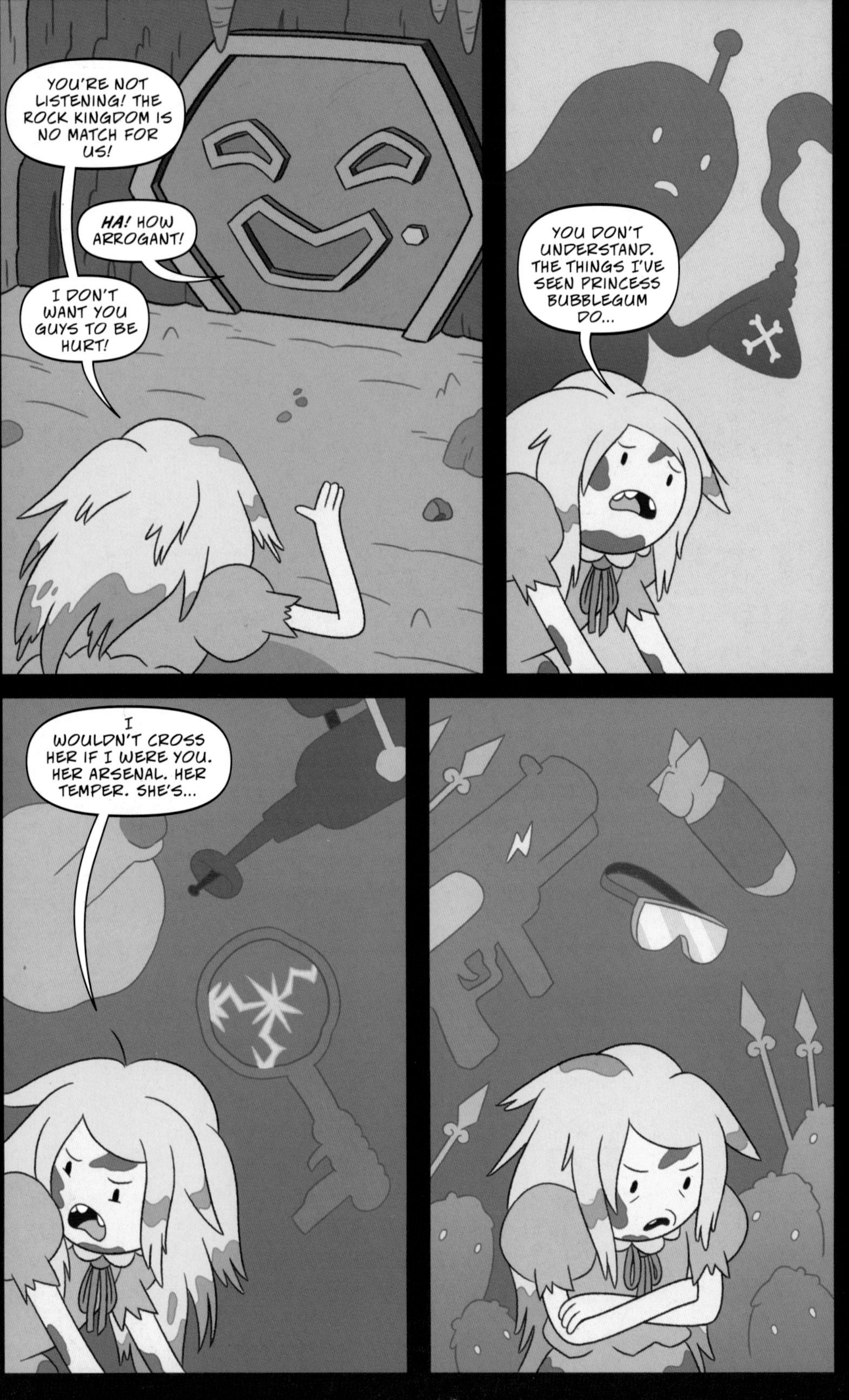
YOU'RE NOT LISTENING! THE ROCK KINGDOM IS NO MATCH FOR US!
HA! HOW ARROGANT!
I DON'T WANT YOU GUYS TO BE HURT!
YOU DON'T UNDERSTAND. THE THINGS I'VE SEEN PRINCESS BUBBLEGUM DO...
I WOULDN'T CROSS HER IF I WERE YOU. HER ARSENAL. HER TEMPER. SHE'S...

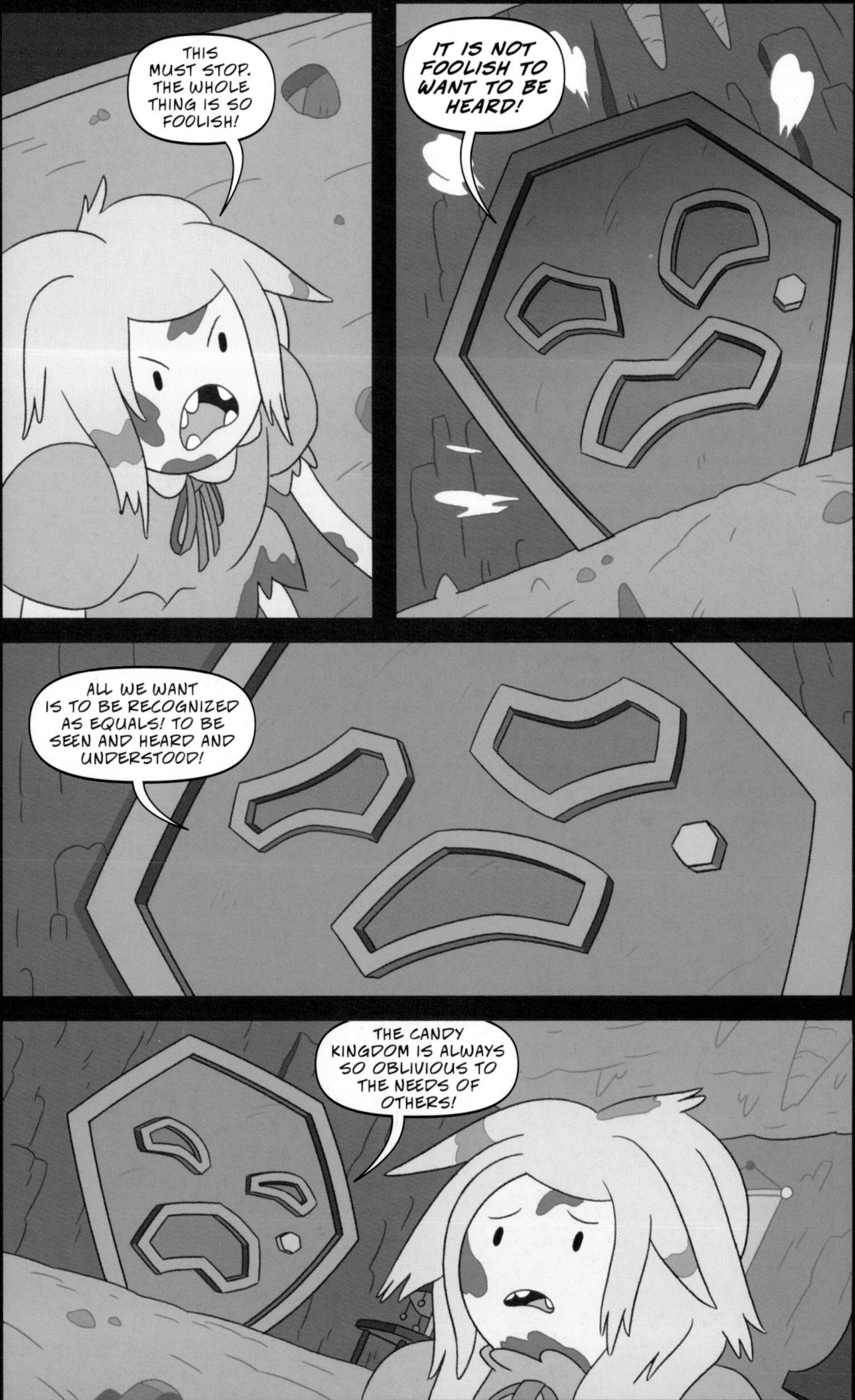
THIS MUST STOP. THE WHOLE THING IS SO FOOLISH!
IT IS NOT FOOLISH TO WANT TO BE HEARD!
ALL WE WANT IS TO BE RECOGNIZED AS EQUALS! TO BE SEEN AND HEARD AND UNDERSTOOD!
THE CANDY KINGDOM IS ALWAYS SO OBLIVIOUS TO THE NEEDS OF OTHERS!

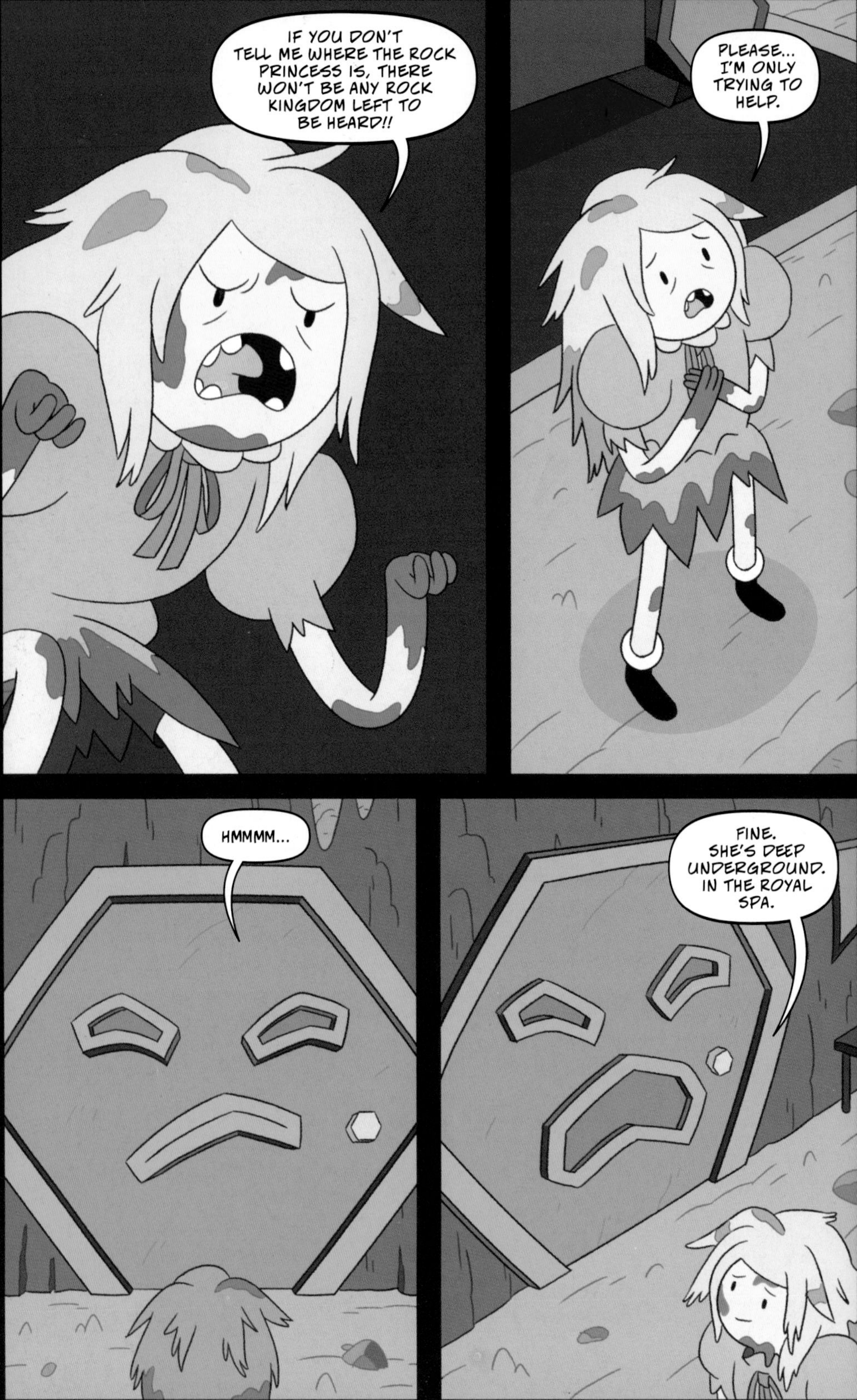
IF YOU DON'T TELL ME WHERE THE ROCK PRINCESS IS, THERE WON'T BE ANY ROCK KINGDOM LEFT TO BE HEARD!!
PLEASE... I'M ONLY TRYING TO HELP.
HMMMM...
FINE. SHE'S DEEP UNDERGROUND. IN THE ROYAL SPA.

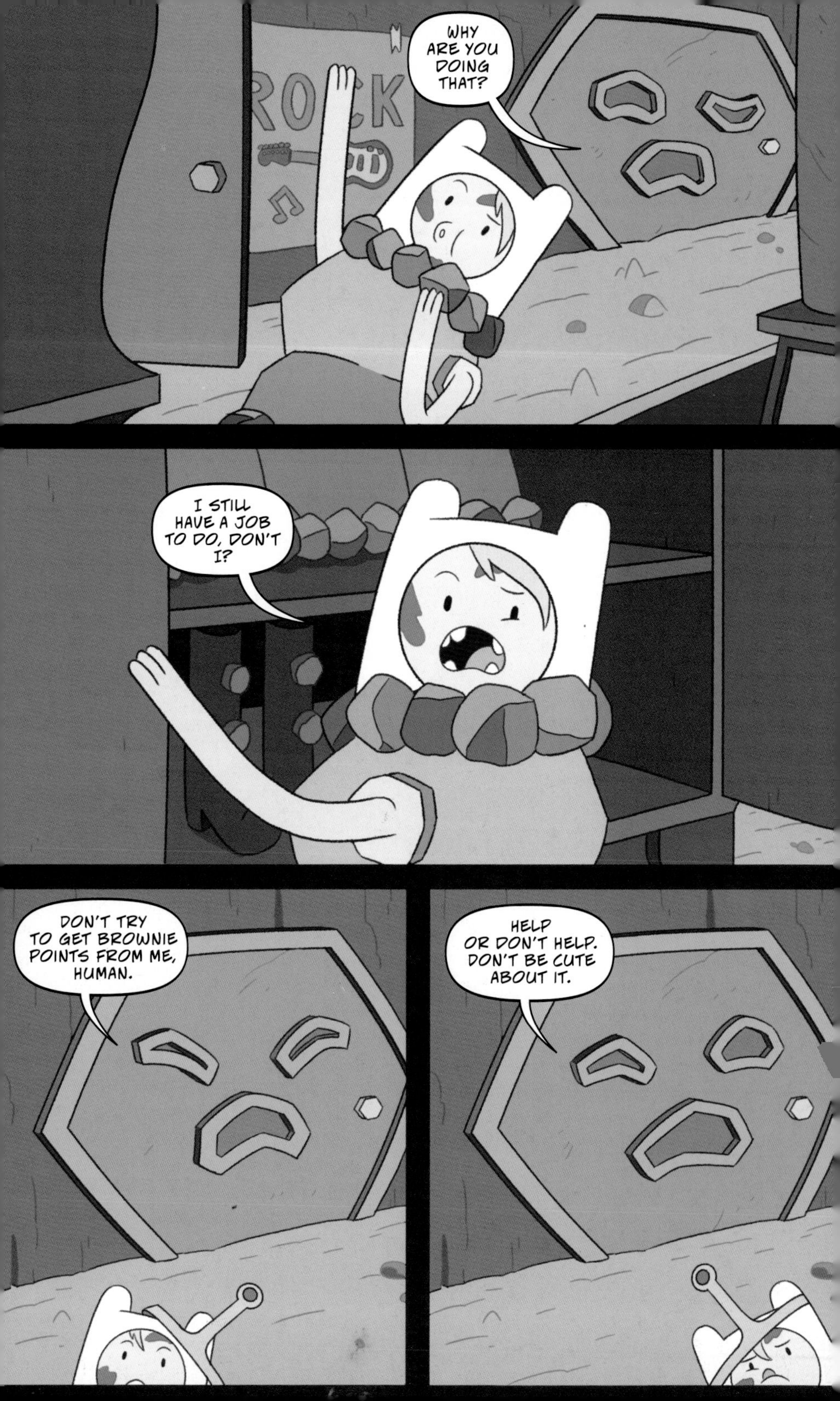
ROCK
WHY ARE YOU DOING THAT?
I STILL HAVE A JOB TO DO, DON'T I?
DON'T TRY TO GET BROWNIE POINTS FROM ME, HUMAN.
HELP OR DON'T HELP. DON'T BE CUTE ABOUT IT.

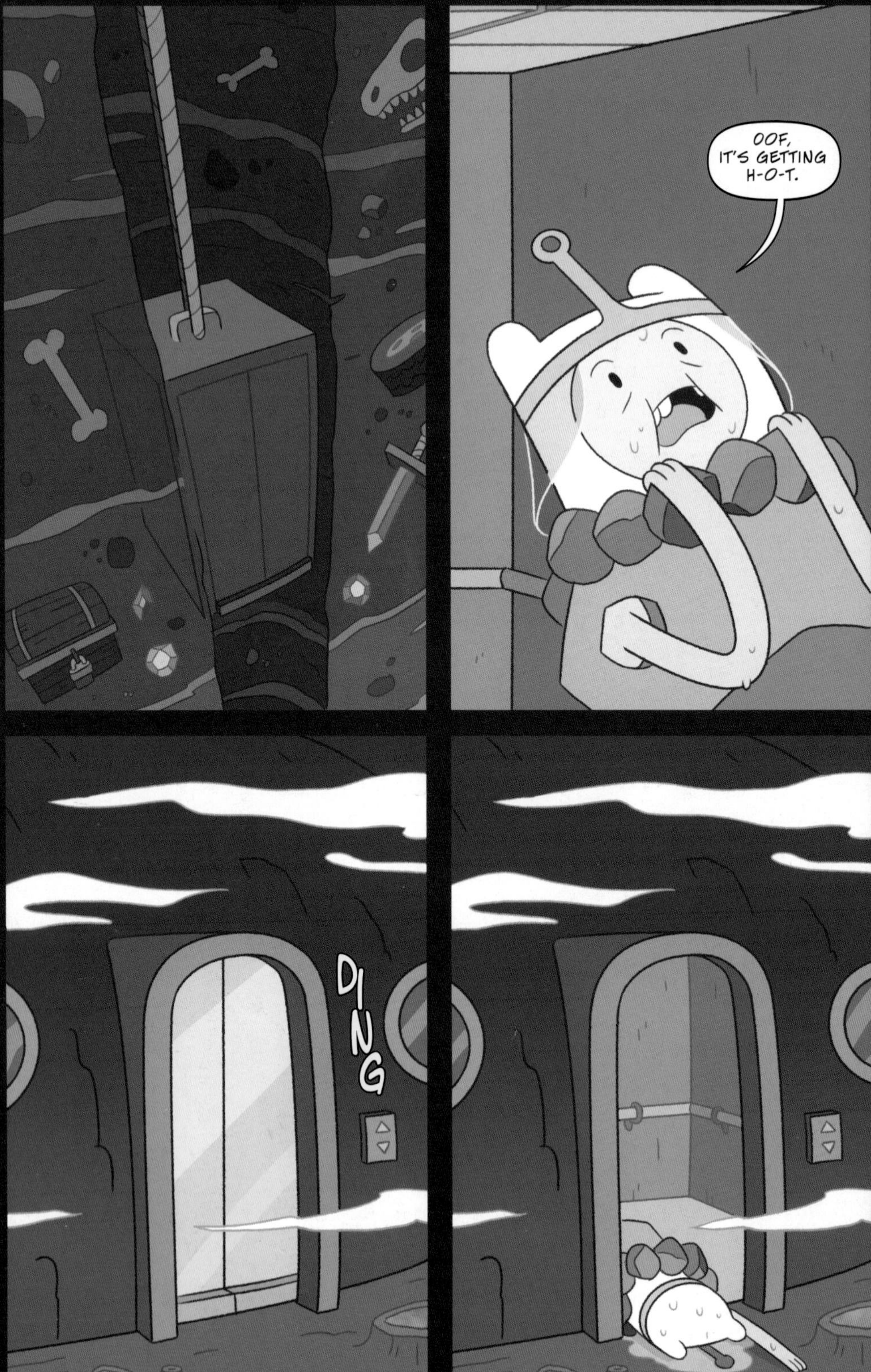
OOF, IT'S GETTING H-O-T.
DING

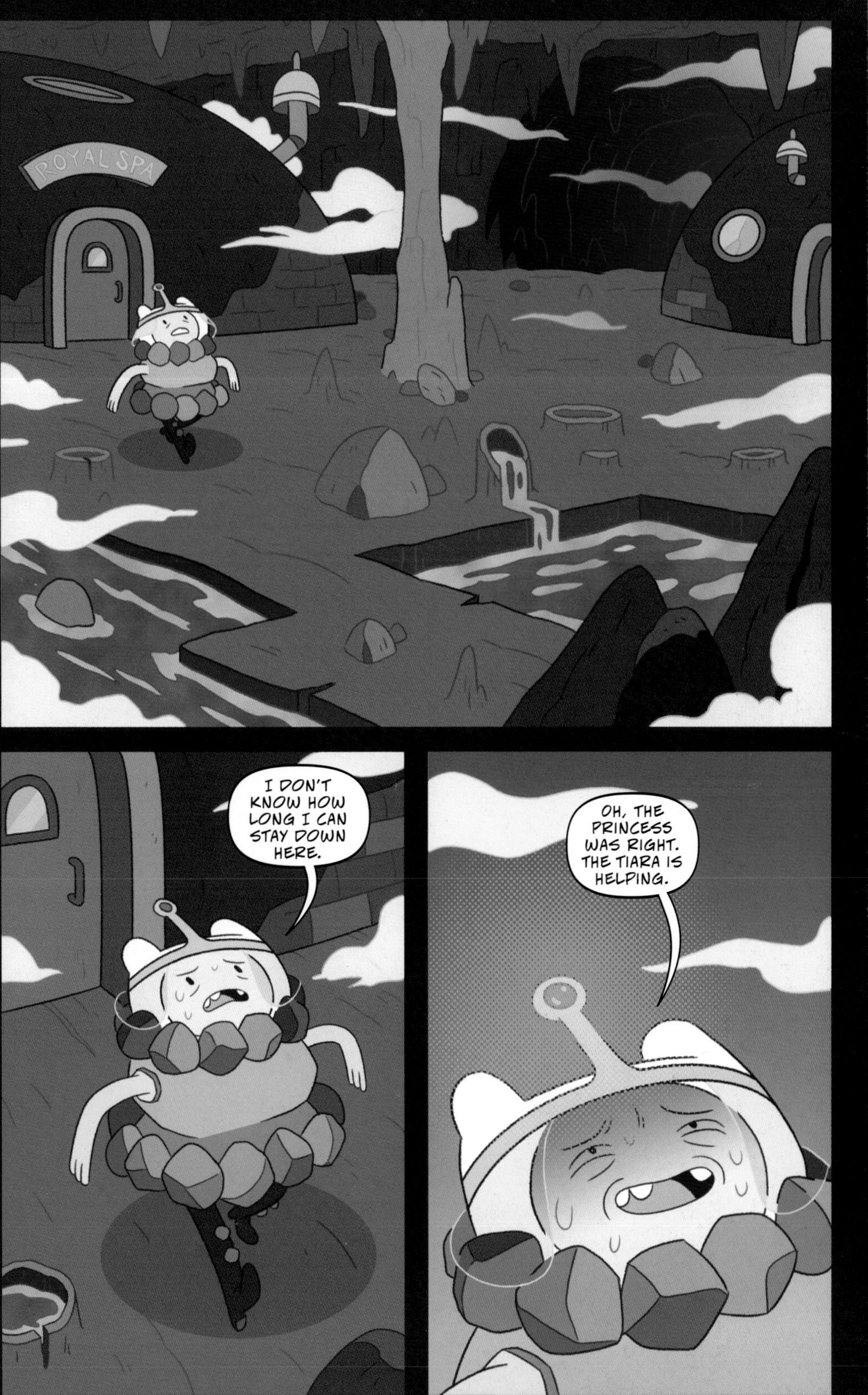
ROYAL SPA
I DON'T KNOW HOW LONG I CAN STAY DOWN HERE.
OH, THE PRINCESS WAS RIGHT. THE TIARA IS HELPING.

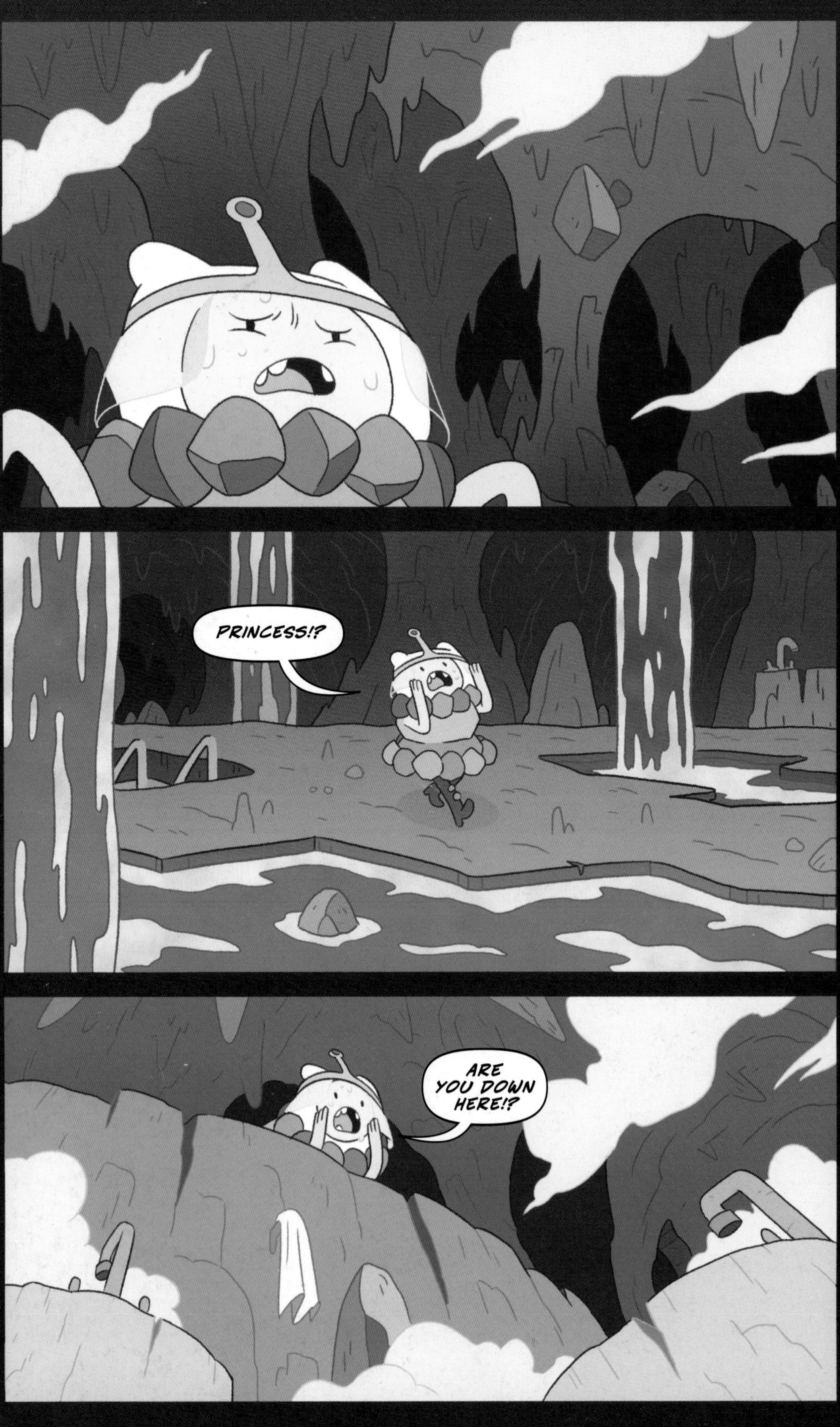
PRINCESS!?
ARE YOU DOWN HERE!?

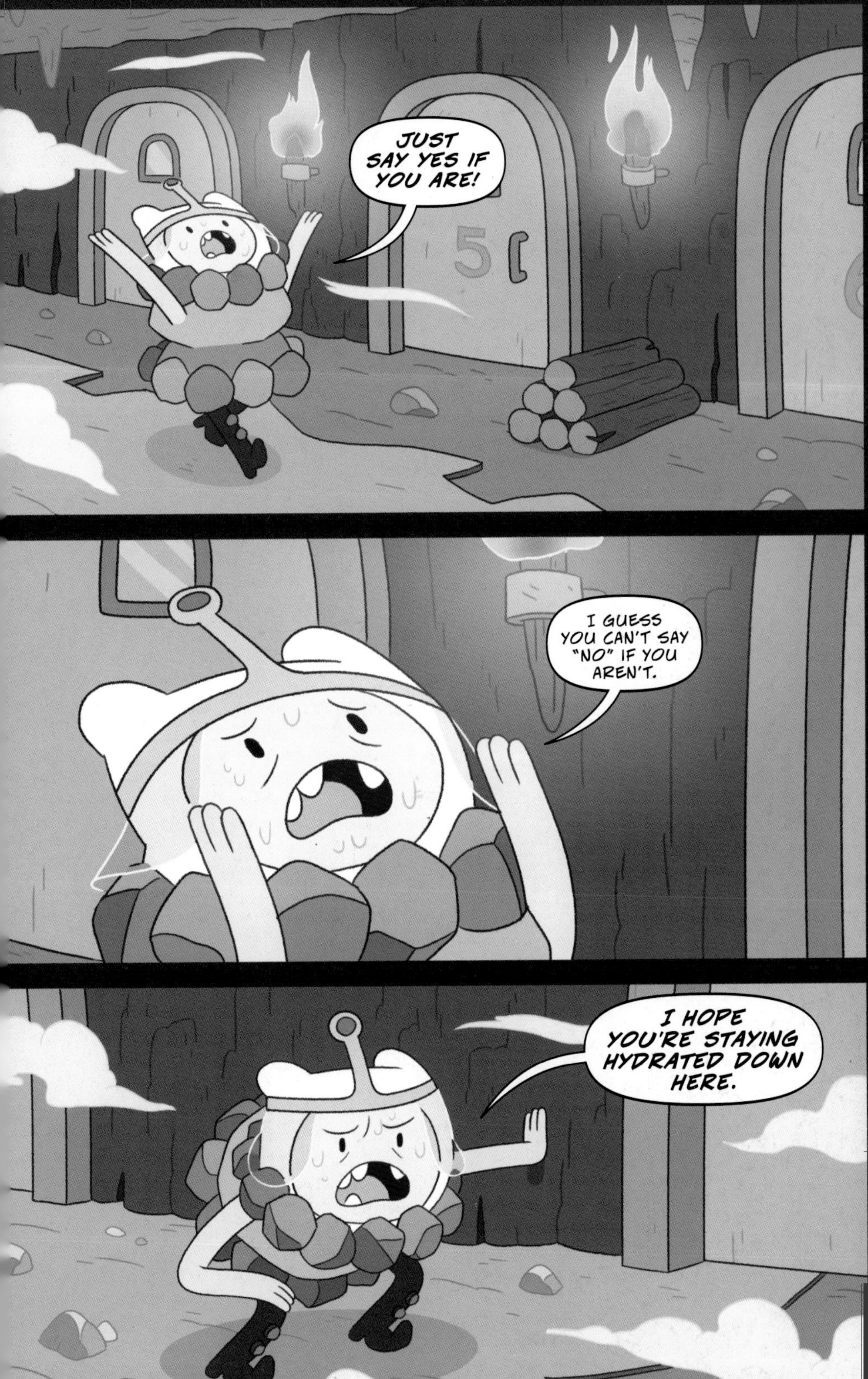
JUST SAY YES IF YOU ARE!
I GUESS YOU CAN'T SAY "NO" IF YOU AREN'T.
I HOPE YOU'RE STAYING HYDRATED DOWN HERE.

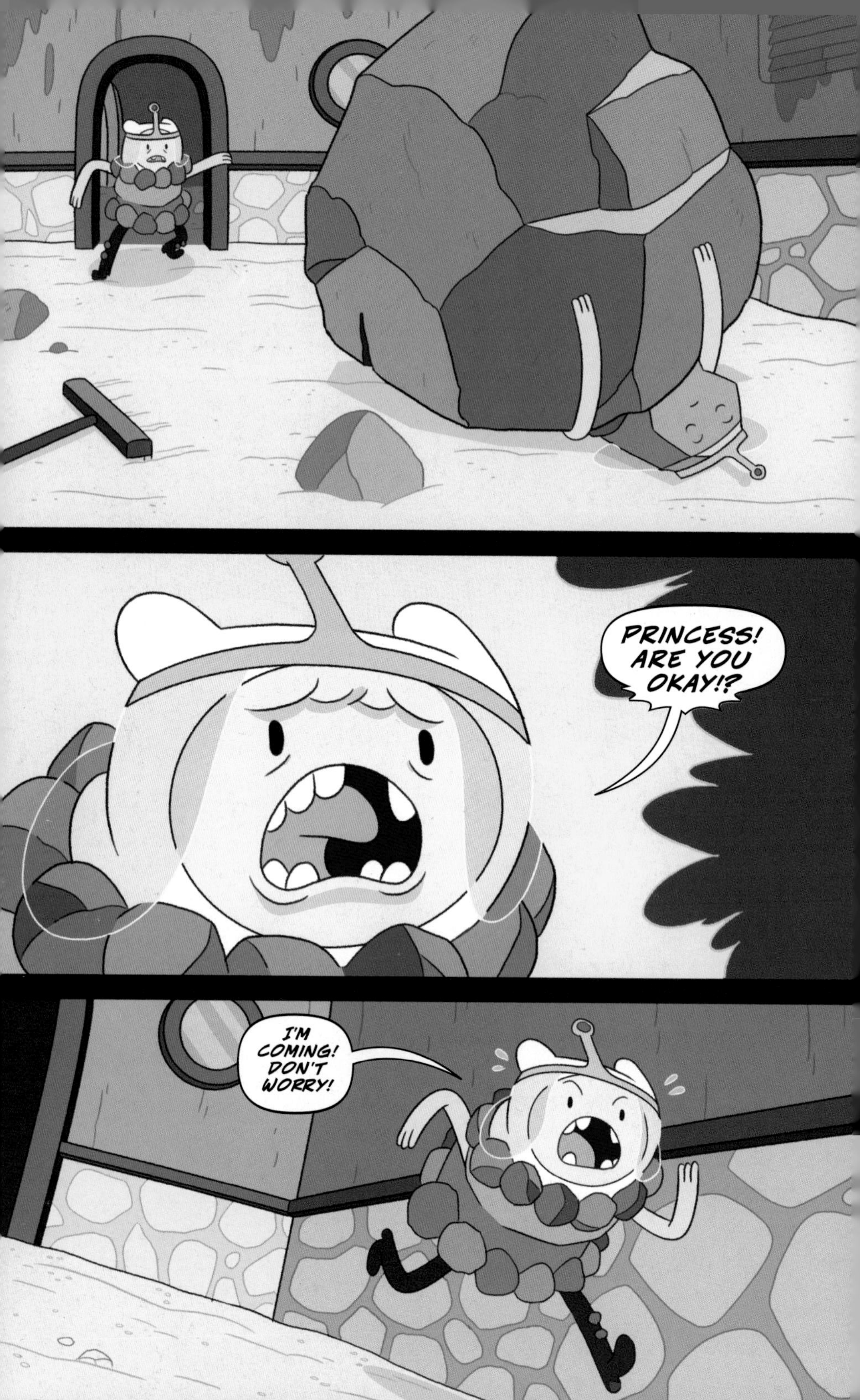
PRINCESS! ARE YOU OKAY!?
I'M COMING! DON'T WORRY!

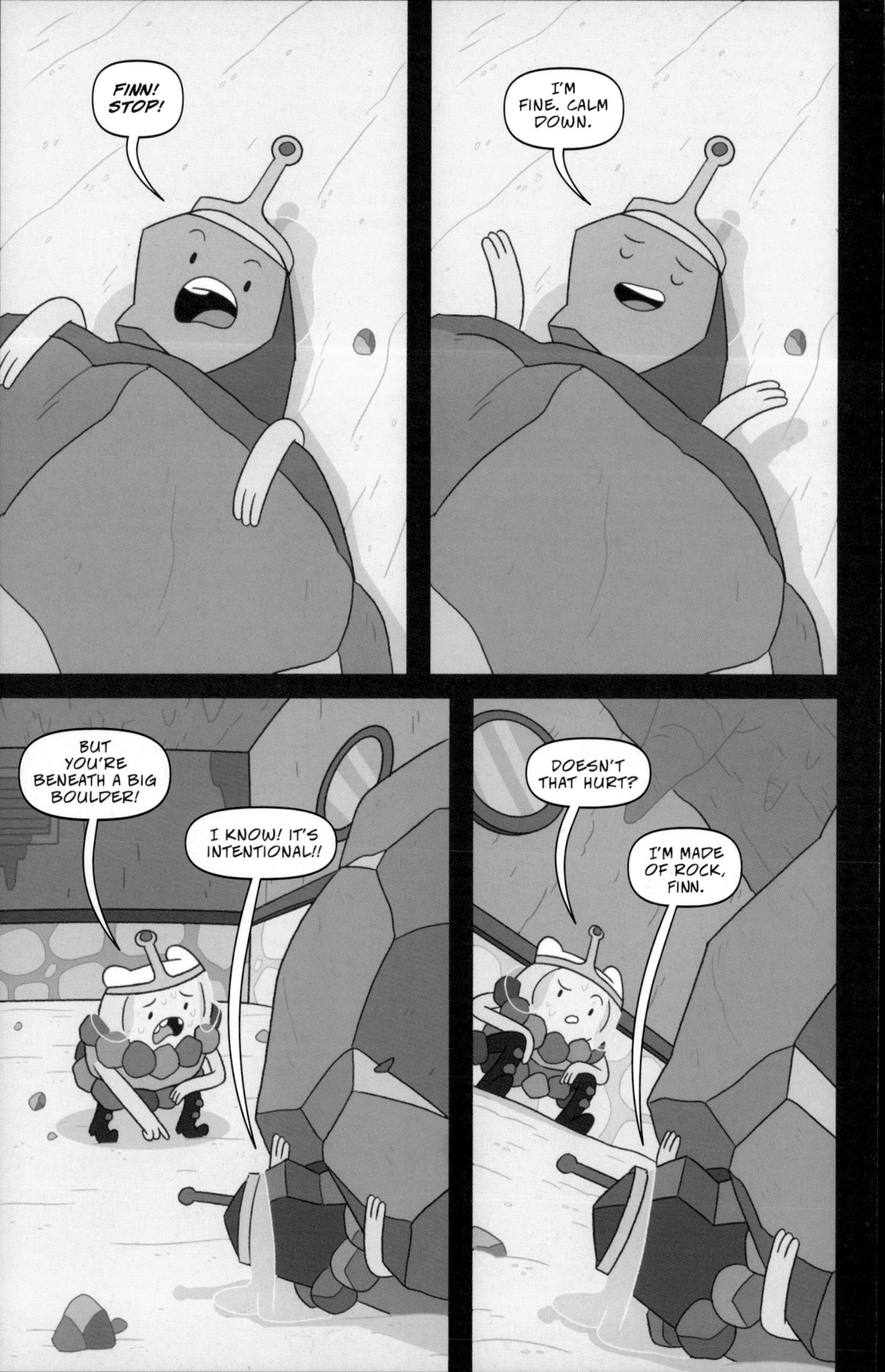
FINN! STOP!
I'M FINE. CALM DOWN.
BUT YOU'RE BENEATH A BIG BOULDER!
I KNOW! IT'S INTENTIONAL!!
DOESN'T THAT HURT?
I'M MADE OF ROCK, FINN.

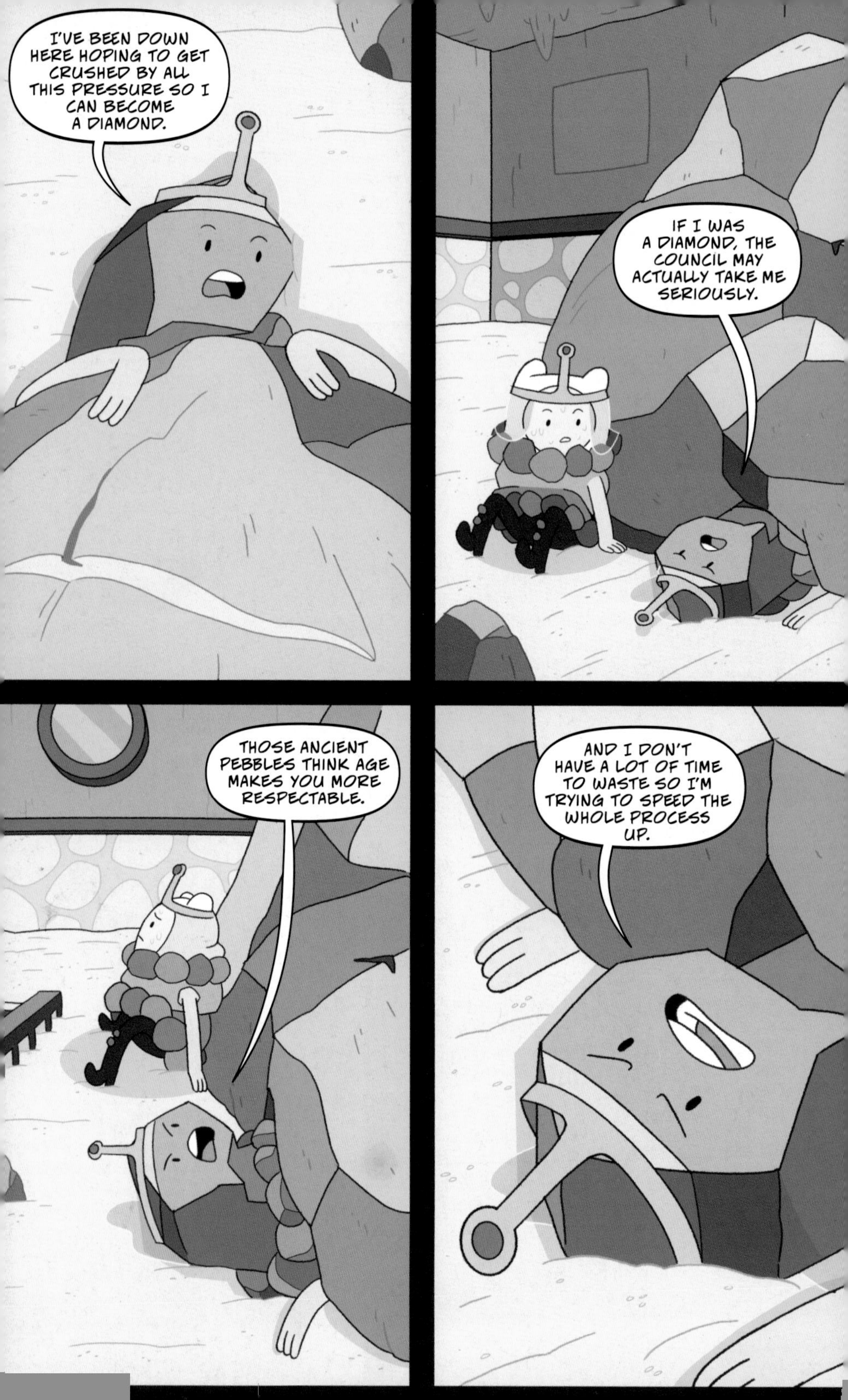
I'VE BEEN DOWN HERE HOPING TO GET CRUSHED BY ALL THIS PRESSURE SO I CAN BECOME A DIAMOND.
IF I WAS A DIAMOND, THE COUNCIL MAY ACTUALLY TAKE ME SERIOUSLY.
THOSE ANCIENT PEBBLES THINK AGE MAKES YOU MORE RESPECTABLE.
AND I DON'T HAVE A LOT OF TIME TO WASTE SO I'M TRYING TO SPEED THE WHOLE PROCESS UP.

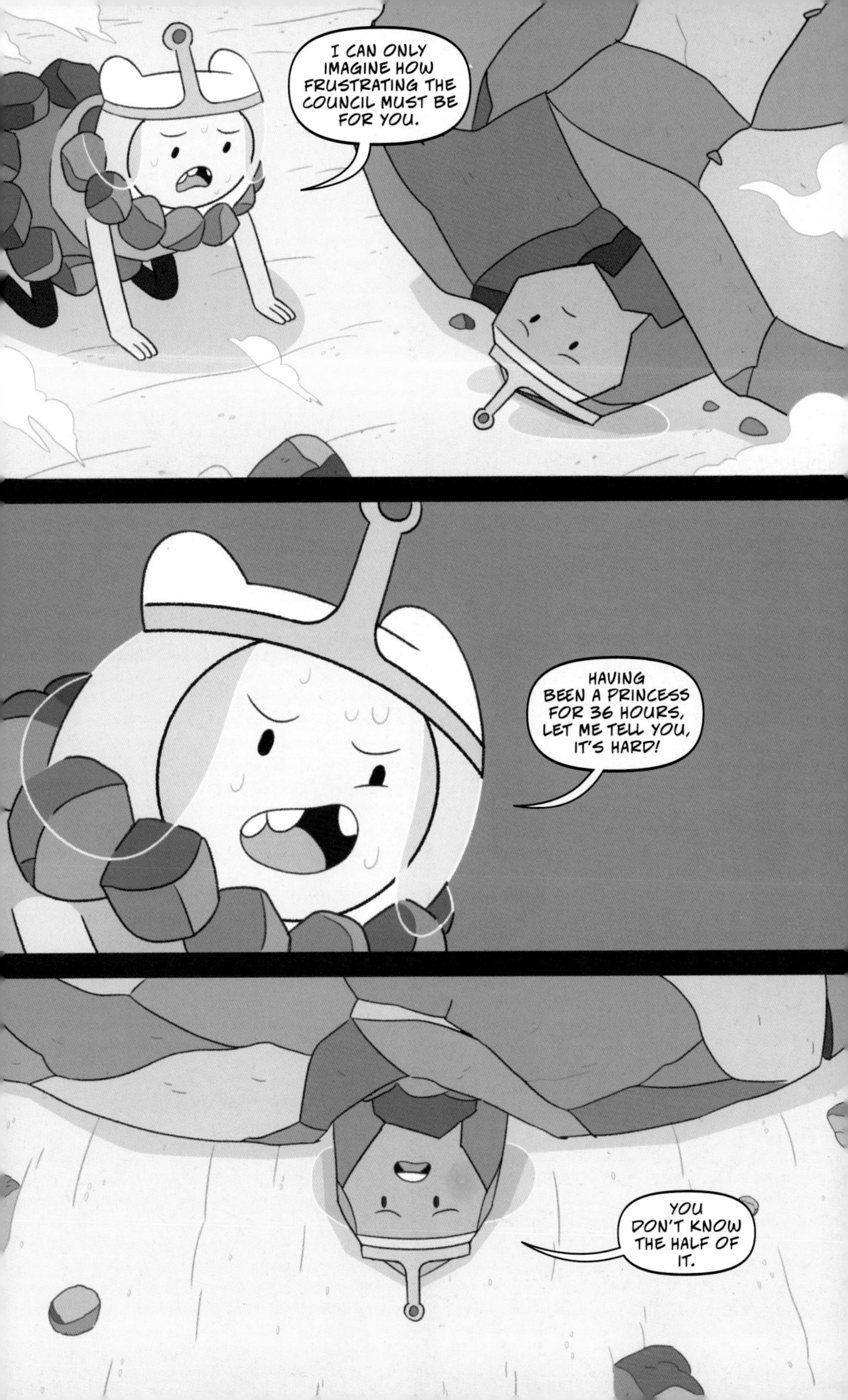
I CAN ONLY IMAGINE HOW FRUSTRATING THE COUNCIL MUST BE FOR YOU.
HAVING BEEN A PRINCESS FOR 36 HOURS, LET ME TELL YOU, IT'S HARD!
YOU DON'T KNOW THE HALF OF IT.

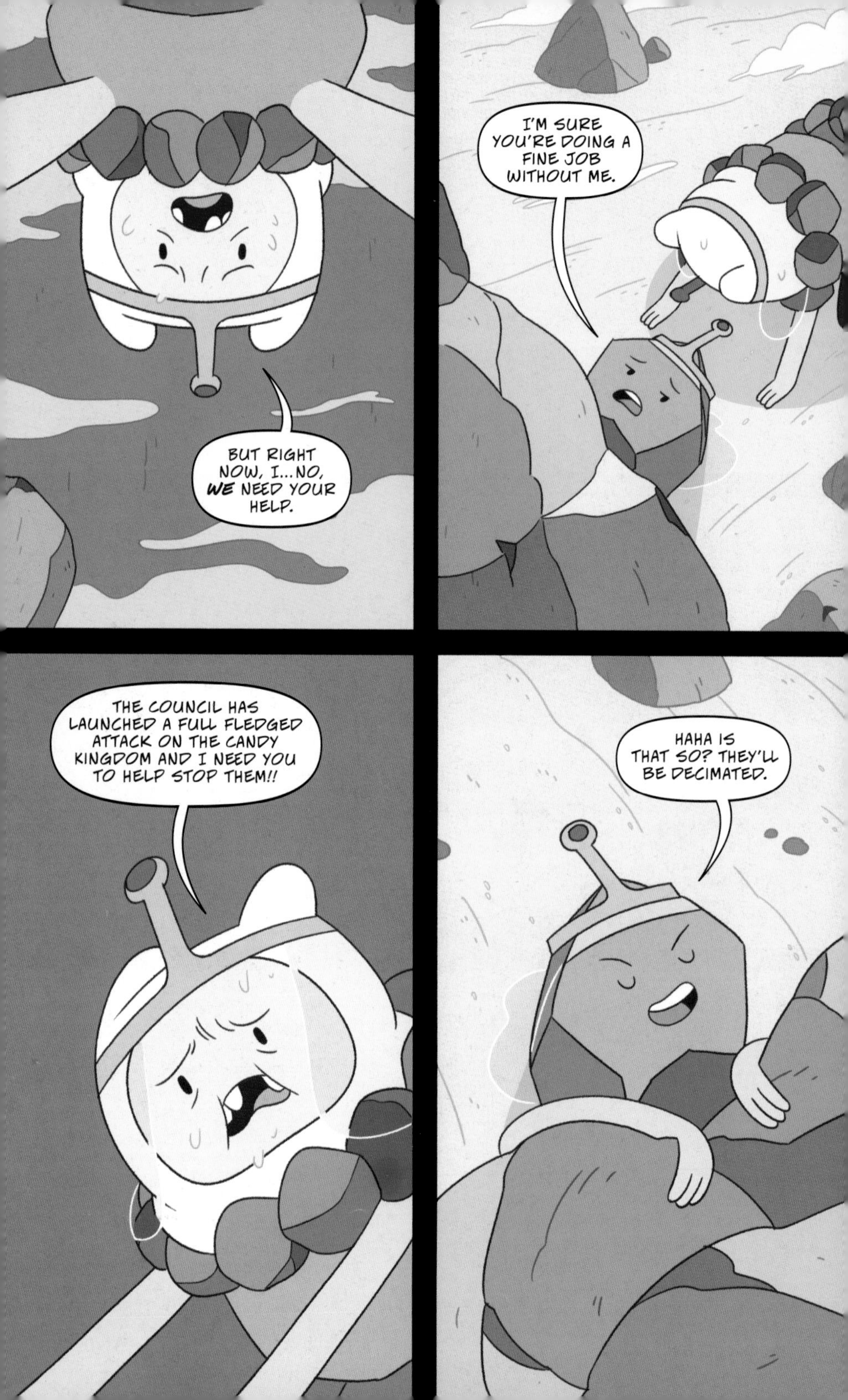
BUT RIGHT NOW, I...NO, WE NEED YOUR HELP.
I'M SURE YOU'RE DOING A FINE JOB WITHOUT ME.
THE COUNCIL HAS LAUNCHED A FULL FLEDGED ATTACK ON THE CANDY KINGDOM AND I NEED YOU TO HELP STOP THEM!!
HAHA IS THAT SO? THEY'LL BE DECIMATED.

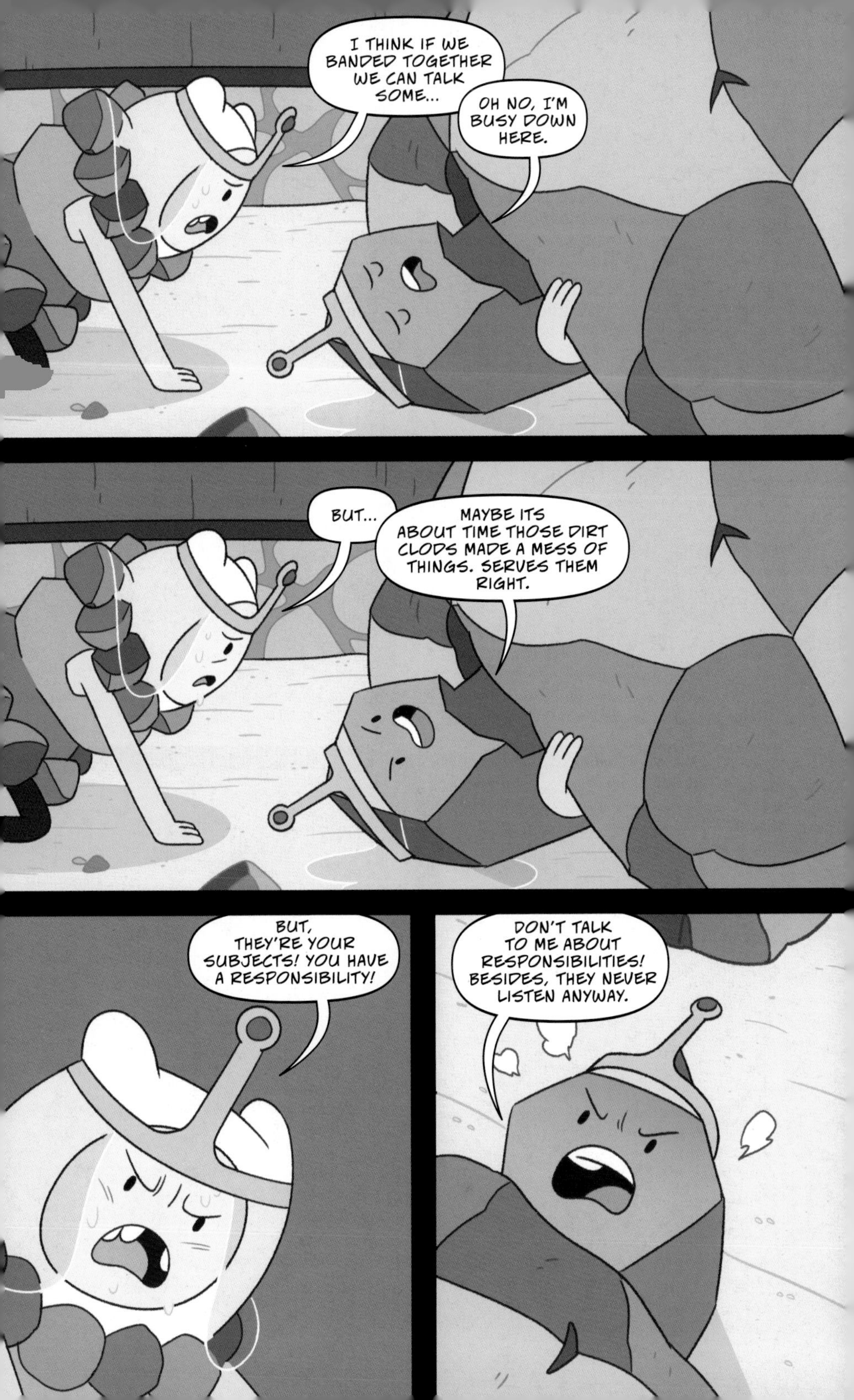
I THINK IF WE BANDED TOGETHER WE CAN TALK SOME...
OH NO, I'M BUSY DOWN HERE.
BUT...
MAYBE ITS ABOUT TIME THOSE DIRT CLODS MADE A MESS OF THINGS. SERVES THEM RIGHT.
BUT, THEY'RE YOUR SUBJECTS! YOU HAVE A RESPONSIBILITY!
DON'T TALK TO ME ABOUT RESPONSIBILITIES! BESIDES, THEY NEVER LISTEN ANYWAY.

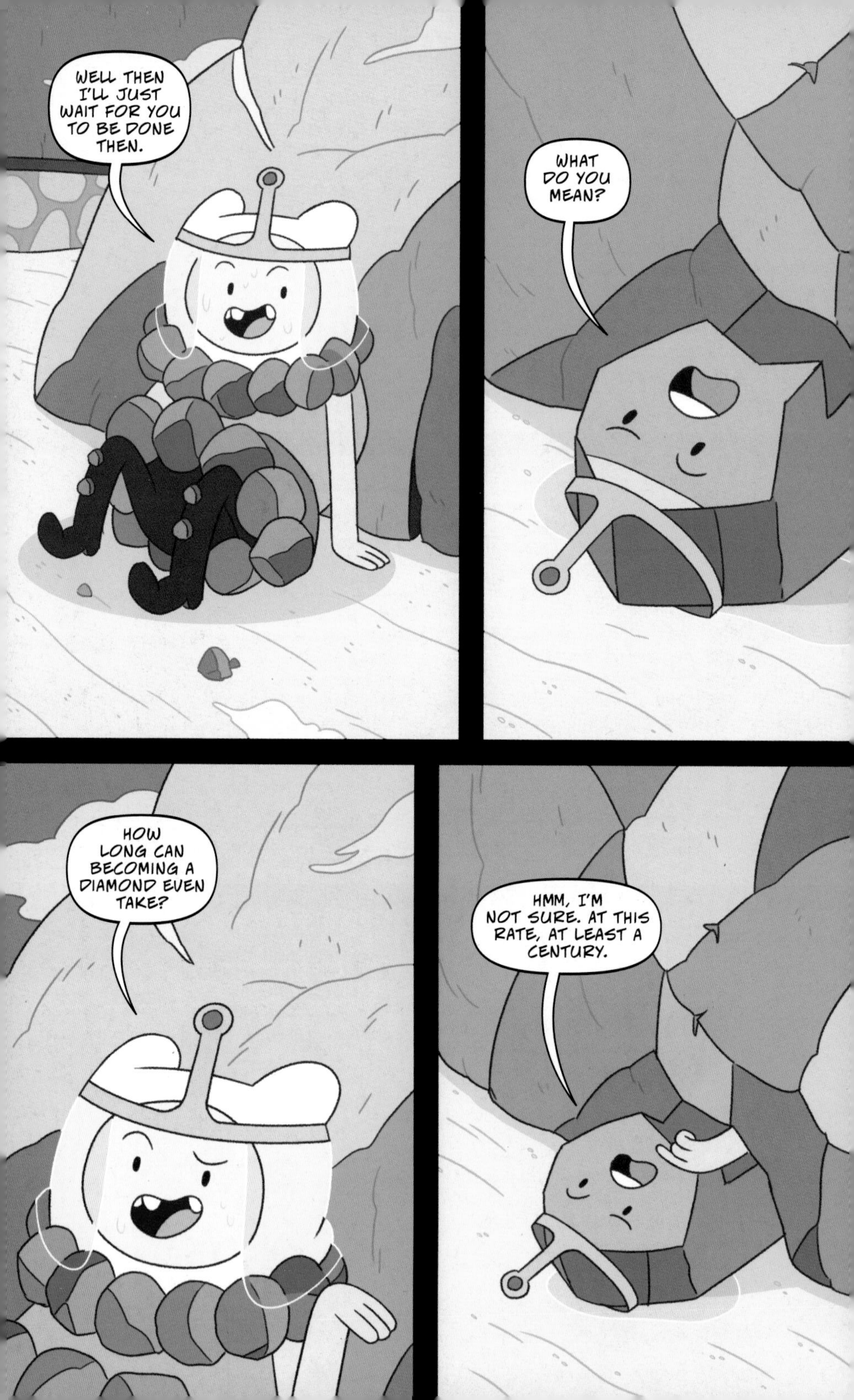
WELL THEN I'LL JUST WAIT FOR YOU TO BE DONE THEN.
WHAT DO YOU MEAN?
HOW LONG CAN BECOMING A DIAMOND EVEN TAKE?
HMM, I'M NOT SURE. AT THIS RATE, AT LEAST A CENTURY.

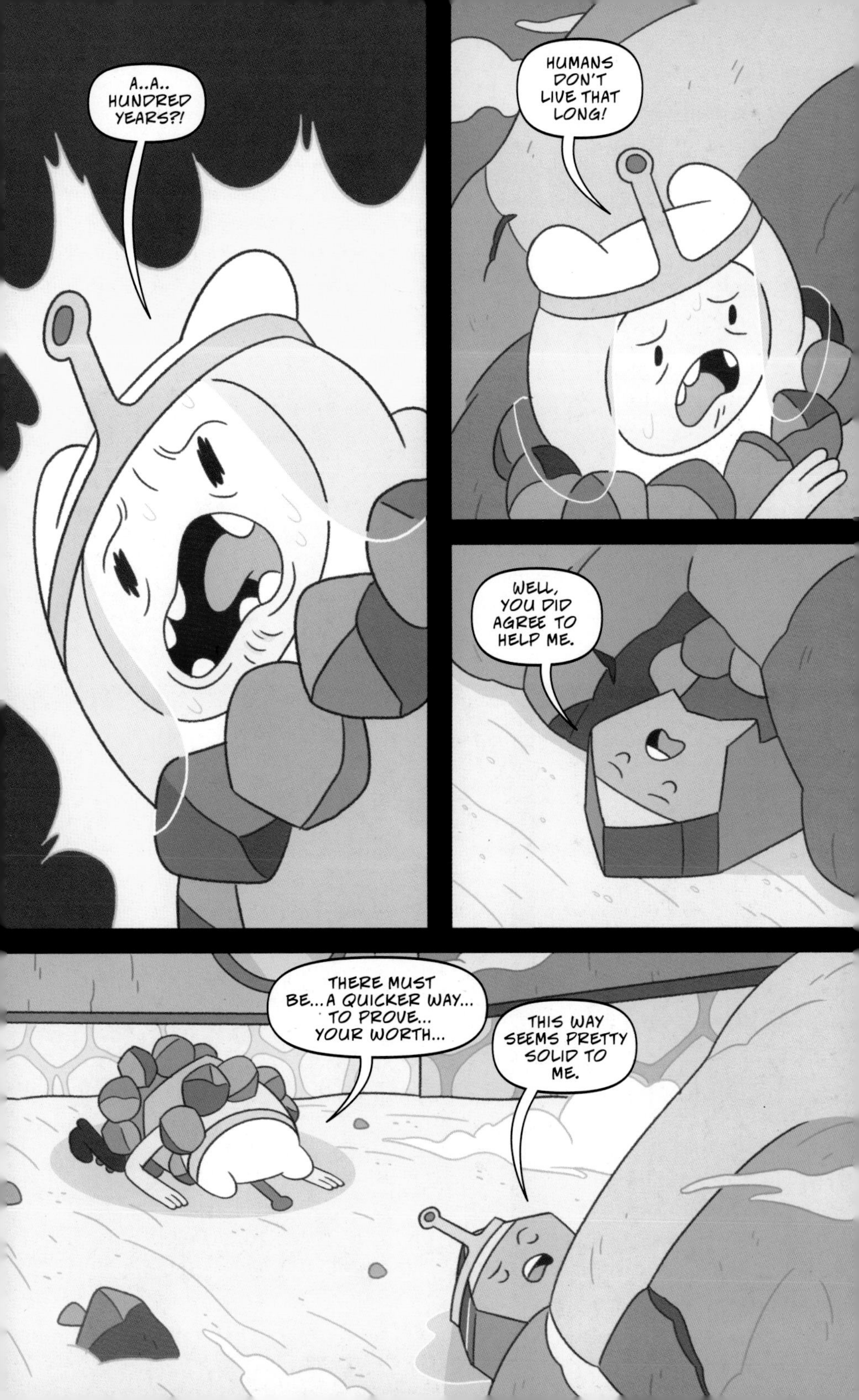
A..A.. HUNDRED YEARS?!
HUMANS DON'T LIVE THAT LONG!
WELL, YOU DID AGREE TO HELP ME.
THERE MUST BE... A QUICKER WAY... TO PROVE... YOUR WORTH...
THIS WAY SEEMS PRETTY SOLID TO ME.

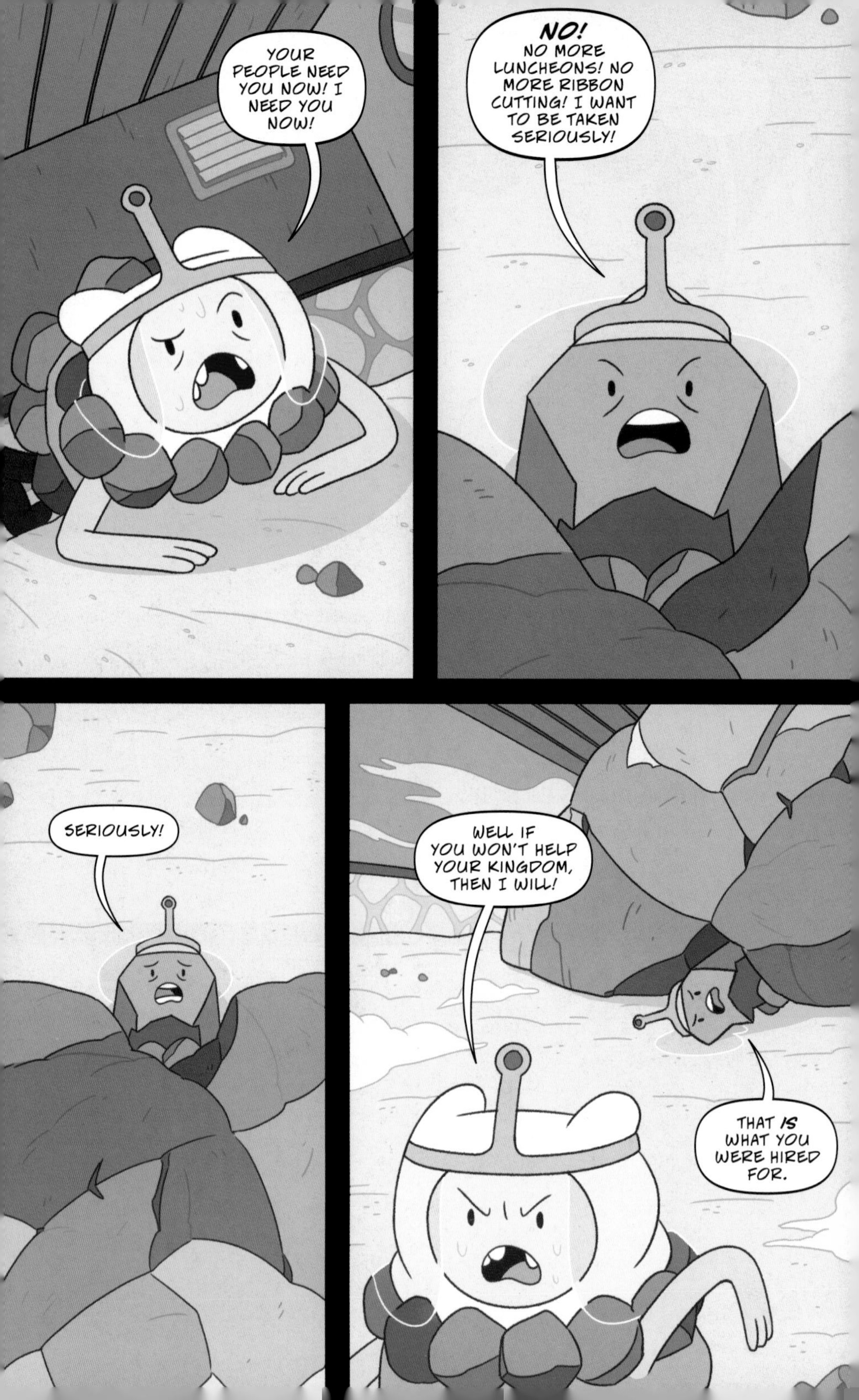
YOUR PEOPLE NEED YOU NOW! I NEED YOU NOW!
NO! NO MORE LUNCHEONS! NO MORE RIBBON CUTTING! I WANT TO BE TAKEN SERIOUSLY!
SERIOUSLY!
WELL IF YOU WON'T HELP YOUR KINGDOM, THEN I WILL!
THAT IS WHAT YOU WERE HIRED FOR.

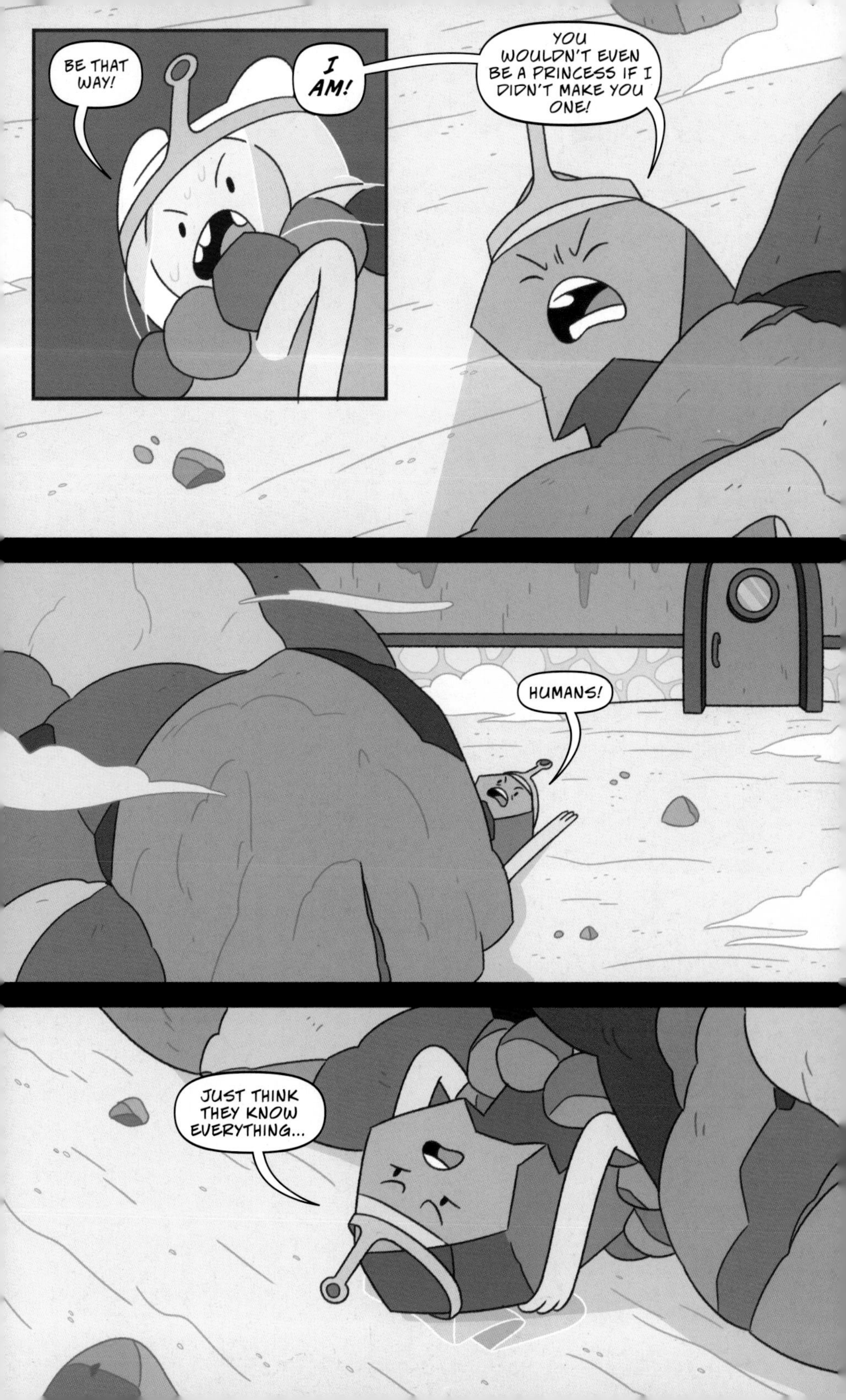
BE THAT WAY!
I AM!
YOU WOULDN'T EVEN BE A PRINCESS IF I DIDN'T MAKE YOU ONE!
HUMANS!
JUST THINK THEY KNOW EVERYTHING...

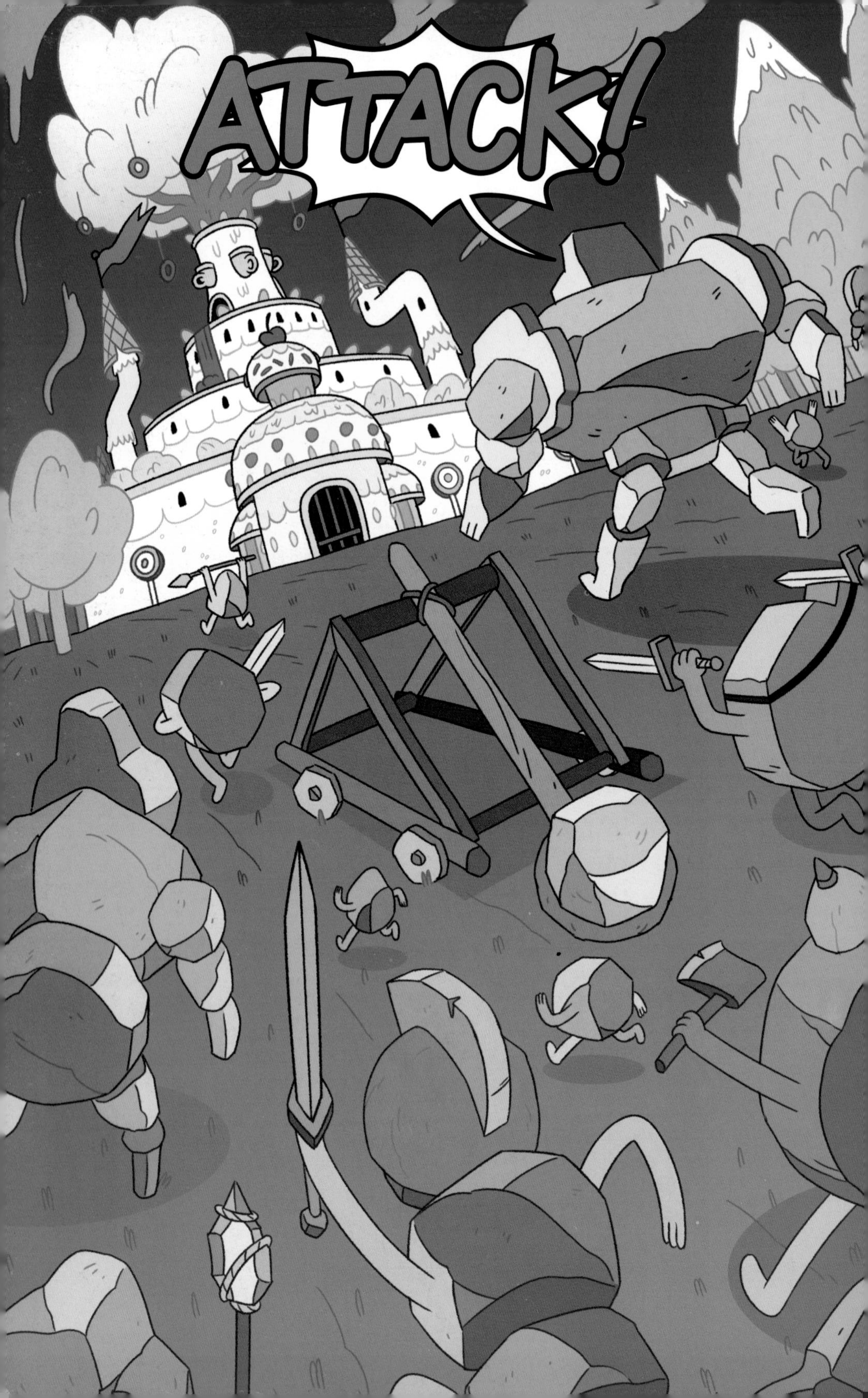
ATTACK!

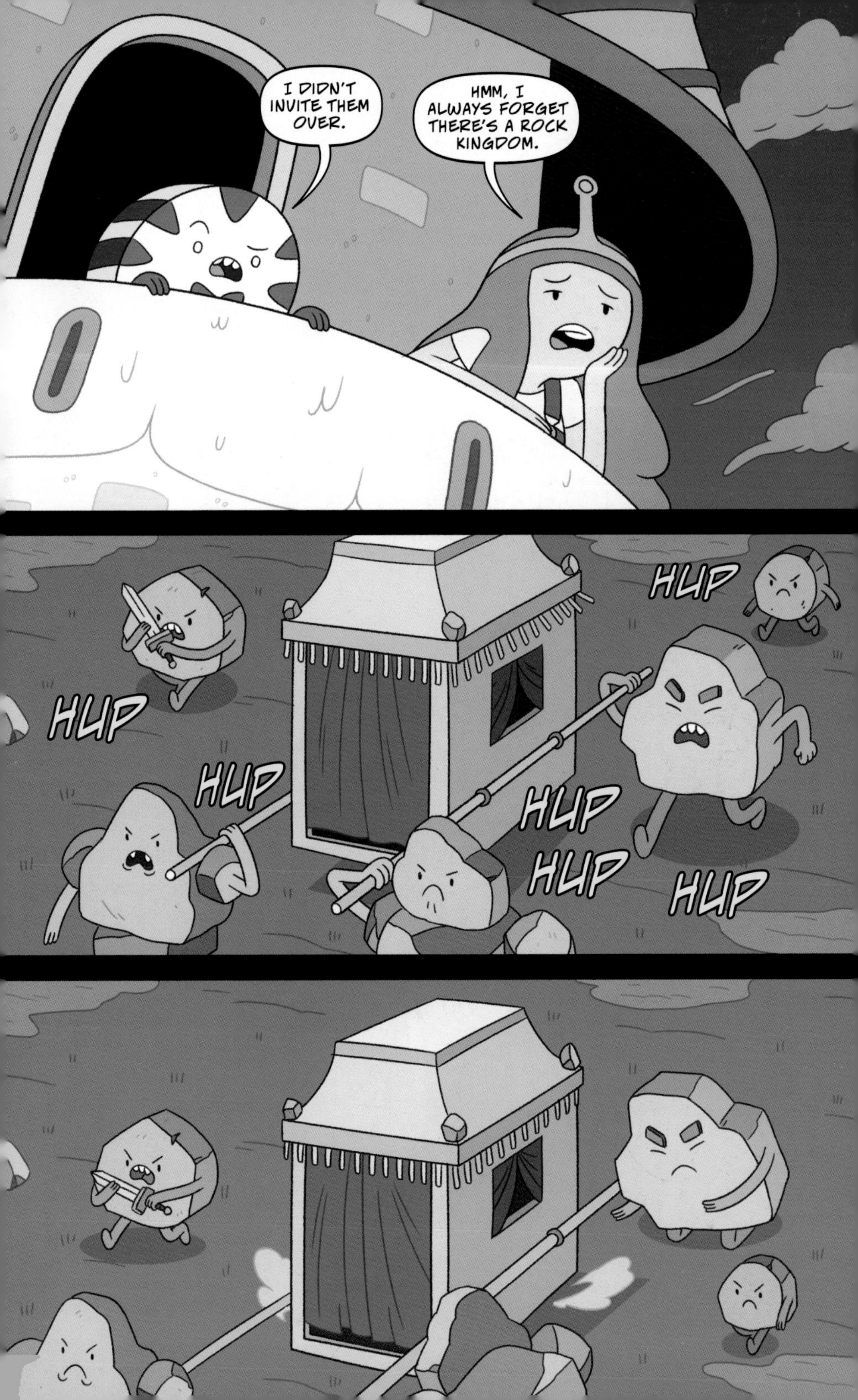
I DIDN'T INVITE THEM OVER.
HMM, I ALWAYS FORGET THERE'S A ROCK KINGDOM.
HUP
HUP
HUP
HUP
HUP
HUP

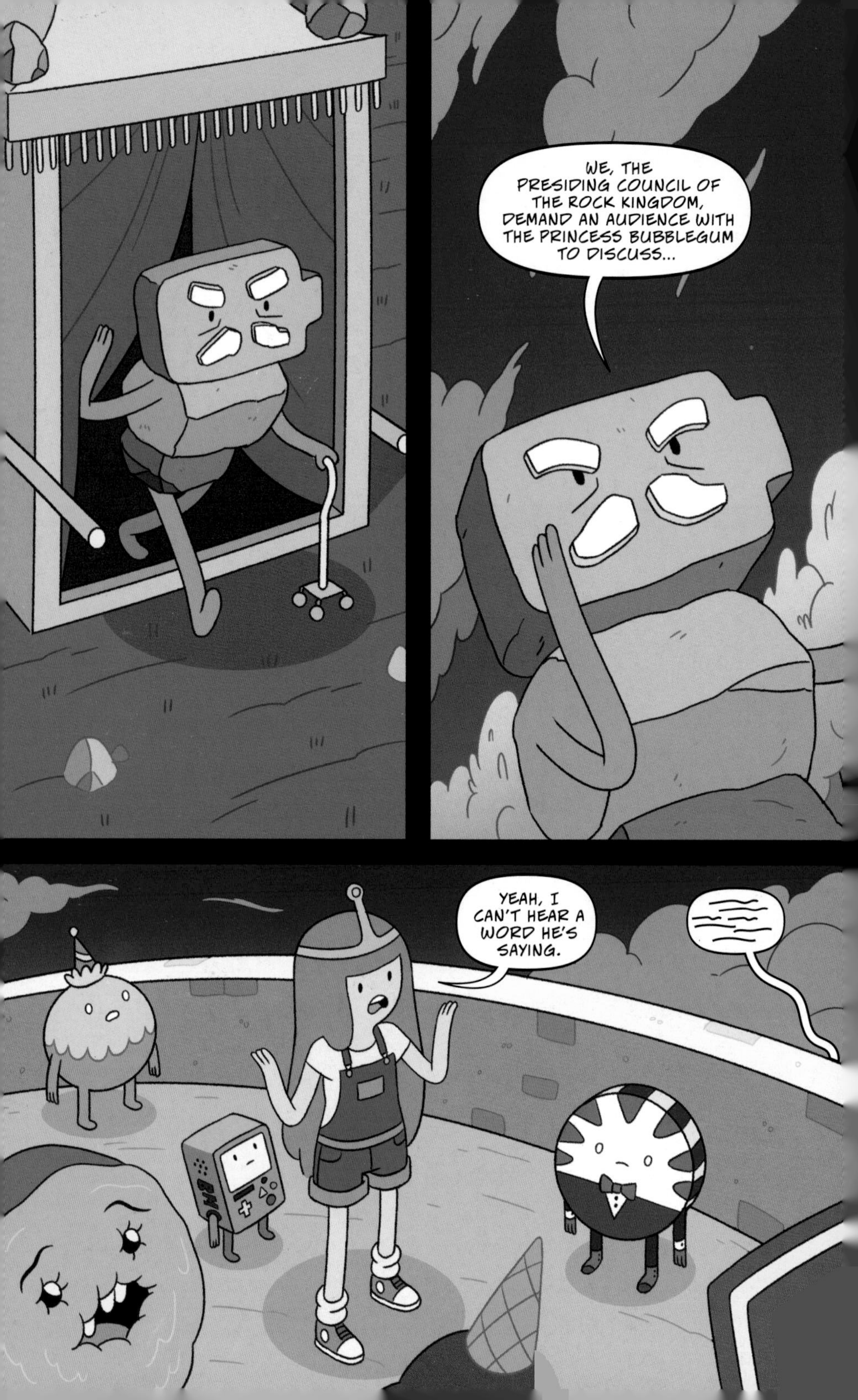
WE, THE PRESIDING COUNCIL OF THE ROCK KINGDOM, DEMAND AN AUDIENCE WITH THE PRINCESS BUBBLEGUM TO DISCUSS...
YEAH, I CAN'T HEAR A WORD HE'S SAYING.

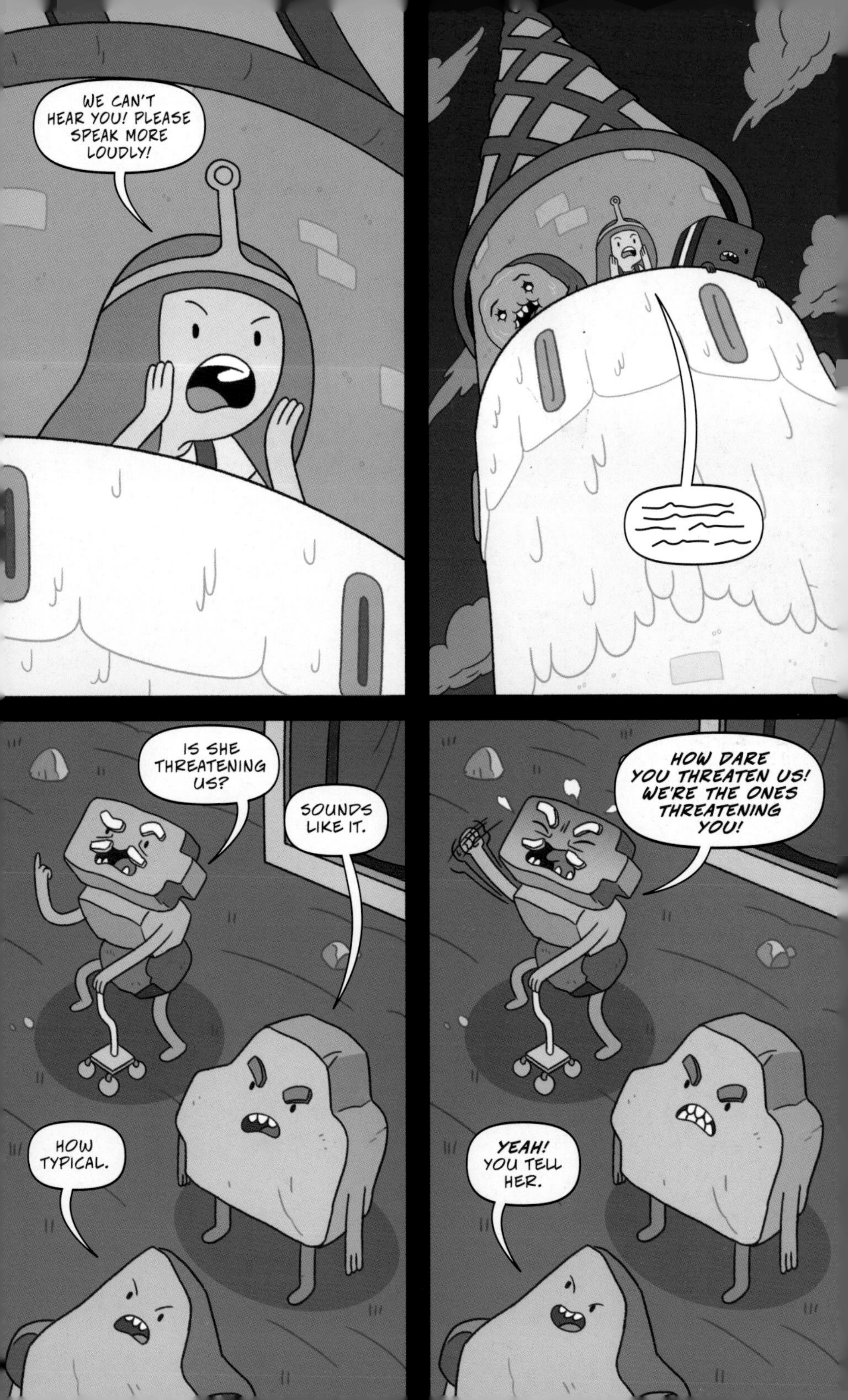
WE CAN'T HEAR YOU! PLEASE SPEAK MORE LOUDLY!
IS SHE THREATENING US?
SOUNDS LIKE IT.
HOW TYPICAL.
HOW DARE YOU THREATEN US! WE'RE THE ONES THREATENING YOU!
YEAH! YOU TELL HER.

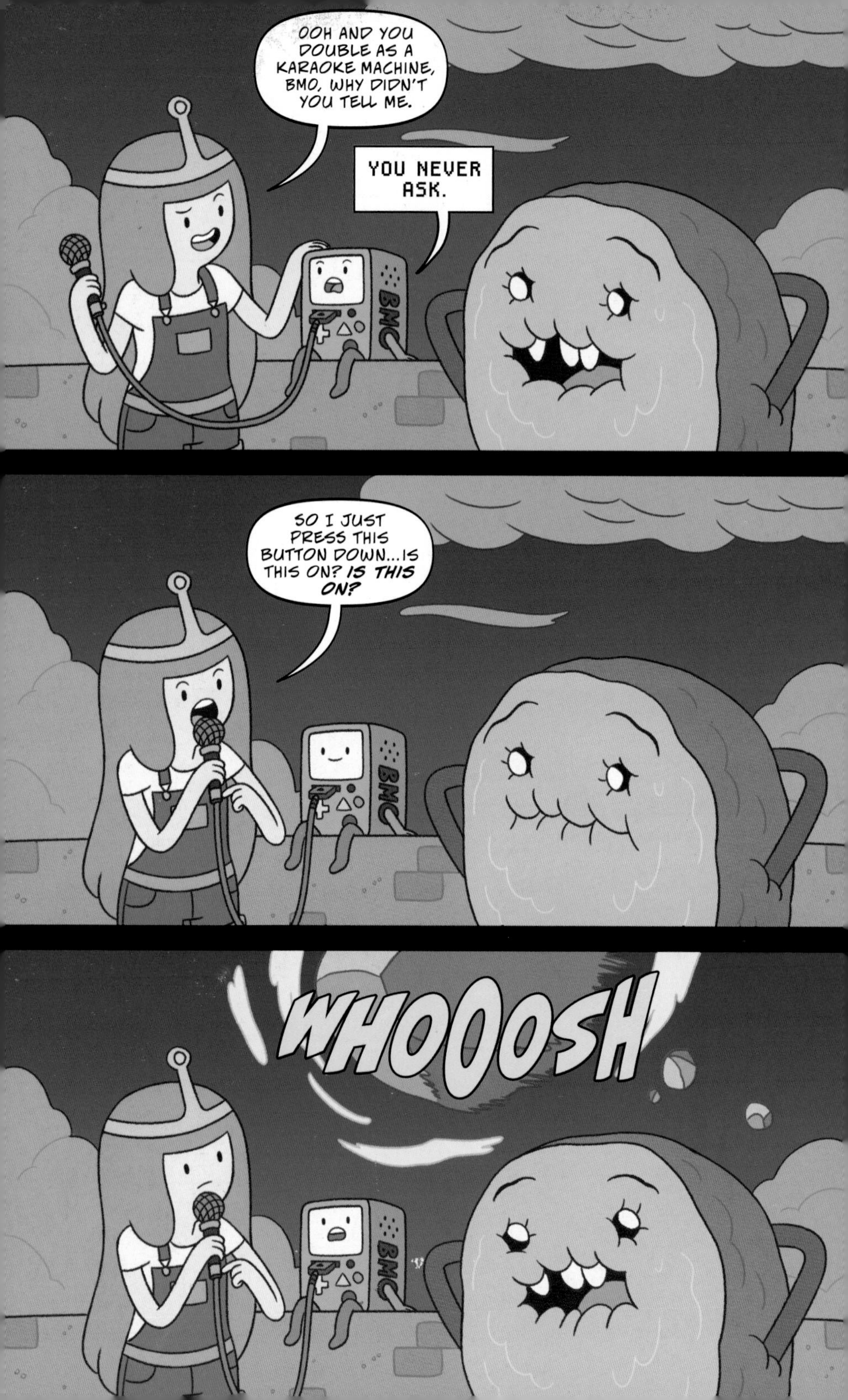
OOH AND YOU DOUBLE AS A KARAOKE MACHINE, BMO, WHY DIDN'T YOU TELL ME.
YOU NEVER ASK.
BMO
SO I JUST PRESS THIS BUTTON DOWN...IS THIS ON? IS THIS ON?
BMO
WHOOOOSH
BMO

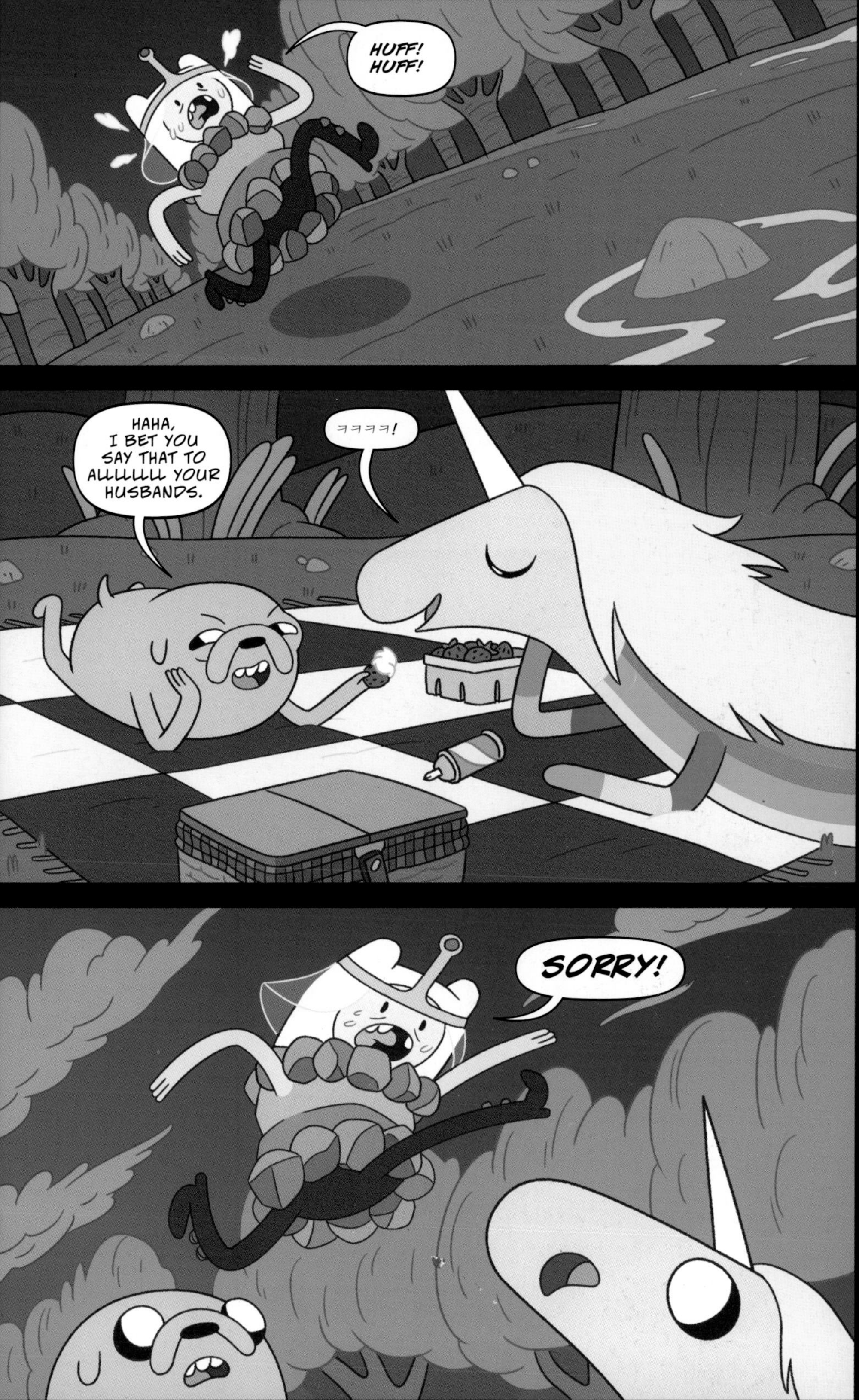
HUFF! HUFF!
HAHA, I BET YOU SAY THAT TO ALLLLLLLL YOUR HUSBANDS.
ㅋㅋㅋㅋ!
SORRY!

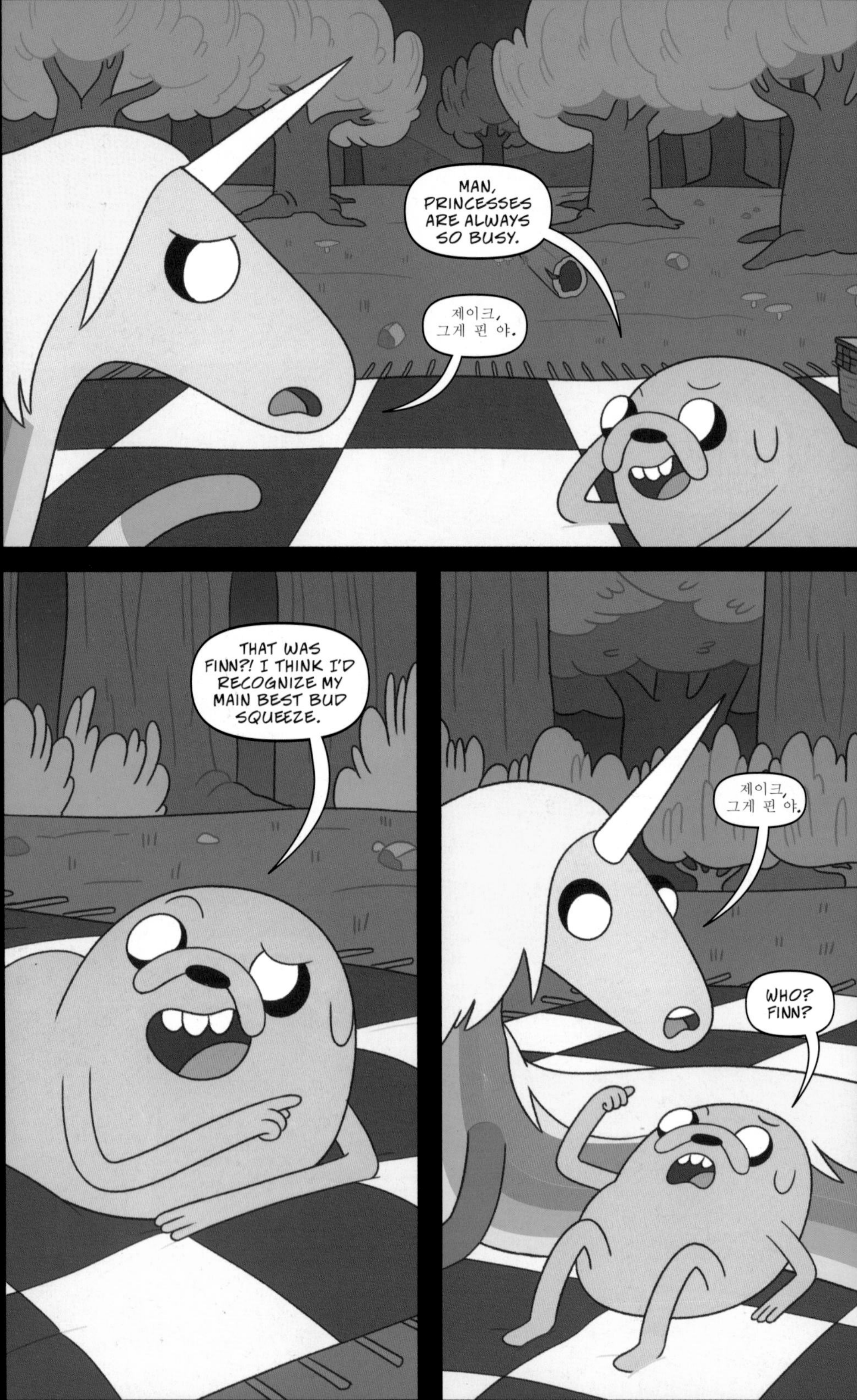
MAN, PRINCESSES ARE ALWAYS SO BUSY.
제이크, 그게 핀 야.
THAT WAS FINN?! I THINK I'D RECOGNIZE MY MAIN BEST BUD SQUEEZE.
제이크, 그게 핀 야.
WHO? FINN?

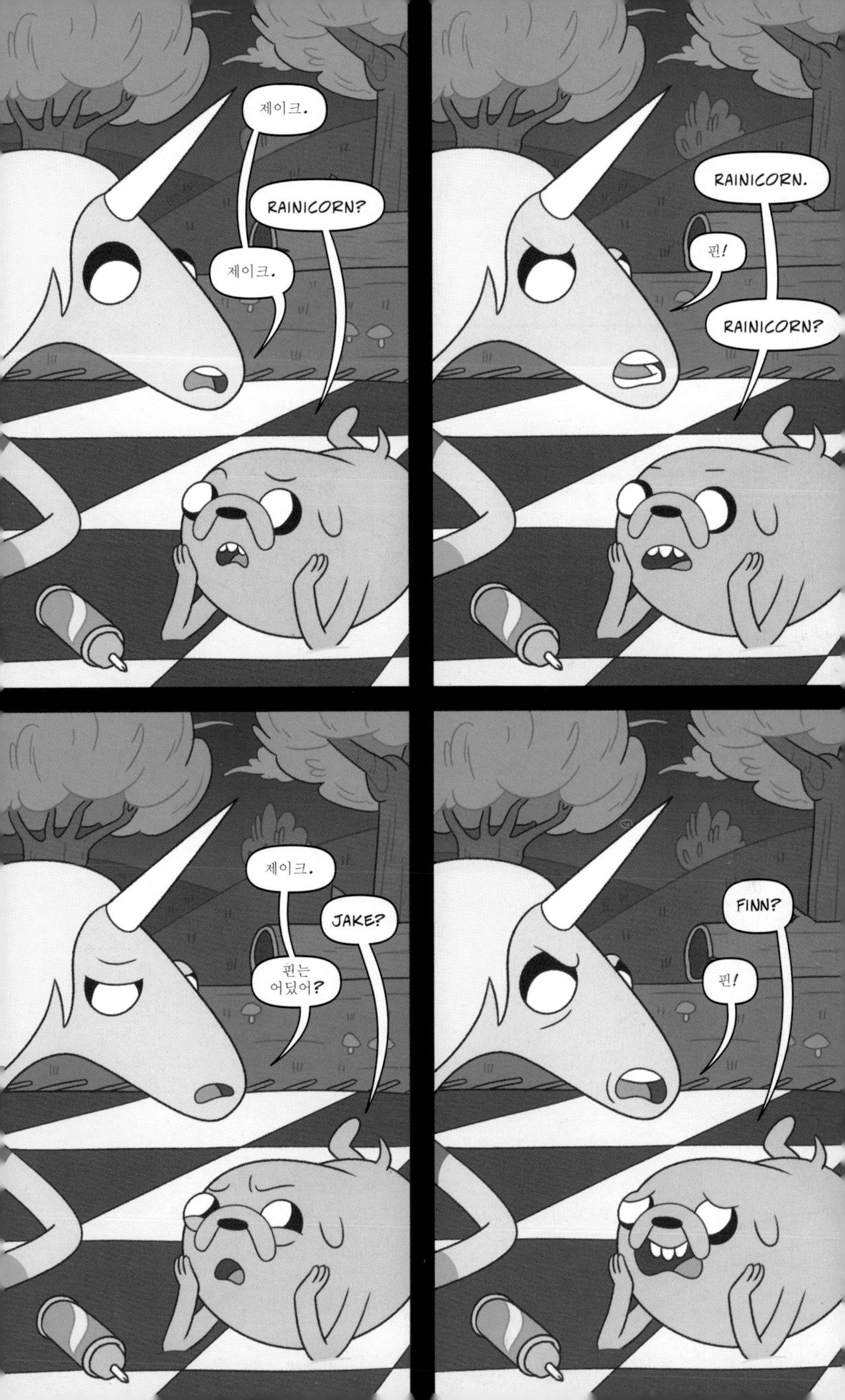
제이크.
RAINICORN?
제이크.
RAINICORN.
핀!
RAINICORN?
제이크.
JAKE?
핀는 어딨어?
FINN?
핀!

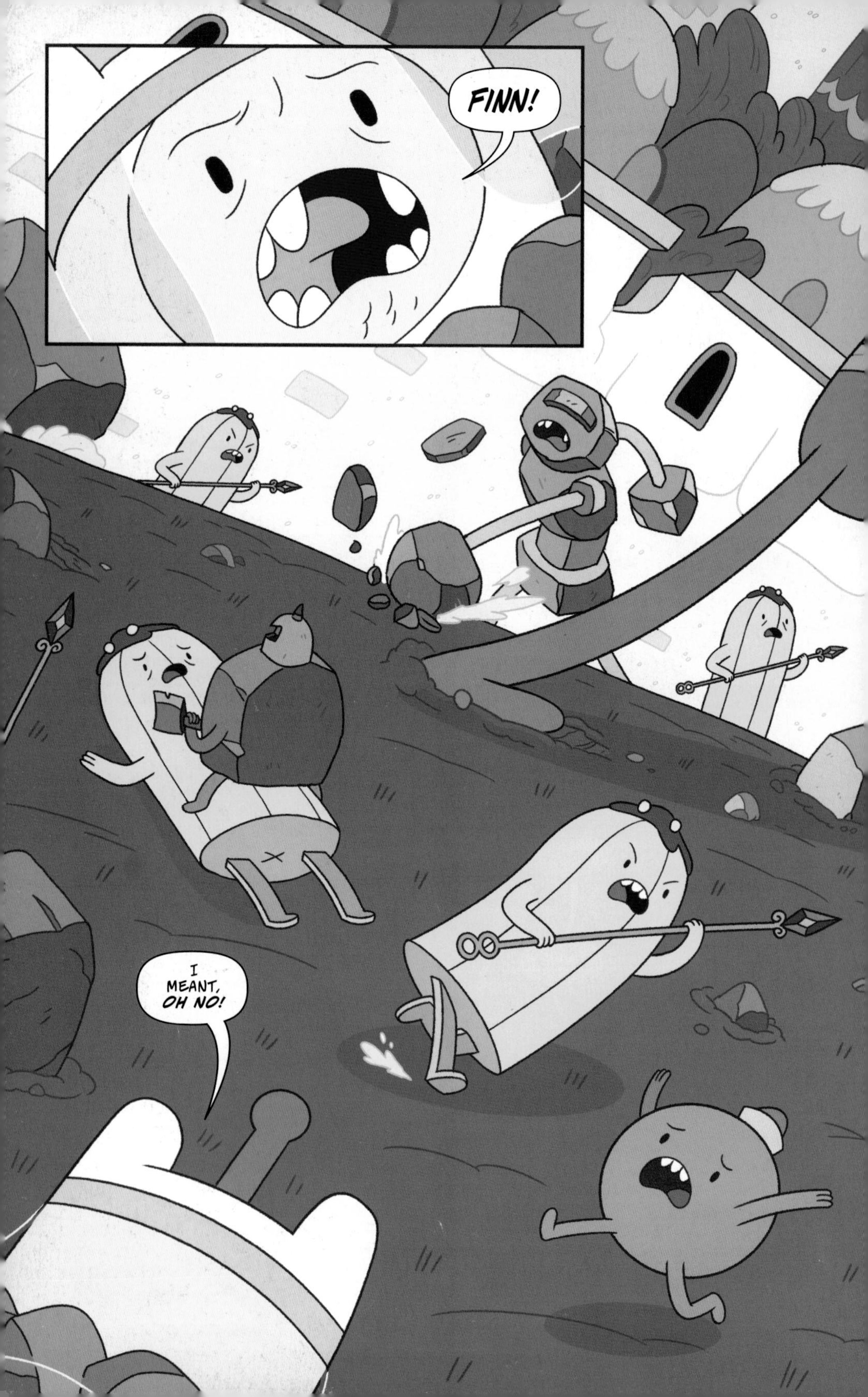
FINN!
I MEANT, OH NO!

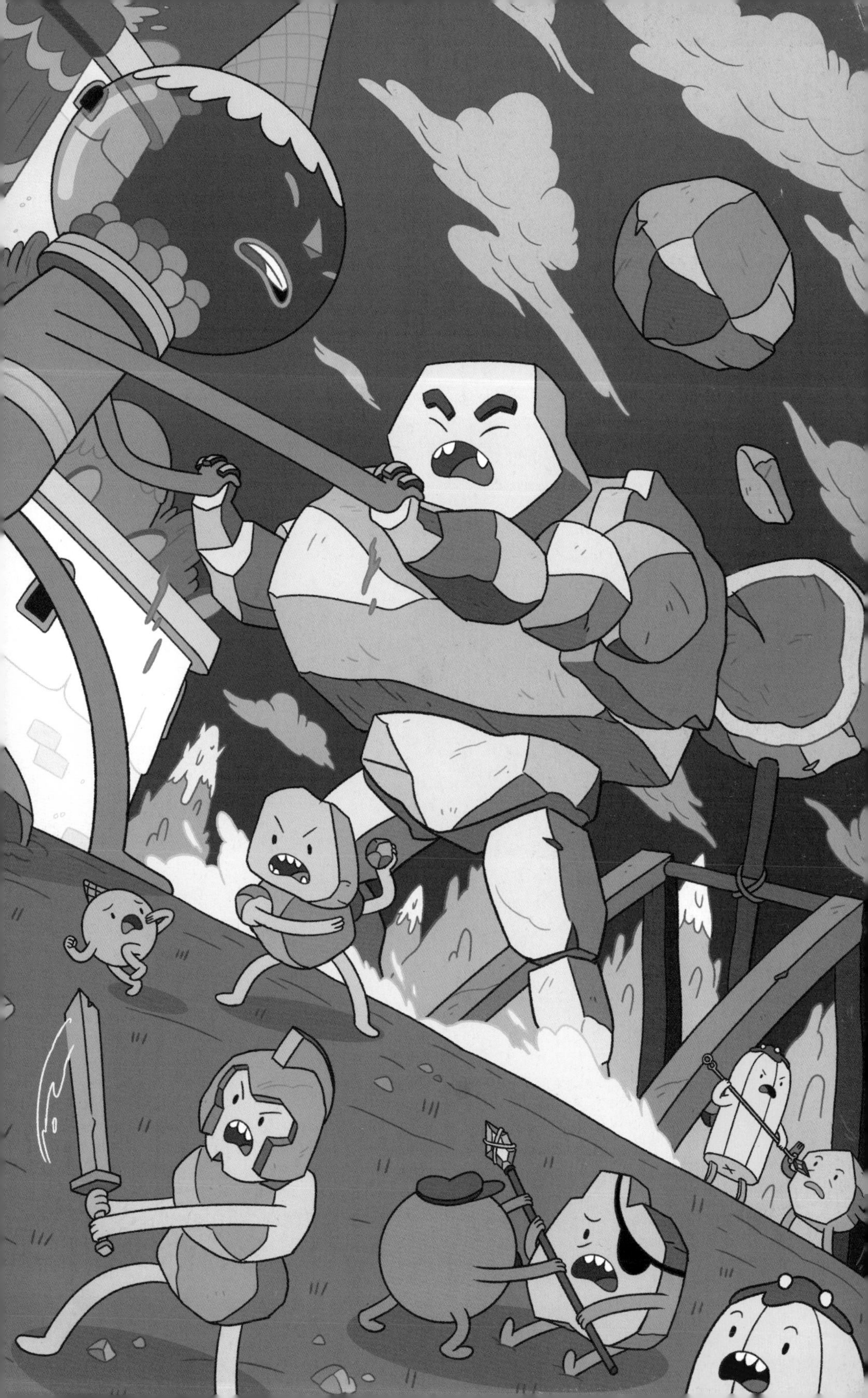

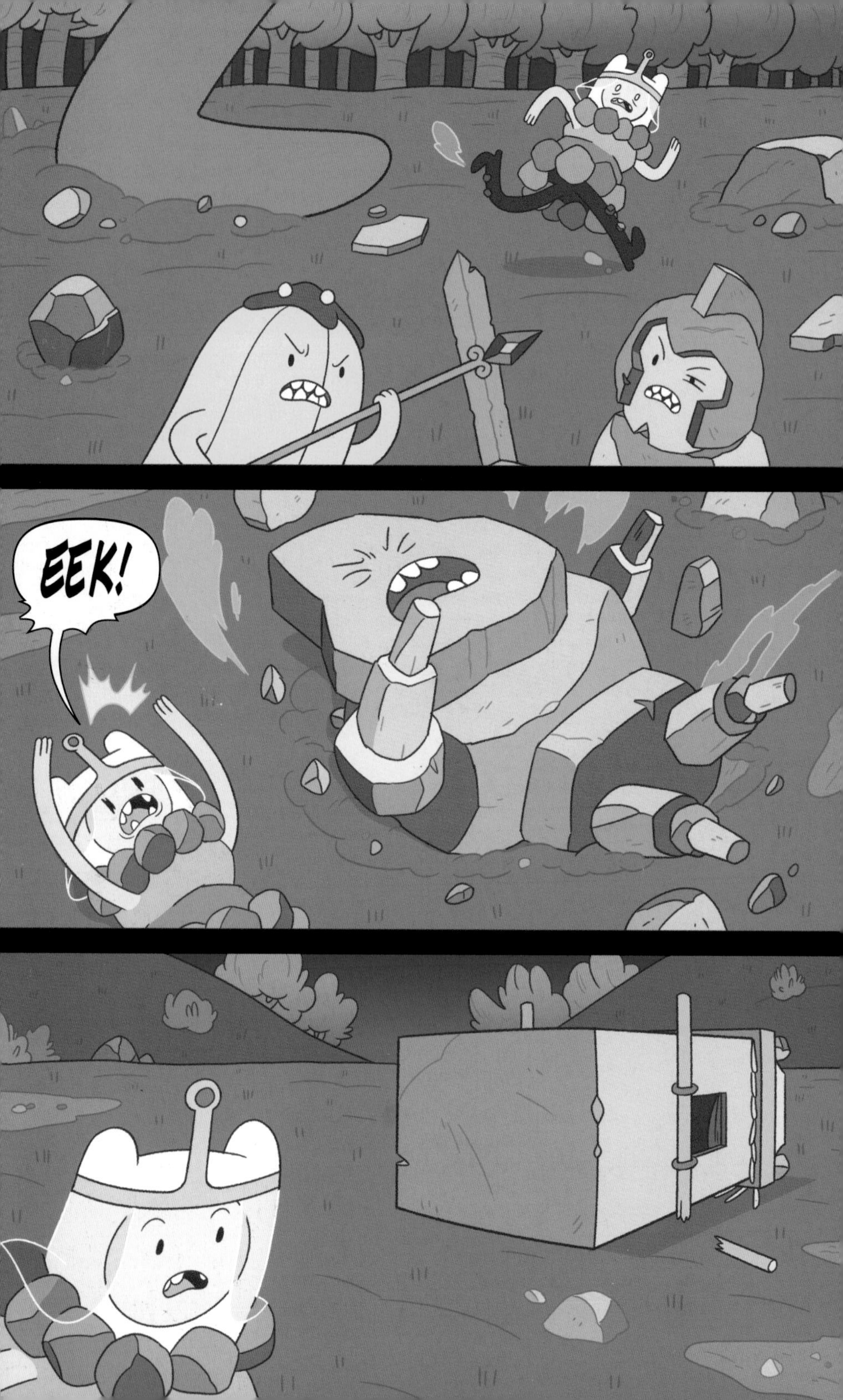
EEK!

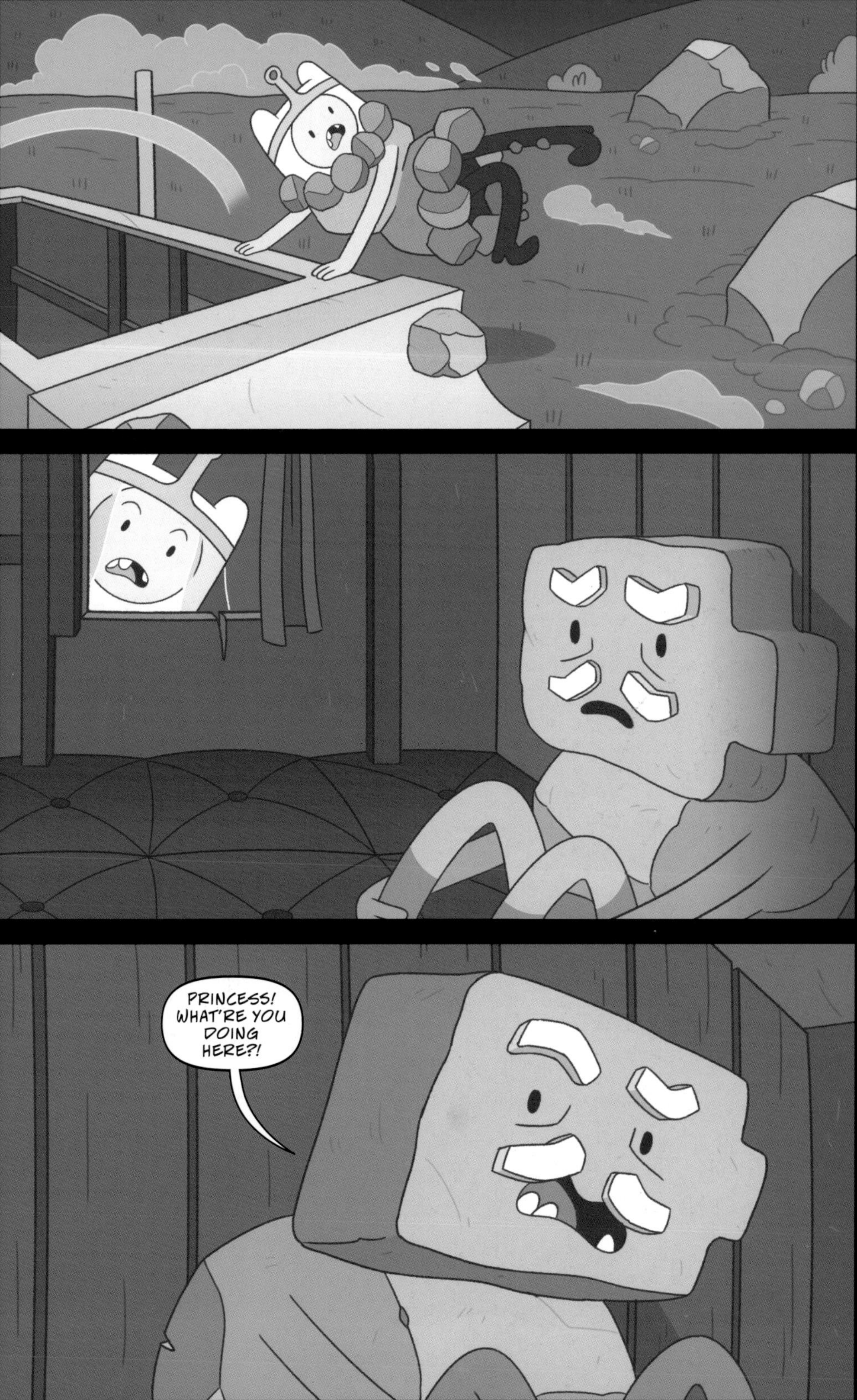
PRINCESS! WHAT'RE YOU DOING HERE?!

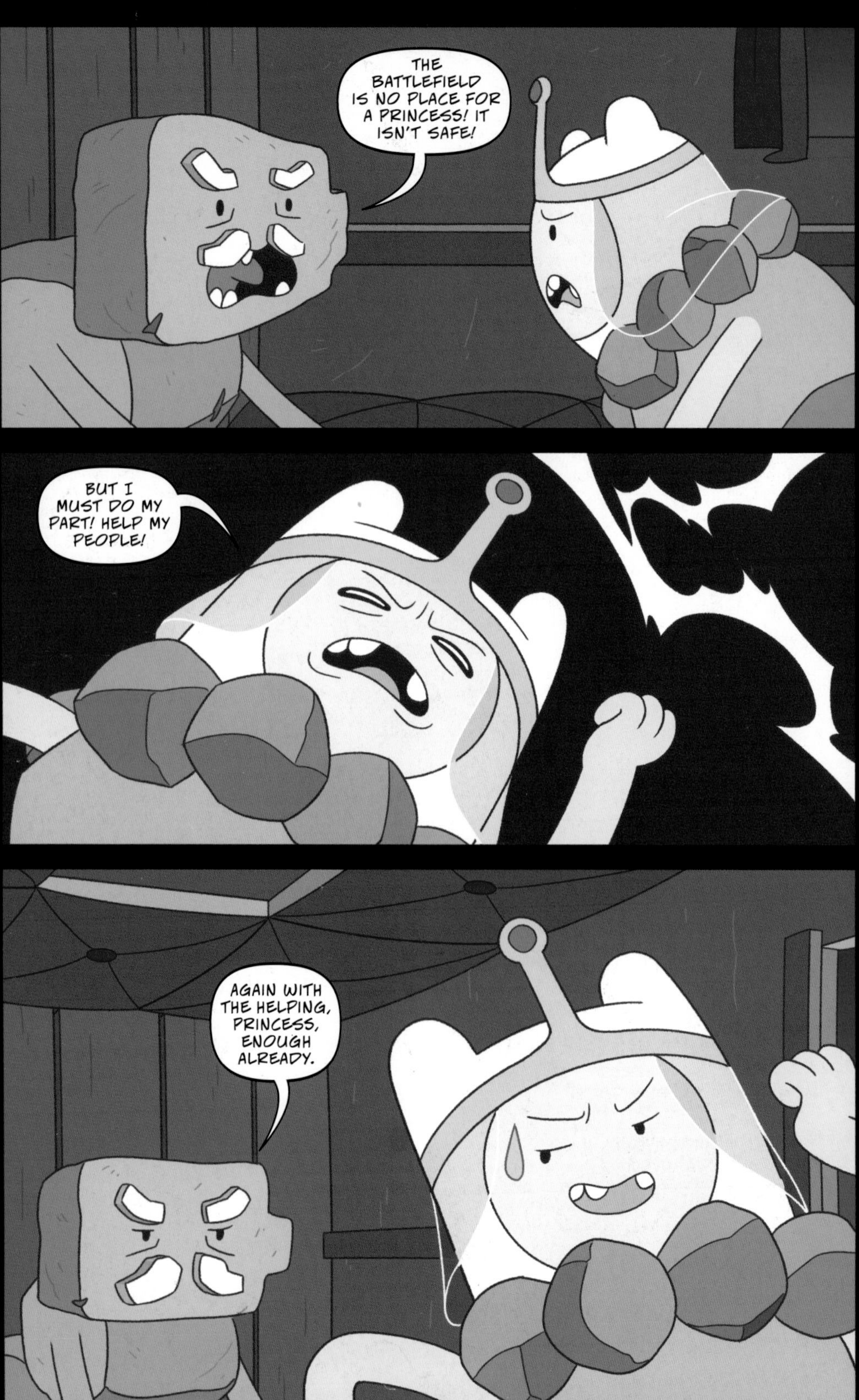
THE BATTLEFIELD IS NO PLACE FOR A PRINCESS! IT ISN'T SAFE!
BUT I MUST DO MY PART! HELP MY PEOPLE!
AGAIN WITH THE HELPING, PRINCESS, ENOUGH ALREADY.

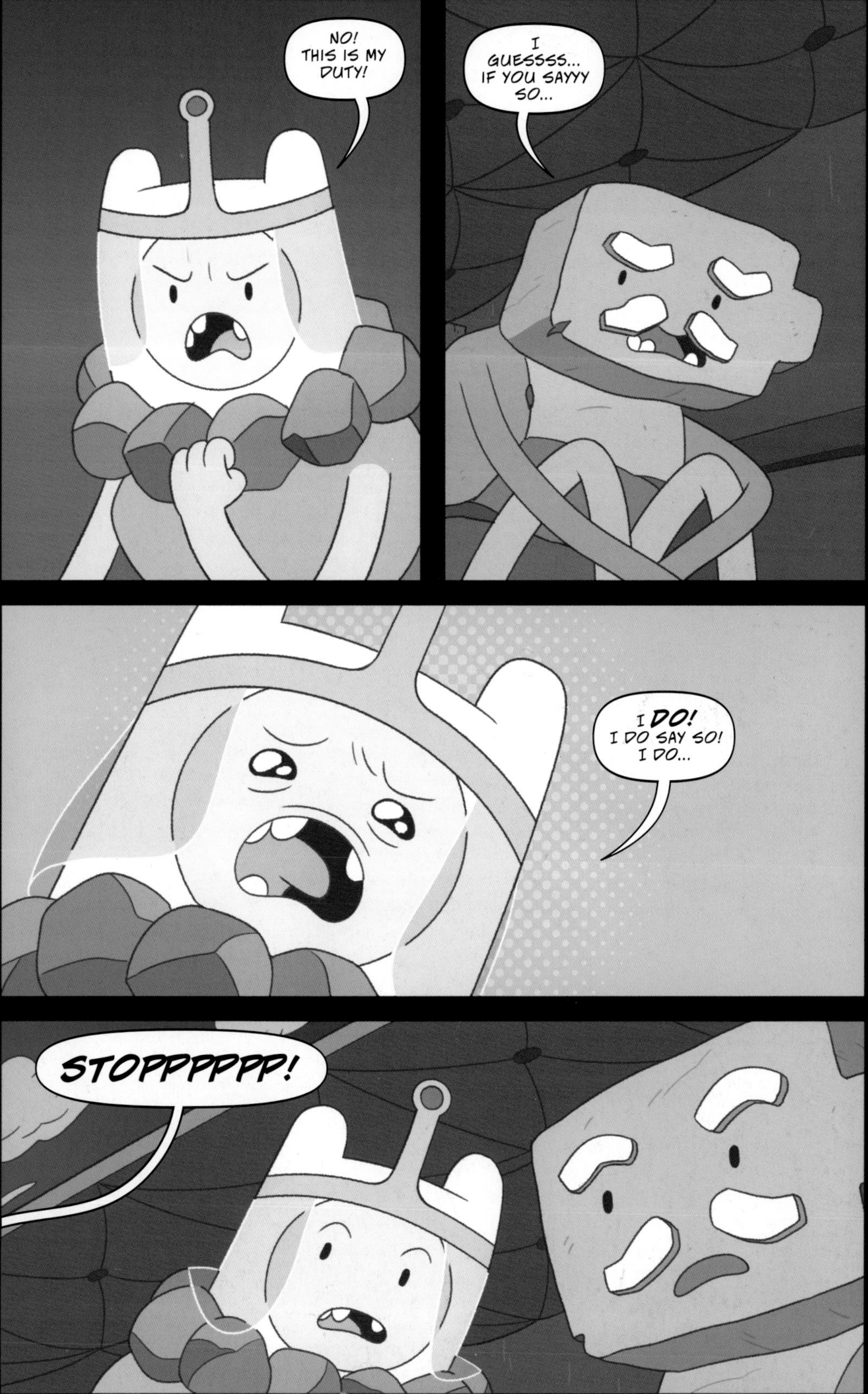
NO! THIS IS MY DUTY!
I GUESSSS... IF YOU SAYYY SO...
I DO! I DO SAY SO! I DO...
STOPPPPPPP!

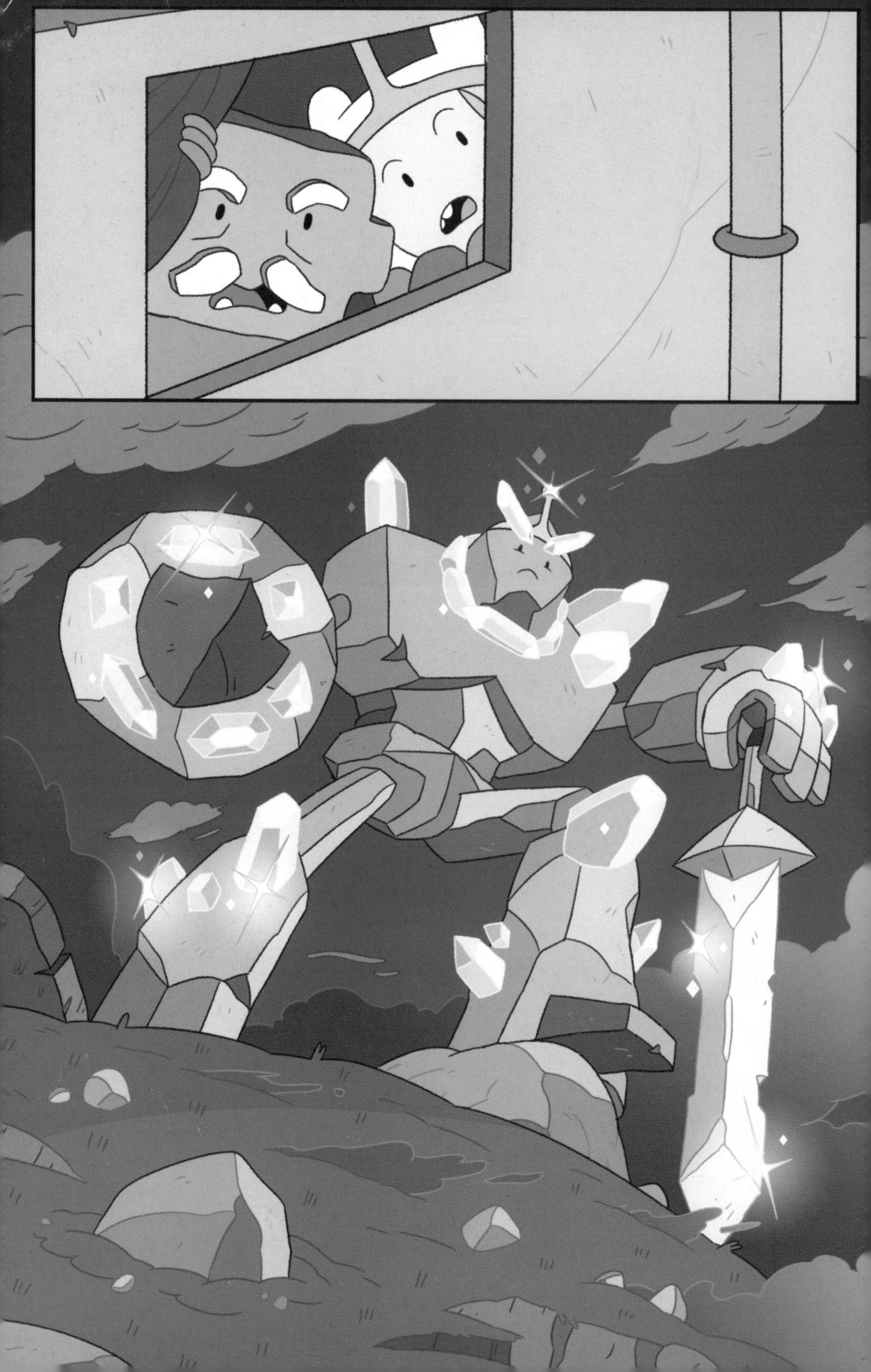

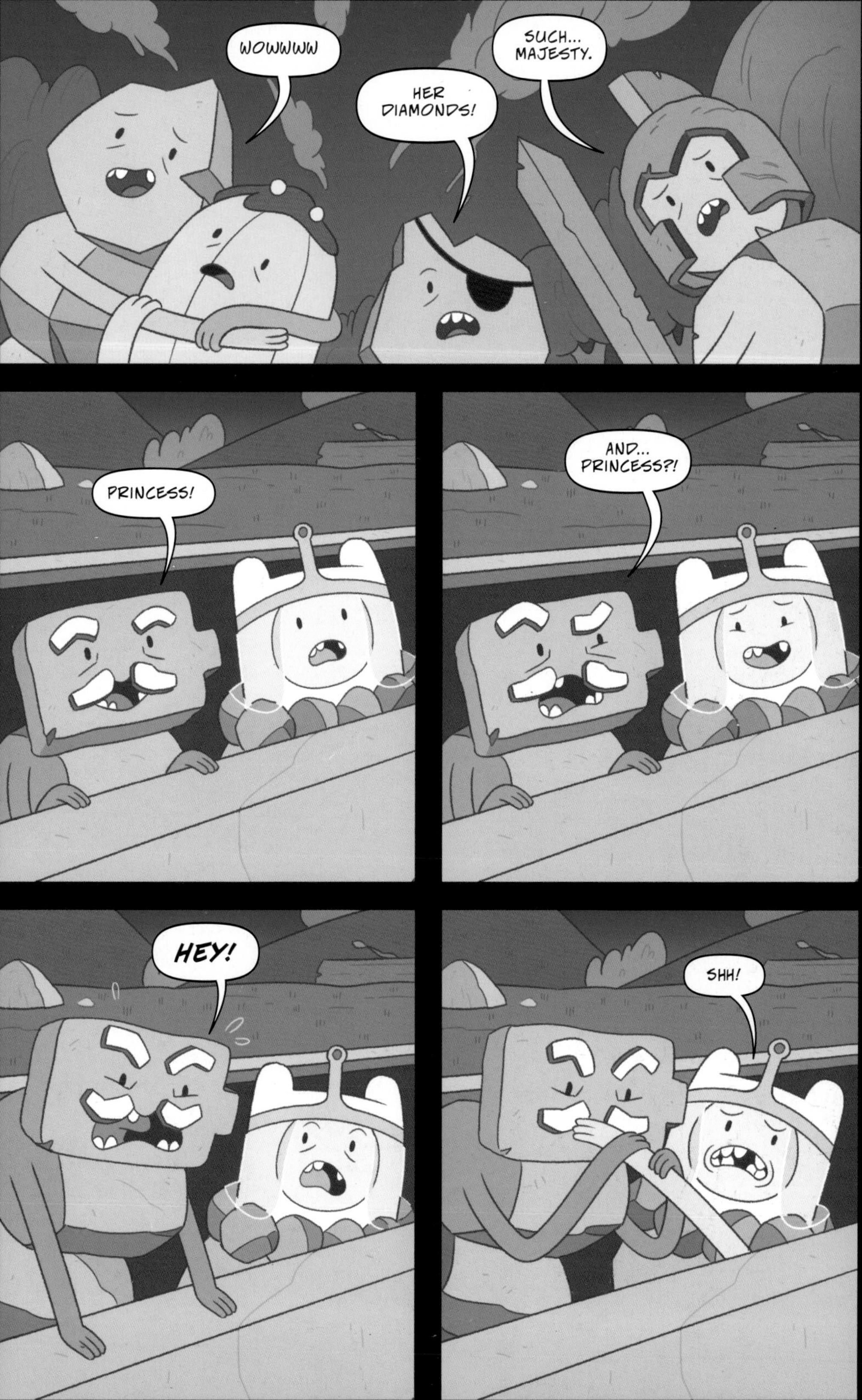
WOWWWW
HER DIAMONDS!
SUCH... MAJESTY.
PRINCESS!
AND... PRINCESS?!
HEY!
SHH!

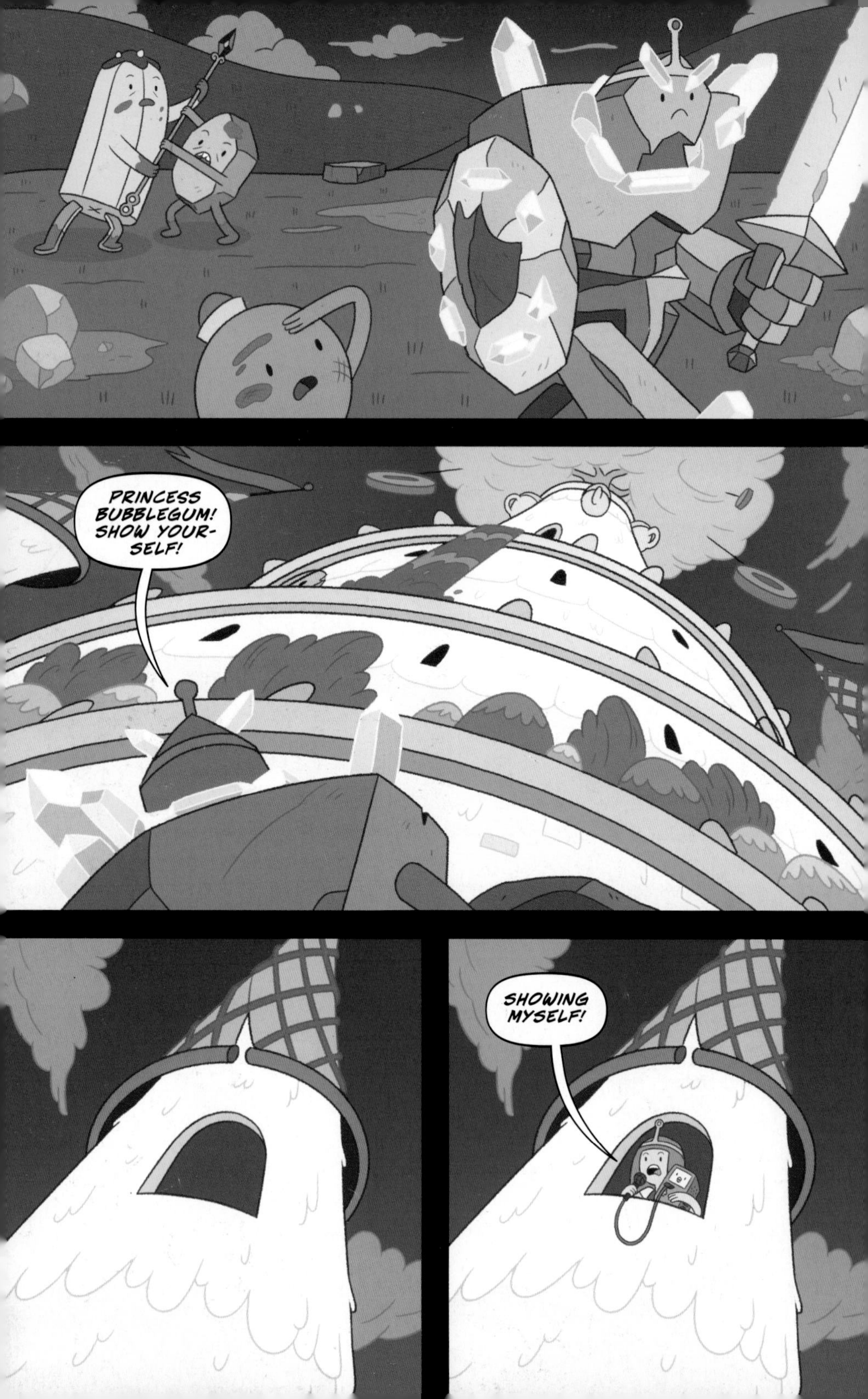
PRINCESS BUBBLEGUM! SHOW YOUR-SELF!
SHOWING MYSELF!

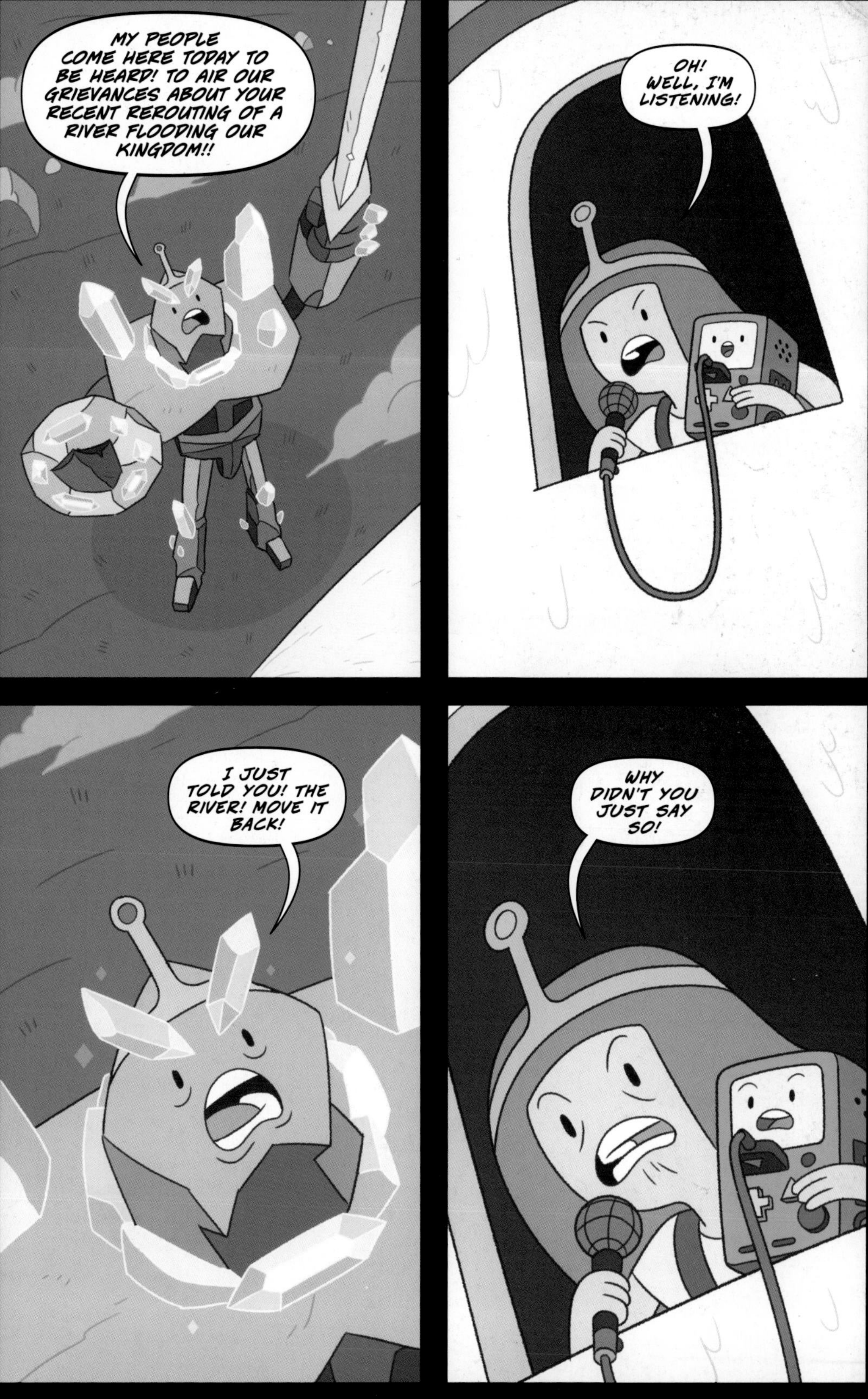
MY PEOPLE COME HERE TODAY TO BE HEARD! TO AIR OUR GRIEVANCES ABOUT YOUR RECENT REROUTING OF A RIVER FLOODING OUR KINGDOM!!
OH! WELL, I'M LISTENING!
I JUST TOLD YOU! THE RIVER! MOVE IT BACK!
WHY DIDN'T YOU JUST SAY SO!

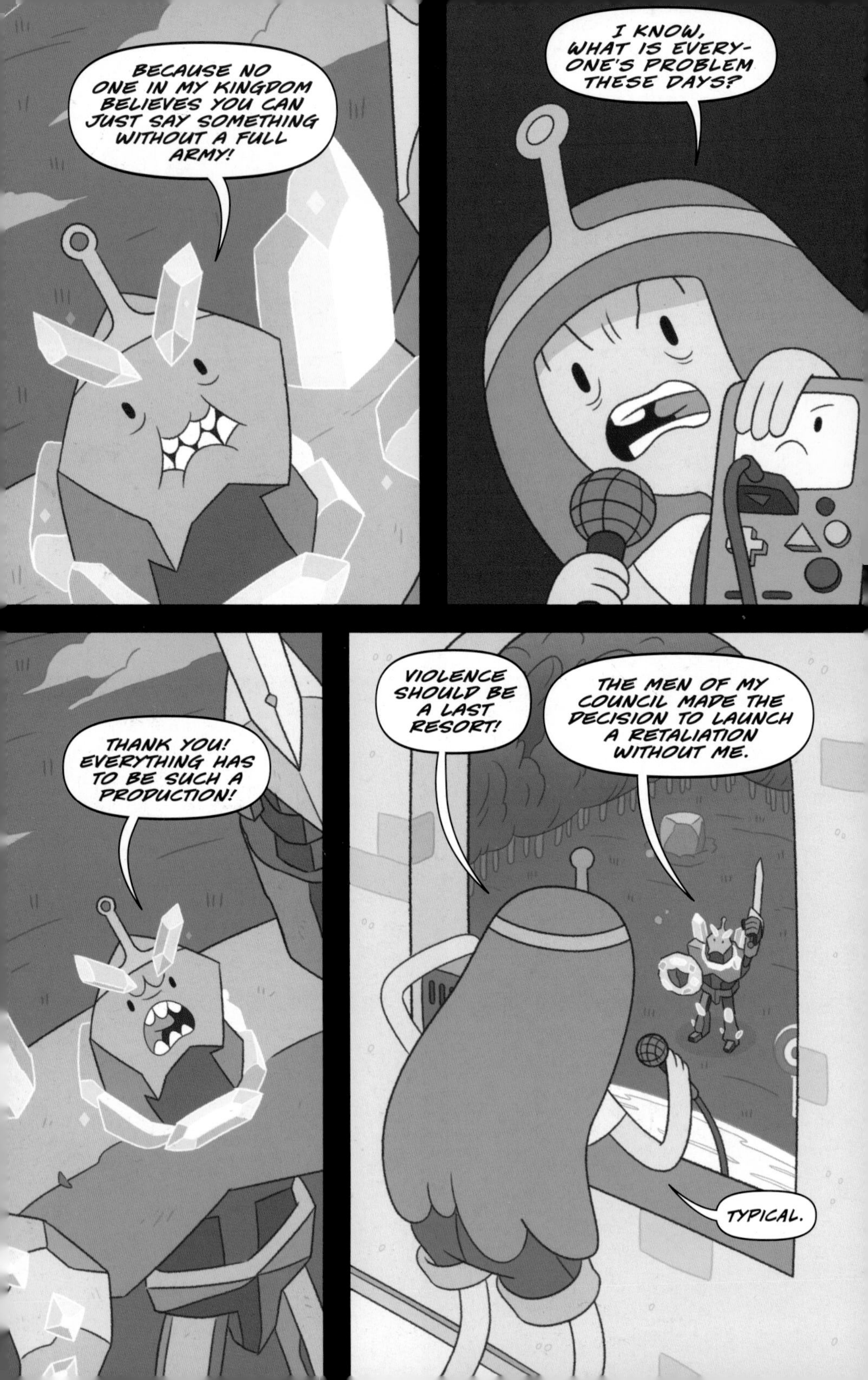
BECAUSE NO ONE IN MY KINGDOM BELIEVES YOU CAN JUST SAY SOMETHING WITHOUT A FULL ARMY!
I KNOW, WHAT IS EVERY-ONE'S PROBLEM THESE DAYS?
THANK YOU! EVERYTHING HAS TO BE SUCH A PRODUCTION!
VIOLENCE SHOULD BE A LAST RESORT!
THE MEN OF MY COUNCIL MADE THE DECISION TO LAUNCH A RETALIATION WITHOUT ME.
TYPICAL.

I JUST WANT TO BE APPRECIATED FOR MY LABOR AND GIVEN THE AUTONOMY TO MAKE DECISIONS ON MY OWN!
I FULLY UNDERSTAND WANTING TO BE HEARD!
HOLD ON, I'M GOING TO OPEN THE GATE! YOU SHOULD COME INSIDE AND WE CAN DISCUSS THIS FURTHER.

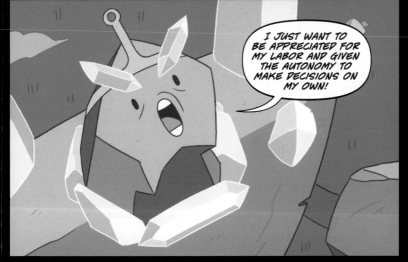

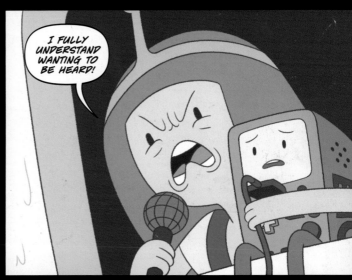

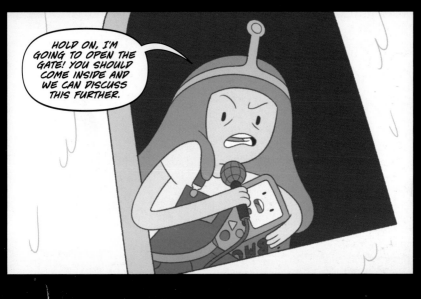

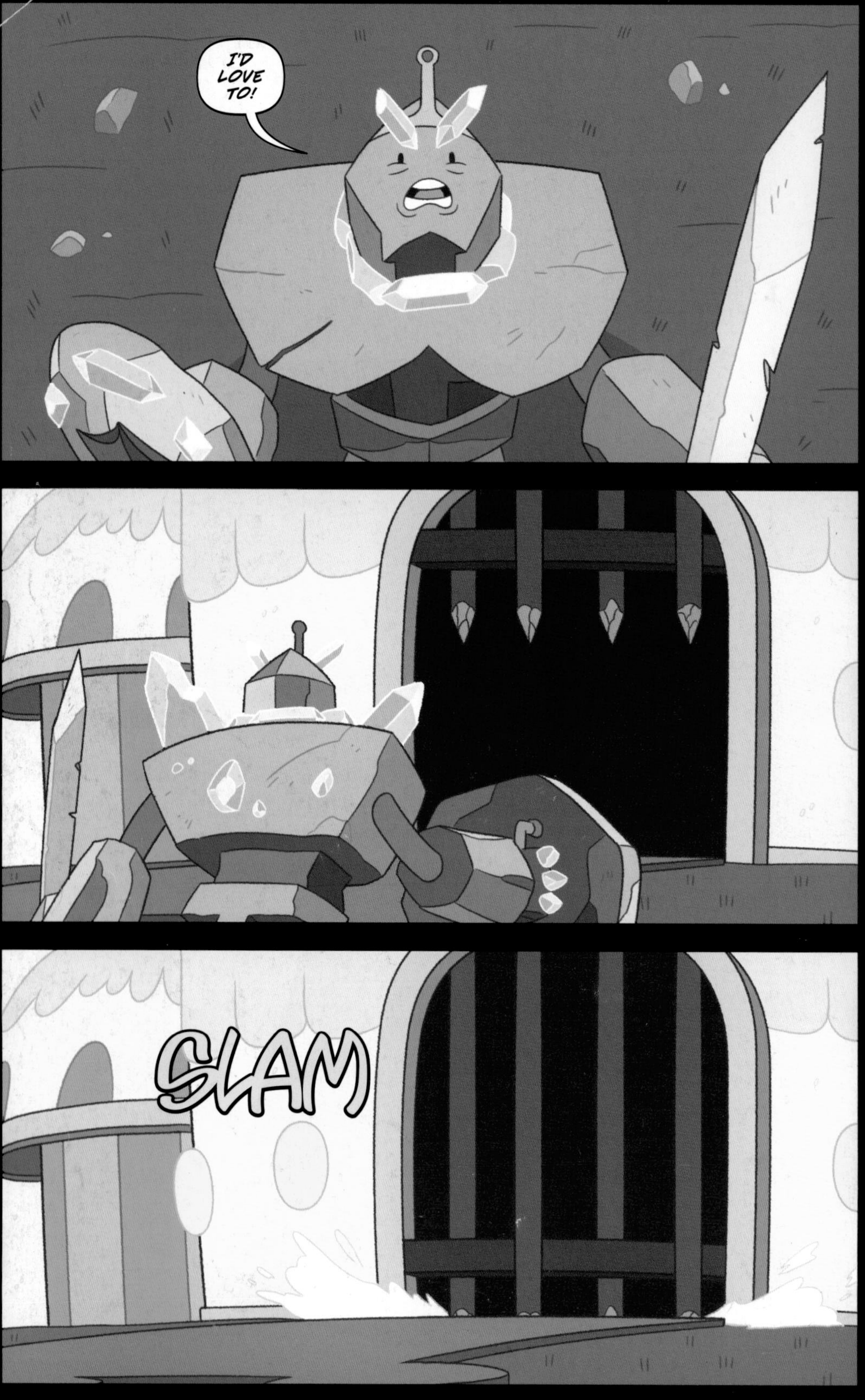
I'D LOVE TO!
SLAM

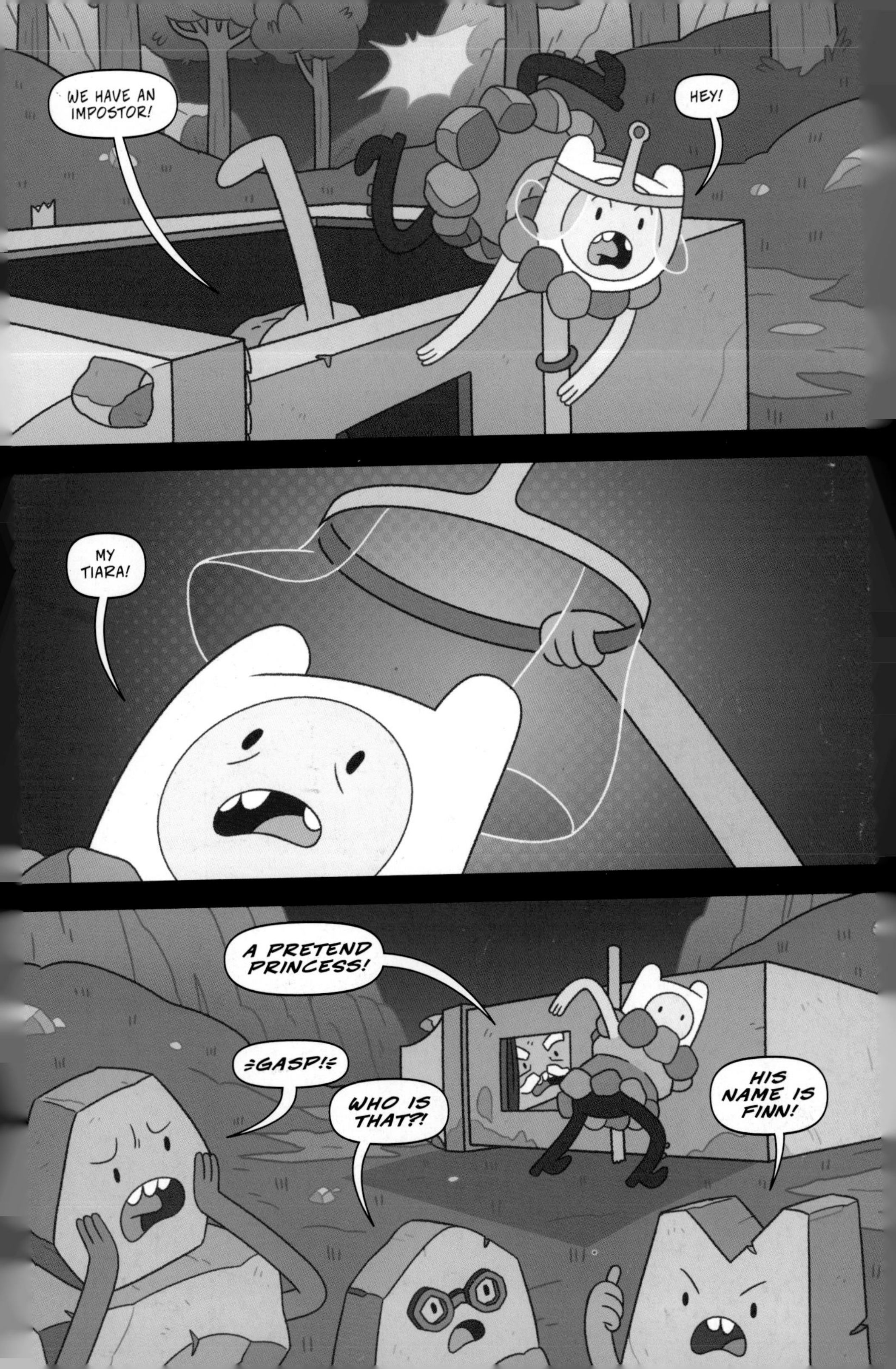
WE HAVE AN IMPOSTOR!
HEY!
MY TIARA!
A PRETEND PRINCESS!
GASP!
WHO IS THAT?!
HIS NAME IS FINN!

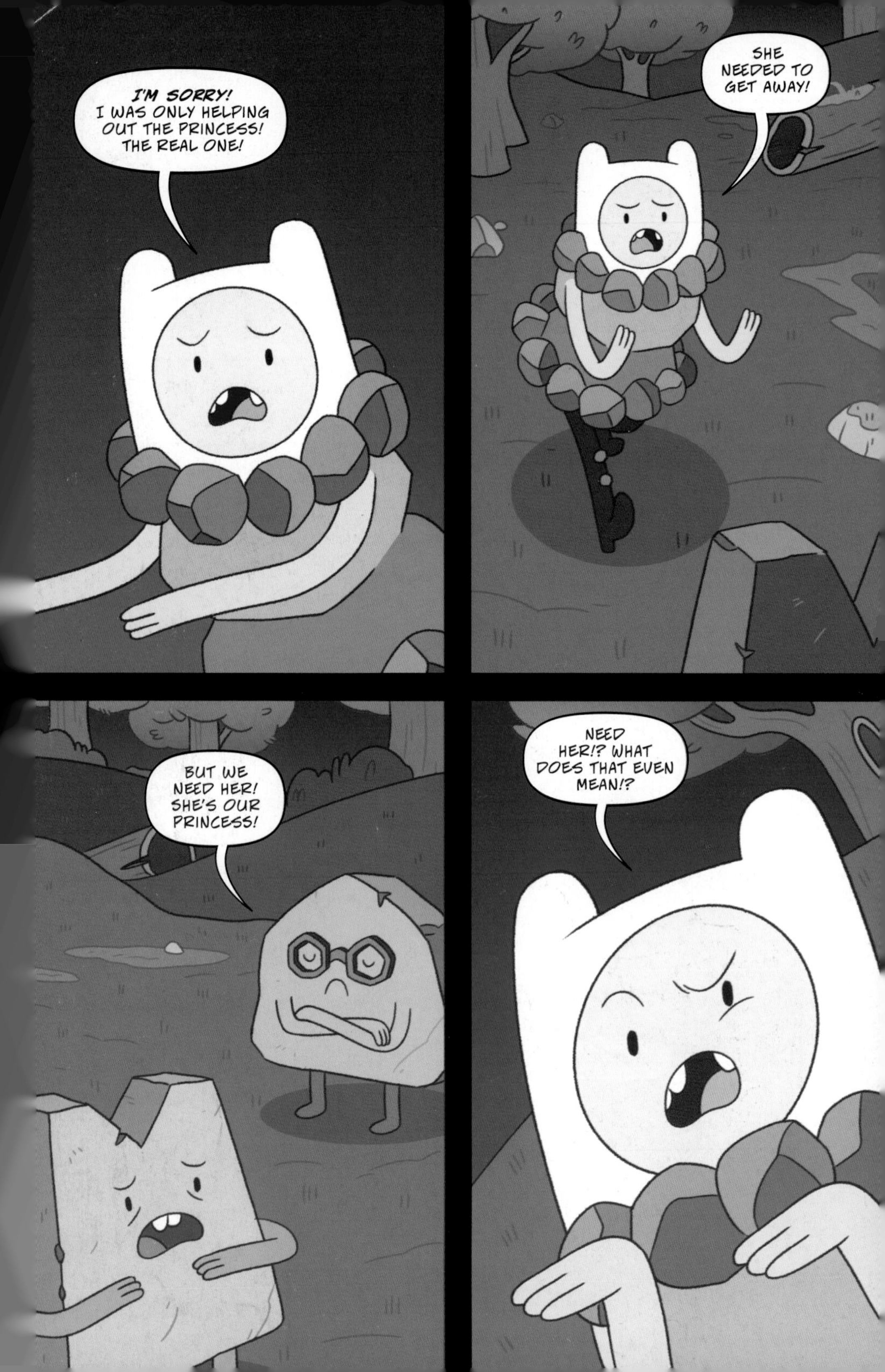
I'M SORRY! I WAS ONLY HELPING OUT THE PRINCESS! THE REAL ONE!
SHE NEEDED TO GET AWAY!
BUT WE NEED HER! SHE'S OUR PRINCESS!
NEED HER!? WHAT DOES THAT EVEN MEAN!?

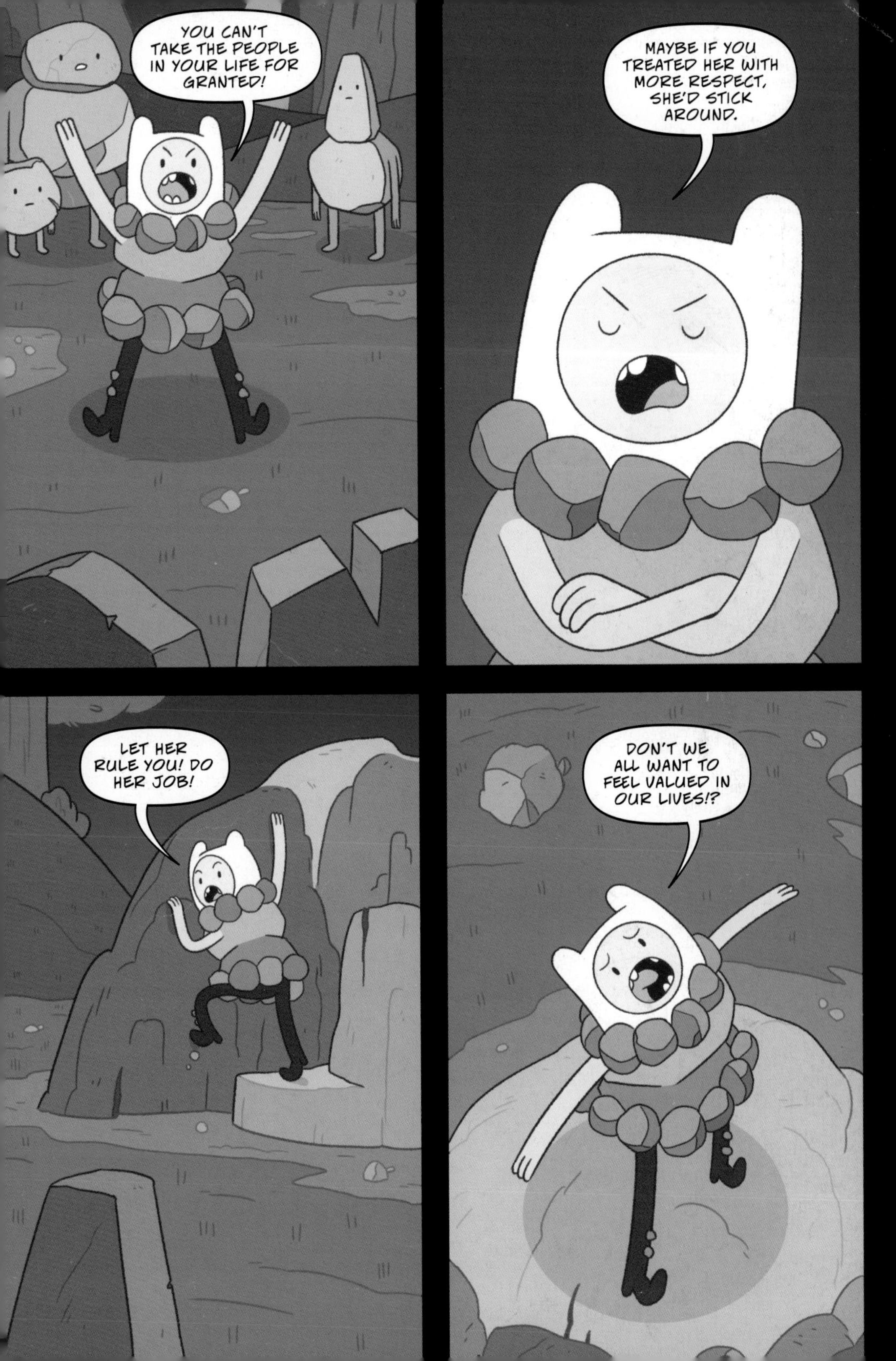
YOU CAN'T TAKE THE PEOPLE IN YOUR LIFE FOR GRANTED!
MAYBE IF YOU TREATED HER WITH MORE RESPECT, SHE'D STICK AROUND.
LET HER RULE YOU! DO HER JOB!
DON'T WE ALL WANT TO FEEL VALUED IN OUR LIVES!?

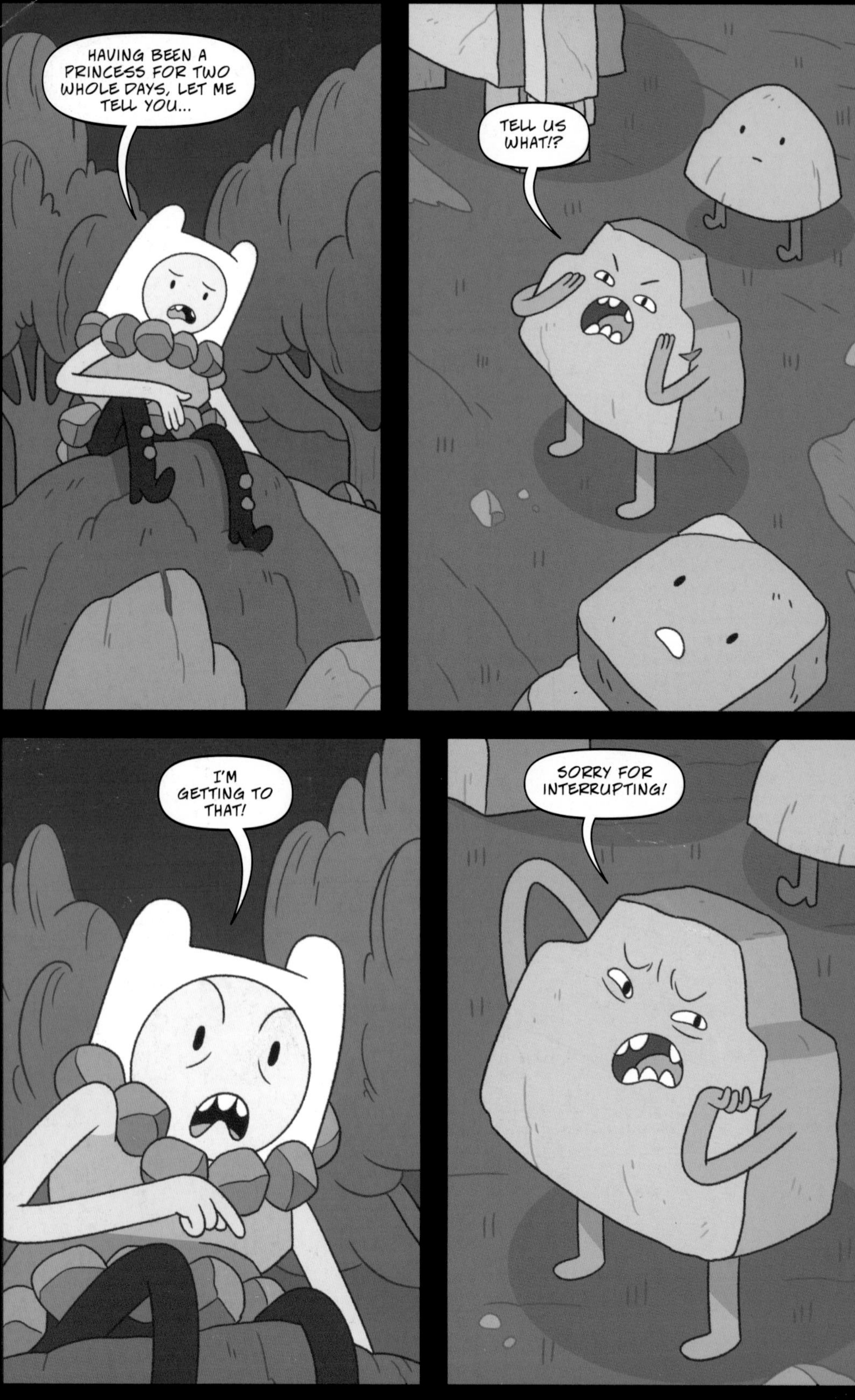

HAVING BEEN A PRINCESS FOR TWO WHOLE DAYS, LET ME TELL YOU...
TELL US WHAT!?
I'M GETTING TO THAT!
SORRY FOR INTERRUPTING!

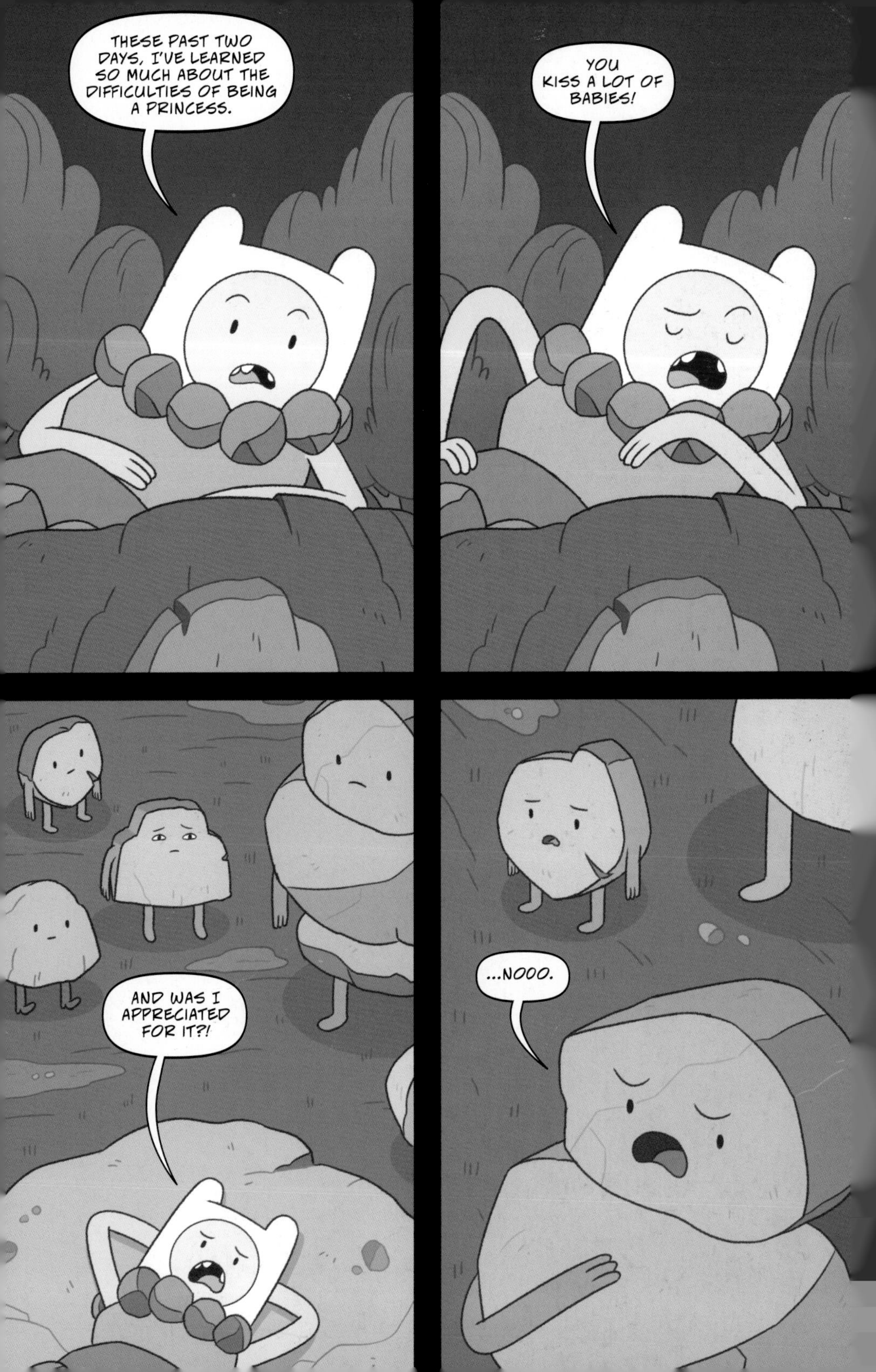
THESE PAST TWO DAYS, I'VE LEARNED SO MUCH ABOUT THE DIFFICULTIES OF BEING A PRINCESS.
YOU KISS A LOT OF BABIES!
AND WAS I APPRECIATED FOR IT?!
...NOOO.

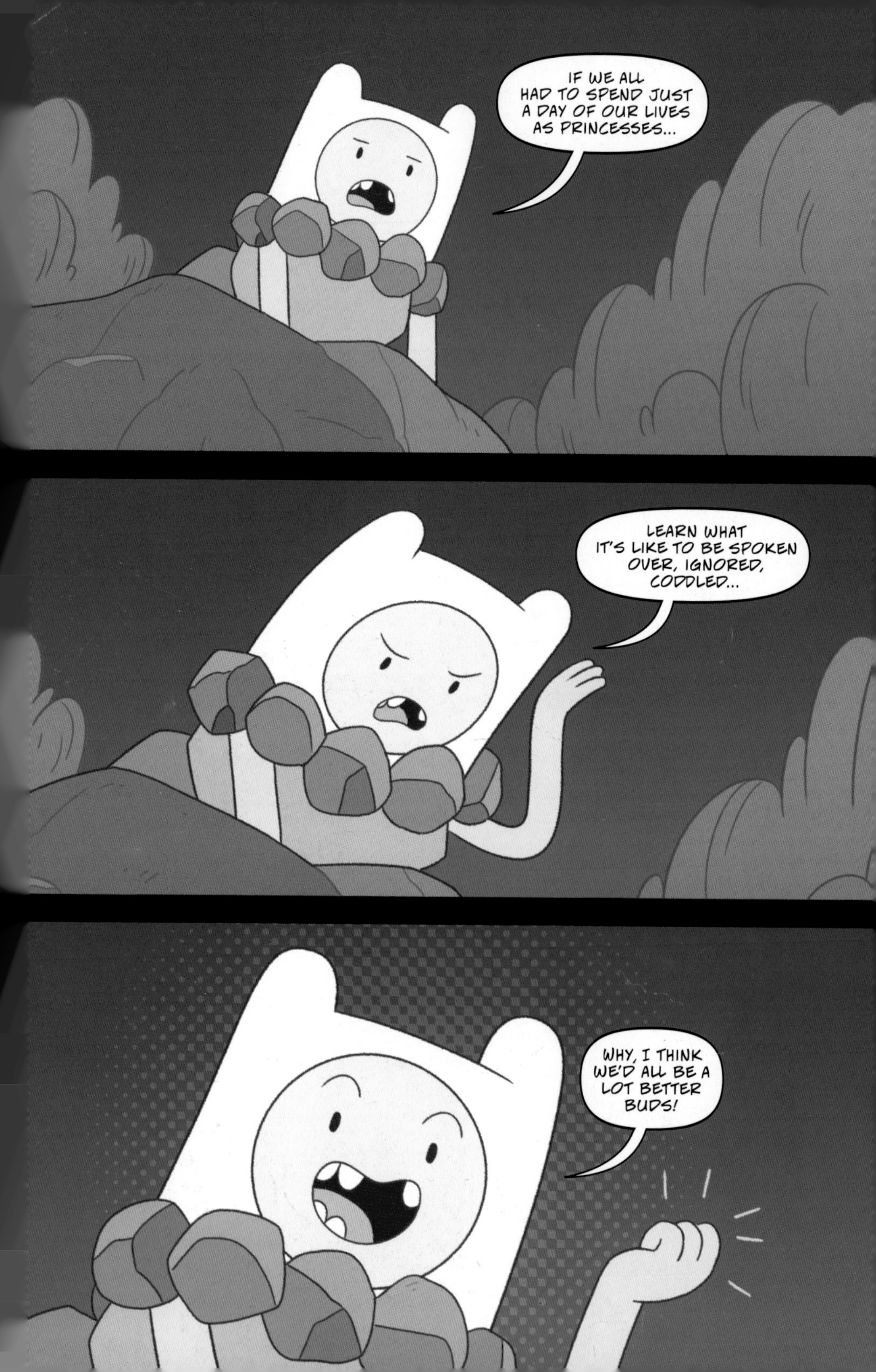
IF WE ALL HAD TO SPEND JUST A DAY OF OUR LIVES AS PRINCESSES...
LEARN WHAT IT'S LIKE TO BE SPOKEN OVER, IGNORED, CODDLED...
WHY, I THINK WE'D ALL BE A LOT BETTER BUDS!

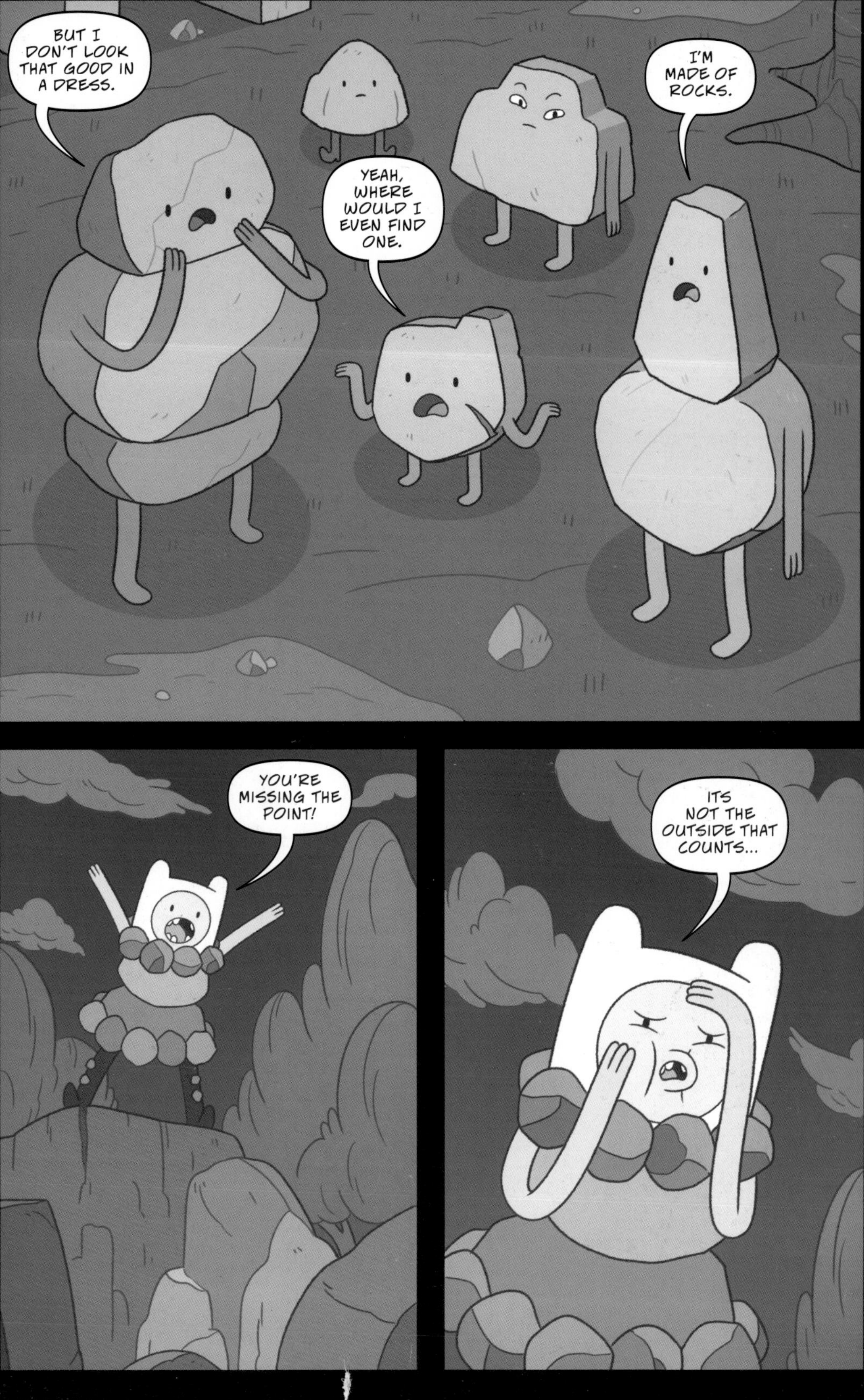
BUT I DON'T LOOK THAT GOOD IN A DRESS.
I'M MADE OF ROCKS.
YEAH, WHERE WOULD I EVEN FIND ONE.
YOU'RE MISSING THE POINT!
ITS NOT THE OUTSIDE THAT COUNTS...

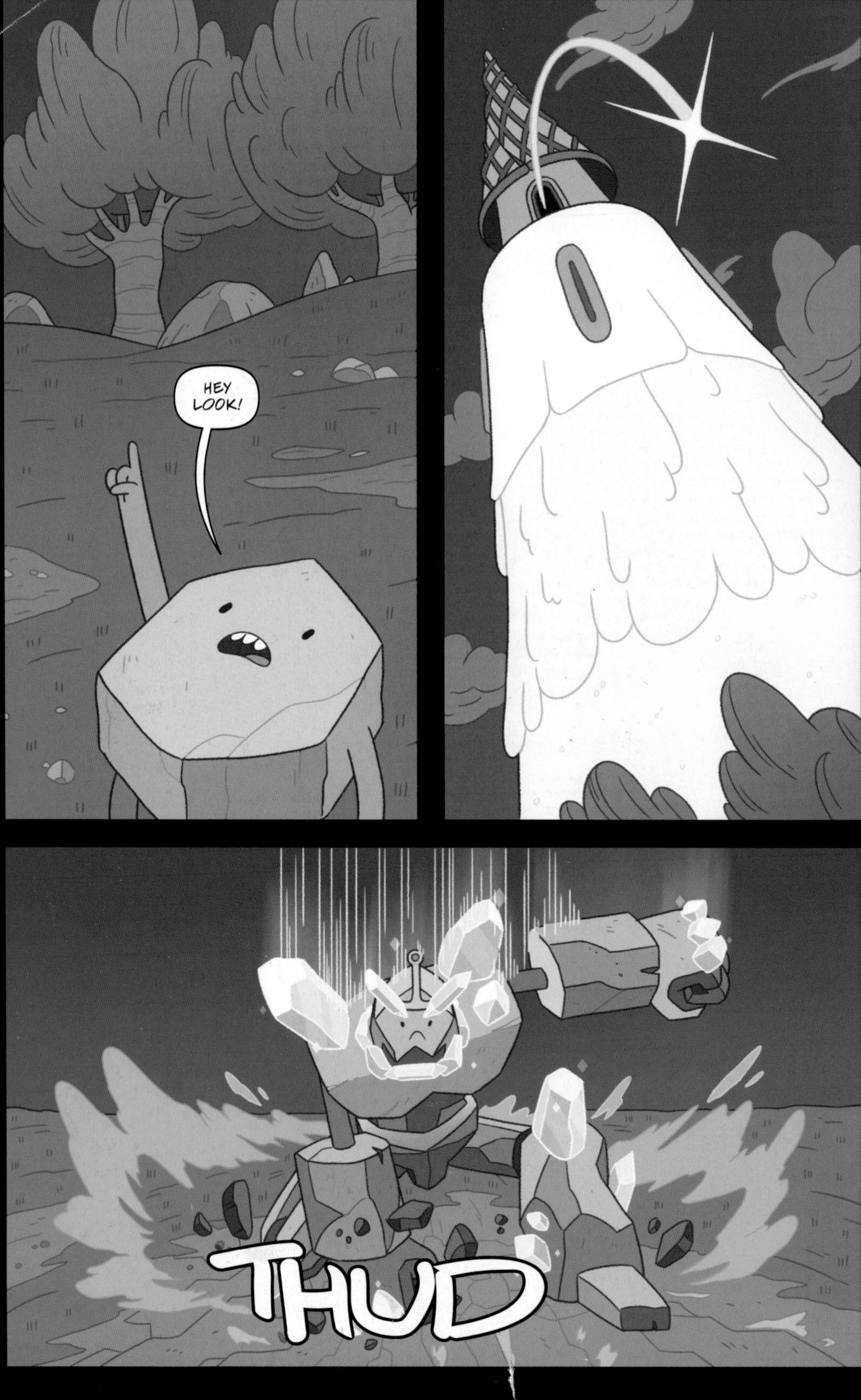
HEY LOOK!
THUD

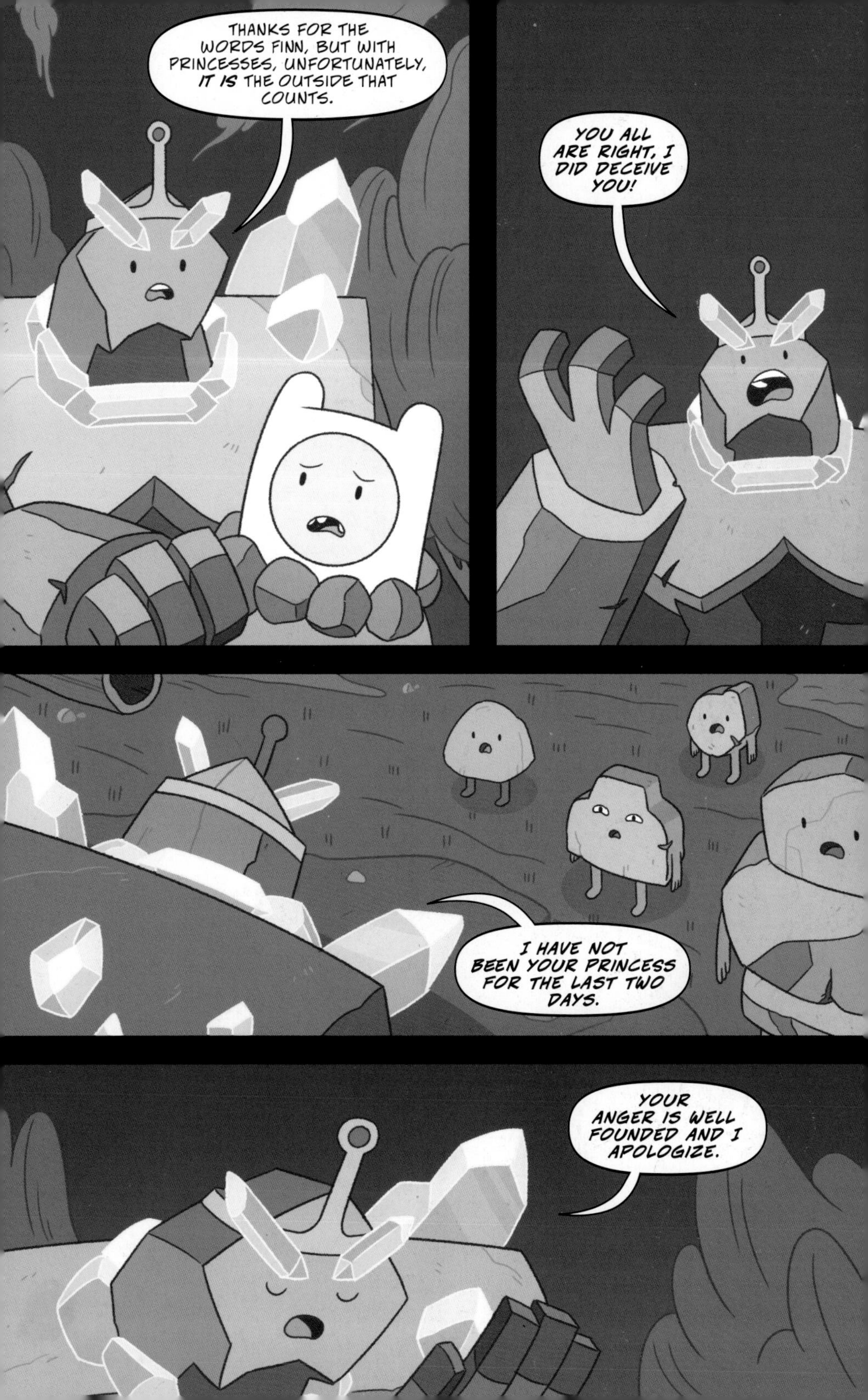
THANKS FOR THE WORDS FINN, BUT WITH PRINCESSES, UNFORTUNATELY, *IT IS* THE OUTSIDE THAT COUNTS.
YOU ALL ARE RIGHT, I DID DECEIVE YOU!
I HAVE NOT BEEN YOUR PRINCESS FOR THE LAST TWO DAYS.
YOUR ANGER IS WELL FOUNDED AND I APOLOGIZE.

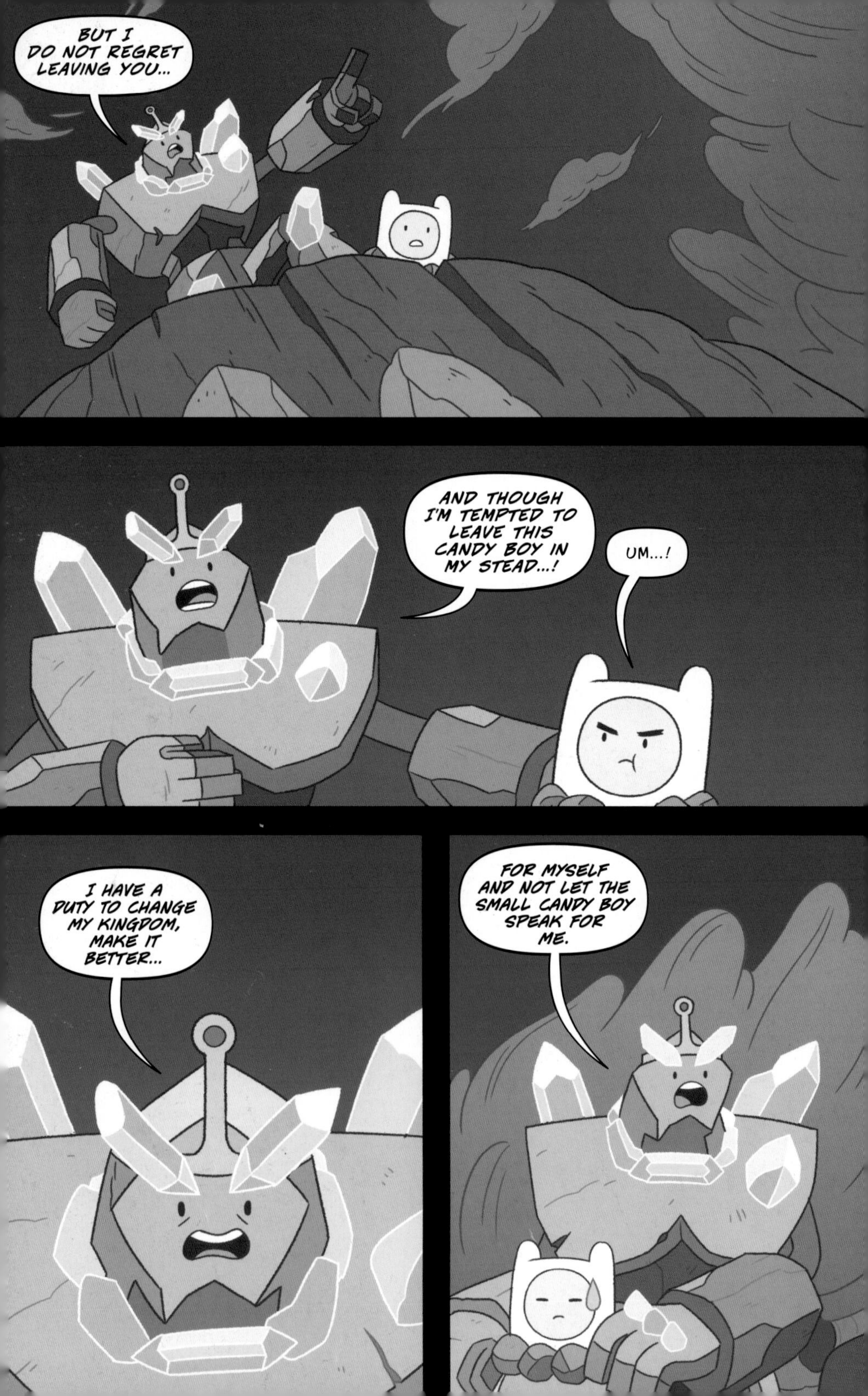
BUT I DO NOT REGRET LEAVING YOU...
AND THOUGH I'M TEMPTED TO LEAVE THIS CANDY BOY IN MY STEAD...!
UM...!
I HAVE A DUTY TO CHANGE MY KINGDOM, MAKE IT BETTER...
FOR MYSELF AND NOT LET THE SMALL CANDY BOY SPEAK FOR ME.

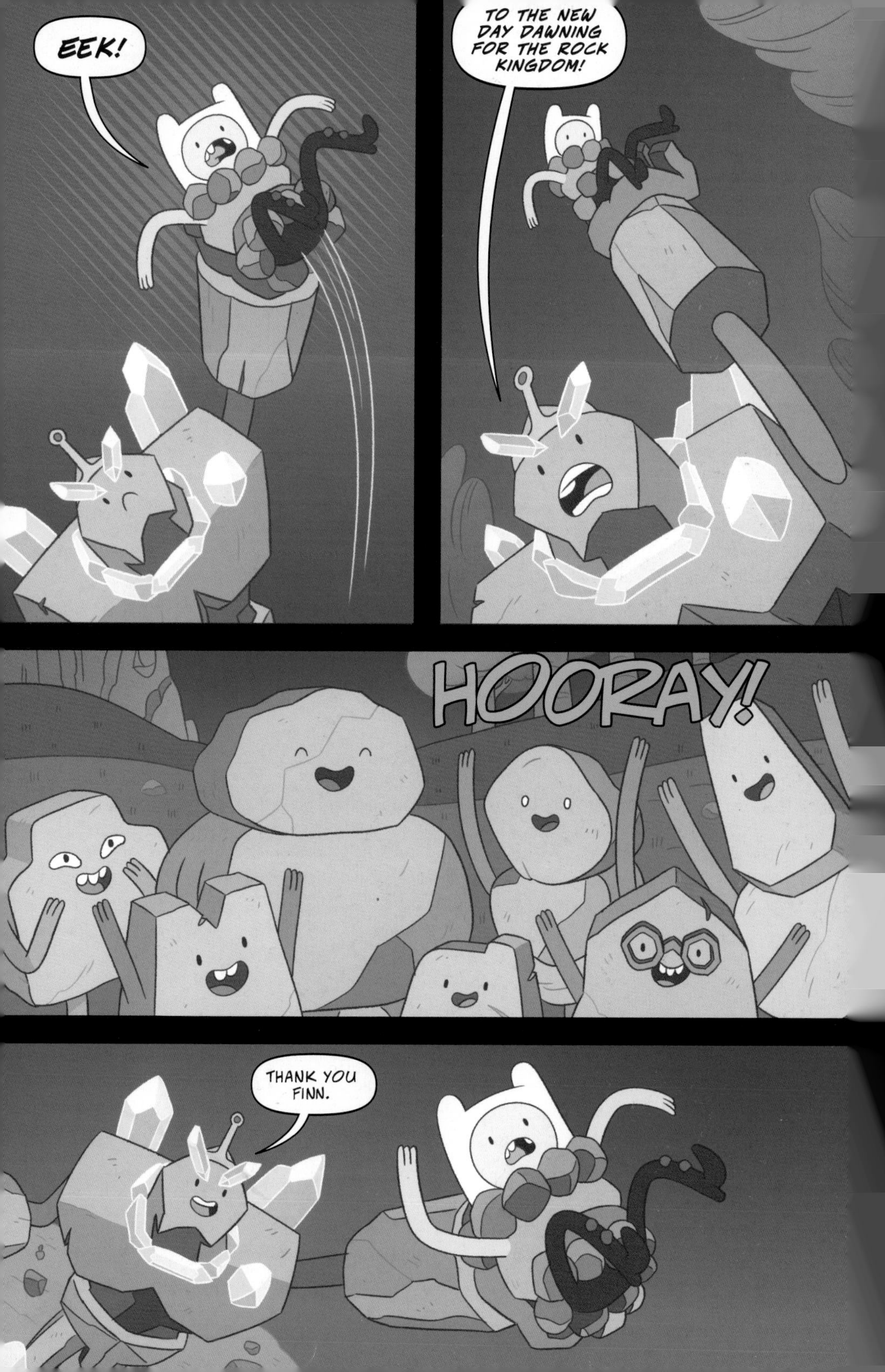
EEK!
TO THE NEW DAY DAWNING FOR THE ROCK KINGDOM!
HOORAY!
THANK YOU FINN.

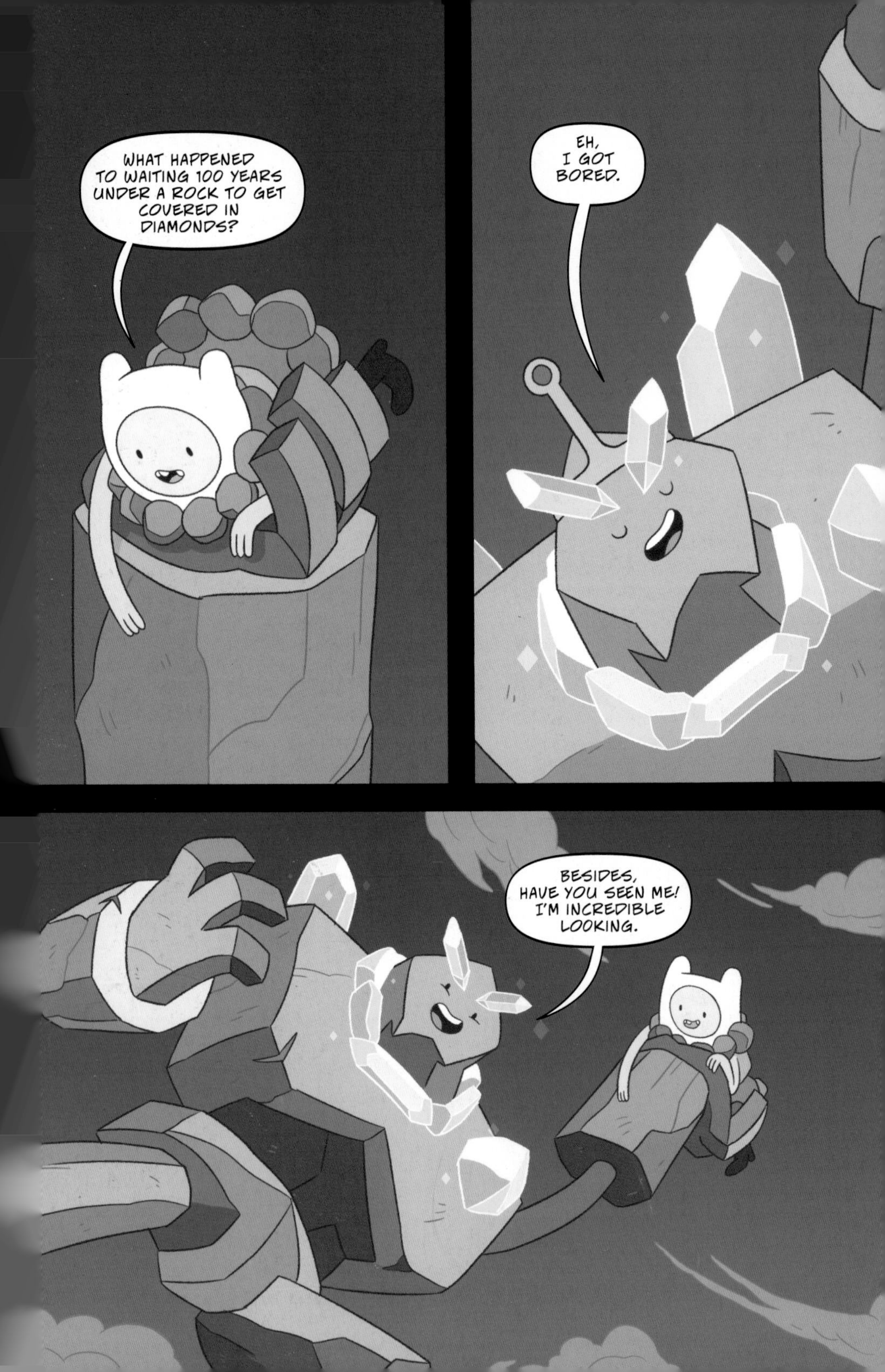
WHAT HAPPENED TO WAITING 100 YEARS UNDER A ROCK TO GET COVERED IN DIAMONDS?
EH, I GOT BORED.
BESIDES, HAVE YOU SEEN ME! I'M INCREDIBLE LOOKING.

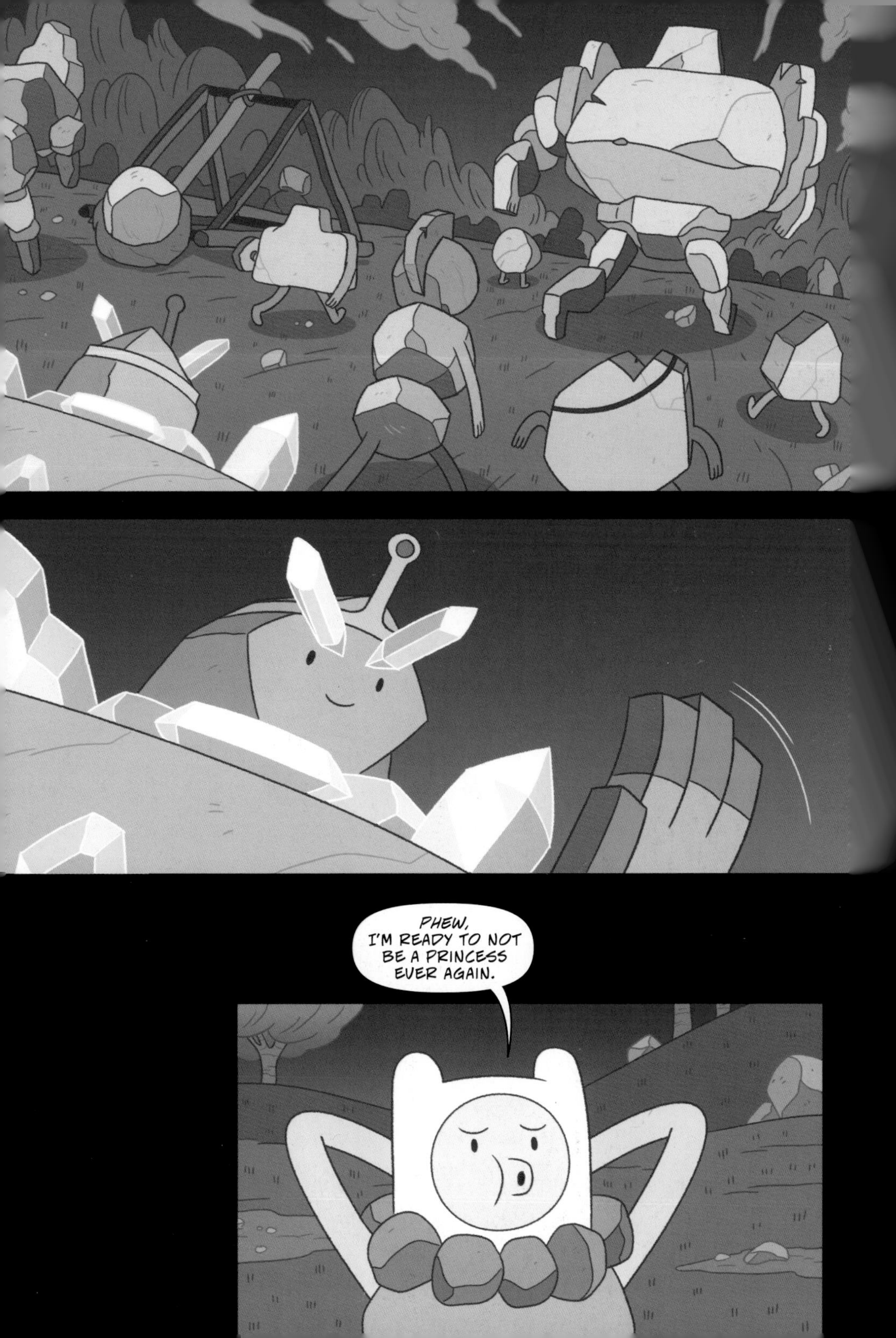
PHEW,
I'M READY TO NOT
BE A PRINCESS
EVER AGAIN.

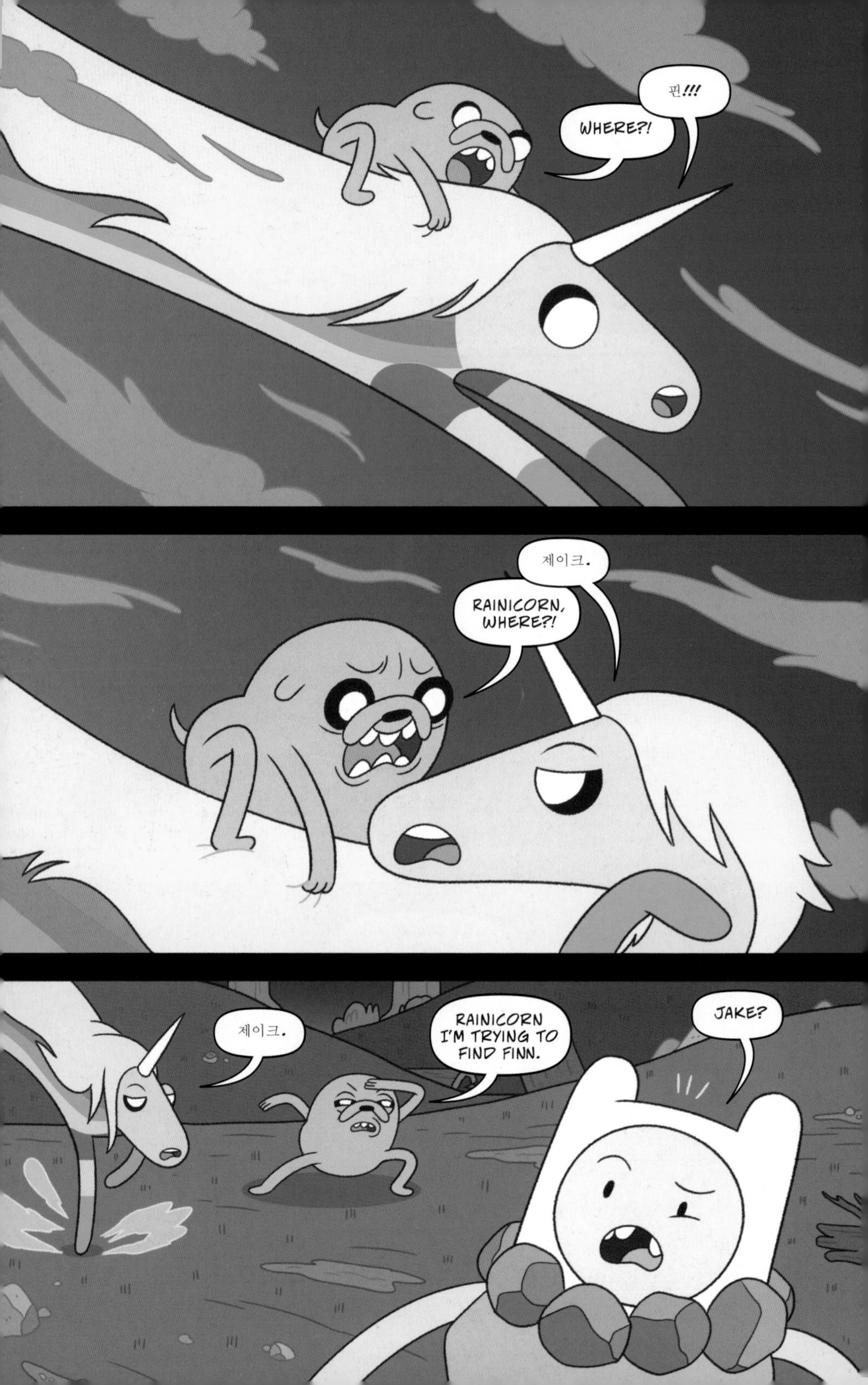
핀!!!
WHERE?!
제이크.
RAINICORN, WHERE?!
제이크.
RAINICORN I'M TRYING TO FIND FINN.
JAKE?

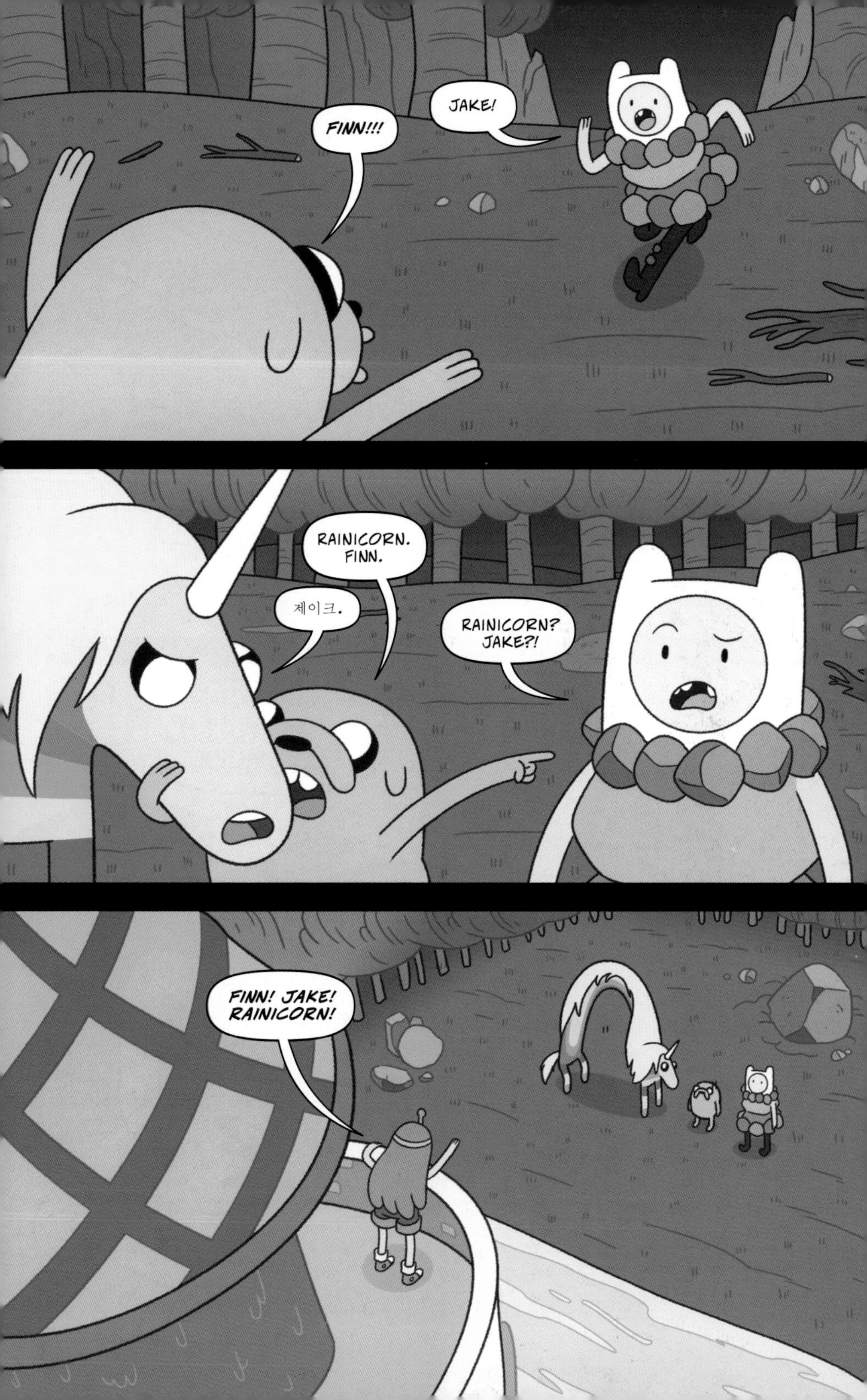
FINN!!!
JAKE!
RAINICORN.
FINN.
제이크.
RAINICORN?
JAKE?!
FINN! JAKE!
RAINICORN!

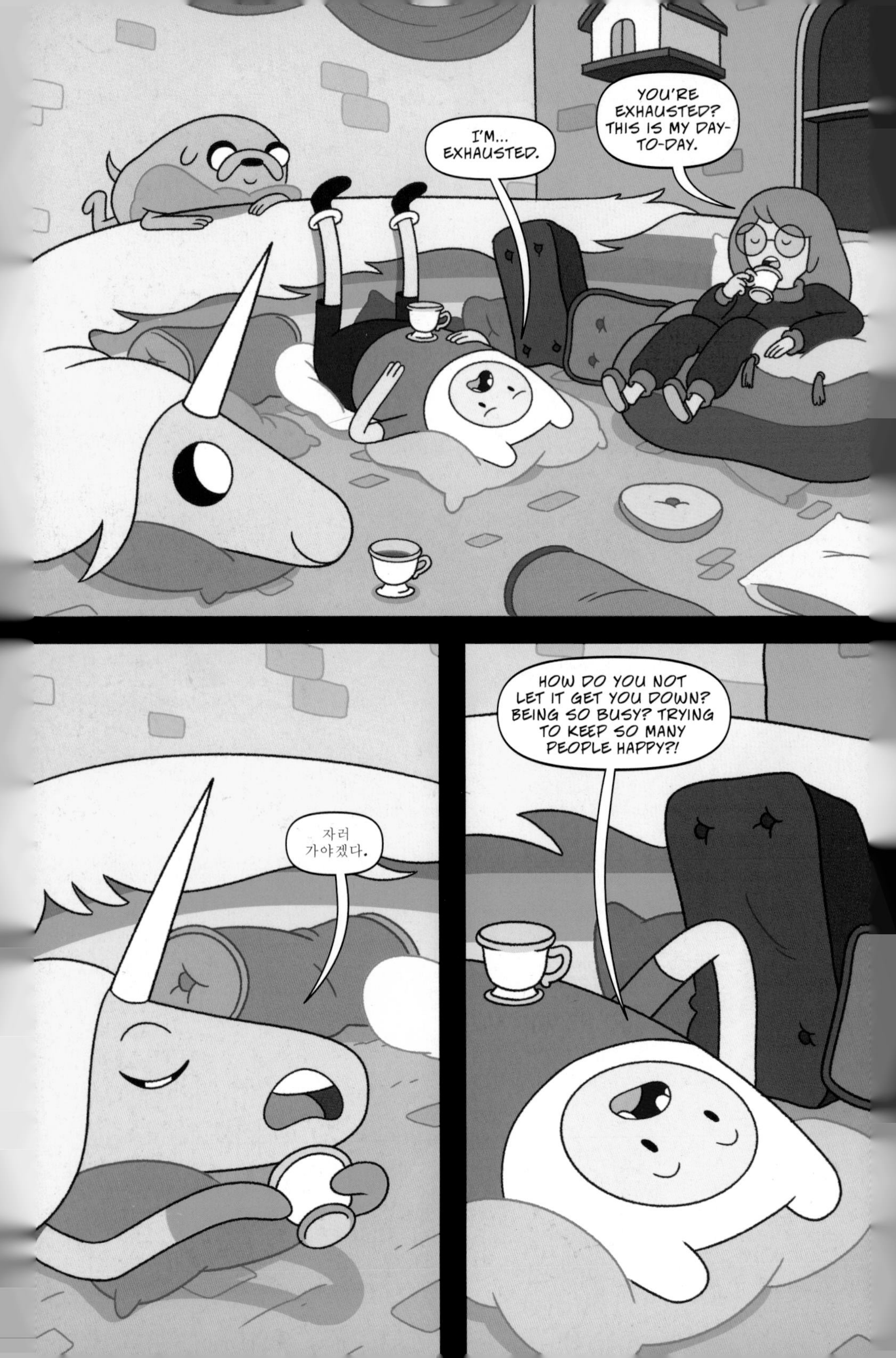
I'M... EXHAUSTED.
YOU'RE EXHAUSTED? THIS IS MY DAY-TO-DAY.
자러 가야겠다.
HOW DO YOU NOT LET IT GET YOU DOWN? BEING SO BUSY? TRYING TO KEEP SO MANY PEOPLE HAPPY?!

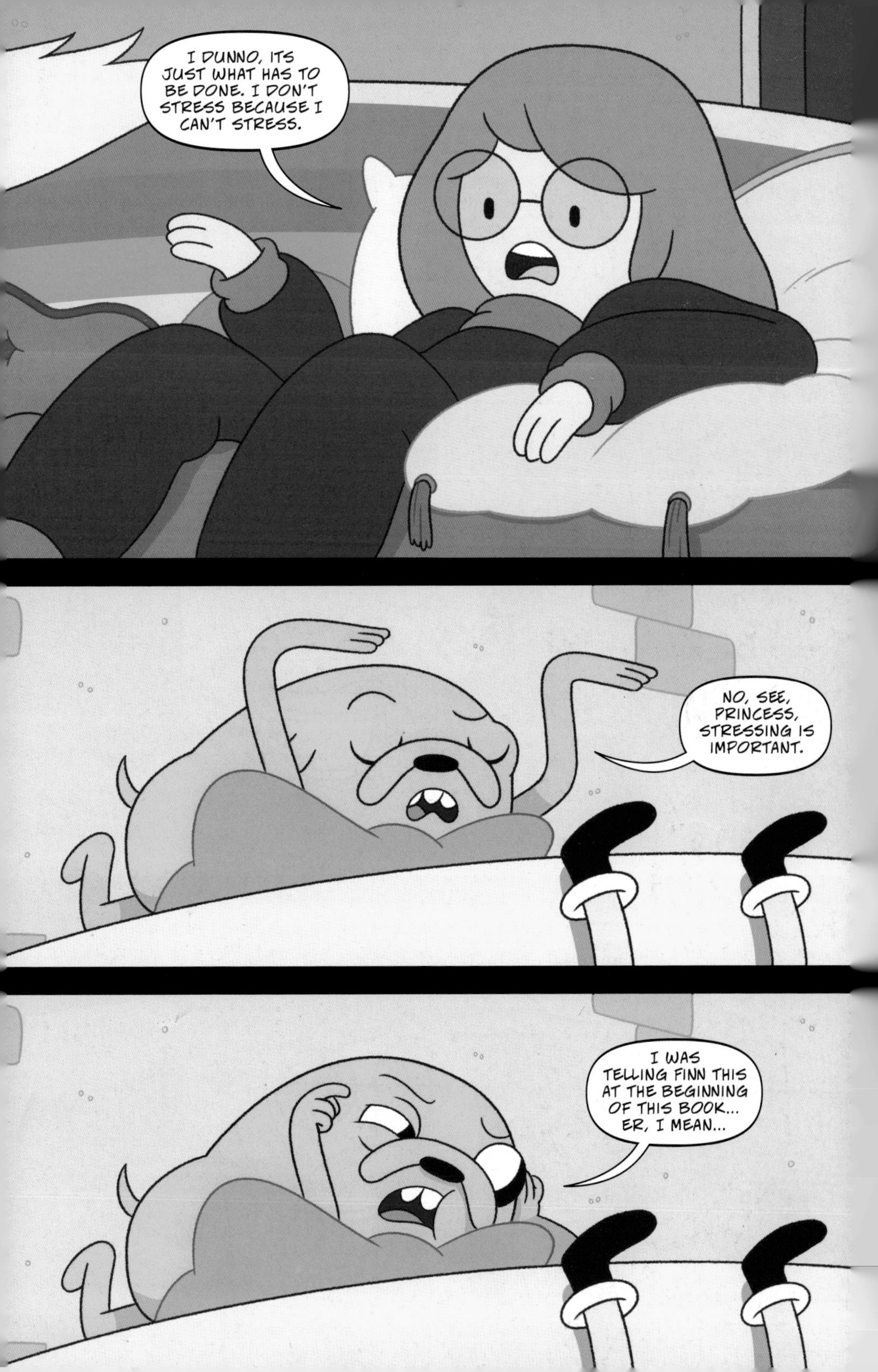
I DUNNO, ITS JUST WHAT HAS TO BE DONE. I DON'T STRESS BECAUSE I CAN'T STRESS.
NO, SEE, PRINCESS, STRESSING IS IMPORTANT.
I WAS TELLING FINN THIS AT THE BEGINNING OF THIS BOOK... ER, I MEAN...

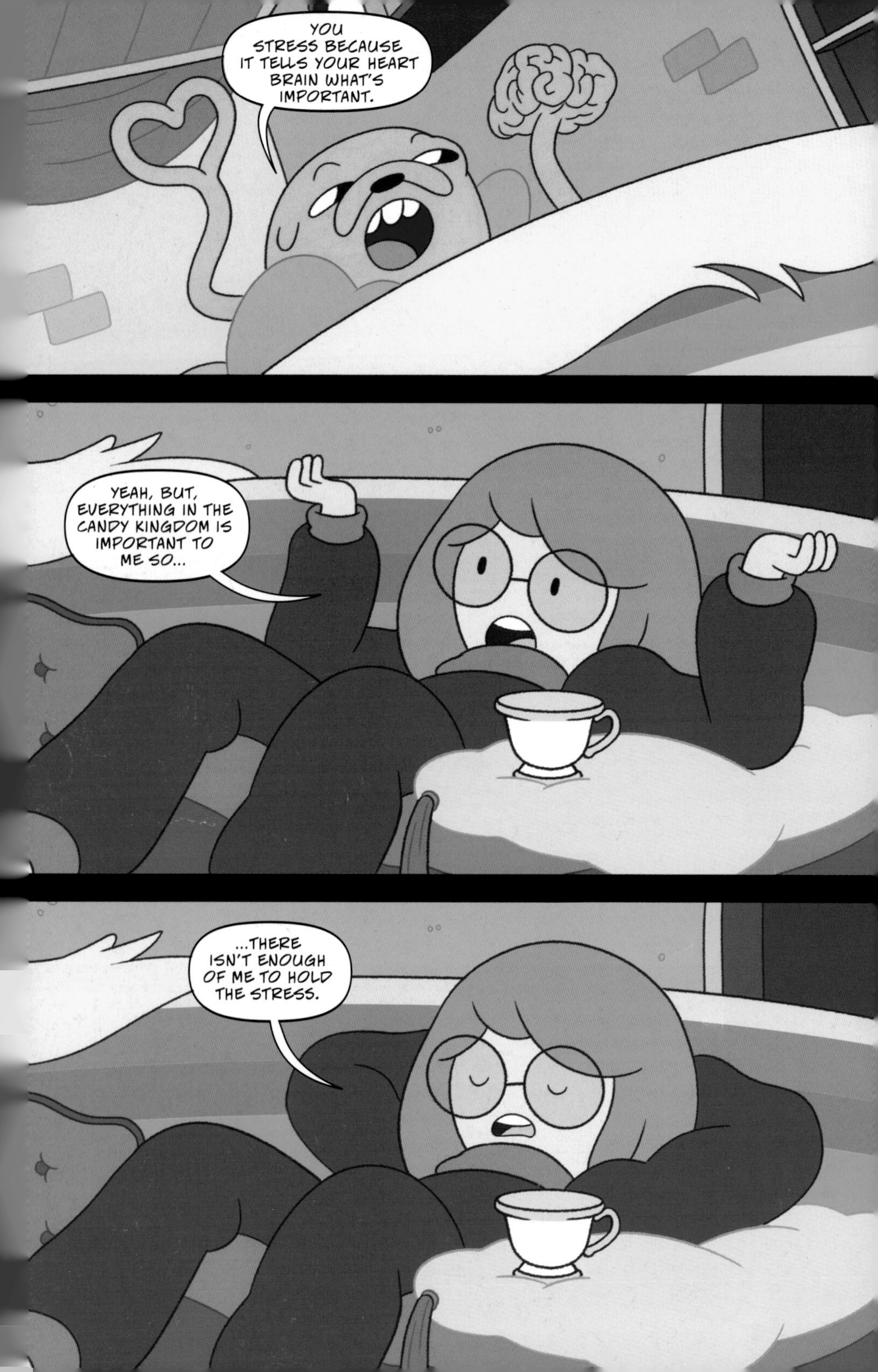
YOU STRESS BECAUSE IT TELLS YOUR HEART BRAIN WHAT'S IMPORTANT.
YEAH, BUT, EVERYTHING IN THE CANDY KINGDOM IS IMPORTANT TO ME SO...
...THERE ISN'T ENOUGH OF ME TO HOLD THE STRESS.

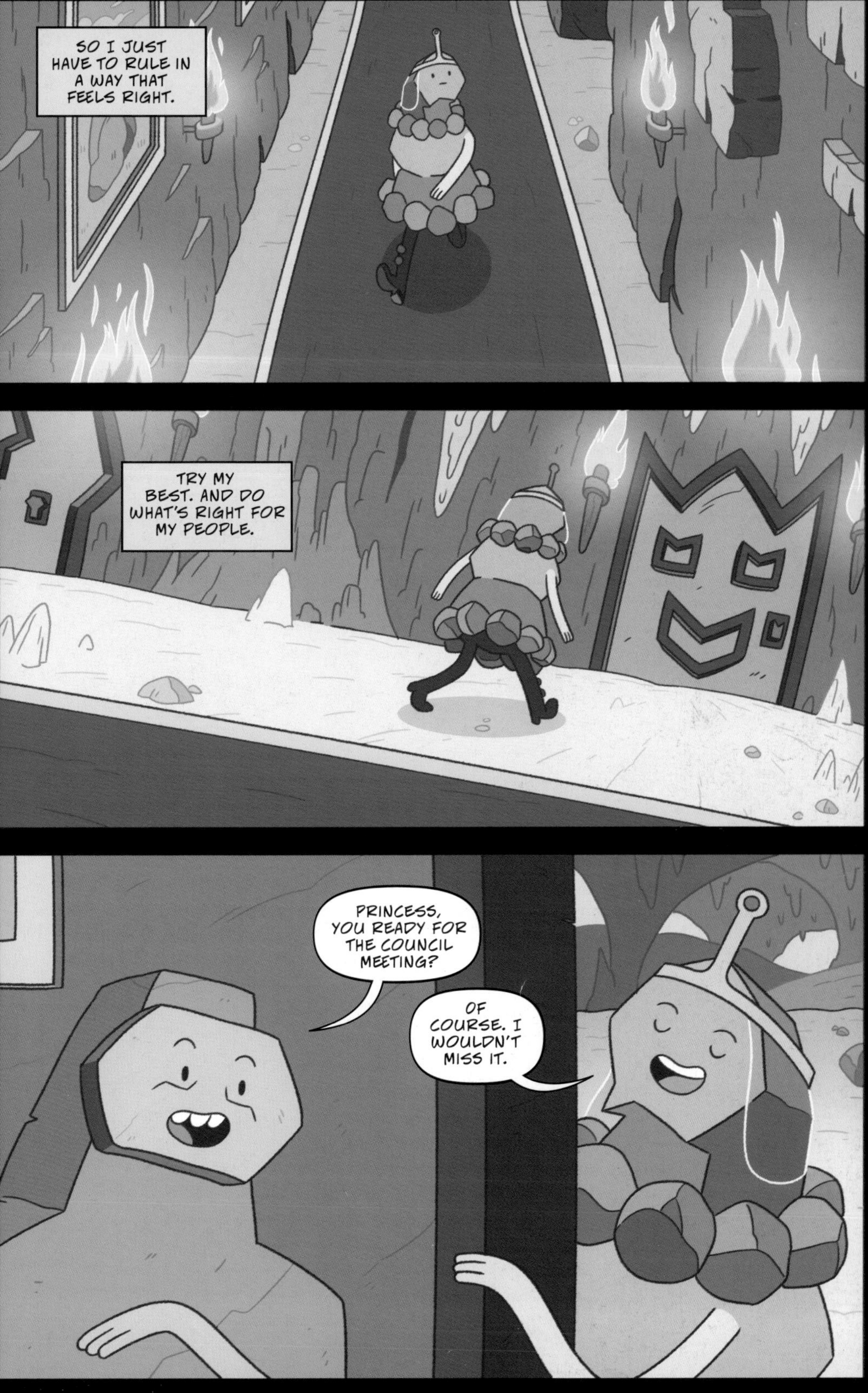
SO I JUST HAVE TO RULE IN A WAY THAT FEELS RIGHT.
TRY MY BEST. AND DO WHAT'S RIGHT FOR MY PEOPLE.
PRINCESS, YOU READY FOR THE COUNCIL MEETING?
OF COURSE. I WOULDN'T MISS IT.

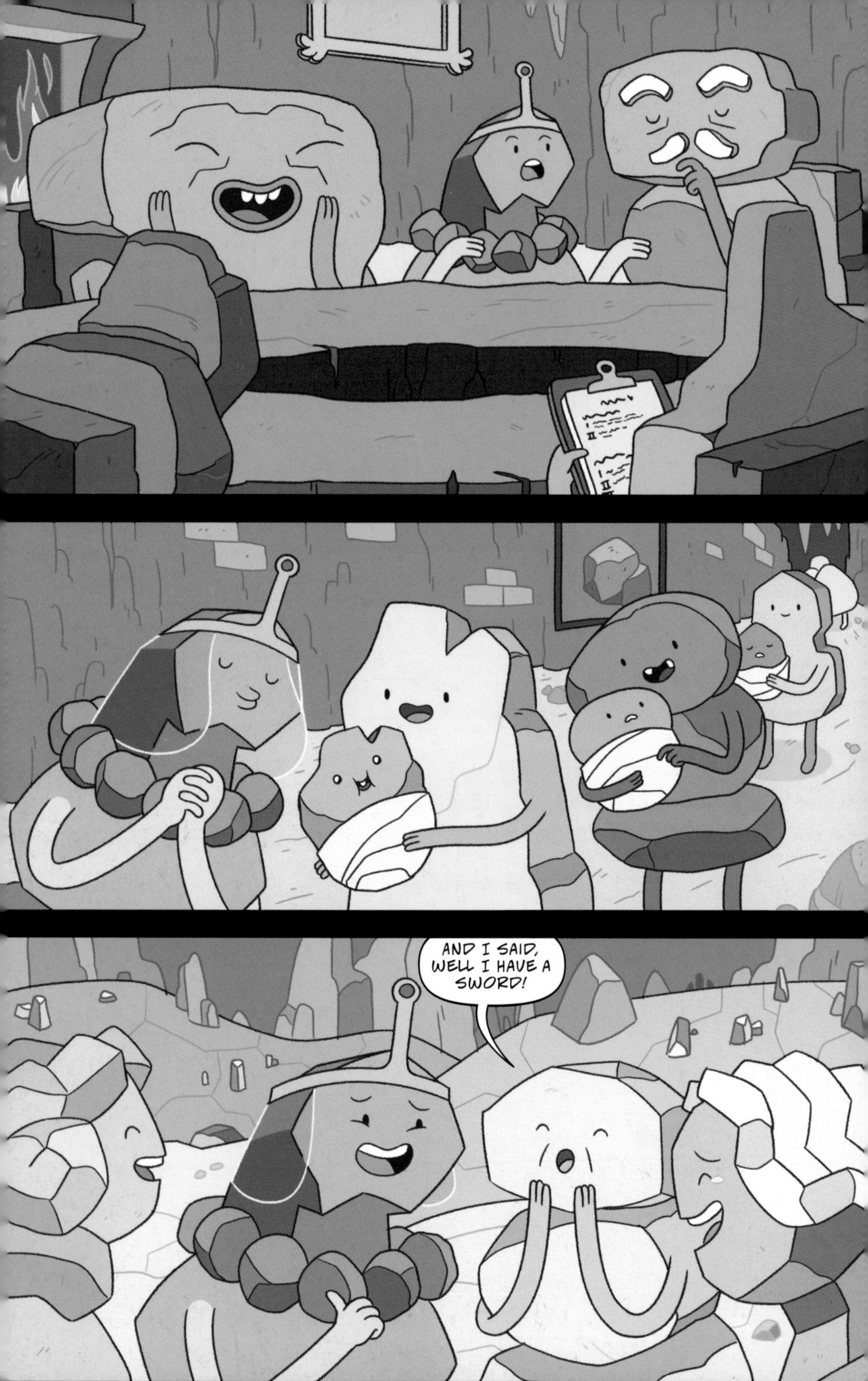
AND I SAID, WELL I HAVE A SWORD!

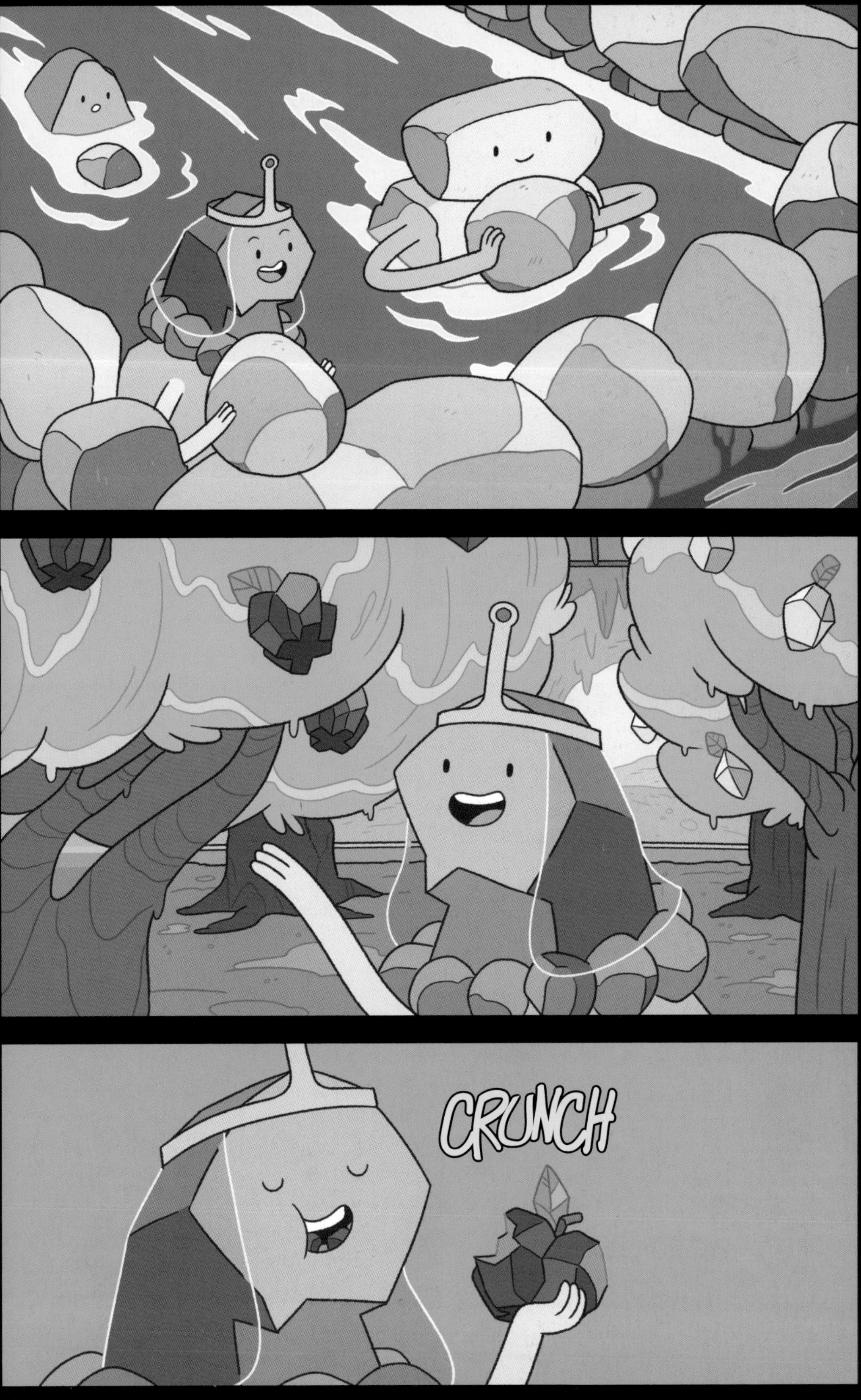
CRUNCH

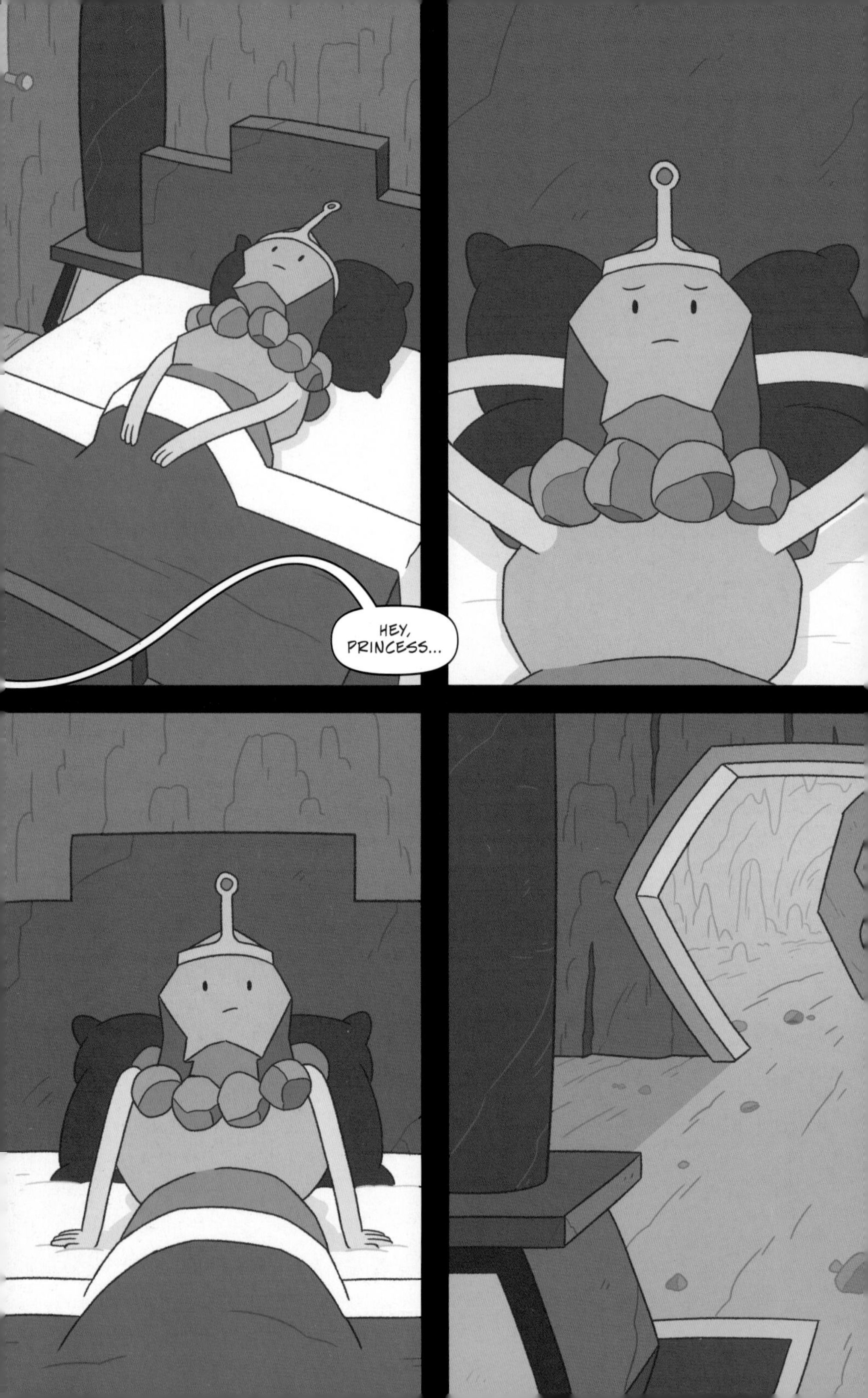
HEY, PRINCESS...

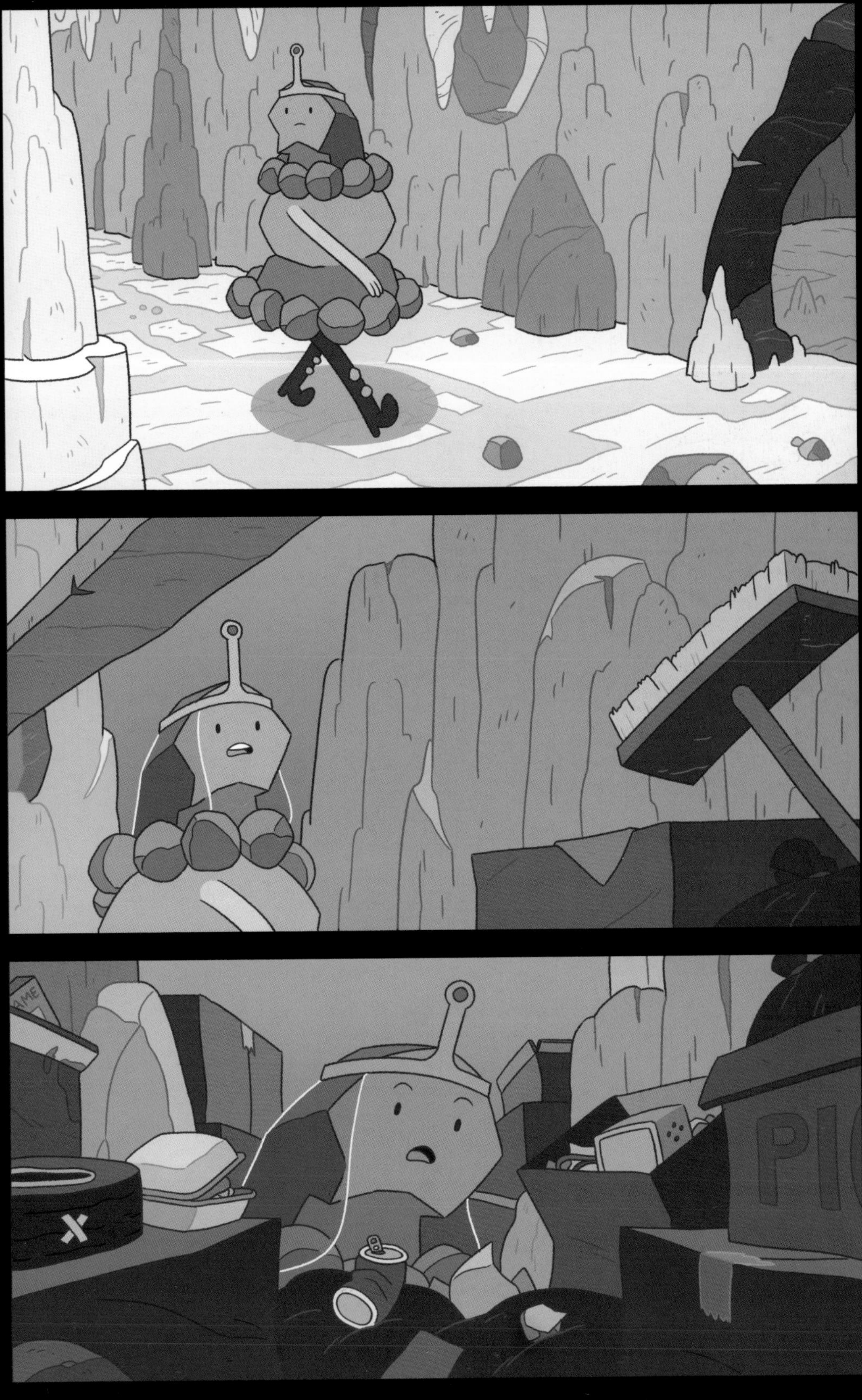

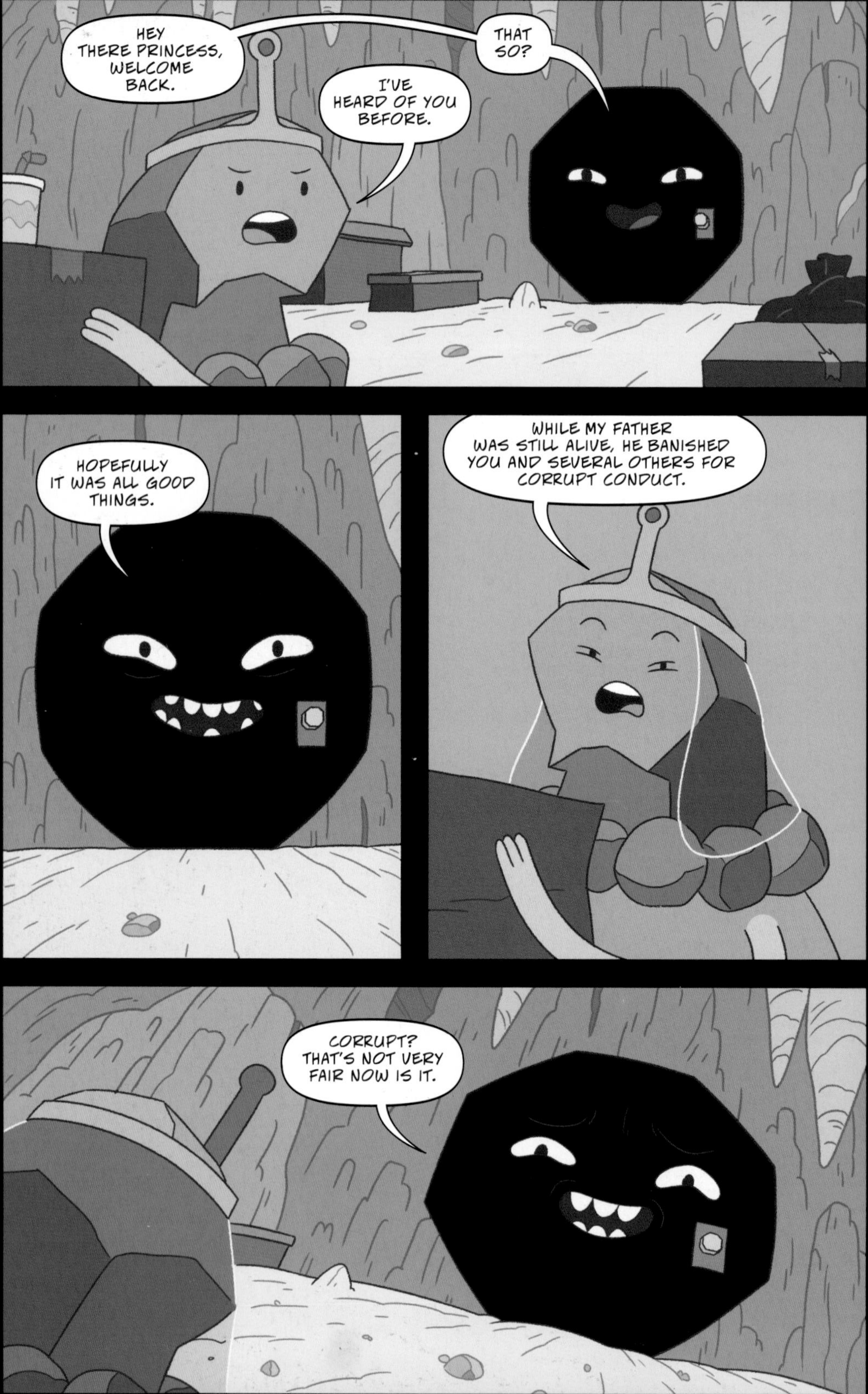
HEY THERE PRINCESS, WELCOME BACK.
I'VE HEARD OF YOU BEFORE.
THAT SO?
HOPEFULLY IT WAS ALL GOOD THINGS.
WHILE MY FATHER WAS STILL ALIVE, HE BANISHED YOU AND SEVERAL OTHERS FOR CORRUPT CONDUCT.
CORRUPT? THAT'S NOT VERY FAIR NOW IS IT.

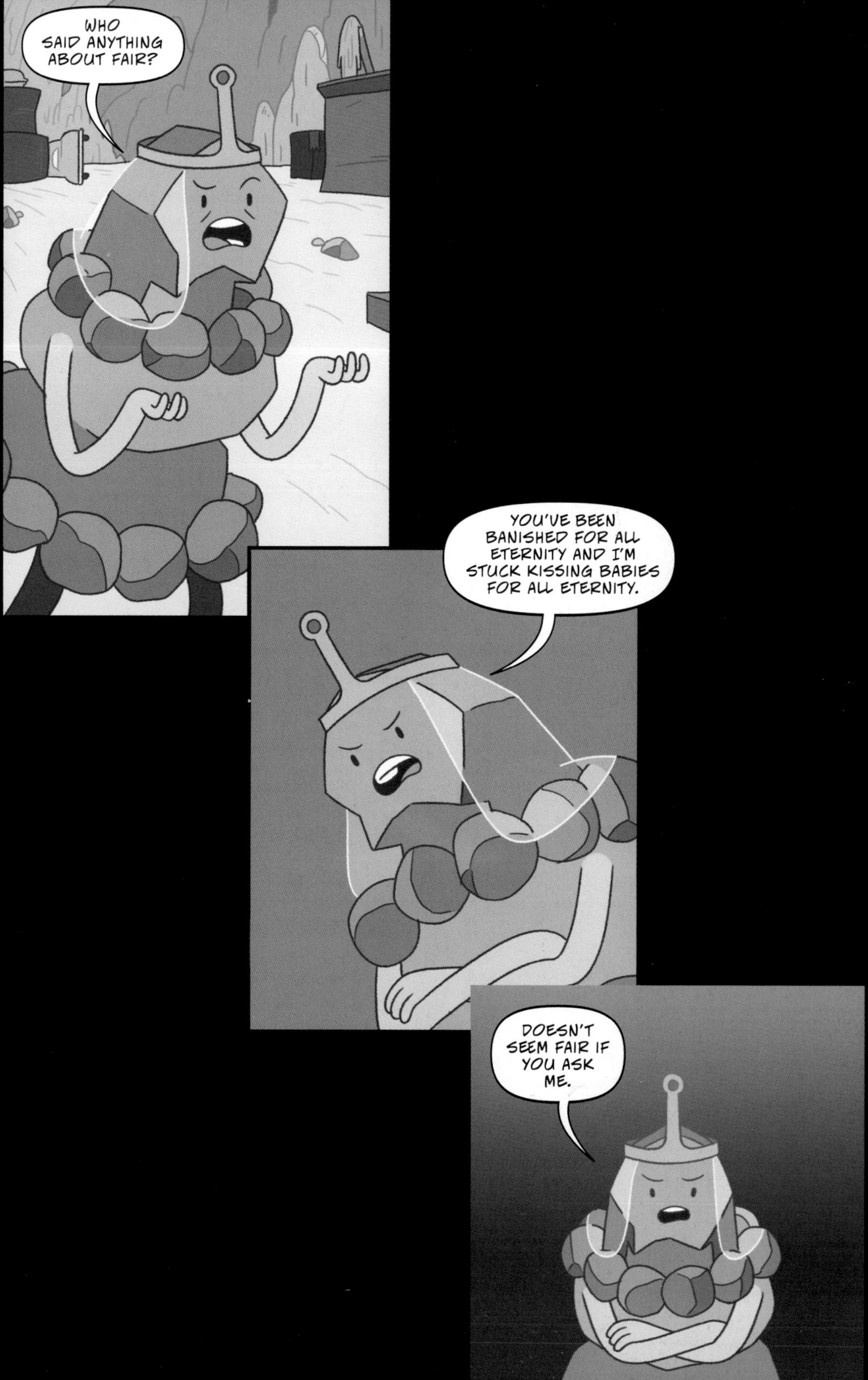
WHO SAID ANYTHING ABOUT FAIR?
YOU'VE BEEN BANISHED FOR ALL ETERNITY AND I'M STUCK KISSING BABIES FOR ALL ETERNITY.
DOESN'T SEEM FAIR IF YOU ASK ME.

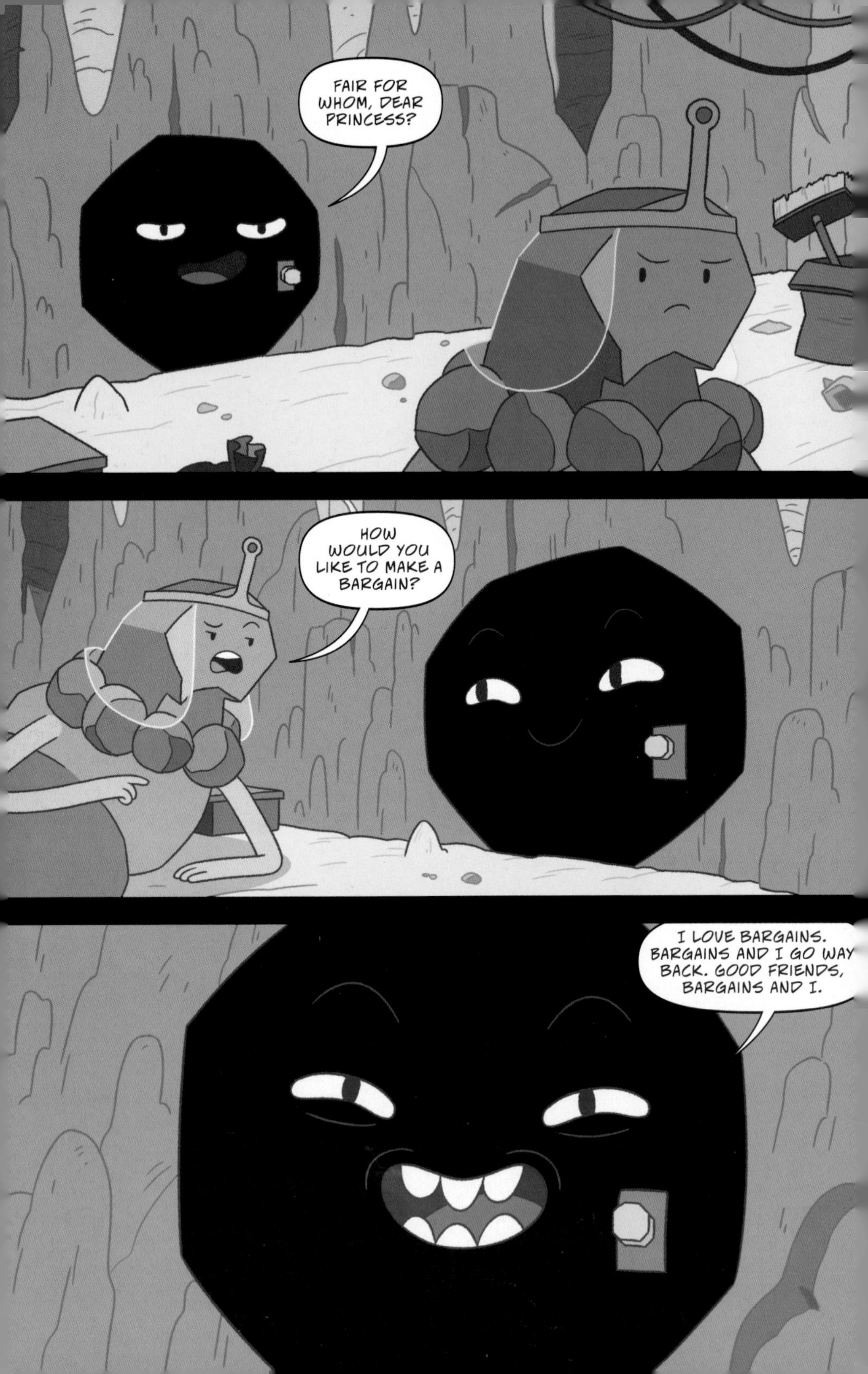
FAIR FOR WHOM, DEAR PRINCESS?
HOW WOULD YOU LIKE TO MAKE A BARGAIN?
I LOVE BARGAINS. BARGAINS AND I GO WAY BACK. GOOD FRIENDS, BARGAINS AND I.

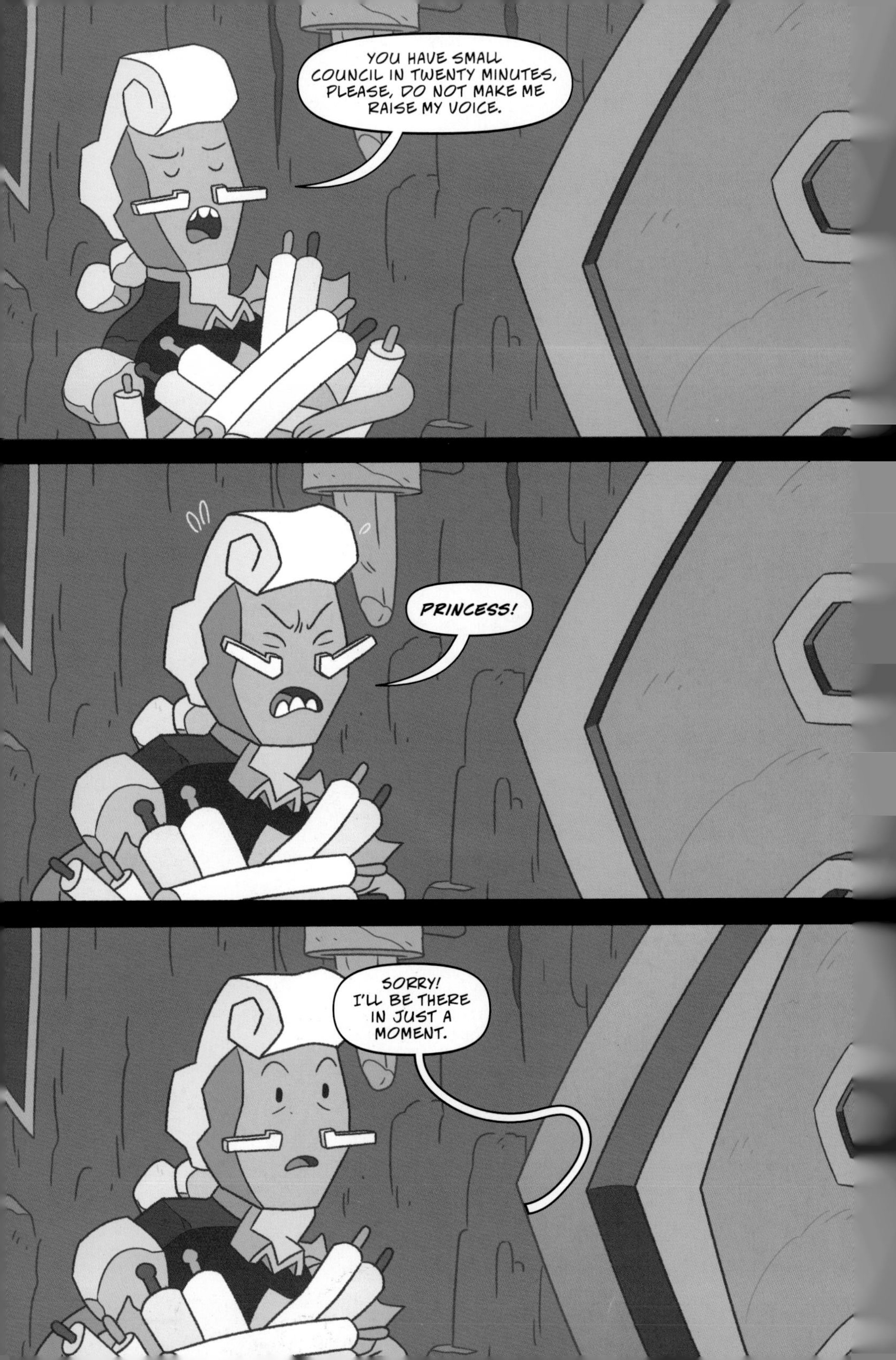
YOU HAVE SMALL COUNCIL IN TWENTY MINUTES, PLEASE, DO NOT MAKE ME RAISE MY VOICE.
PRINCESS!
SORRY! I'LL BE THERE IN JUST A MOMENT.

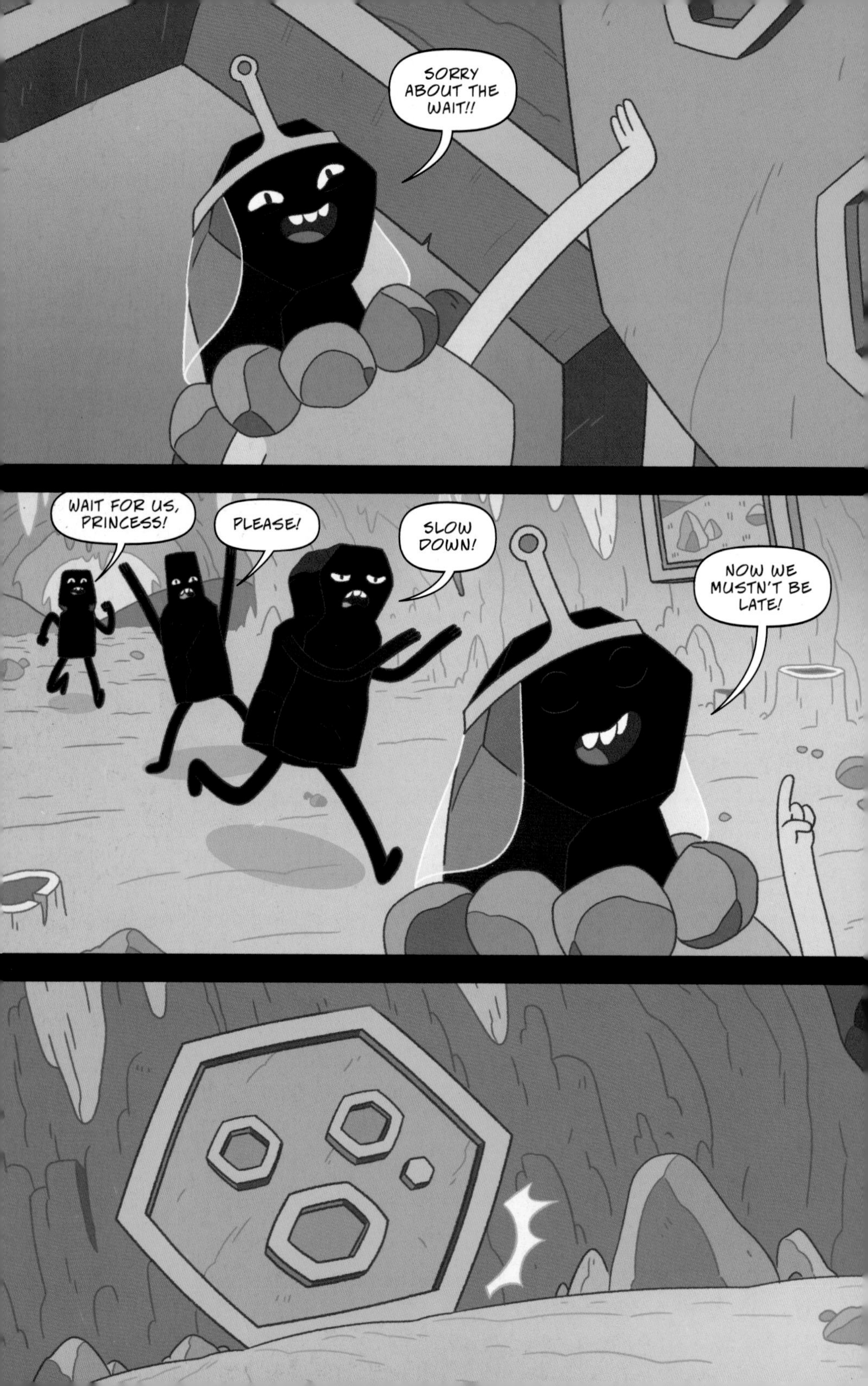
SORRY ABOUT THE WAIT!!
WAIT FOR US, PRINCESS!
PLEASE!
SLOW DOWN!
NOW WE MUSTN'T BE LATE!

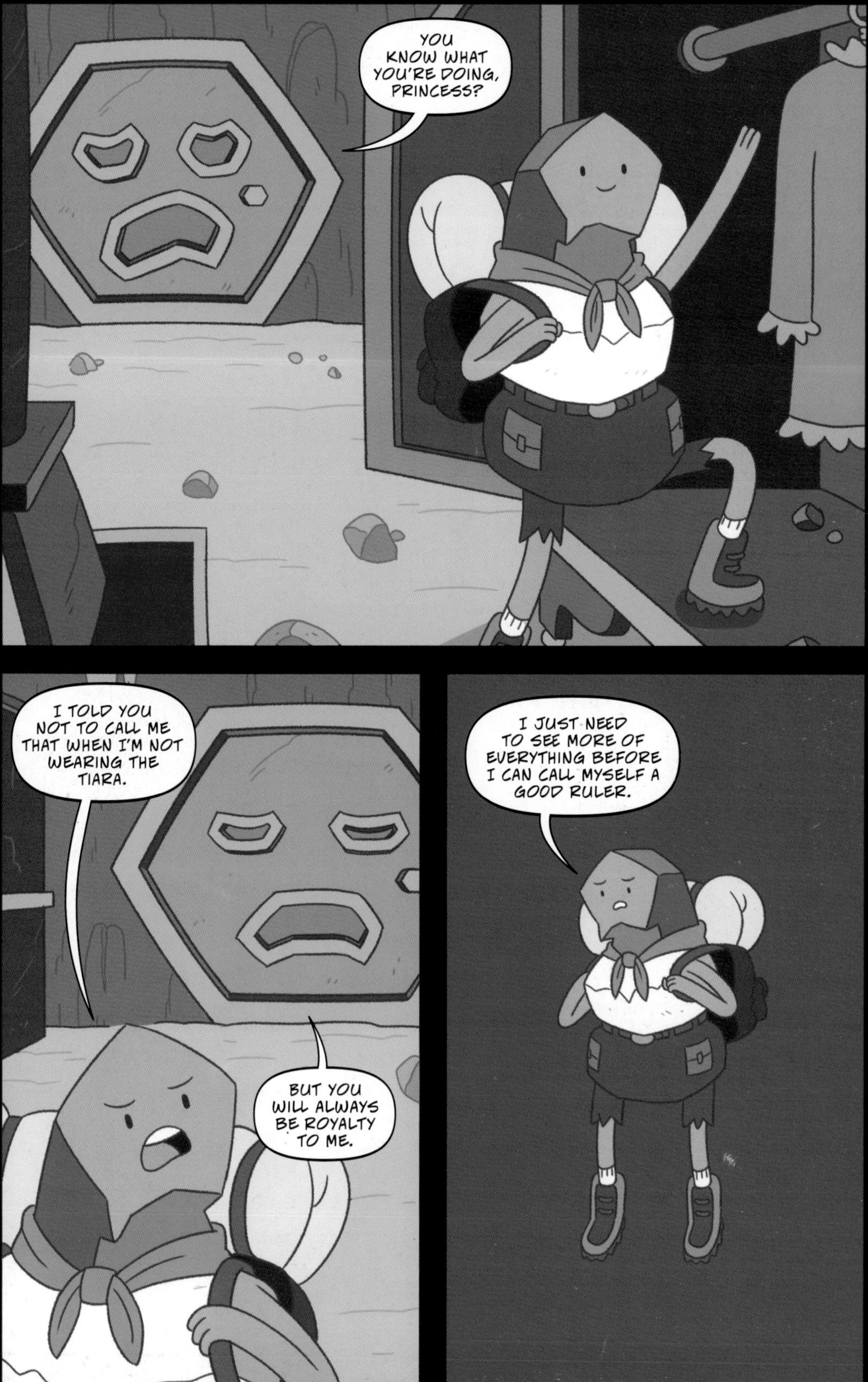
YOU KNOW WHAT YOU'RE DOING, PRINCESS?
I TOLD YOU NOT TO CALL ME THAT WHEN I'M NOT WEARING THE TIARA.
BUT YOU WILL ALWAYS BE ROYALTY TO ME.
I JUST NEED TO SEE MORE OF EVERYTHING BEFORE I CAN CALL MYSELF A GOOD RULER.

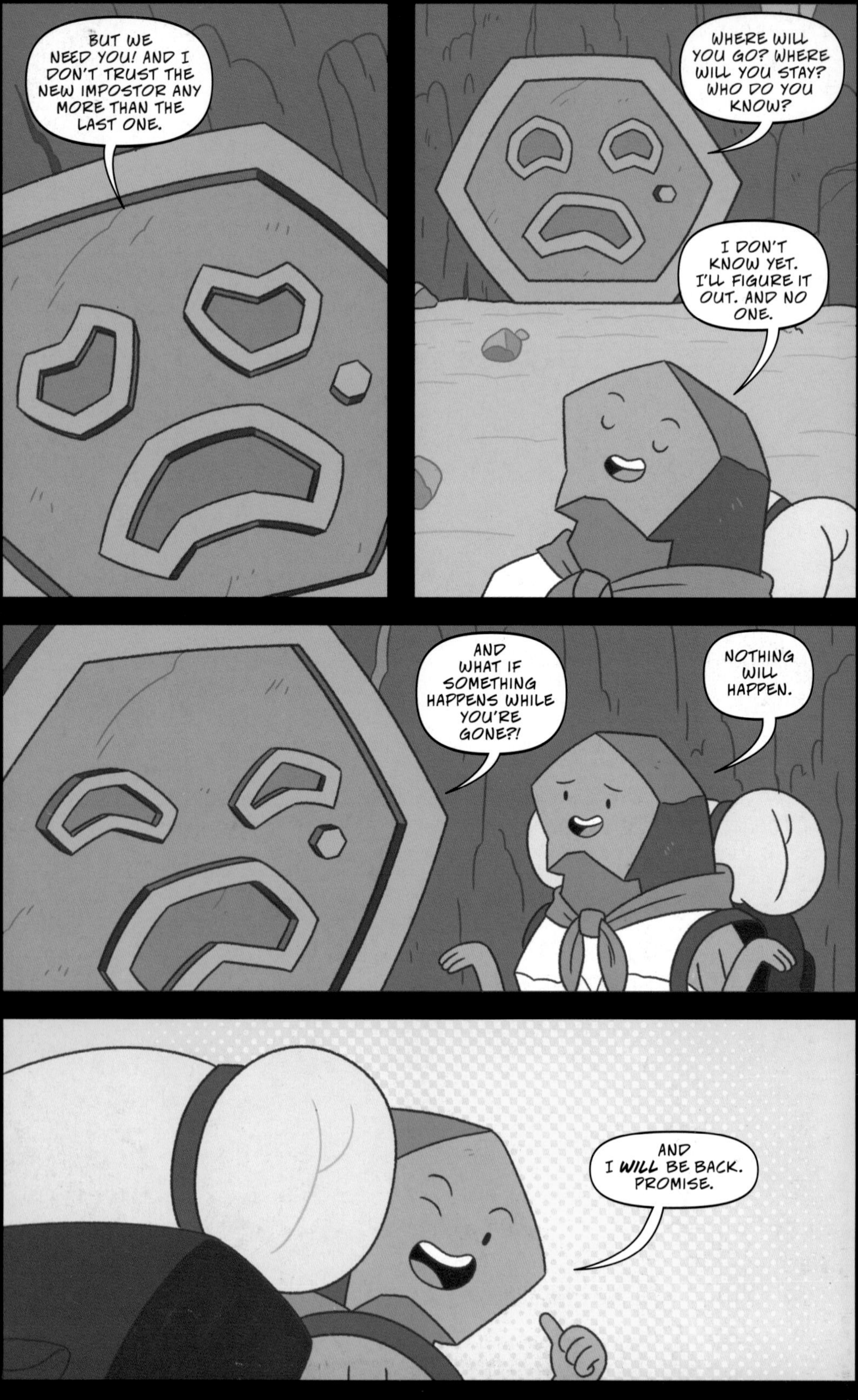
BUT WE NEED YOU! AND I DON'T TRUST THE NEW IMPOSTOR ANY MORE THAN THE LAST ONE.
WHERE WILL YOU GO? WHERE WILL YOU STAY? WHO DO YOU KNOW?
I DON'T KNOW YET. I'LL FIGURE IT OUT. AND NO ONE.
AND WHAT IF SOMETHING HAPPENS WHILE YOU'RE GONE?!
NOTHING WILL HAPPEN.
AND I WILL BE BACK. PROMISE.

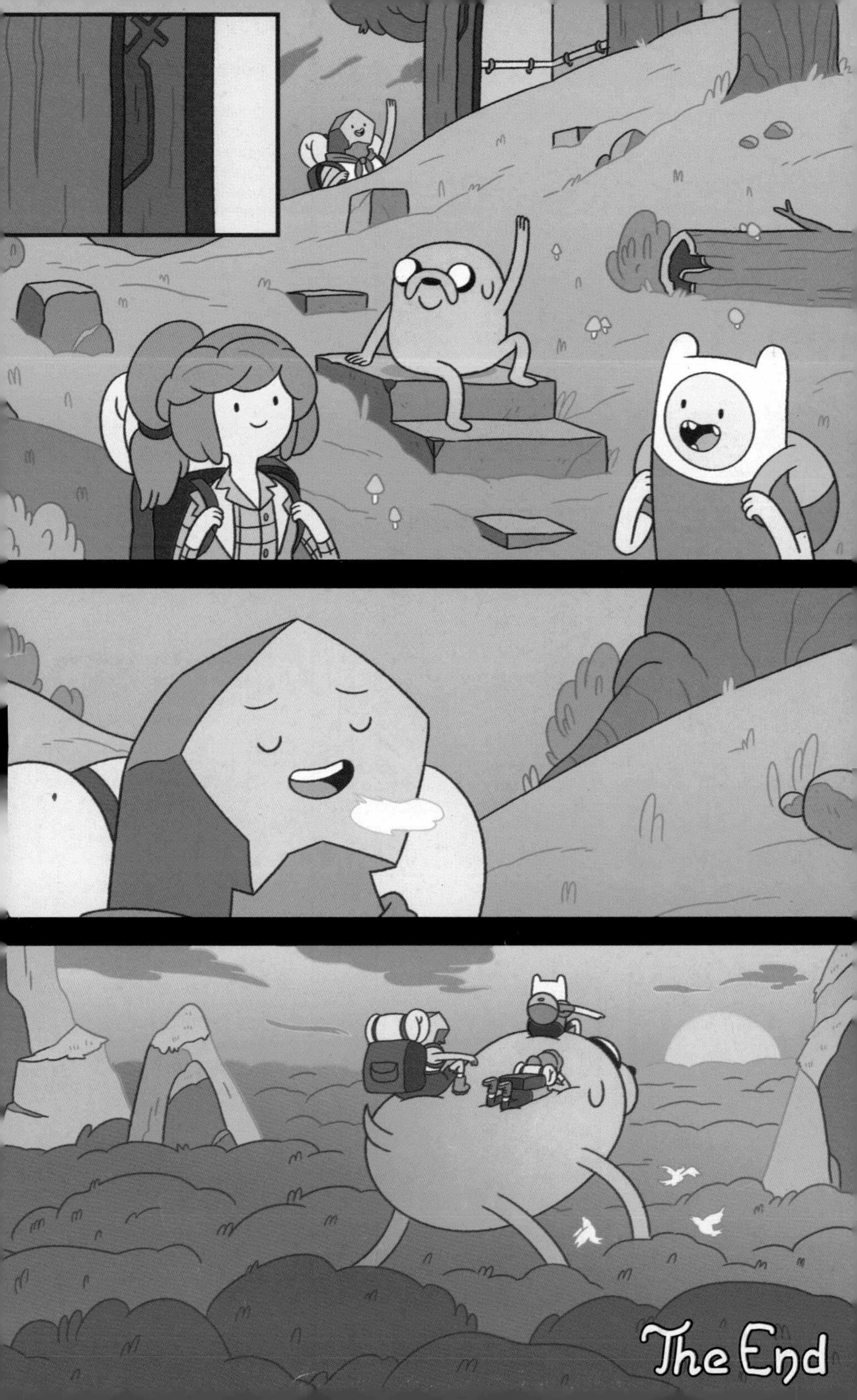
The End

DISCOVER
EXPLOSIVE NEW WORLDS

ADVENTURE TIME

Sam Sykes · Selina Espiritu · Sarah Stern
Brave Chef Brianna

KELLY THOMPSON BRIANNE DROUHARD M. VICTORIA ROBADO
MEGA PRINCESS

THE NOT-SO SECRET SOCIETY
DALEY · CRAFTS · CLARK · BRUNI

OVER THE GARDEN WALL

STEVEN UNIVERSE
VOLUME ONE

AVAILABLE AT YOUR LOCAL COMICS SHOP AND BOOKSTORE

kaboom!™

To find a comics shop in your area, call 1-888-266-4226

WWW.**BOOM-STUDIOS**.COM

Adventure Time
Pendleton Ward and Others
Volume 1
ISBN: 978-1-60886-280-1 | $14.99 US
Volume 2
ISBN: 978-1-60886-323-5 | $14.99 US
Adventure Time: Islands
ISBN: 978-1-60886-972-5 | $9.99 US

The Amazing World of Gumball
Ben Bocquelet and Others
Volume 1
ISBN: 978-1-60886-488-1 | $14.99 US
Volume 2
ISBN: 978-1-60886-793-6 | $14.99 US

Brave Chef Brianna
Sam Sykes, Selina Espiritu
ISBN: 978-1-68415-050-2 | $14.99 US

Mega Princess
Kelly Thompson, Brianne Drouhard
ISBN: 978-1-68415-007-6 | $14.99 US

The Not-So Secret Society
Matthew Daley, Arlene Daley, Wook Jin Clark
ISBN: 978-1-60886-997-8 | $9.99 US

Over the Garden Wall
Patrick McHale, Jim Campbell and Others
Volume 1
ISBN: 978-1-60886-940-4 | $14.99 US
Volume 2
ISBN: 978-1-68415-006-9 | $14.99 US

Steven Universe
Rebecca Sugar and Others
Volume 1
ISBN: 978-1-60886-706-6 | $14.99 US
Volume 2
ISBN: 978-1-60886-796-7 | $14.99 US

Steven Universe & The Crystal Gems
ISBN: 978-1-60886-921-3 | $14.99 US

Steven Universe: Too Cool for School
ISBN: 978-1-60886-771-4 | $14.99 US

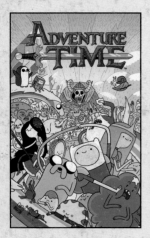

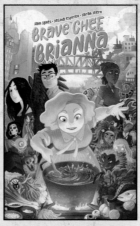

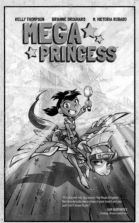

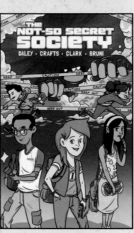

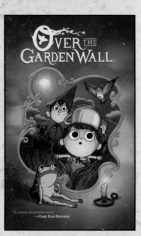

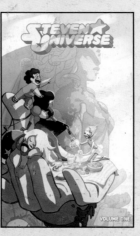

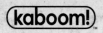